About the Author

The author has worked all her life in offices and doctors surgeries, then finally taking on a pub/restaurant with her family before retiring.

She has always nurtured a passion for books and a secret need to write one for herself. Then, at the age of seventy-six, the author finally took the bull by the horns and produced this work.

Her other passions in life are gardening and enjoying her family, especially her grandchildren.

Making Memories:

Patricia Goring

Making Memories

Vanguard Press

A CIP catalogue record for this title is available from the British Library.

ISBN 978-1-83794-564-1

This is a work of fiction. Names, characters, businesses, places, events and
incidents are either the products of the author's imagination or used in a fictitious
manner. Any resemblance to actual persons, living or dead, or actual events is
purely coincidental.

Vanguard Press is an imprint of
Pegasus Elliot Mackenzie Publishers Ltd.
www.pegasuspublishers.com

First Published in 2025

Vanguard Press
Sheraton House Castle Park
Cambridge England

Printed & Bound in Great Britain

Dedication

To my wonderful husband Ian.
To my beautiful grandchildren Charlie, Trafford,
Aston, and Fynn.
You make my life complete.

Acknowledgements

Charlie, my beautiful granddaughter, for convincing me to take this journey; without her help and encouragement, this would never have happened.

Also, Dom, Matthew, Vicki, Trafford, Shellie and Lilah. Corinne and Aston Kim and Fynn.

Thank you all for your unwavering faith and support and the encouragement I needed along the way…

Ella Rose Speight

I'm scared, always have been, always will be. I was born scared. I don't ever remember a second of my life when I wasn't afraid. From the moment I drew my first breath I was meant to suffer in silence and take whatever punishments came my way.

I had been told my parents were good people but they had never had any formal education to speak of and so had to take work wherever they could get it. I'm not sure who told me that but someone had, probably one of the numerous farm hands that came and went.

Most of my parents' short lives had been spent on the road, travelling from one town to the next. They met when they were not much more than children themselves and, as usually happens, very quickly I was on the way.

My father, Joseph Charles Speight had managed to find work as a farm labourer, The job came with a run-down cottage and a little money. My mother, Adele Rose also worked on the farm doing whatever she could. Helping in the farm kitchen, doing any jobs that needed to be done right up to her going into labour with me. There were always lots of jobs to be done.

The farm's owner, Will Adams, was a cruel, vicious, wicked man who thought nothing of beating his farm hands if they didn't do as he said. Sometimes, he would beat them just because he could. He only seemed to employ people that were either in this country illegally and so were unable to go to the authorities, or people like my parents that didn't know any better. Some would stick it out for a while but would then disappear overnight.

I was born on the scullery floor apparently and named Ella Rose Speight. There wasn't a midwife or doctor to see to my mother and check everything was okay. The farmer's wife, Dot, was the only person there and the only births she had ever attended had been with the animals.

It would seem that my mother managed the delivery on her own, but she suffered afterwards. Some of the afterbirth had been retained in the womb and eventually it festered and poisoned her. She died before I was one month old, she was just nineteen years of age, and so it was left to my father to care for me, but still do his job.

The farmer's wife, Dot, would take charge of me during the day whilst my dad worked out on the farm, then it was down to him for the rest of the time. It's a miracle I survived at all. I don't think Dot was very keen on me, but someone had to keep an eye on me and so it was left to her to do the job.

My earliest memories are of pain and suffering along with hunger. My dad told me I was allowed to crawl around the filthy floor in the kitchen of the main farmhouse once I was mobile. He also told me that I would share the dog's meals because I was so hungry. The dog didn't like me eating his food and would often snap at me leaving scars on my legs, hands and arms; scars that I still carry today.

It's a miracle I have turned out as well as I have. With losing my mum and only Dot and my dad to care for me I was very short of affection. Dad loved me in his own way, but he was out of his depth when it came to looking after me. He was still only twenty-one himself.

Social Services were never alerted to the conditions on the farm. I am certain that if they had been made aware then something would have been done.

Once I started school, things got worse. Five-year-olds can be every bit bullies as older children. Because I wasn't cared for like them they decided that I smelt bad, and my clothes were little more than rags.

When I was eleven and just going to secondary school, my dad became ill. Because of the poor conditions we lived in any illness would soon be made worse. It was not the done thing to go to the doctor, the farmer thought it a waste of time so by the time my dad did see a doctor it was too late. He died from pneumonia very quickly.

This left me having to care for myself and do lots of the jobs that my dad had done. I hated the animals, they scared the life out of me, and they seemed to sense my fear. Even the chickens tried to bully me. I was scared to death of the farmer and his wife who would think nothing of using a belt to beat me with. They were both bullies and very unkind leaving me to cope on my own as best I could.

I struggled on, going to school, doing my homework, and working around the farm. I didn't have any other choice.

Amazingly, I did quite well at school. I didn't have any friends at all, the other kids all thought me weird, so my time there was spent with my nose in a book instead of running around the playground with the other kids or staring lovingly at the older boys. No boy would look at me anyway and why would I want them to?

I was allowed to use the bathroom in the main farmhouse once a week, other than that I had to make do with the poor conditions in the cottage where I lived alone. No hot water and the toilet was outside and disgusting. As hard as I tried to get it clean it was impossible.

There had never been any visits from the authorities, if there had been I am now certain I would have been taken into care, but it just seemed that no one knew that I existed, except for the fact that I went to school every day. Because I turned up each day, did my work and always handed my homework in on time, it was assumed that everything in my existence was good. No one asked and I was too scared to complain.

I was dropped off at school in Marchpool in the mornings by Will and then collected at the end of the day. I was never allowed to join any clubs or groups at school which meant my existence was very lonely.

I should have been brave and told the school about the things that went on at the farm, but I was so scared all the time. Fearful that if I did rock the boat, then I would be made to suffer at the hands of Will. It took all the effort I could muster just to exist and go to school. I had traded one set of bullies for another. There was no escape.

When I was fifteen Dot became ill. She was taken to hospital and never came out again. I was never told what had happened to her, only that she had died and now it was me that would have to do the work that had been hers to do. How much worse could my life become? A lot as it happens.

On my sixteenth birthday, I was told that I was to be married that same day to Will, the farmer. That was the only time it was discussed with me. Although it wasn't so much a discussion as a statement of fact. I didn't have any choice. This was to be my life from now on.

And so that is what happened, I was driven to the registry office in Marchpool by Will in his battered old Land Rover. I wore some of my mum's old clothes that were still hanging in the wardrobe in the bedroom of the cottage. They must have been at least twenty years old. Mum had lived a life like mine and so all her clothes and shoes were old when she got them. I was shaking with nerves and fear, no idea what would happen.

The ceremony was quick, thank goodness, with no guests, just two people Will had dragged in off the street to be witnesses.

I was then driven back to the farmhouse in time to cook a meal for Will at lunchtime and then help with the chores around the farm. All the other farm hands were terrified of Will and I could understand why. He got everything he wanted by beating and bullying anyone and everyone.

Bedtime was a revelation and the most frightening experience. I had no idea what went on between a man and his wife in bed and I hated it. Obviously, I had seen the animals doing 'it', but it hadn't occurred to me that I would have to do that same thing with the horrible Will that was now my husband. I was told to get upstairs to the bedroom and take all my clothes off. I was then told to lie on the bed and wait for Will. I was shaking all over, terrified.

He came into the room smelling of drink, whisky I think. I had noticed a bottle on a shelf in the pantry. He took his trousers off and I could see his naked bottom half. That sight made me shake even more. Whatever would happen next?

He said I was to lie on my back and open my legs. What did happen next was just so awful. He climbed on top of me and thrust himself into me really hard making me cry out with pain. That earned me a hard slap across the face.

He just kept pushing himself into me and I was crying with pain. Eventually, he climbed off and lay next to me breathing heavily. I was too scared to move.

Then he growled at me saying, "You had best go and clean yourself up girl. Then you can change these sheets, you've got blood on them."

That first night set the tone for the rest of my life, or so I thought. Each and every night I would be told to get upstairs and get myself ready. Each night he would do the same thing, just thrust himself into me and keep thrusting until he had managed to finish his mission.

Being so young and not at all worldly I couldn't understand why my periods had stopped. Will noticed and said that I must be pregnant. That really scared me so much. There was no way I could have a child and bring it up in the way that I had been. No, that would never happen.

I decided that the best thing I could do was take on lots of heavy-lifting jobs around the farm. I tried to do these jobs when Will was elsewhere so he couldn't see and realise just what I was doing. I would pick up the heaviest things I could find. Pick them up, put them down, pick them up again. Then I would climb on anything high up and jump off, I would throw myself around landing heavily on the stone floors.

It worked, I had what appeared to be a really bad period that knocked me off my feet for two days, but I knew that the child had left my body. I could then breathe easy for a few days.

This happened many times over the next nine years. I would not and could not bring a child into this awful world.

I was never allowed any money at all so couldn't leave the farm to try to get help. We were so remote it would take almost half-an-hour of walking before reaching a road, and then what if I did actually make that walk.

The farm didn't have a television, Will wouldn't hear of having such a thing, only a radio but I was never allowed to listen to it. I had bought books home from the school library and would transport myself to another world where Will didn't exist and only kind people came into my world, but of course as soon as I had left school then my reading had to stop.

Life became more unbearable with each day being exactly the same as the previous one. Rising early to do jobs before having to cook breakfast for Will, then back-breaking chores around the farm, washing, no such thing as a machine to do this job for me, it was all done by hand. Then there was all the cleaning, so much cleaning. Then it would be time for Will's lunch then more chores till late in the afternoon when he would turn up looking for a hot meal.

The evenings would revolve around him listening to the radio in his office or doing work there. I would sit and mend clothes, darn socks, anything to keep me occupied. Then he would march into the kitchen and demand some supper and a glass of whisky before finally announcing it was time for me to go to the bedroom and get myself ready for him. I dreaded this time knowing exactly what would be happening to me. I was so terrified.

My whole life was full of fear and pain. I dreaded nighttime the most though. How could anyone, any woman or girl actually want to go through this torment? I was in constant fear of finding myself pregnant yet again.

One of these days I wouldn't be able to rid myself of the child, if that happened I would kill myself. I might actually do that anyway. At least my pain and suffering would be over. My life was a thing of nightmares and there was no way out.

Once in a while. Will would go off for the day saying he had to see his accountant or the lawyer that looked after all the legal things he was required to do. On those days I had to do more of the work that Will would normally do and keep an eye on the other workers.

I remember not so long ago a really nice man turned up at the farm one day and he and Will shut themselves away in the office. I had taken a tray of drinks into them, not speaking or looking at them, just placing the tray on the desk and then turning to leave. Will called me back saying, "Don't run off, let me introduce you to my lawyer, Scott Ryan. He lives in London you know."

I just smiled at him and went to leave, but Will said I shouldn't be so rude and should speak to the man. How could I speak to him, I hadn't a clue what to say?.

He smiled up at me and asked "how did I enjoy life living on a farm". What could I say? "I just said yes it's fine" then turned and left the room.

I heard Will say, "Ignore her, she's a bit strange, but she does her wifely duties okay, so I put up with her".

I left the room, closed the door behind me then broke down in tears. Now I knew for sure. He didn't care one jot for me, never had, never would. I just did as I was told without argument.

About an hour later, the two men left the office and came into the kitchen. Mr Ryan said "it had been a pleasure to meet me and if I ever found myself in London then I was to call in to say hello". I muttered a thank you and thought, yes, fat chance of that happening. London sounded so exotic to my ears, so far away. I would never be going there, not if I lived to be a hundred. I would be far too scared for one thing and how would I manage to find my way around?

Our nearest towns were Marchpool and Newburn and I had never been allowed to visit either of those places except for my 'wedding day' that took place in the registry office in Marchpool. What an adventure that had been.

Once Mr Ryan had left, Will seemed in a good mood for a change. He said he fancied taking me to bed. "Get up the stairs girl," he growled at me. "I think we could manage it twice today."

This was getting worse by the day. Now, not only did I have to go to his bed every night he now wanted to do it in the day as well. I just wanted to die.

Shortly, after this daytime sex session, I noticed my period was late once more. No way, Not again. The same thing had happened the month before and I'd had to resort to my usual way of dealing with this problem, a lot of very hard manual work. So far this had rid me of the children I would have carried.

How much longer though? I simply could not bring a child of his into this awful toxic world in which I lived.

Another quick trip around the barn, lifting all the heavy pieces of equipment that were stored in there was the only way to deal with this constant problem. Pick it up, put it down, pick it up again. Eventually, I would feel the gush of blood leave my body and run down my legs. I could breath another sigh of relief.

Will's demands on me increased as the weeks went by. He wasn't working on the farm as much as he used to. I asked him one day why he didn't tend to the animals any more. He laughed and said that he was getting rid of them all. More trouble than they were worth.

I had noticed several lorries arriving on the farm recently. They would load up some of the beasts and off they would go. I assumed they were going to market but no, apparently Will has decided to give up farming. He had received a very good offer for his land from a building company that wanted to build a small, new town on the land. He said he would be rich beyond all dreams once the deal went through.

He said he would buy either another small farm, just a smallholding really so that he could retire from all the hard work and he and I would be able to spend many happy hours every day in bed having fun.

I baulked at this suggestion, Will noticed and shouted at me. "What the hell is wrong with you, girl? Anyone would think I treated you badly. You have food in your belly and clothes on your back and me in your bed each night keeping you happy." He reached over and smacked me hard across my face.

I fled from the house and ran bare foot through the yard and up the lane. I could hear Will coming after me. Why had I done that? Now I would get another beating into the bargain.

I slipped into one of the fields next to the pathway and dropped down on my knees, praying that Will wouldn't follow me. I should have known better. I could hear his boots hitting the cobbles as he ran after me. I would just have to take my punishment and hope he got tired before he killed me.

I kept very still, hardly daring to breath. I could still hear his footsteps getting closer. I put my fingers in my ears and I prayed.

When Will failed to reach me I removed my fingers slowly and listened? I couldn't hear him any more. He must have gone back to the house. I stayed very still and continued to listen but no, he definitely wasn't coming any nearer to me.

After what seemed like an age I stood up slowly and looked towards the house, but there was no sign of him. I crept around the gatepost and began to walk back slowly towards the house. There he was, lying on the pathway and all bent up. He looked odd but I was too scared to go close. I stayed watching him for a long time but there didn't seem to be any movement.

Finally, I thought I would have to go to him and help him up. If he has hurt himself then I will have to do the work on my own. Will had got rid of the other workers several weeks before so there wasn't anyone else to do the jobs or anyone to help me now.

I was thinking, thank goodness almost all the animals have gone now so I won't have to deal with them. Still, looking after Will when he was well was hard enough, he will be a nightmare if he is laid up for any length of time.

As I reached him I could hear him making gurgling noises. He was face down on the path and he looked awful. I moved to look at his face then turned his head to one side. Something was very wrong with this awful man. Should I try to help him? No, I should not. I walked past him and just left him lying there.

I went back into the farmhouse and made myself a cup of tea then I set about preparing vegetables to make a stew for his evening meal. I would wait till the stew was ready then go out looking for him. Hopefully, he wouldn't last that long, and I will find him dead.

It had begun to get dark and a drizzle of rain had set in by the time I put my coat and wellington boots on and made my way slowly along the path.

He was still there, still in the same position I had left him in. I approached him cautiously. I bent down and touched his face. Stone cold, as were his hands. I tried to feel for a pulse but wasn't sure I was doing it right. He looked dead and I felt nothing but relief.

I felt in his jacket pocket for the key to his office. I was never allowed in there. The only phone in the place was in there and I would need to use it if only I knew how.

Once I had found the key I then hurried back to the house. I pulled my boots off by the door and went to the office. The key turned easily, and I entered his domain. The phone was on his desk. I had never used a phone before and wasn't sure what to do.

I picked up the receiver and listened, just a strange noise. I put it back down for a minute trying to think. I remembered hearing some of the girls at school some years before saying they had needed to ring 999 for an ambulance once so I tried that. I had no sooner dialled the number when I heard a woman's voice say, 'Emergency, which service do you require?'

I stumbled over my words, but she was very calm and kind, and eventually, I was able to tell her that "my husband hadn't come back for his supper and when I went to look for him I had found him on the pathway and I thought he was dead".

It took a while for me to give her directions to the farm, after all, I rarely left the place. It took a while but eventually, an ambulance arrived, and I was able to direct them to where Will still lay.

I could see them doing tests on him, but I knew it was far too late. I could breathe easily at last. The ambulance people were very calm and said that Will was definitely dead. It looked as if he had suffered a heart attack but there would be a post-mortem to confirm that.

They asked if there was anyone that could come and stay with me but of course, there wasn't. I said I would be fine on my own.

They said that under normal circumstances they would have to ask a funeral director to come and remove the body but because of this situation, they would take Will to the mortuary where a doctor would be sent to confirm the death.

A strange calmness had spread over me. At long last, at the age of twenty-five, I would be free. There was a flurry of activity as Will's body was loaded into the ambulance. I thanked them both for all the help and assured them that I would be fine, and of course I was. More than fine really.

I set about sorting out the few remaining animals and made sure they were fed, had water, and were safely locked up for the night. I then went back into the house and ate my supper. For the first time in my life, I actually enjoyed my meal.

Once I had cleared away my tea things I went upstairs and ran a steaming hot bath. I allowed myself to sink into the lovely, soothing water and then closed my eyes. My thoughts began to wander, what would I have to do next? Who did I need to speak to? God, that was going to be hard. The only person I had spoken to for a very long time was Will and once that fancy lawyer from London.

First thing in the morning I would have to check that the animals were all okay then set about looking through all the papers in the office. I suppose I will have to ring people but who and what did I say?

That will take a lot of thinking about. Time enough for that tomorrow. Tonight I was going to sleep and really enjoy being in bed by myself. Heaven.

By eleven o'clock the next morning all my jobs were done. The animals had been checked and were now in their relative fields. The dog and cats had been fed and then let out into the yard for the day. The cats would be looking for mice and good luck to them.

I felt as if a heavy weight had been lifted from me. The whole world lay in front of me but what I was going to do about it remained a mystery.

I had left the office door open and so could hear the telephone ringing. Another first, answering the bloody thing. I gingerly picked up the receiver and put it to my ear. "Hello," I said.

"Hello, is that Mrs Adams?"

"It is," I said.

"Hello, this is Doctor Morgan from the surgery. I am so sorry to hear about your husband Mrs Adams. Is there anything we at the surgery can do to help you?"

I said, "Yes, please. I don't have a clue what I need to do or who I need to contact or anything."

"Is there anyone with you, Mrs Adams?"

"No," I said. "I don't know anyone and all the workers from the farm have left. I am here on my own."

"That's not good," said the doctor, "how about if I ask someone from social services to come around and advise you on what needs to be done?"

"Would you, doctor? That is so kind of you. I am so alone here and don't know a soul."

"Leave it with me, Mrs Adams, I will ring them now, then you should receive a call from them shortly."

"Thank you so much doctor, it means such a lot to me."

"Not a problem, Mrs Adams and if there is anything else we can do for you then please give us a call."

"I will doctor," I said, "and thank you once more."

I put the receiver down and breathed a big sigh of relief.

Right, first a cup of tea and a slice of toast then into the office. See what joys await me in there.

I took another cup of tea with me into the office, Will would not agree with that for sure. One cup of tea was sufficient. Any more was wasteful.

I sat in Will's chair in front of his desk and wondered, 'where do I start'?

I was shaken when the phone began to ring. Goodness don't think I will ever get used to that.

"Hi, is that Mrs Adams?"

"Yes," I replied with a shaky voice.

"Caroline Young here, Social Services. Doctor Morgan has asked me to give you a call to see if we can be of any help to you."

"Thank you so much, I can use all the help you can offer. I am drowning here, don't know what I am supposed to do first."

"Right, I can come over now for a couple of hours then we can decide what we need to do first, then make a list and work our way through it."

"Would you really do that for me? I will be eternally grateful. Do you know where to find me?"

"Not really, can you give me some directions?" I did my best and then prayed she would make it. She did, about forty minutes later I saw a car bumping down the track that was supposed to be a lane.

"You weren't wrong, were you? Definitely remote." I had walked out into the yard to meet her. She seemed nice. A bit older than me, I guessed. "Come in," I said, "would you like a drink?"

"I would yes, tea would be lovely." I made the drinks and placed them on a tray with a plate of homemade shortbread. "Shall we take these through to the office?" I asked.

"Good idea, if there are papers to be gone through then I guess that is where we will find them." I made a big sigh and Caroline looked at me. "Are you okay, Mrs Adams?"

"Please, call me Ella, I hated being Mrs Adams?"

"Really? Why is that?"

I felt that I really needed to explain my life to this kind woman.

I began my story and I told her everything. For the first time in my life, I was able to reveal the whole terrible story that was my horror of a life. I told her of all the abuse I had suffered, the forced marriage, and how I had rid myself of all the unwanted children that the beast kept forcing on me. The beatings, so many beatings. I tried to explain everything in a short space of time. I think she got the gist of it.

"Ella, I am so sorry. What a dreadful thing to happen to you. If you had been stronger and had told someone about it then we would have been bought in and sorted a foster family for you. I do understand all the fear you felt though. It must have been dreadful."

"It was, I have been scared all of my life till now. Is it too late for me to find a brave new me? I can't see how I will be able to go forward until I am able to man up, is that what they say? Or should it be a woman up?"

"Look Ella, let's not get ahead of ourselves. The first thing we need to do is sort out the funeral. I guess there won't be many mourners there."

"I doubt it, everyone that he knew was scared of him, oh, just a thought, apart from his fancy lawyer from London. I only ever saw him once, he seemed nice though."

"Well, we will need to contact him to find out if there is a will for a start, then you will need to decide what you want to do next."

"Caroline, I have no idea. My whole life has been here, this is where I was born, and I don't want to stay here a minute longer than I have to."

"I can understand that, Ella. This place has nothing more than bad memories for you. But you do need to find out where you stand legally. You say that your husband was planning to sell the place. Let's see if we can find out if that offer is still on the table."

"First things first though, the funeral. Do you have a preference for a funeral director?"

" I don't know what one of those is. I am sorry, you must think I'm a complete idiot."

"No, Ella, I don't but I do think that you are going to have to learn how to live a normal life very quickly indeed."

"I know. I have spent my entire life being scared of everything but now I need to act like a grown-up. I just don't have any idea how to do that. This here has been my entire world since the day I was born. How and where do I start?"

"Like I said, first things first. Let's set the wheels in motion for the funeral. If you don't have a preference then how about we just go with the Co-Op?"

" I can live with that," I said.

Caroline rang the Co-Op funeral place and they arranged to come out the next day to discuss what I wanted for the service et cetera. They would be out at two-thirty the following day. So Caroline wrote that down on the calendar we had found in the office.

"I needed to go to the surgery at some point to collect the death certificate and then go to register the death. How I'm supposed to do that is beyond me."

We set about looking through the drawers and filing cabinets to see what we could find. "We needed an address book as well. I would have to ring the lawyer as soon as possible."

Will's records were remarkably well kept, and we soon found the address book we needed. Caroline found a copy of his will also and so we made a fresh pot of tea and then sat down to read through the document.

It didn't take long, everything, the farm, its contents, and several thousand pounds in his bank accounts was all left to me. It would take time before I could access any of the money though and I needed to live in the meantime.

Further investigations in the office revealed a safe that wasn't even locked. Inside, there were bundles and bundles of bank notes. Looked like a fortune to me. I had no idea where any of this money had come from.

Caroline suggested that I use some of this money to pay for my day-to-day living expenses. I would need to keep a record of what I spent and what it was spent on. Keeping receipts for as much as I could.

Once all that had been sorted out we found an insurance policy. It would appear that it was for two hundred and seventy-five thousand pounds and payable on Will's death to me.

Perhaps, he had cared for me after all, in his own weird way. Then again, there was no one else to leave it to. None of this made me feel anything for him though. I was still glad he was dead.

As the afternoon wore on, I said to Caroline that perhaps I should ring the lawyer. "Good idea. He should know all about this sale of the farm and lots of other stuff as well."

I had told Caroline how I had never used a phone before finding Will collapsed. I said that it scared me, having to speak with people I didn't know. But there again, I didn't know anyone anyway.

She said she understood, "It must be very strange suddenly having to deal with all this stuff when all I had ever done before was cook, clean, and work on the farm."

She said that she would ring Mr Ryan and explain what had happened if I wanted her to. "Oh, Caroline, please, I will be forever in your debt."

"Nonsense, now where is that number?" She rang the number and spoke to someone saying who she was and who she needed to speak with. After a few moments, Mr Ryan must have answered the call. I could only hear Caroline's side of the conversation, but he was obviously listening and commenting.

Once she had finished speaking with Mr Ryan, she turned to me and said, "Right, that's all sorted. Mr Ryan will come up to see you the day after tomorrow. He said he should be here by about eleven in the morning. I will make a note of it on the calendar for you."

"Now Ella, do you want me to be with you tomorrow when the undertakers come, and also if you need me to be here for your meeting with Mr Ryan, I can do that as well."

"Thank you, Caroline, I would really appreciate it. You must think I'm a real idiot but honestly, my life has been a living nightmare for as long as I can remember. Meeting you today has given me hope that I will be able to lead a different life in the future. The times I have just wished I could die and get it all over with.

I am still very scared though. I have no idea how the world works. I have never been on a train or plane or been in a taxi. I have never even been on a bus. I have never been to the coast. In fact, the farthest I have been is Marchpool and Newbern a couple of times. I was never allowed to go with other people, only with Will and before that my dad. I could only go if there was something specific that needed doing. Doctors, dentists that sort of thing but even then it didn't happen very often. In fact, I struggled to remember exactly when I had been to either of these places.

I had never been allowed to look in shop windows or go into a shop and buy things. I have never been allowed to have any money. I don't have a clue how to actually go into a shop and buy something or how to go into a library to borrow books. That is something I always wanted to do but Will wouldn't allow it. I used to borrow books from the school library but of course, I haven't been there for a very long time. This whole business really frightens me. I have a lot to learn, and I guess the first thing I have to learn is how to stop being so scared of everything."

Caroline was watching me, "You poor, poor girl. How have you managed to survive?"

"To be honest, Caroline, I have no idea. Every day has been exactly the same as the one before and the next one would be the same as well. I would never dare question anything, if I did I would receive a smack around the head or a slap across my face, so hard it would knock me off my feet. So, I quickly learned to say nothing. Tell me something Caroline, do you have many cases like mine?"

"To be honest, Ella, I have been doing this job for more years than I care to remember, and I can honestly say this is the first and only case of this type I have heard of. True, we have many, far too many dreadful cases of cruelty in our country but this is unique as far as I can tell. It is like something from out of the dark ages.

But I promise you, things are going to change for you and change for the better. I promise I will help you as much as I can. I will speak with my boss tomorrow and put her in the picture. I want to be assigned to you so that you won't have to deal with several people; it will always be me. Would that be all right for you?"

"Yes, Caroline, it would be amazing. I am so used to being on my own and being very lonely but until now I have never had to sort things out, or make decisions. I have only ever been allowed to do as I was told. This talking with you is something I have never done before either. The only person I spoke with was Will but I tried not to do that unless I really had to. I have led a very lonely life."

"Well, my friend, things are going to change for you from now on. It would appear that you won't be short of money. So that is a very big plus for you. Let's wait for Mr Ryan to come up though, and he will be able to explain everything for you. Try not to worry too much, I am certain things will turn out well for you in the end."

"Right, are you happy with everything so far?"

"I am," I replied. "I'm not worried about being here on my own, it is when other people arrive that I begin to lose the plot."

"Do you know, I have never been to the hairdressers? My hair has never been cut, I mean, just look at the state of it, look at the state of me. Will would never allow a television in the house and I wasn't allowed to read papers or magazines.

The only time I went anywhere else was on the rare occasion I had to see a doctor or dentist. Usually, if I needed a tooth taken out then Will did it.

He has a radio, but it is in the office and he wouldn't let me listen to it. I have no idea what is going on in the world. I don't know how a woman of twenty-five is supposed to dress, how I should act, what is and is not allowed out there. It feels as if I have just been born and I have to learn all about everything. I'm not even sure how I am supposed to speak with people."

"Ella, please don't worry. I will help you navigate everything. I will be here with you for the whole journey. Now, I will have to go but I will be back tomorrow. Are you sure you will be okay here on your own?"

"I am and thank you so much. I will spend a couple of hours going through this paperwork then have my supper before sorting the animals out. I need to find out who bought the other livestock and see if they want the rest of them. They can just have them, I don't want payment, I just want them gone. That will be a big weight off my shoulders. So that is my mission for the rest of the day."

"Right then my friend, until tomorrow. Bye for now. I will see you in the morning."

Once Caroline had left I made another cup of tea and went back into the office. I set about looking through the mountain of paperwork. Most of it meant nothing to me at all so I just checked over it and then put it back where it had come from.

I checked again in the safe. Earlier we had found several thousand pounds and thought I should just check it again, count it, and write down a record of what is actually there.

I knelt down and started taking everything out of the safe.

There were piles and piles of bank notes, goodness knows where it came from. There were lots of papers too, so I took those out and put them on the desk as well. Underneath all of that, I found three boxes. Not very big but they did look expensive. They were covered in leather and they really did look very expensive to my eyes anyway but what did I know?

I carefully opened the first one and then took a deep breath. Inside was the most beautiful necklace, earrings, and bracelet. They all matched, and they took my breath away. Where had they come from? The little stones, I think must be diamonds and the main ones were green and gorgeous. I had no idea what they were but I loved them. I closed the box and put it to one side.

The second box was similar, again diamonds but with red stones, I closed that box and put it with the first one. Finally the third box, I was trembling as I opened it. Again it contained a necklace, earrings, and a bracelet but the stones were all black. It was stunning, I have never seen anything like it. In fact, I have never seen any jewellery apart from my silver wedding ring. I wonder who they belonged to?

I closed all the boxes and quickly put them back in the safe.

I had a quick glance at the paperwork. It seemed to be the deeds for the farm and several insurance documents. I will have to get Mr Ryan to look at all these. I have no idea what to do with them.

I began counting the notes, but it all became a bit too much, so I bundled them all back into the safe and decided to leave them till Mr Ryan arrived. It was all too much for me. I was way out of my depth.

I quickly did a tidy-up of all the papers and left the room looking quite clean and tidy.

The following morning Caroline arrived before I had finished sorting the animals out. She walked across the yard and asked how I was.

"Okay, thanks. I slept well for a change."

"Have you had breakfast yet she asked?"

"No. I need to finish sorting these beasts out first then it is my time."

"How long will you be?" she asked.

"About twenty minutes or so I think."

"Right, I am going to put the kettle on and make tea then I have picked up some croissants for our breakfast."

"Sorry, picked up what?"

"Croissants, they are French pastries and delicious."

"I am looking forward to tasting those then. Something else new for me to get my head around. I was only ever allowed toast for breakfast and porridge in the winter."

"Do you know where everything is in the kitchen?"

"Don't worry about me, I will find what I need."

Caroline went back to the house and I quickly finished what I had been doing with the animals. I was looking forward to my breakfast now. I strode across the yard and entered the kitchen. What a glorious smell greeted me.

"Blimey! Caroline, that smells lovely."

"Sit yourself down and it is all ready when you are." I quickly washed my hands and sat down waiting.

Caroline removed a tray from the oven and placed it in the middle of the big kitchen table. All the tea things were there as well waiting for me.

She poured the tea and passed me a mug. "Right young lady, help yourself. The first lesson in living your new life."

I reached over and took one of the pastries. I held it under my nose and took a deep smell of the lovely, light croissant. Heaven, then I took my first bite. "*Wow*, this is amazing Caroline. So light and buttery, it just crumbles in my mouth."

Caroline laughed, "I just knew you would enjoy these. Now come on, get them eaten." She sat down opposite me and reached for her own pastry. We were both in heaven.

I managed three of these delicious treats and then poured a second cup of tea for us both. Once finished, we placed all the crocks in the sink and left them till later.

We made our way into the office. I said to Caroline to sit in the big chair as I had some things I wanted her to look at.

Once seated I began to empty the safe again. I placed all of the money in one pile and then the paperwork in another pile. Finally, I reached in and bought out the three boxes. I placed them in front of her and said, "Go on, open them."

Caroline looked at me with a puzzled expression on her face. "What are these Ella?"

"Go on open them," I said, "I found them last night. I had no idea they were here or who they belonged to." She carefully opened the first box and gasped when she saw the contents.

"Bloody hell Ella, this is amazing, you say you have never seen them before."

"No, I haven't, I was just trying to sort stuff into piles ready for when Mr Ryan gets here tomorrow. I was so shocked when I saw them I just put everything back in the safe and pushed the door to. Dot, Will's first wife was a scruffy, fat woman and like me never left the farm. Why would they be hers?"

"I have no idea, Ella. Let me look at the others." She opened the second box and again gasped. "These are stunning Ella, they must be worth a fortune."

"Open the last one, I think I like that one best." She did as I asked and again gasped at the sight. It was the black stones, they certainly looked amazing.

"What are they, Caroline, do you think?"

"Well, I have never seen anything like this before, but I would imagine they are black diamonds. If that is what they are they are very rare and very expensive. The red ones I would say are rubies and the green ones are emeralds. They must all be very valuable."

I shook my head. "None of this makes sense. Will was always on about cutting back and saving money. He said he wasn't made of money. If I

29

couldn't make savings then we would be homeless. Something else that frightened the life out of me."

"I am not surprised Ella, what a dreadful man. Playing on your vulnerabilities, causing you even more pain, and filling you with fear."

"Perhaps, Mr Ryan will be able to tell us more about these and everything else. Let's put it all back and wait for him. He sounds like a really nice man. I'm sure he will have answers for you."

"Before the funeral people arrive I think we should try to find out about these animals. If we can get them sorted out it will be a big weight off your shoulders."

"It will Caroline, I have never liked dealing with them, they scare me, to be honest."

"Right, let's see if we can track down the paperwork for the other beasts that Will got rid of. That will be the first place to start."

We set about looking through as much stuff as we could.

"Finally. Caroline said, 'Bingo'. Got it, I will give them a ring and see if they want the rest of the stock." I breathed a big sigh of relief and then crossed my fingers.

She was on the phone for quite a while but when she had finished she turned and smiled at me. "Sorted my friend," she said.

"Really" I couldn't believe it. "How many will they take?"

"If you seriously don't want payment for them they will take the lot."

"I don't," I said, "I just want them gone along with all the sacks of feed and anything else that may be useful to them."

"Right, well the guy I spoke to says he will send some wagons over later today and see how many he can take, then if there is still some left, he will come back tomorrow."

"He asked about some paperwork that he would need regarding the health and history of all the animals. I said he was welcome to come into the office and look for what he needed himself. He is happy to do that so long as one of us stays with him. Just to make sure he only takes what he needs. We can do that, can't we?"

I was feeling happier and lighter by the minute. "If they leave the dog and cats I can manage them for now, but the rest have been a nightmare for me. I know how to look after them short-term, but they really do scare me, especially the big cows".

Caroline managed to locate some of the paperwork she thinks will be needed so that will help.

There was a knock on the kitchen door, so I hurried through, followed by Caroline. I opened the door to find a man standing there carrying a briefcase.

"Mrs Adams?"

"I am," I said. He held out his hand to shake mine, this was something very new for me as well. Physical contact with other humans.

"Milo Harrington, funeral director for the Co-Operative Funeral Services."

"Hello," I said, "come in please."

He followed me through to the kitchen and I introduced him to Caroline. "I am sorry about all this," I said. "I have no idea how to go about any of this so Caroline has offered to help me. I don't know what I would have done without her."

"That's fine, Mrs Adams. I will do all I can to help you sort this side of things out." I asked if he would like a drink and he said that tea would be lovely.

I busied myself making the drinks whilst Caroline began discussing what we would need to do regarding the funeral.

"As I understand it, there is to be a post-mortem, so the funeral won't happen until that has been completed. We can, however, discuss what you require regarding the funeral itself. I understand there won't be many mourners? Is that correct?"

"Yes," I said, "Will was a very private man and didn't have any friends that I know of and he certainly doesn't have any relatives."

"Right, this shouldn't take long then."

We sat for about ten minutes discussing the funeral and how it should be arranged.

It was then that Caroline said that Will had actually left instructions regarding the funeral. It is all in the papers attached to the will. I looked at her, "I didn't know that."

"I know," she said. "I thought you had enough to worry about. I will get the paperwork from the office."

She went off to fetch the document. I made a fresh pot of tea and poured it out before she returned. "Here it is," she said,

"Okay, let me have a look at what he wants," said Mr Harrington.

"This all looks quite straightforward. Mr Adams says that he wants to be cremated and his ashes scattered over this land. He requests that no mourners are to be present. Not even you, Mrs Adams."

He stresses that there should be "no hymns or prayers or people making speeches and talking about him and his life".

"Given his requests, I think this can all be sorted and dealt with very quickly once the post-mortem is completed."

He swiftly filled out a form and asked me to sign it. "This document states that there is money set aside for the funeral and it gives details of how we can access that money. It would seem that Mr Adams has thought about everything, so you have nothing to worry about after all."

"Yes," I said, "it would seem that he has spared me that problem." Perhaps he did like me a bit after all."

"Well, that was easy," I said to Caroline after the funeral director had left. "This experience won't teach me much though. If I ever need to do something like this again in the future I will still be in the dark."

Caroline laughed, "Does this mean you might give marriage another go?" she asked.

"Good God no, I have had enough of men, well one man to last me a lifetime. I will be quite happy on my own for the rest of my days. I won't ever be able to let another man anywhere near me, thank you very much."

"Don't say never Ella, not all men are like Will. There are some really lovely, kind, and gentle men around. I know, I had one of those and he was amazing. He died too. It's been nearly seven years now. He was a construction worker on a building site. There was a terrible accident and Martin was killed."

"I would love for you to find some true happiness in your life. You are too lovely to remain single. There will be a man out there for you and when you meet him you will know."

"I am so sorry for you Caroline, all this must bring it all back to you."

"It never leaves me, Ella some days are better than others, but it is still always there, just bubbling away beneath the surface."

"But, this is not about me. It is all about you and how to make you live once more. Or should I say learning how to live from the bottom up?"

"Living these past twenty-five years has taught me never to trust a man, ever again. Not that I ever trusted Will, I can't live like that again. I will just spend the rest of my life being me and sod the men. I will be fine on my own once I get rid of this fear, and I will get rid of it. I will be stronger on my own."

Caroline looked at me and smiled, "What?" I said.

"We will see," she replied.

We were quickly becoming good friends. I certainly can't manage without her yet. I hope we remain friends forever.

The lorries began arriving mid-afternoon. The man in charge came into the farmhouse and spoke with Caroline. She showed him all the paperwork she had managed to find, and he seemed happy with that.

I showed him where everything was kept and said he could just take whatever he wanted. He seemed very pleased with the deal.

The remaining animals were checked over and then loaded onto the lorries, all the feed, hay, etc. was stacked in another lorry. Soon they were all happy and they set off for the new homes this man had arranged for them.

Caroline and I sat down at the kitchen table and let out a joint sigh. "Well, that's that then," I said. "No more running around after animals I don't even like. I hope Mr Ryan has good news for me tomorrow," I said. "I really don't want to live here any more."

"Where do you want to live?" asked Caroline?.

"I have no idea," I replied. "I have never even stayed away from this place for one night before so wherever I end up will be a journey of discovery."

Caroline left at five o'clock and promised to be back the next day in plenty of time to meet with Mr Ryan.

As I didn't need to feed the animals, the rest of the night was mine to do as I wished. I still had the dog and cats to feed but that was a simple job. Ten minutes and they were sorted.

I decided to treat myself to another hot bath. This was luxury. Will would have gone mad, wasting water. I went into the bedroom and looked at Will's wardrobe. A great big monstrosity that took up almost the whole of one wall.

I wondered if he had anything in there I could put in the bath water, something nice smelling. Maybe some shampoo as well. All my life I have had to wash my hair in cheap washing-up liquid. When I let my hair down it reaches right down past my backside. It has always been a nightmare to wash. I would love to have it all chopped off. Something else to do in the near future.

Before running the bath I began looking in the wardrobe. There were a lot of clothes in there. Most I have never even seen before.

"Why buy all these things and then just leave them hanging in the wardrobe? Complete madness. I will have to sort through all these things and then ask Caroline what I should do with them".

It would take an age, whereas my clothes could be looked through in two minutes. That is something else I will have to do, buy new clothes. Where would I go to buy them though remained a mystery. Caroline will help me.

The big exploration of Will's wardrobe could wait, but I would just have a quick look in the bottom of it to see what I could find to use in the bathwater. Tucked away at the back of the wardrobe I found what I was looking for. Several bottles of shampoo and conditioner, I will have to read the instructions for that. I also found a pack of six bottles of bubble bath. Great, now I might be able to smell a bit better than the cattle did.

I took all my finds through to the bathroom and began running the water. I had a quick read of the bubble bath bottle. Just pour a small amount in the water and watch the bubbles. I laughed to myself. *"Get me, having a bubble bath".*

I would have my bath and then attempt to wash my hair. There is a shower head that I have used before to rinse the soap out of my very long, very thick auburn hair. It just fastens on the taps.

I sank down into the gorgeous-smelling water. The bubbles felt so luxurious. I could have stayed there for days.

These regular baths were working wonders on my skin. It now looked clean and after this, it would smell nice as well. Even my hands were looking clean, just my nails to try and get clean now, they looked a mess.

Eventually, I got out of the cooling water and wrapped myself in one of the old, threadbare towels that I always used. I began to shiver so went back into the bedroom and put my dressing gown on. This was a very old one that had belonged to Dot and was enormous. Something else I would have to treat myself to.

Once I warmed up a bit I went back into the bathroom and read how to use the shampoo and conditioner. Seemed easy enough. *"Let's give it a go"*.

It was quite a long job because my hair is so long and thick. I always tie it up and plait it to keep it out of the way.

'*The sooner I get it chopped off the better*' I thought.

The shampoo smelt lovely, and I could feel how different my hair was. I finally used rather a lot of conditioner rubbing it through the long lengths. It advised to leave it on for ten minutes and then rinse it out. It smelt good enough to eat. '*It had the smell of apples*' I thought. "*A very fresh smell*".

After what seemed an age, I had rinsed all the conditioner away so wrapped my hair in another towel and began rubbing it to try and dry it a bit. That is the problem with hair this long, it does take such a long time to dry. I will sit by the fire when I eat the remainder of the stew for my tea, that may help it to dry.

I got the old hairbrush that had belonged to Dot and began to brush the long lengths of my hair. It felt so different. Really soft, I liked the feel of it. Perhaps it wouldn't be so bad if I kept it washed and conditioned regularly. Will have to wait and see.

I had asked Will once if I could have a new hairbrush and he had gone mad, said he wasn't made of money and the brush that I had was quite good enough.

I warmed my tea up then sat in front of the fire and ate it, enjoying every mouthful. I would have to make some bread in the morning. I will have to offer Mr Ryan something to eat as he is coming all the way from London. There was cheese in the fridge, and I had cooked a piece of gammon ham at the weekend intending to make dinner with it.

Never mind, I will use it for sandwiches and not care how wasteful it is. There were homemade pickles still in the pantry to go with the sandwiches and I would knock up a quick sponge cake as well. Sorted.

By the time I had eaten my stew, my hair had almost dried. Still damp underneath but if I kept brushing it then that would help it to dry.

I couldn't believe how soft my hair felt and the smell was divine. I spent some time just brushing it from the scalp to the very ends, always plaiting it I hadn't realised there was a natural curl to it.

When I was satisfied it was dry I took the brush with me back upstairs. I sat on the edge of the bed and looked in the long mirror hanging on the wardrobe door. I looked so different. I brushed my hair one way then the other, pushing it behind my ears and then having it hang just straight down over my ears. I couldn't decide which way looked best. I will leave it down tomorrow and then ask Caroline what she thinks.

I wandered back down the stairs and washed up my supper things. This was so different, nothing to do. I could get used to this. After a while, I decided to go and make a start on Will's wardrobe.

I opened the doors and looked at the rail, rammed full with clothes I had never seen before. There were labels still hanging on most of them.

This was complete madness, when had he been shopping? He did have the odd day away, but I never saw him bring bags into the house. He must have waited till I was busy in the barn then took his purchases in without me seeing. But why? That is what I couldn't understand. He really had been a very strange man.

I closed the doors once more, couldn't face it yet. Caroline will know what I should do with all this stuff. It can't stay there especially if the place is sold. Then where would I live? I really hope Caroline means what she says about staying friends with me. I won't have a clue if I am left to deal with all this on my own.

I will have a look in the chest of drawers, they might be easier to get through. I opened the top drawer and found his underpants, there didn't seem to be anything else in there so closed the drawer. The next one was full of socks, and pushed down the side was a big envelope. I opened it and found yet more money. I looked for a note or some writing, anything to explain what this money was for. Nothing, just a large brown envelope stuffed full of money. I put it to take downstairs to put in the safe with the other money.

I had managed to find the key to the safe in a desk drawer so I could at least lock the money away. None of this seemed real. We had lived mostly hand to mouth, never buying anything we could manage without. Oh well, let's see what else I can find.

The third drawer was almost empty apart from three boxes, I opened them and found a watch in each box. All very different and looked very expensive. I put those to go in the safe as well.

The rest of the drawers held various pieces of clothing but little else, so I pushed those back in and then took the money and watches down to the safe. Mr Ryan would have a lot of sorting out to do.

I need to find out everything that is hidden in this house. If it is sold then the house will probably be knocked down and any of Will's things hidden away will either go to whoever knocks it down or be buried. This is going to be a very long job I guess.

I slept so well that the next morning I was late getting up to sort out the dog and cats. The dog was always locked up overnight, but the cats were just left to roam, they always found their way back by breakfast time the next day though.

I quickly sorted them out then went back into the kitchen to make the bread and whip up a cake. Caroline will be here soon and then Mr Ryan. I wonder how much he knows about all the money and jewellery? If he doesn't know about it then he is in for a surprise.

Once the bread was made and set to rise and the cake was in the oven I went upstairs to get ready. My hair was flying loose around my head and it felt very freeing.

My usual style is very severe. I plait it then wind it round and around my head holding it in place with pins. There is so much of it I struggle to keep it restrained.

I searched through the clothes of Dot's that were still in the wardrobe in the second bedroom. She had been a very large woman so this stuff will be way too big anyway. There were some trousers that were massive and a couple of skirts that would be equally too big. There were a couple of blouses that might make dresses for me but nothing I could use straight away.

Back to my own meagre clothes offerings. I settled on an old check shirt that had been my dad's and didn't look too bad and a pair of black work trousers that were at least clean.

I went to the bathroom and washed my face and hands then cleaned my teeth. I put on the chosen clothes and then set about doing my hair. I brushed it as best I could. The brush itself was very old and not good for untangling bed hair. I did what I could. It didn't look too bad and at least it was clean and shiny.

As I put the brush down I heard the back door open. That will be Caroline, I flew down the stairs, hair flying all over the place.

I dashed through the door into the kitchen, breathless with excitement. Caroline looked up at me. "Blimey! what have you done with Ella?" she said.

I laughed, "I found some bubble bath, shampoo, and conditioner. So I went to town. Do you like it?"

"I do," she said, "you look like a new woman. Your hair is amazing, I hadn't realised just how long it is. How long did it take you to grow it?"

"All my life," I said, "it has never been cut. I almost put the scissors to it last night".

"Don't do that," she said, "it is beautiful. I would change my mousy locks for that rich mane in an instant. It is fabulous, such a gorgeous colour."

"Did you find anything of interest when looking for the bubble bath"?

"I did. Another pile of money and three men's watches. They look expensive. I put it all in the safe with the other stuff. Thought we could present it to Mr Ryan when he gets here."

"He will be as surprised as us I should think," she said. "It is like Aladdin's cave in this place. Wonder what the total sum will be. He was a very unusual person, this Will of yours."

"Please, not my Will, more like my nightmare. I cannot understand why he made us all live the way he did when he had all this money lying around. Total madness. I have been looking through his wardrobe and it is full of clothes still with the labels on. He only ever wore the same few things, very old and full of holes."

"I will just get the cake out of the oven and then put the bread in. If I don't hurry up, Mr Ryan will be here."

"Right," said Caroline, "sort your oven out then I suggest we start on that big filing cabinet in the office. We should be able to do a couple of drawers before Mr Ryan gets here."

I did as she said, the cake had risen well so I put it to cool down and then popped the loaves into the oven. *"Mustn't forget them, they soon burn"*.

I went into the office to join Caroline just in time to see her pull out a large envelope. "Wow," she said, turning to me then said, "then there's more."

"More bank notes, Oh God," I said, "whatever shall we do with all this money?"

"Well, you and I could go on a trip around the world to start with but perhaps we had best put it in the safe with the other things."

I had just opened the safe door when I heard knocking in the kitchen. I pushed the envelope into the safe and then went to see who it was.

Mr Ryan stood just inside the doorway, he saw me and smiled. "May I come in? My name is Ryan, Scott Ryan and I have an appointment with Mrs Adams."

"Sorry, Mr Ryan, come in. I was expecting you."

He looked a little puzzled, "Mrs Adams, is it you? My goodness, you look a lot different to the last time I was here."

"Sorry," I said, "I have tidied myself up a bit since you were last here. Come on in, don't just stand there. We have an awful lot to tell you."

"Of course," he held out his hand to shake mine. "Come on through," I said, "Caroline is in the office. I will put the kettle on. You must be ready for a drink."

"I am Mrs Adams, the traffic was bad on the motorway, it seems to have taken an age to get here."

"I really appreciate you taking the time to come. I have been in a real tizzy since Will died, I don't have a clue what to do first. I don't know what I would have done without Caroline."

"Well, friends are always welcome at times like these. Now, let's see if we can make things even easier for you."

I quickly sandwiched my sponge cake together with some jam I had made earlier in the year. It all smelt nice. I assembled a tray with the tea things and the cake together with plates and a knife. That should do.

I checked on the bread and decided it was ready so took it out of the oven and left the loaves to cool.

I carried the tray through to the office and placed it on the desk. Caroline had begun taking all the things out of the safe. It looked like rather a lot. The money was stacked on one part of the desk then the jewellery and watches on another.

I glanced at Mr Ryan, he looked as puzzled as I had done. He looked up at me as I placed the tray down and said, "I see what you mean. I guess you had no idea about all this stuff."

"I did not," I said, "Will was a miser, we didn't have any luxuries and had to live a frugal life. He hated having to spend any money, especially on me. I have lived a nightmare life since the day I was born and then was forced to marry him when I was just sixteen. He has abused me ever since.

Will dying has given me the chance to live a normal life at long last. I am twenty-five years old and have never been further than Marchpool and that hasn't happened very often. I have no idea how to live a normal life, to be honest."

Mr Ryan looked horrified, "I had no idea all this was going on Mrs Adams. Had I realised I would have done something about it."

"Please don't call me that, my name is Ella and that's what I want you to call me."

"Okay Ella, just as long as you call me Scott."

"Deal," I said. "Meet my saviour, Caroline." They shook hands and they seemed to hold a gaze between them for what felt like an age.

"Now let's have a cup of tea and a slice of cake before we tackle all this stuff, shall we?"

We all sat eating cake and drinking tea, making small talk. Once finished I cleared all the pots away and made room for all of the money.

Caroline asked, "Where do we start? We have both begun counting the money then got overwhelmed and put it all back in the safe."

Scott said that he thinks the first thing he wants to do is to give me all the details of the will. I said that we had found a copy of it but didn't really understand it.

"Okay, the will that you have a copy of is slightly different from the latest one that had been amended the last time I had been to the farm. So not that long ago really."

"I won't bother with all the legal jargon, it is very boring but basically wheels have been set in motion to sell the farmland and all the buildings and machinery. Everything really. There is a buyer ready and waiting with the money to complete that sale."

"Had Will lived he intended to buy a smallholding or a house with a fair amount of land. In the event of his death then everything passes to you, Ella. I assume you will want to go ahead with the sale."

"Yes, Scott, I do. The only thing is I have no idea what to do next. I am so used to living without people. I don't think I could live in a city or a town. The thought of a village scares me so anything bigger will be out of the question. I was actually born here, on the kitchen floor I believe, and never lived anywhere else.

I have no idea how to buy a house or furniture or anything, not even a pair of knickers. I haven't ever been to a cinema or theatre, not even a public library. I am going to need an awful lot of help and advice. I hadn't used the phone before until I found Will dead down the lane". I had begun to shake thinking about all the changes that were going to happen.

Scott was smiling at me. "Please don't get ahead of yourself, Ella. Me and my company are at your disposal anytime you need help and advice. I am sure that Caroline will also be on hand to give help whenever needed."

"All you need to know for now is that whatever you decide to do there will be money available. You will be a very wealthy young woman."

"Does that mean I will be able to get my hair cut I asked.?"

"Well, yes of course but why would you want to cut your hair, it's beautiful."

"That's what I told her," said Caroline.

"Well, I have never had it cut and it really does get on my nerves. If I am going to be this new woman then I should perhaps have a new look." They both laughed at me.

"I think you have far more things to make decisions about before worrying about your hair." They both said it was glorious as it was and not to do anything just yet.

"I won't," I said.

"So, what should we do first," I asked.?

"Well, I suggest we get all this money counted and put into your bank account." I looked blank.

"Go on," said Scott, "tell me, you don't have a bank account."

"No, I don't, never needed one because I have never had any money."

"Right, we need to think about this a bit more. We will get it counted first. Is this it? No more hiding anywhere?"

"I have no idea, Scott. It feels like every time I open a cupboard or drawer I find more money. I will need to start at the top of the house and look through everything I guess. I began to get frightened to open any more drawers in case there was another surprise."

"Not only the money but the watches and jewellery. It is all a mystery to me. I had no idea any of these things existed."

Scott said, "The only thing I can help you with is the jewellery, it was all left to Will by his great-grandmother many years ago. Will never told me about any of the other stuff.

Look, Ella, will it help if I stay for a couple of days and help you go through it all?"

"Would you do that Scott, it doesn't seem fair on you. Your family will be needing you back at home."

" Don't worry about that Ella, I will go back tonight and come up again tomorrow. I can then stay either one or two nights. Will you be here as well Caroline?"

"Yes, certainly through the days but I will have to leave in the late afternoon".

"Does that mean you are staying here on your own Ella?"

"Yes, of course?. That doesn't bother me, I have virtually lived on my own anyway. Will only ever had anything to do with me at bedtime and I can live without that, thank you very much."

Scott looked horrified, "Has your life really that bad?"

"It has," I replied. "When you have several hours free I can give you the facts."

"No need for that, my dear, I believe you."

"Tell me something Scott, why did Will use your company? There must be more lawyers that live closer."

"Our connection goes back many years, since before Will or I had been born. Will's father and grandfather used our company. I think my grandfather and Will's grandfather had known each other since childhood. Then, once my grandfather began the business Will's grandfather used us and the connection has stayed ever since. That is how I know about the jewellery although I have never seen it.

It hasn't been a problem being in London. With trains and cars, we can get anywhere in a short space of time. Will normally came down to our offices whenever there was something needed doing anyway."

"Well, all I can say is thank goodness for those two grandfathers. I can't imagine being so comfortable in the company of other lawyers."

"I will take that as a compliment then. Now, let the great forage begin."

I had noticed how Caroline seemed to be watching Scott a lot. She fancies him, I thought. Bet he is married though.

"Tell me, Scott. Are you married?" I saw how Caroline's head shot up at the question.

Not any longer came the reply. "I was married, my ex-wife's name is Flora. We stay friendly for the sake of the children, we have two girls, Becki and Melisa. They are eight and six. I manage to see them regularly and they come to stay with me some weekends and holidays. It works quite well."

"I am sorry," I heard myself saying.

"That's okay, it was a long time ago and we have all moved on.

"Do you have a girlfriend then?" I asked?.

"Goodness me, no. Don't have time for that, I'm afraid."

I smiled at him, "Never say never," I said.

" Maybe, one day," was his reply.

We set about counting all of the money we had found so far. There was a lot of it. Scott was amazed at the sight of the jewellery and the watches. He had no idea where they had come from.

It was decided over lunch that we would go into Marchpool, open a bank account and put the money in there.

Scott wanted to use a London bank, but I said I would never be going there so that wouldn't work. I also needed to collect the death certificate and go to register the death.

"The thing is Ella, banks have branches in most towns throughout the country so it won't really matter so much where we go to open the account. You will be able to use any of the branches, wherever you go. We can do your other jobs whilst we are out."

"I doubt very much I will be going far," I said. "I am out of my depth if I go as far as the farm gate. Any further and I begin to shake with fear of the unknown."

Scott said, "All that is for the future. Let's deal with today first. We need to get this lot into a safe place and then begin the great excavation of the rest of the house."

"Will it be okay for me to stay here for a couple of nights? I don't want to put you out."

"Your company will be welcome," I said. "There are plenty of rooms here. The only thing is, apart from the bread, ham and cheese we have here for lunch there is little else to eat. Will always fetched any shopping we needed. Will you be able to collect some food for us to eat?"

"Of course I will, unless Caroline would like to meet me at the supermarket tomorrow, then we can get something that we will all enjoy."

"I can do that," said Caroline. I thought to myself, "*you little madam, getting your foot in the door there*".

I wish I had her courage, she has seen something she wants and will go for it. I could never be that brave. Anyway, after Will I can't see me ever wanting to have another relationship with any man. I found the sex side of things disgusting. Why any woman would want to willingly do *'that'* with a man is beyond me. As far as I am concerned "*once more would be once too many*". No, not going there ever again".

After lunch, Scott took me into the town, what a revelation. I am told that Marchpool is a small town compared to some others. We went straight to the bank, Scott asked if it would be possible to speak with the manager. A few minutes later we were taken through to the manager's office. I left all the talking to Scott, I managed to shake hands with the manager then just sat back and listened.

Scott explained a little of what had happened and what we needed to do. The manager, Mr Jenkins was very helpful. He suggested what we should do with the money and Scott thought his idea would work. One hundred and seventy thousand pounds should be put in a separate account that will gain interest. The remaining fifty-eight thousand pounds was to be put into a current account giving me some money with which to pay all the bills that would be coming my way before too long.

He arranged for a chequebook and bank card to be issued in my name. All that done, we set off for the surgery then to the registry office which is where I had married Will. We registered his death with a lot of help from Scott who also requested several copies of the death certificate so I can claim on the insurances.

On the drive back to the farm I couldn't help but bring up Caroline. I wanted to know if she was in with a chance and from his replies to my questions I think she is. That would be so nice for two people who were helping me to cope with all this trauma. I liked the idea of a happy ending for them.

We arrived back at the farm by three o'clock, Caroline had the kettle on, so the first job was to have a mug of tea and another slice of cake.

Scott had kept three thousand pounds back in cash which we had put back into the safe along with the jewellery and watches. It remains to be seen if we can find anything else in our great explore.

Scott left for home shortly after with the plan to return the next day, meeting Caroline in Tesco's car park at ten the next morning. I had made a list of things I thought we might need over the next couple of days. I would have to get used to doing the shopping myself eventually but not just yet. So much was happening and so quickly, it scared the life out of me if I'm honest.

Once they had left I sorted the dog and cats out with some food and fresh water then locked myself away in the house. I wouldn't venture into the attic on my own. Only ever been in there once before and I didn't like it at all. Scott was welcome to go up there on his own.

There are still so many cupboards and wardrobes to be sorted, I think the best thing I can do is go through one room at a time. Make sure I get everything out that is of interest then decide what to do with the rest later on.

I suppose I should start on the room that Scott will sleep in first, clear out the cupboards and drawers then put some fresh sheets on the bed. I will need to put a couple of hot water bottles in the bed to air it first.

I set the kettle to boil and then found two hot water bottles to fill. Once they were ready I set off up the stairs. The rooms are all clean at least. I pulled the eiderdown back, put the bottles onto the mattress then pulled the eiderdown back up.

I went in search of decent sheets and blankets. Most of the bedding was very old but a search through a blanket box in another of the rooms revealed what looked like newish sheets and pillow cases plus several blankets. I pulled them all out, draped them around the room to see if they needed washing, to begin with then left them out to air properly.

I have never seen any of them before. I wasn't allowed to look in bedrooms or go through drawers or cupboards. I could only use certain things and they were all threadbare. No idea where any of these things had come from.

I went back into the bedroom I was preparing for Scott. There is a small cabinet at the side of the bed, a chest of drawers and a small wardrobe. That wouldn't take long. I will go through those and then put fresh hot water bottles in the bed. I will then go and find something to eat before having another long soak in the bath.

There was little to be found in that room. Just rubbish really, I have no idea what I am supposed to do with it all. I will ask Caroline tomorrow, to see if she has any ideas.

I did a quick tidy round and decided I would make the bed up in the morning. I went downstairs and made a sandwich, cheese was all that was left apart from this morning's bread. I made a mug of tea and sat thinking about all that had happened over the past few days and all that was going to happen in the future. *God, I hope I can cope with all the changes. What would I do without Caroline and now Scott?"*

Next, I ran a tubful of lovely hot water. I wouldn't wash my hair again, I had only done it the day before. I did one of my long plaits then wrapped it round my head, pinning it in place to keep it from getting wet.

I carefully climbed into the tub which I had scented with yesterday's find. The smell was gorgeous. I lay back in the bubbles and began to relax.

This is such a new feeling to me. I seem to have been tense and anxious all my life and now I can let all that go and look forward, forward to what though. I just have to trust in other people now. People I don't know, people I have only just met. People I have yet to meet.

That thought is very scary. I have never been good with strangers and have never been given the opportunity to meet many people at all. I have always just stumbled around saying yes, or no and thank you. Since meeting Caroline and now Scott properly I have begun to come out of my shell a bit and can actually hold a conversation with these two-lovely people.

My one worry at the moment is that before long I will have to venture to do things on my own. I can't expect them to be my help and support forever.

That thought made me tense up for a moment then I thought, oh, sod it. I have got to do this now. No other way but forward. I just hope and pray the world and all its people will be kind to me.

I slept really well again and didn't get out of bed till seven-thirty. That is some lie in for me. Will would insist I got up with him at five am then of course we always had to go to bed early so that I could suffer the almost daily trauma of sex. I shudder every time I think of it. Still, don't have to do that ever again.

Once up and dressed I made tea and put two slices of bread in the toaster. Of course, it was a bit stale by now but at least it was food. I put my pots in the sink then went upstairs to make the bed up for Scott.

It will be strange having someone else sleep in the same house as me. We never had visitors at all really, except for those needing to speak with Will about farm matters and of course, they didn't stay over.

I opened the bedroom window to let a bit of fresh air into the room. Everywhere felt musty and old to me. There was a gentle breeze blowing so that would soon blow away the bad smells.

I then went to sort out the dog, yes that really is his name, and the cats that don't have any names. I was thinking about what to do with them when it was time for me to leave when I heard the telephone ringing in the office. I ran back in and picked up the receiver holding it to my ear, "Hello," I said cautiously.

"Morning," came the reply. "Ted here, Ted Griffiths, you remember, I came to your farm the other day to take your animals away?"

"Oh, yes," I said, "are they all okay?"

"Yes, they are my lovely. Even the chickens seem happy with their new surroundings. I was only wondering what you intend to do with your dog and cats. I'm assuming you won't be taking them with you."

"It's funny you should say that," I said, "I was just wondering what to do with them myself."

"Well, if it will be of help to you I can take them as well. My old dog has been put to sleep this morning. He was very old and this morning he couldn't get up. Poor bugger. So that made me think about your dog and cats."

"Well, Mr Griffiths, if you can make use of them then they are yours. I don't really like any of them very much and I don't think they like me either. I wouldn't be cruel to them, but they are farm animals and not pets so with me not having a farm for much longer it would be a big relief to me to know they were going to a good home. The cats are amazing mousers, by the way."

"That's sorted then, my lovely. Can I come round this afternoon to collect them?"

"Certainly, you can," I said, "I will be here all day trying to sort out all the rubbish that is in the house."

"Whilst I am on the phone, can I ask what you will be doing with all Will's old clothes? Only I have a few farm labourers working for me and some of them are not very well turned out. If there is anything that I can take to give to my men it would be very helpful."

"Mr Griffiths, you are my saviour, I will sort some of the better stuff out so you can take it with you."

" Great," said Mr Griffiths, "see you later today."

I sat back in the office chair and breathed out a very long breath. *"This man was turning out to be a Godsend".*

So, Scott's room is sorted, and the animals have been fed and watered. Now I will go and sort all those clothes out. *"Get them gone"* is what I thought. One more job ticked off the list.

I went up to the bedroom first as that is where most of Will's clothes seemed to be. I began pulling them out of his wardrobe and lying them on the bed. I guess I will need to go through the pockets before letting them go.

It was a long job and didn't reveal much apart from handkerchiefs and bits of paper. I put the papers to one side thinking I will need to read them before throwing them away, just in case. I folded all the clothes up and put them into five piles. Shirts, trousers, jackets and jumpers, then underwear and socks. They were all in good condition and a lot were brand new.

The chest of drawers was next. Vests, pants, tee shirts and socks. *"There was an awful lot of them too. I can't understand why Will spent all his life in just the same few things with me having to mend them constantly when this lot lay unused in the drawers. Madness".*

All of those went into two more piles. I will have to make several trips downstairs to get them all together for when Ted arrives. At least this stuff would do someone some good.

It was the bottom drawer that revealed some more jewellery. The drawer was mostly filled with rubbish again. Old combs with some of the teeth missing. Boot cleaning brushes and clothes for the same purpose judging by the colour of them. Then right at the back, I found seven little boxes. Wasn't sure what I would find in them.

The first one I opened was empty, but the others all had a ring in each. Very elaborate and looked very old. It was whilst looking at these rings I started thinking about the other jewellery from the safe. "That all looked very old too. I wonder if these rings had belonged to Will's great-grandmother as well, maybe. Something else for Scott to look at".

I heard the kitchen door open, and Caroline shouted upstairs, "Hi, Ella, are you up there?"

" I am I replied, coming down now."

I gathered a pile of clothes and carried them down with me. I will just put these in the front room then I will make you both a cuppa.

I then went through to the kitchen wondering what they had managed to buy.

The kitchen table held rather a lot of plastic carrier bags and a box with bottles in it. Caroline had already put the kettle on.

"You look as if you have been busy," she said, "and why is your hair all tied up again?"

"I have been busy," I said, "and I put my hair up last night whilst I had my bath then forgot to take it down again. I will do it later."

"You two look as if you have been busy as well."

Scott was beaming. "You like shopping then, do you, Scott?" I asked.

He laughed, "Not usually but Caroline made it fun. She is a very funny lady you know."

"I do know that," I said. "Her humour has kept me going this past few days. I don't know what I would have done without you both."

"Well, we have some news on that front as well," said Caroline. "Scott has invited us both down to London to stay in his house in Wimbledon. That is a place outside of the city and where his family home is. I have rung work and booked three weeks' holiday starting today. So, once we have sorted everything out here, we will go back down with Scott and be able to enjoy a couple of weeks living in luxury."

I must have looked horrified, "Whatever is the matter Ella?" asked Caroline.

"I can't go to London, I won't know how to be, what to do, anything."

Scott came over and put his arm around my shoulders, "Now Ella, enough of that. We have arranged this so that you won't be on your own. We will be with you and we can then gently introduce you to your new life. I have a big house so there is plenty of room."

"My younger brother, Jacob, is staying with me at the moment as well. He has gone through a very nasty split with his pain of an arse ex, and he is feeling delicate. A home for waifs and strays is what I have. You two are more than welcome to share it with me.

I will have to go into the office a few times, but I am clearing my diary as best I can so that I can take you both sightseeing. You won't be able to say you have never been to London again."

"I can't," I said, "look at me. Everyone will laugh at me."

Caroline said. "I have thought of that and have bought you a few things from Tesco. They will be fine until we can go shopping in London."

I felt myself draw in a big breath. I suddenly felt very small and scared. "I can't go shopping, that will mean speaking to strangers, I can't do that, and I don't understand the money yet."

"Nonsense," she said, "Scott and I were strangers to you a couple of days ago and now look at us all. You won't have to do anything or go anywhere on your own. We will be with you every step of the way. Now, stop fretting about it. We are going to have a lovely time, a real adventure."

"Right, first things first, tea." She went off and made a pot setting it down on the table. "I have bought some cream cakes as well for a treat. Now sit down and tell us what you have been doing."

I sat down in a daze. Me going to London, unbelievable. I tried to put it out of my mind for now.

Scott was busy emptying the bags and putting stuff in the ancient fridge. Cakes appeared on a plate and little plates were spread round the table, so we had one each. The cakes looked lovely. Caroline poured the tea and then sat down next to Scott.

I am sure there is something going on between those two, they look very comfortable together. Time will tell.

Caroline began pulling clothes out of the bags. "Blimey! Caroline," I said, "how much do I owe you?"

"Don't worry about it yet, let's eat first then you can tell me about your day so far." Before we could choose a cake Scott placed a big pork pie on the table along with a jar of my pickle. He had bought a loaf and was cutting huge slices from it. Butter was put on the table so we could help ourselves.

"Are you two trying to fatten me up?" I asked. "I won't fit into any of those clothes at this rate."

We all laughed and then began to eat. What a lovely lunch we had.

We all enjoyed the bread and pork pie with the pickle then the cakes. Oh my goodness, I have never tasted anything so wonderful. I ate two then had two mugs of tea. I am turning into a right pig.

Whilst we had been eating I had filled them in on my morning. I said,"It's a good job Mr Griffiths is taking dog and the cats. I have sorted a load of Will's clothes out for him as well to give to his workers. Still a load more to do but at least I have made a start."

"Why do you always refer to the dog as 'dog'?" asked Caroline.

"Because that's his name," I replied. We all burst out laughing at that. I told them that Ted Griffiths was coming to fetch dog and the cats and all these clothes later in the day.

"You have been busy," said Scott.

"Yes, I have. I found seven more boxes in a drawer upstairs. One was empty but the others had rings in them. I was wondering if the empty one had this wedding ring inside. It's only silver so don't imagine it's worth a lot."

Scott asked if he could look at it, I pulled it off my finger and looked at it, "You can keep it as far as I'm concerned."

I handed the ring to him and he began examining it. He smiled, "This is not silver Ella, this is platinum. Looks expensive to me, not that I'm an expert. We could take the jewellery to London when we go and get it all valued."

There it was again. The mention of going to London made me feel sick. I will have to pull out before they set off. They will have a better time without me anyway. Just go along with it for now.

I got up and went to fetch the other boxes. I put them all on the table and left them to examine the contents whilst I cleared the table and began to wash up.

"Ella, these rings look very valuable to me and very old as well," said Scott. "Did you find any paperwork with them?"

"I don't know," I replied, "the drawers are full of bits of paper and rubbish? The papers are in the drawers in the bedroom I have made up for you so if you want to have a look then be my guest."

"I will later on, usually these old pieces have some sort of paperwork with them. If not we will do as I suggested and take them to London. I know a couple of jewellers. They can decide what they are worth."

"Right madam," said Caroline, "let's go and try these clothes on, make sure they fit."

We gathered up all the things she had chosen for me and went up to the bedroom. Right then she said, "What do you want to try first?"

There was so much, jeans, blouses and jumpers, a pretty dress. Some smart trousers, a couple of jackets, underwear, nighties and a dressing gown plus two pairs of shoes.

Caroline had good taste and it all fit. "Will I need all this stuff," I asked, I usually just wear the same things for several days. Saves on the washing and ironing.

"You will need more than these few things," she said. We can hit the London shops and get you properly rigged out."

"Oh, Caroline, I don't think I can go to London. The thought of it scares me to death. Leave me here and you go with Scott. I think he likes you, a lot."

"Well, I like him a lot as well, but this is all being done for your benefit, not ours. You will go to London and you will have a fabulous time. We will be there with you every step of the way so stop worrying."

"Okay," I said reluctantly. "But I won't enjoy it, I know I won't."

All she said was, "We'll see."

The phone in the office rang and Caroline ran in to answer it. It was the Co-op Funeral directors. Will's body has been released so they can arrange his cremation. So this is it, the final piece of the puzzle.

Caroline arranged for us to go to their office the following day to sort the final things out. There really wasn't much we could do though. Will had left instructions for his own funeral. No mourners, not even me. Not that I would mourn him. It was just a case of checking that I was happy with everything. The funeral was already paid for, so I don't have to bother with that either.

We went back into the kitchen where Scott was patiently waiting. "All good?" he asked. We both said, "Yes, no problems for a change. Will's body has been released so they can get on with the cremation. I don't have to go to that thank goodness. I would feel like a fraud pretending to care."

Scott said, "I am pleased about that, Ella. You have enough to cope with. I have a suggestion for you. How about if we leave someone else to sort all this lot out?"

"What do you mean?" I asked.

"Well, a friend of mine runs an auction house. I have spoken to him on your behalf, and he says that they can come in and sort everything out. Rubbish to be burnt then if there is any furniture or ornaments worth selling they will take that away to be cleaned up and sent to auction. If they find anything else that might be valuable then that can be kept separate, and a price put on it. This is the guy I thought of asking about the jewellery. He assures me his workers are very trustworthy and have tackled similar jobs before."

"Once all that can be sold is disposed of and everything completed then you will get a cheque from them. Obviously, they charge for this service, but I wondered if you would prefer to let someone else take the problem out of your hands. You need to remember you are going to be a very wealthy woman once all this and the sale of the land is completed. It would free you up to start living again."

"What do you mean, again? I have never lived before so it will be like I am just being born. So yes, I think that is a fabulous idea. Ted will be here to collect dog and the cats soon." I feel lighter all of a sudden.

"Does this mean you will be going back down to London then?" I asked.

"Well, yes it does but you will be coming with us.'

" I don't think I can do that Scott."

"Yes, you can and you will. Let's get all the stuff ready for Ted to take then sort out what you will be taking with you. We can set off first thing in the morning if the funeral directors can manage without you, so you won't have time to worry about it. I will ring them to check."

"Caroline, have you got to go home to sort your stuff out?"

"Yes, I have but I can do that tonight then be ready when you are. I will leave my car locked away in the garage and travel with you."

Ted arrived to collect the animals and the clothes, he was pleased with everything. Dog came over quickly and was put in the back of Ted's car. The cats took longer but eventually, they were rounded up and put in the cage that Ted had bought with him. I had a box ready with the remaining food so that went with them as well.

I told him that I would be away after today for a week or two, but that people would be here sorting everything out so if he did need anything he would probably be able to deal directly with Scott's friend, Ed.

He went off happy. Scott and I went into the office and checked that all the things we wanted to take with us were handy. Scott had a lot of paperwork he would be taking with him.

"Right then young lady, let's go and eat and perhaps have a glass of wine to help us relax."

"I have never had wine," I said, "in fact, I have never had any alcohol at all."

"Well, this is your day to start trying all these new and exciting things."

"If you say so, Scott. I am really not comfortable with this though."

"Stop being so worried. Caroline and I will be with you all the time. Also, my brother Jacob will be there and he's a nice guy. I told you he was staying with me for a while. He has had a rough time and I think having you around will be good for him as well."

Ted had bought the post down with him when he'd arrived. He had met the postie at the end of the lane. Saved her a trip down here he said. I rarely had any post but there were three envelopes with my name on them.

Scott saw me eyeing them and said, "they won't bite".

I laughed, "Okay," I said, "let's see what we have here. The first one contained a bank card. No idea what I would do with that. The second one held a chequebook and paid in slips. The third was all the information I would need regarding my bank account. There was also a statement telling me how much money I had. Blimey! this is going to take some getting used to."

I was going to need some money to pay Caroline for the clothes she has bought me and also for when I go shopping in London. Get me, shopping in London. Just thinking about it made me shudder. I still had the cash from the safe so that will last me a while. I would need to buy a purse to keep some money in. I will need to make a list.

Caroline had brought me a suitcase of hers so I could put all the new stuff in there later on. All my old things could stay here and be burnt along with all the other rubbish.

We decided to eat, Scott had bought steaks and frozen chips plus a salad already in a bowl. Who would have thought it? If we had chips I had to melt lard in a saucepan to cook them in. We didn't have them very often, they tasted disgusting.

Scott said for us both to sit down and have a glass of wine, he would cook. A man, cooking, this I needed to see.

Caroline chose a bottle of red wine and then poured three glasses out. Not wine glasses I might add. We didn't have any of those, so we used the glasses we normally had for water.

She assured me the wine would taste better in proper glasses, but these would do for now. I picked up my glass and smelt it. It didn't smell like anything I had ever smelt before. I wasn't sure this was for me. I took a sip then another. Not as bad as I thought it would be.

Scott said that he's no expert, but he does enjoy a glass with his evening meal. He said that his brother, Jacob, knows far more about it than he does. He will teach you what are good wines and what to steer clear of.

"Does he know he has to babysit a twenty-five-year-old woman?"

Scott laughed, "He does. Obviously, I had to fill him in on some of your history but by no means all of it. He is a good listener and very good company. If you want to tell him everything then that's up to you and if you don't want to tell him anything that is also up to you. He will be fine no matter what."

"Right, the food is ready. Sit and eat."

It turns out that Scott is a good cook after all. I have never had steak before, but this is wonderful and frozen chips, another revelation, so much nicer than the greasy ones I cooked. Salad already made in a bowl, how easy would life be with these things at hand? We all tucked into the meal and talked as we ate. *"Is this what real life looks like"* I wondered. It was a most enjoyable time. Perhaps the best time I had ever spent.

Meal over and cleared away we decided to do a quick check of each room to make sure there was nothing obvious being left behind. Once that was done I decided to pack my new clothes into Caroline's case and just leave the things out I would be wearing the next day. I had drunk a whole glass of wine and it had a good effect on me.

I suddenly realised I could do this. With Caroline and Scott helping me I had nothing to fear. Maybe I should take up wine drinking-regularly.

The final check around the house hadn't revealed anything so Scott said we should leave the jewellery and money in the safe overnight and then take it all with us the next morning.

Caroline left for home at six, I noticed Scott kissed her lips as she left. We arranged to pick her up from her house at nine the next morning. I had another long soak in a hot bath. How extravagant am I, don't care though. No more having to watch every penny for me.

Scott had his bath after me then we both sat down in the lounge and had another glass of wine. It made me feel really relaxed and calm. I could get used to this I thought.

Scott is such a nice man. He seems to have dropped everything to come and help me. I hope we can remain friends.

Once we were happy that everything we could do had been done we decided to go to bed, and get an early night. There would be a lot to do in the morning.

I slept well again, woke at seven o'clock and could hear Scott doing something downstairs. I quickly got up, had a quick wash and dressed in my new clothes. I felt really different. I pulled all the bedding off my bed and then left it in a pile on the floor. Couldn't be bothered folding it all up.

I arrived downstairs to the smell of bacon frying. "Scott, what are you doing? I should be cooking you breakfast. You fed me well yesterday. You are really spoiling me."

"Stop worrying, sit down. Bacon sarnies are almost ready. The tea is made so you can pour that out if you will." I did as he asked then sat down at the old kitchen table. The smell of bacon cooking made my stomach rumble. I shall be the size of a house if I keep eating like this.

Once our breakfast was finished, we began packing all the food from the fridge and the bottles of wine that Scott had bought. We couldn't take everything so left it for Scott's friend to deal with. He and his team would be arriving the next day.

The bags and my case were stacked in the boot along with the food and wine bottles. We put as much rubbish in the bins as we could manage then finally we went into the office. I got all the jewellery out and put it onto the desk while Scott assembled all the paperwork he needed. I fetched a couple of bags from the kitchen, and we put all our booty in those.

One more quick look around then I locked the door whilst Scott put the last of the bags safely in the boot. I put the key under an old plant pot by the door so that Ed would be able to get in.

I turned back to look at the house, hopefully for the last time. Scott had rung the electricity and water suppliers along with the council to inform them that the building would be empty in two weeks so that should stop any more bills being forwarded. "This is it then," I said, "Bye old life, hello new life."

"That's the attitude I have been looking for," said Scott. "Let's go and pick Caroline up then get on our way."

We drove up the lane leading to the main road with both of us shouting 'Bye' at the tops of our voices.

Jacob Ryan

Jacob Ryan, 30 years of age. Successful, wealthy and should be happy, but I'm not.

After suffering from exhaustion and depression for several months and trying to cope without medication I really thought I had hit the jackpot when I met model and girl about town Cleo Roberts. We seemed fairly well suited or so I thought.

Being the impulsive sort I went ahead and bought a beautiful old house close to where my brother Scott lives in Wimbledon. I had plans drawn up to have the house totally renovated and the gardens landscaped. I must have been in a really bad place, why did I do that?

We had viewed the house together and Cleo seemed as smitten with it as I was. I did have an uneasy feeling about her though but me being me I just ignored all the warning signs.

I thought all my dreams had come true when Cleo announced that she was pregnant. Something I had always wanted was a family of my own. Sex with her was a rare occurrence but something must have worked.

Cleo didn't seem as thrilled as I was, but I thought it was just that this pregnancy had come out of the blue and not planned. I had always used condoms on the few occasions we'd had sex and just assumed that one must have split, with no other explanation. Once she got over the shock she would begin to see what I could see. A brilliant future with a family to share it with.

Wrong on all counts. Without telling me or even discussing it she had an abortion. I was and still am devastated. The rows began as soon as I found out what she had done. How could she deliberately kill my child?

Eventually, the truth came out. She had been having an affair with a very close friend of mine and didn't know which of us was the father. Like I said, I had always used protection so I guess that more or less ruled me out. She may well have been able to pass the child off as mine except that my friend Arlo comes from Jamaica.

Not only have I lost Cleo and what I thought of as our child, I have also lost my best friend. Arlo and I had been the best of friends since University days.

At least I still have my work to keep me sane. Whilst at University studying law, I was 'discovered' as being the new 'West End' star. I had always been able to hold a tune and was always called upon whenever a singer was required for University productions.

It was whilst performing in one of these shows that a record producer was in the audience supporting his daughter who was also in the show.

Long story short, he liked what he heard and signed me up. He found a good manager for me who got me into shows in the 'West End'. Since then my career has gone from strength to strength.

I have performed all over the world and am now very confident on stage. I still do musical theatre but also go out on my own doing whatever takes my fancy. I prefer easy listening music myself but can also take on more serious roles when asked to. Acting has always been my first love and I have done several films and a couple of plays.

When the shit hit the fan with Cleo I took to my bed for a couple of weeks. Then when I finally got up I began drinking. I have never been a big drinker, but I do like a glass of wine with a meal. I have taught myself about wine and feel comfortable now ordering in restaurants.

That bit is not the problem, I began drinking whisky, a lot of whisky. It was my brother Scott who finally dragged me out of my apartment and took me back to his house. I have been there ever since. He has been amazing. He finally made me realise that life will go on. He took time away from our family's law practice and managed to get me back to some sort of normality.

The thing that has given me hope for the future is the new show I am doing. It is my show, everything that I want to do. A one-man show. My own songs, songs that I want to sing, some songs that I have written myself. I am really enjoying it. Perhaps there is light at the end of the tunnel after all.

For the time being I am staying with Scott. He is away from the house a lot, so I have some peace and quiet. When he is there he is very supportive and always just a phone call away if I need him. We get on well, always have.

My apartment has since sold and all my furniture along with my beautiful piano have been put into storage, now all I need to do is decide about the house. Sell it as it is, do the renovations then sell or carry on with the renovations then move there on my own. Not sure yet what I want to do. There's no rush to make a decision, the house will still be there.

Very slowly my life was improving, just needed to keep positive. Don't need any more hassle. Not had another woman in my life as yet and I'm not sure I could cope with one. Perhaps I am too picky, being in this position leaves me open to all sorts of offers and I really don't like that way of living.

I have dropped out of the party scene, never did like it really. Always lots of pretty young things offering to transport me to heaven. No, thank you very much.

I am led to believe that sex can be wonderful but only with someone you care about not just because it's on offer. That means nothing at all. Won't hold my breath on that score.

Scott is all of a flurry at the moment. Seems he has met someone he really likes. He was married at a very young age and has two adorable daughters. His wife went off with the milkman and took the girls with her. When I say the milkman, he actually owns the dairy along with several other businesses.

A very rich man and he seems to make her happy. Not that Scott is poor, he is the senior partner now in our family's law practice. The one that I would have joined if I had completed my time at University.

As soon as I was signed to the record company I left University which left just Scott and my sister Ingrid to manage the business. Since then Ingrid has also left. She married and now has three children with another one on the way. She won't be going back to work anytime soon.

Poor Scott has the family business to run, a wife and children that no longer live with him and no life outside of work. I was so pleased when he told me that he had met this amazing woman from the Midlands.

It appears he went up there to sort out a client whose husband has died, and he has fallen for the social worker assigned to this poor woman who appears to be a bit of a recluse and has been ill-treated all of her life. I guess she needs the help. At least it has got Scott away from the office and now it seems that he has met someone he feels he can care for. Good for him.

He is bringing both women down here with him later today. He thinks that the widow needs to see that there is a life outside of the farm where she was born and has lived all her life. Sounds a bit like hard work to me. Hope he doesn't expect me to sit talking to her all day. Older women and widows in particular fill me with dread. To have one that is both those things really will freak me out. Might give me the kick up the arse I need to make some decisions regarding my house.

Hopefully, I won't be here when they arrive as I need to be at the theatre to get ready for tonight's show. It will mean I leave a bit earlier than usual, but it will also mean I don't have to sit and make small talk with this woman till tomorrow.

Scott has mentioned that he wants to take the two women to see the show one night, so I had better sort out some decent tickets for him. I will never hear the end of it if I forget.

I will need to eat something though before I go. Didn't bother with breakfast today so will need to fuel up before long. I really must get into some sort of routine. *"This wandering around from one thing to the next is getting me nowhere"*.

Scott's housekeeper is here today, wonder if she will rustle something up for me. I can't be arsed to do anything more than a sandwich.

"Mrs Harris, are you free?" I shouted. She came bustling into the lounge where I was sitting doing bugger all.

"What can I do for you, young Jacob?"

"Are you in a rush to get off today?" I asked as sweetly as I could.

"No, why? I expect you are wanting me to feed you, idle sod," she said. It was all in good humour though. She loves me really.

"If I ask nicely, pretty please?"

"Okay, what do you want, anything special or just what I decide to do for you?"

"Mrs H, you are my saviour and I love you for it."

"Less of the flannel lad, I will see what I can find in the fridge."

Half an hour later she called me through to the kitchen, "Right lad, sit yourself down." She pushed a plate of scrambled eggs with smoked salmon and toast on the side in front of me. "Tea coming up."

"Anyone ever tell you, you are a wonderful woman?"

"Yes, your brother tells me the same thing most days. It's a good job I love the pair of you to bits."

"I should say it is. Who else would look after two such dreadful menfolk as us?"

"Well, there you have it, young Jacob. At least you both own up to your faults."

"This is wonderful Mrs H. Just what I need to set me up for tonight's show."

"You know we have visitors later today, don't you?"

"Yes, Scott did mention something. Two women I think he said, one recently widowed."

"Correct," I said, "I am so looking forward to spending time with her. A widowed old woman, just what I need. Will do my street cred no amount of good."

I was still talking to Mrs Harris when we heard the front door open.

"Are you there Jacob?" Scott shouted, "Come and give me a hand with this luggage."

"Be there in a minute, just finishing my lunch. You are earlier than I thought."

Scott appeared in the kitchen and said, "Yes, there was nothing to hang about up there for and the motorway was kind to me today."

"Come on through ladies, let me introduce you to my brother."

First through the door was Caroline, "Jacob this is Caroline, the lady I was telling you about. Caroline meet my brother Jacob."

She held out her hand and said, "Pleased to meet you, Jacob. Hope we won't be too much trouble for you."

"Ella, come on through, he won't bite I promise. Right, Jacob? Meet Ella, Ella this is my brother, Jacob. He is the one to ask about all things wine."

A stunningly beautiful young woman came into the kitchen very slowly. She looked like a startled fawn. Terrified. She has the most amazing head of very long auburn hair, fabulous. I felt my heart skip a beat when I looked into her lovely deep blue eyes.

"Come on in Ella, I am pleased to meet you," I said. She held out a trembling hand. "All a bit much for you, I guess," I managed to say.

"Sorry, she said. I am not used to meeting people and I get very scared. I will be all right in a minute."

Mrs H was watching all this and smiling. "See you tomorrow boys," she called as she left.

Scott has assured me that this woman would have no idea who I was so I couldn't understand what was making her shake so much.

Very often when meeting fans they would be so excited they would shake but this seemed different somehow.

'Please, continue your lunch," she said, "I don't want to upset your routine."

"Almost finished," I said. "I will go and help Scott with your luggage then."

"Thank you," she managed in a whisper, "you are very kind."

I will need to ask Scott about her later. Such a stunningly beautiful young woman but no confidence at all. Will have to find out her story. See if we can't make her feel a bit better about life. Scott never said she was a young widow, I had just assumed she would be elderly. This is so much better than I expected.

"I suddenly realised I was looking at this stunning young woman with interest. The first time in over a year that I have looked at any female with interest. Does this mean I am moving on? Maybe"

"This frail, frightened young woman was not normally my type at all but there was something drawing me to her. Tread carefully was the warning that flashed up in my head".

I quickly finished my lunch and then went with Scott to bring in the luggage. Scott had Caroline's and I had Ella's. I would really like to know this woman. She intrigues me and I only met her ten minutes ago.

Scott took Caroline along the landing to her room, next to his. Funny that.

I carried Ella's to her room, next to mine. I hadn't realised where she would be sleeping.

"Right Ella, if you want to freshen up, then come down to the kitchen I will put the kettle on and make us all a nice cup of tea, how does that sound?"

"Oh, Jacob, that sounds wonderful. I have been so scared all the way here, my mouth has gone all dry. You must think of me as a total idiot. The thing is I have never been to London before, well to be honest I have never been anywhere before. It is all very strange for me.'

"Really, why is that?" I asked.

"I lived on a remote farm with my horrible husband that I was forced to marry when I was just sixteen. Apart from the day I went into the town to get married, I have been nowhere. Please forgive me for being weird. I will get over it."

"I can't imagine that Ella," I said. "I don't know how you have survived. It's no wonder you are so scared and frightened."

I have lived and worked all over the world and really enjoy seeing other countries, and seeing how other people live their lives. I don't think I have ever come across a story like yours though. Women in some countries are treated as second-class citizens and little more than the animals the menfolk keep but not in this country. Do you mind talking about it?"

"I do not, it will help me deal with stuff I should think. It is only this past few days that I have been able to hold a proper conversation with other people. That is thanks entirely to Caroline and your brother. I think those two make a good couple, don't you?"

"I hadn't really noticed, to be honest, Ella. I couldn't take my eyes off you when you came into the kitchen. Scott did tell me he has met a nice young woman that he really likes. It's about time he started to live again. He has been a bit of a recluse since Flora left him. He sees the girls regularly and loves the bones of them, but he has been lonely. Let's hope Caroline is good for him and him for her."

"Then of course there is you, I think it's about time you started to live. Your life must have been hellish. I can't really imagine it."

It has been a continual nightmare since the day I was born. I will tell you about it if you are interested but can we have that cup of tea first, please?"

"You can," I said, "I will go and put the kettle on now. Come down when you're ready. Your story may have to wait until tomorrow though as I need to be at work shortly and then won't be back till quite late. I will be free to talk as much or as little as you want in the morning though. I will be very interested to hear from you. Can I just tell you something though, I don't want to upset you or frighten you off"

"I promise not to be scared off, what do you want to say?"

"Here goes," I said. "Ella, I find you to be the most fascinating and beautiful woman I have ever met, I would really like to get to know you. There, said it. I hope I haven't upset you."

"No, Jacob, you haven't upset me, but I do think you need to get your eyes tested. I mean, look at me."

"I am looking at you Ella, you are mesmerising, and my eyesight is perfect."

"Right," I said, "enough of that. Tea, be ready in five minutes, okay?"

"Yes," she said, "I will be down in a minute."

I left her to freshen up or whatever you women do then went down the stairs to make the tea. Scott and Caroline were very quiet. Seems that they really do like each other.

The sight of Ella as she came back down the stairs and into the kitchen, well, she quite literally took my breath away. She is stunning, with no makeup, wild hair and wearing very ordinary jeans and a jumper. Definitely not my type at all, well until today that is. I had this mad urge to gather her into my arms and kiss her. Hadn't better do that though. That would really scare her off.

"Come on in," I said, "treat the place as your own. We don't stand on ceremony here. Come on, sit down on the couch and I will bring the tea over."

She walked through to the seating area and sat down on the big squishy sofa.

"Oh, wow," she said, "this is so nice. It feels like the sofa is giving me a hug. Will you have time to sit with me for a while before you go to work?"

"I will," I said, all my stuff was ready, so I only had to put it in the car before setting off.

"You go to work in these beautiful clothes?" she asked. Scott had told me that she wouldn't know who I was so I just kept the conversation neutral. Didn't want to frighten her off now.

"Yes," I said. "I get changed when I'm there then change back into these before coming home".

I carried the tray over and placed it on the coffee table.

"Would you like a slice of Mrs 'H's cake? She keeps Scott and I filled up with her delicious cooking."

"Who is Mrs 'H'?" she asked.

"That is Mrs Harris, she is Scott's housekeeper. We end up doing very little around the place. She just floats around like a fairy, and everything is clean and tidy by the time we appear. That was her just leaving as you arrived."

Ella laughed, she had the nicest, most infectious laugh. Genuine, a really nice young woman.

"This is the first time in a very long time that I haven't been consumed with thoughts of Cleo, well more what Cleo had done to the baby and me. Perhaps there is light at the end of the tunnel after all".

I sat down next to Ella and went to pour the tea but before I could get there Ella had taken over the pouring and slicing of cake. She handed me a plate with a huge slice of lemon drizzle cake on it then she placed my mug of tea on a coaster on the table. She then sat back with her own slice of cake. "This is wonderful," she said. "I must ask her for the recipe."

"You bake, do you Ella?" I asked.

"Yes, I do, it was a case of having to learn quickly or starve." She giggled.

"What's so funny?" I asked.

"Oh, I was just thinking back to when I was a toddler. My mum had died less than a month after I was born so I never knew her at all. It was left to my dad to bring me up, he was only twenty-one himself and so had no idea about raising a child. We lived on the farm in a cottage but when Dad had to work I was apparently taken over to the main farmhouse and the farmer's wife, Dot, had to keep an eye on me. I don't think she liked children. Well she didn't seem to like me for sure. I was just left to crawl around the filthy kitchen floor.

When I was hungry, which was often, I used to eat the food left out for the dog. The dog didn't like it too much. He used to nip me and when I continued to eat his food he would bite me. That is where I got all these little scars from. Mostly on my hands and arms but also I have a few on my legs and this one here by my eye."

She lifted her hair so that I could see the faint white scar that ran very close to her eye.

"My God Ella, you have had a rough time," I said.

"That's nothing," she said, "when you have more time I will tell you about my delightful upbringing and about how, at the tender age of sixteen I was forced to marry Will, the farmer after his wife died."

"Ella, I don't know what to say. You have been made to suffer badly but that doesn't mean you will continue to suffer. There is someone out there that will give you a much better life. Someone that will love you for who you are. Don't give up."

She smiled at me and her whole face lit up. God, I wanted to kiss her, to run my fingers through that gorgeous hair.

"I doubt that very much Jacob," she said, "I am resigned to living the rest of my life on my own with the help of my new friends, and you too if you don't mind having a raving idiot as a friend."

"Don't say that Ella, you are a gorgeous woman. Just the sight of you makes my heart sing." There it was again, that beautiful laugh. "I will be that friend if you let me, but would also hope that in the future, when you are ready we could perhaps become a little more than friends."

"Don't joke with me, Jacob. I know I am damaged, very brittle really. It wouldn't take much to break me completely. I have to concentrate on learning how to live my life on my own. I don't have any problem with being alone.

What I can't do is live with another man for fear of things turning out how they did in my past, previous life. I will not be that person ever again. I have lived my whole life terrified, frightened of everything and everyone."

"I am sorry Ella, it is just that meeting you today and finding you so beautiful, gorgeous, a fabulous young woman, well, it filled me with hope. I suppose you know that I have had a bad time recently. This is the first time since then that I have felt a bit of joy, a bit of hope. I know we only met a couple of hours ago, but I find you intriguing. Let's forget this conversation ever happened then start again tomorrow, please?"

Ella smiled at me and my insides melted.

"Okay Jacob, I can live with that, tomorrow we begin again."

Time was marching on and I felt that I had made a sufficient fool of myself for one day. *Whatever is wrong with me? Before meeting Ella I wasn't looking forward to meeting this widow that Scott had lumbered himself with.*

Now, well I am smitten if I'm honest. She is wonderful, beautiful, gorgeous, sexy as hell. Perhaps if I back off a bit she might come round. She is here for at least a couple of weeks, so I have time. I will get some tickets for the show then Scott can bring them along. They might enjoy a night out.

All the while my mind was going into overdrive, Ella was watching me.

"What Ella? Have I got cake crumbs on my face?"

She laughed again, "No, Jacob, you don't have crumbs on your face. I was just enjoying looking at you. I have never seen such a handsome man if I'm honest. This is a novelty. I thought Scott was the most handsome man I had ever seen and then I met you. The only men I have seen before have been farm hands, my dad and the awful Will.

He was horrible to look at and worse to have to be close with. He smelt awful as well. When he decided it was time for bed and came close to me I would gag. He couldn't understand why I wasn't falling all over him. If I protested too much I would earn a smack across the face. It really was awful, I hated having to do it with him and I just can't imagine being like that with anyone else willingly. The thought of it fills me with horror.

Don't get me wrong Jacob, I think you are a lovely man, a really lovely man but honestly I just can't even think about being intimate with anyone."

"Look Ella, it is early days. You have only just lost your husband and I understand that it is impossible to think of being with anyone else but let's give it some time, spend time together and see how it goes. I really do have to move now. My car will be here in ten minutes, so I have to move. Can we start again in the morning?"

"Yes, we can and I am sorry for making you late."

"No worries. May I kiss you goodnight?"

She looked horrified, "or not if you feel uncomfortable," I said.

"No, sorry, you caught me unawares. Yes, I think I would like you to kiss me. I have never been kissed before."

"I had better get it right then," I said. I put my arm gently around her shoulders and pulled her to me. She looked terrified.

I need to do this properly I thought. Don't want to scare her off.

I placed my lips on hers very gently and waited for her to pull away, but she didn't. I moved a little and put a little pressure on her lips. Still, she didn't pull away.

I couldn't hold myself back any longer, I put my other hand on her shoulder and pulled her into my embrace. She responded to my kiss. She likes it I thought. I really wanted to open her lips with my tongue and explore her mouth but thought that would be too much. We both became breathless but clung on to each other in a desperate frenzy. God, why do I have to work tonight?

We kissed for what seemed an age then gently separated. "My God Ella, that was a very special kiss. I wish I could stay here with you all night just kissing your beautiful lips."

"Oh, Jacob, that was amazing. I honestly have never been kissed before. I would like to spend all night kissing you too."

"Really Ella," I gasped, "did you really like it?"

"I did," she said, "hope I did it right."

"You did it perfectly, I loved it."

I heard my car pull up at the front of the house.

"I have to go, Ella. I will be in so much trouble. I will be back as soon as I can. Don't wait up for me though. It will be late."

"Okay," she said. "Until tomorrow," she then leant forward and kissed me once more." Whatever is wrong with me?

A blast from the car horn brought me back to myself. I got up and said, "I have to go." I kissed her once more then left as quickly as I could collecting my bag from the hall as I left. God, I was going to be late tonight.

Thankfully, I did make it in time. It didn't take me long to get ready so was able to take to the stage at the right time. Another full house. This show is so rewarding after the year I have had but now I feel positive and meeting Ella has given me hope.

The band were playing their intro then the spotlight came up and lit the side of the stage where I stood. I took a deep breath and stepped into the centre of the light and began my walk to the centre of the stage.

My first song begins with just me singing alone and then the band joins in halfway through. We went from one song to the next without a break then it was time for a little bit of chat.

The ladies in the audience seem to like this, some of them ask some very saucy questions and make some improper suggestions but I manage to deal with them in a flirty manner usually.

We have a comedian on for the first half of the show then the second half is all me. Exhausting at times. I am usually on stage for at least ninety minutes and very often longer than that.

Tonight I was lucky, just over the hour and a half and I was taking my final bow. I had been given several bunches of flowers, some cuddly toys and what I think must be wine in bags. I carried them all off the stage and handed them to my assistant, Sam. He carried them to the dressing room for me whilst I went back on and performed one last song then left the stage and walked back to the sanctity of my dressing room.

"Are there many fans waiting?" I asked Sam.

"Not too bad," he said. "I've seen it worse. Ten minutes and you should be on your way home."

"Would you do something for me, Sam?"

"Yes, of course, what do you need to do?"

"Can you sort out some tickets for some of my family? There will be three of them counting Scott. They are here for the next couple of weeks, but if you can get something decent this week it would be good. We have that awards thing next Thursday so that might make it awkward. I am hoping they will come with me to that as well. Hate being Johnny no mates on the red carpet."

"Well, Jacob there are thousands of women that would accompany you".

"That's as maybe Sam, but you know I don't do those things."

"I know Jacob, just saying. Are you ready?"

"Yes, I am now. Get the car around, please. I need my bed tonight."

"On it, Jacob. Be here in five minutes."

"Right, let's go and chat."

I left my dressing room and made my way to the stage door. Sam was right, not too bad tonight. About ten or twelve people waiting. Most of them are regulars and I know them by sight if not by name.

There was the usual chat and the clamour for photographs but nobody trying to take chunks out of me. Ten minutes later my car pulled up and I climbed in the back and settled into the leather seats.

Lots of waving and blowing kisses then we were on our way. The traffic was remarkably light on the way home so made it in record time. Home before midnight and the lights are still on.

I wonder if Ella is still up. I can still taste her kisses on my lips. God, she is gorgeous.

Ella and Jacob's Story

We arrived at Scott's gorgeous home and were hurried inside. Scott called out for his brother to come and give him a hand with the luggage. This place looked very posh, never seen anything like this before.

We were taken into the fabulous kitchen. A very handsome man came to greet us, shaking our hands. He has the most wonderful smile, square dimpled jaw, longish curly hair black as coal and eyes the colour of the stones in the necklace that Caroline said were emeralds. I could feel myself drowning in his gaze. Why couldn't I have met someone like this instead of Will? Just my luck.

This house is absolutely beautiful. I really have never seen anything like it. We were offered refreshments then Scott carried Caroline's case and Jacob carried mine taking us up to our respective rooms. I felt out of my depth. Posh surroundings and this gorgeous-looking man, I just know I will make a complete fool of myself before the day is done.

I have never seen such opulence, how can I be expected to sleep in such a posh room? I bet the Queen's bedroom isn't any better than this one. Jacob put my case onto the bed and then said he would go and organise the drinks. I felt bereft when he left me.

Jacob had handed one of the bags to me and our fingers touched. That felt like a very special moment to me. I really like this man. Both he and Scott are lovely. They are both so kind and gentle and very handsome.

I had a quick wash then changed into clean jeans and a jumper. I brushed my hair as best I could, but it was flying in all directions.

I was going to knock for Caroline then thought better of it. She and Scott seemed to be getting very close. I closed the door to my room behind me then went down the stairs and back into the kitchen. Jacob had the tea made and was assembling a tray with pots and cake. He said for me to take a seat, so I went over to a lovely white couch and sat down. It was amazing, so soft and comfortable. It felt like the sofa was giving me a hug.

Jacob brought the tray over and was going to pour the tea but I got there first, then I sliced the cake.

We sat side by side eating our cake and then sipping our tea. He caught me looking at him and asked if he had crumbs on his face. I had to be honest and told him I had never seen such a handsome man before. I found him quite intimidating but there seemed to be a real spark between us. If not a spark then something special. Unless it's just me reading too much into the situation. After all, I don't have any experience with other men, just horrid Will.

Jacob began talking about how he'd had a few bad months and so I told him a bit about my life with Will. He seemed horrified.

Then he began telling me that he found me very attractive and all sorts of nice things. He said he loved my hair. I felt as if this conversation was getting out of hand so I tried to tone it down a bit by telling him that I could never have another man touch me after Will. It was out of the question.

It seemed to work. He would be leaving for work shortly so not long to keep him at arm's length. As time went on we became more comfortable in each other's company. I filled him in with a bit of my story and so he seemed to accept that I was damaged and needed careful handling.

He said that he would have to leave shortly to go to work, but we could spend time the following day getting to know each other better.

Then he asked me something completely out of the blue.

May I kiss you goodnight he asked?. I was gobsmacked. What could I say to that?

I thought for a moment then decided I would like him to kiss me. I have never been kissed before so wasn't sure what I should do. I said that yes, it was okay to kiss me. I could feel my heart thumping really fast and hard against my chest. Do I really want him to kiss me? Yes, I do.

I sat quite still and waited. He reached forward and put his arm around my shoulders. He pulled me gently towards him then placed his lips on mine. We stayed like that for a moment. When he realised I hadn't pulled away from him he pressed his lips onto mine a little firmer then it was as if he couldn't hold back any longer and neither could I.

He placed his other hand on my opposite shoulder and pulled me to him. The kiss deepened and it was so special. We kissed like that for what seemed a very long time.

Jacob then pulled away from me saying that he could stay here all night kissing me, but he would have to leave for work in ten minutes.

I thought that's a shame. I was just getting into this kissing malarky. He reached forward and kissed me some more then made to get up to leave. A car had pulled up outside and he said he really had to go so I kissed him once more then let him go. He stood up just as a car horn blasted. That's for me, I really do have to go. I will be home late so don't wait up. Okay, I said. He reached over and kissed me one final time then turned and left.

I sat there in a happy, warm stupor. I really like Scott and Jacob and I was beginning to relax in this posh house.

After Jacob had left I set to washing the few pots and putting them tidy. What to do next? Nothing that I could think of.

I hadn't seen or heard anything from either Scott or Caroline since he had taken her case upstairs. I hope they manage to get together. They seem such a lovely couple. I will keep my fingers crossed for them.

I decided to go up to my room and unpack. That would be a start.

As I reached the landing Caroline was just coming out of Scott's bedroom door. I gave her a knowing smile.

"Everything okay?" I asked.

" More than okay, thank you, Ella. I think that Scott and I may decide to try to build a future together. It's only been a few days, but we really like each other. So, thank you for bringing us together."

"Me, nothing to do with me," I said.

"Oh, yes it is. If I hadn't come to see you last week and then rung for Scott to come and help we would never have met. Anyway missy, never mind me and Scott, what about you and the gorgeous Jacob?"

"What about us, we have been sitting in the kitchen drinking tea, eating cake and talking."

"And kissing," she said.

I felt myself blush. "How do you know that?"

"Well, I came downstairs to see if you were okay, but I could see that you were definitely more than okay, so I crept back out the door and went back upstairs. You really like Jacob, don't you?"

"I do," I said "but nothing will happen. He asked if he could kiss me goodnight, that's all."

"Right," she said, "it looked like a goodnight kiss from where I stood. He fancies you too. It is written all over his face. You could do worse, you know."

"Caroline, Will hasn't been cremated yet, how can I think about someone else?"

"Because Will was a bastard and treated you appallingly and you deserve to be happy now that he has gone. Don't think about him any longer, think about yourself and what you want. It's time to wake up Ella and smell the roses."

I laughed at that, "I have never heard that said before, but I know exactly what you mean. Anyway, Jacob has gone to work, and he said not to wait up for him, he will be home late."

"Okay," she said, "have it your own way, but I am telling you he fancies the pants off you girl."

"No, he doesn't, he was just being kind."

Scott came through the door then and asked, "Has Jacob gone to work then? It's a miracle he could pull himself away from you Ella, he is smitten with you and I am really pleased for you both."

"He has," I said, "he said not to wait up for him though as he will be late."

"I should thank you, Ella," he said.

"Me? Why?"

"Well, you have managed to put a smile on his face for the first time in over a year. And it looks to me as if he has done the same for you."

"Well, I do like him very much, but I also like you so have I put a smile on your face as well?"

We all laughed; then Scott said, "I think it's time for food but I guess none of us feels like cooking so I guess takeaway will have to do."

"What is takeaway?" I asked.

"Ella, have you never ordered food in to save you cooking?"

"No, I have no idea what you are talking about."

Scott went to one of the drawers and took out a bunch of leaflets. "Here, have a look at these and decide what you both fancy."

Caroline said, "I can always go Chinese, what about you Ella?"

"Like I said I have no idea what you are talking about, so just order me the same thing that you have."

"Right," she said, "Scott, what about you? What do you want to order?"

"Same as you two will be fine. I eat anything when I'm hungry."

"Come and sit down here and let's decide which ones we will have for our feast then I will ring them."

Scott took out his mobile phone and rang whoever did this service. He read out a list of numbers. They obviously knew him the way the conversation went. He said that he had ordered extra so that Jacob could eat once he got back home.

In no time at all our delivery of takeaway arrived. There is a whole world out there that I know nothing at all about. The food smelt amazing, like nothing I have ever eaten before. Hope I like it.

We sat around the kitchen island and Scott placed all these containers around the space. We had a plate each and apparently, you just helped yourself. I tried everything and I liked it all. This was a revelation, and I am sure I will soon get the hang of ordering my own food.

After we had eaten and then cleared the debris away Scott asked what we wanted to do. We can walk down the road to the pub and have a drink there or if there is something on the TV you fancy we can watch that. There is also a music/cinema room if you want to listen to something soothing.

I said, "If you two want to spend time alone I can go to my room. I can find a book somewhere, I guess."

Scott said, "You are not spending your first evening in London sitting in your bedroom alone."

"Why not?" I asked?. "Because you have spent far too much of your life alone so far and you are not going to be alone ever again."

"Okay," I said, "what do you suggest then?"

"Have you ever watched the television?"

"No, Will wouldn't have one in the house."

"Right, let's have a look what's on, see if there is anything interesting."

We went through to the lounge and sat down. I took a big chair and left the sofa for the lovebirds. Scott switched the television on and began pressing buttons. He flashed through several things and then settled on a film (apparently) something else I have never seen. I thought you had to go to a cinema to see films and didn't realise you could watch them at home.

He said that he thought this one would be a good place to start, 'Love Actually'. "Of course, I didn't know any of the people in it, but it was good, I enjoyed it very much."

Halfway through, Scott went and fetched a bottle of wine and three glasses. He poured some out for us all. *"This is a very civilised way to spend an evening,* I thought. *Pity Jacob had to work, it would have been nice for the four of us".*

The wine was lovely, a white one this time. If I sipped it then I wouldn't feel dizzy like I did with the red one. Or maybe I had drunk too much of that one.

"Right Ladies, do you have any plans for tomorrow?"

"I have no idea," I said. "It is all new to me so I will have to be guided. Just don't take me to the centre of London and then leave me there."

"As if we would do that to you," Caroline said. "Scott, have you got to work tomorrow?

"Only in the morning," he replied, "why?"

"If it's not being presumptuous, could Ella and I come into town with you to do some shopping?"

"You can, I can collect you at lunchtime then come back here or we can pick Jacob up and go out for lunch. I will ask him, see what he fancies doing."

My eyes must have lit up at the mention of Jacob's name. They both looked at me and smiled.

"What?" I asked. They both said, "Nothing, nothing at all."

At just after eleven thirty we heard a car pull up. Scott said that must be Jacob, who managed to finish earlier than usual. Wonder why that is? They both looked at me and smiled again.

"What is it with you two?" I asked.

"Like we said, nothing at all."

Jacob put his head around the door and said, "Hi folks, didn't expect you to still be up."

We all chorused Hi back. Scott asked, "Good night, mate?"

"It was," he said. "Thankfully most people wanted to get home tonight, so I was able to slip away quickly. Smells like you all had a good time without me, Chinese I guess."

"It was really nice," I said, "never had takeaway before. We saved some for you."

"You did? Great, I am starving."

I asked him if he would like me to warm it through for him.

"Do you know how to work a microwave?" he asked.

"A what?"

"Don't worry, I can do it. If you want to come with me I can show you what a microwave is and how to use one."

"Okay," I said and got up to follow him.

As I walked past Caroline and Scott I caught them looking at each other and smiling. I stuck my tongue out as I passed them.

Jacob was still standing by the door waiting for me. "Come on then," he said, "first lesson in microwave cooking." As I walked past him he caught hold of my hand and held it as we walked down the hall towards the kitchen. My heart was beating so fast.

Before we entered the kitchen though he pulled me back and put his arms around me, pulling me into a wonderful, warm embrace. He looked at me then placed a gentle kiss on my lips. This was followed by a more urgent kiss, so passionate.

"God Ella, I have been wanting to do that all night. Trying to work but thinking of you constantly. Please say I'm not overstepping the mark."

"No, you're not Jacob, I have been thinking about you all night as well."

He held me so close and kissed me again then he kissed my face, my neck then back to my lips again. I was breathless but loved it.

"Come on, let me eat before I take a bite out of you."

" Really, are you that hungry?" I asked.

"For you Ella, yes I am, I am desperate to hold you, to kiss you, to take you to my bed. Don't worry, I know I am going at a hundred miles an hour and I need to slow down. I don't want to scare you off."

"You won't," I said. "Just don't rush me."

"I won't Ella, just tell me when you are ready. I can live with your kisses till then."

We went into the kitchen and Jacob loaded a plate up with the leftover food. He then gave me a quick lesson on how to use the microwave. Amazing, I couldn't get my head around how quick it was.

I sat with him as he ate his supper. We sat close together, and he kept touching me, my hands, my hair, my face.

We had a glass of wine each whilst he was eating. He fed me a little of his meal and then shared his wine with me. He drank a little then put the glass to my lips so that I could drink. I never knew what erotic meant but I am beginning to find out. I have never known what love is, but I am beginning to know what that is as well.

Jacob finished his meal and then held out both hands to me. I took them and he gently pulled me up putting his arms around me, holding me tightly. He put his mouth on my neck and I could feel his breath on my skin. I shuddered involuntarily, this small act made me tingle all over.

I have gone from never wanting another man anywhere near me to wanting this man as close as he can be, and all within less than a day.

This is madness really. I suppose it's all because I have been so lacking in affection all my life then this handsome man shows me a different way and I can't say no, and why would I want to?

We were still in the kitchen holding each other and kissing when the door opened.

Scott popped his head around the door and said, "Excuse me folks, we are going up to bed. Goodnight."

Jacob pulled away from me and said, "Hang on Scott, got something for you." He went into the hallway and got something from his jacket pocket, handing it over to Scott.

"Thanks, mate," said Scott, "I owe you one."

Jacob came back into the kitchen and began kissing me again. He really did take my breath away. I began thinking about what would happen next. We couldn't stay here all night kissing as much as I would enjoy that.

"Aren't you tired?" I asked?

"Not really, no," he replied. "Are you?"

"Yes and no," I said. I am tired but I doubt I will sleep."

"Do you want to stay down here?" Jacob asked.

"I want to stay with you," I said. "If you stay here, then so will I."

"What will you do if I go to bed?"

"Can I go with you?"

"Oh God, Ella, are you sure?"

"Jacob I have been having sex daily since my sixteenth birthday and never wanted any of it. It was horrible and Will smelt badly of sweat. He made me gag. He never kissed me, ever. Not that I wanted him to, half of his teeth were bad. He was a gross old man and I hated him."

"Then today I met you and suddenly my resolve to spend the rest of my life alone and definitely never have a man do that to me ever, well let's just say you have made me change my mind. Take me to bed, Jacob, please. Before I change my mind.

"Only if you are really certain, my love. I want you so badly, but I don't want to spoil anything."

"You won't, Jacob. I want you too. For the first time in my life, I really want to make love, and I want it to be with you."

"Okay," said Jacob. "If you are really sure, let's do this before I burst."

I giggled at what he'd said. Must be the wine making me brave. Ever since Jacob had begun to kiss me I was having strange feelings low in my tummy and between my legs. Made me want to squirm. Jacob has the knack of making me want to do all sorts of things that I have never dreamed of doing before.

"Come on I said, before we both had second thoughts."

"We climbed the stairs holding hands, and then Jacob took me into his bedroom. As we went in and closed the door behind us he asked me once more if I was really sure.

"I am," I said, "stop wasting time."

Jacob took me into his arms and held me close. He kissed me thoroughly and passionately. My breath caught in my throat. He began putting his hands under my jumper, eventually finding my breasts. I have never been touched there except when Will decided to hit me and would catch me there. Very painful. This was something very new.

He gently lifted my bra and took my breasts into his hands. Very slowly and gently he began to tease my nipples. *Wow*, this I liked.

I lifted my jumper and pulled it over my head, dropping it onto the floor. My hair was all loose and getting in the way.

Jacob reached round my back and undid my bra, letting it slide down my arms, landing on the floor with my jumper. He paid my breasts a lot of attention. God this had a big effect on me. Never have I known such pleasure, so many feelings popping around me.

I undid his shirt and pulled it off him throwing it onto the floor with all the other things. We stood facing each other and just taking in the sight of each other. This man has one gorgeous body. I really want to do this and to do it with Jacob.

If my life is going to change then let this be the first thing to change.

Jacob took a step back and just gazed at me. Taking in every inch. "May I remove your jeans, please?"

"You may," I replied "just so long as I can remove yours. He smiled at me. "You most definitely can."

I very slowly undid the buttons on his jeans and pulled them down followed very quickly with his pants. His hardness sprang free making me jump.

"Goodness," I said, "I wasn't expecting that."

"What were you expecting, he asked?"

"Sorry, all this is so new to me. I have never undressed a man before. Will would just tell me to get upstairs and get ready then he would come up, do the business, roll of and go to sleep, the same thing night after night. I have no idea how any of this works. I am just doing what feels right. If I get it wrong, you will have to tell me," I said.

"You are doing fine, my darling. Just do what you want and stop if you want."

"I don't want to stop, I want you to show me how all this should be done. I really want to enjoy sex and not be scared stiff of it. I want to enjoy it with you. If I go weird on you though you will have to forgive me."

"I will be very gentle with you and I will stop the second you tell me to. Now may I remove your jeans?"

"Please," I said, "I feel as if we are wasting a lot of time talking."

I am feeling so brave, it must be the wine. I don't feel at all awkward with Jacob, he is lovely.

He slowly undid the zip on my jeans and pulled them down. Then he removed my knickers as well. He began kissing my body, the mound above my legs, then a little lower. God this is driving me insane.

We both stood then completely naked looking at each other. Jacob is a very beautiful man, he has a lovely body and very fit by the looks of things.

We moved together again, and he wrapped his arms around me. We kissed some more, I love his kisses. He slowly lifted me up into his arms and carried me over to the bed, laying me down very gently. He rose over me then bent to kiss my lips, my neck then my breasts.

I could feel something very different happening between my legs. Feelings I have never felt before. These feelings made me want to have Jacob inside me. "Jacob, please, will you make love to me now. I don't want to wait any longer. I need you."

"Okay, my sweet girl," he said, "I want you so much." He lifted himself up and I opened my legs. Very slowly and very gently he pressed himself into me. He looked into my eyes to check that I was happy to continue, I was, very happy.

He moved inside me and very quickly I could feel a very strange feeling begin. It built and built the more Jacob moved inside me. I moved with him and that increased my feelings. I couldn't stop myself. I moved with Jacob moving back and forth and the feeling still kept building then all of a sudden it was out of control. "God Jacob, what's happening?"

"Just lie back, my sweet girl and enjoy it," he said.

A pulsing deep inside me and wrapping itself around Jacob. It suddenly burst with a great rush of feelings. The pulsing kept going, all around Jacobs girth, I felt him explode inside me and still it went on. More and more, such an amazing feeling. We finally slowed then stopped.

Jacob looked at me, "Bloody hell Ella, that was absolutely amazing. Was that really the first time you have done it when wanting to."

"It was, Jacob. You are amazing. I have never felt anything so fabulous. Until tonight I have hated sex. I have never experienced those feelings before. It was wonderful, I loved it."

"It was pretty good, wasn't it?" he said. "It has been a very long time since I last had sex and honestly, I have never experienced anything so amazing. I loved it. You are one very sexy, gorgeous woman."

We lay side by side just gazing at each other. Jacob reached over and pulled me to him then kissed me with such a passion. "Oh, Ella," he said, "what have you done to me? I want you so much."

"I feel the same, Jacob. We don't know each other at all but I really want to be with you. Kiss me again, please."

He did, more and more kisses then he began moving down the bed kissing my body as he went. Finally, he reached my tummy and began to kiss me all over finally going lower and kissing the mound above my legs.

Slowly, he opened my legs and then moved his head between them still kissing me everywhere. What happened next blew my mind.

"Jacob, that was amazing. I never in all my life realised sex could be so wonderful. Thank you for showing me a different life. I came here today with no expectations, then I met you and *Wow!* The best of it is I wasn't even looking when I found you."

"I am so pleased you enjoyed it, my darling girl. It doesn't have to stop there either. We can do this whenever we want. We can explore each other's bodies and get comfort and relief from each other all the time, hopefully for years to come."

"Jacob, do you really mean that? We only met today, and we really don't know each other at all. All I do know is you have shown me a very different side to life, and I love it. I love it with you Jacob. You are one very special man."

"Thank you Ella, that is a real compliment. In truth, I am just a man, nothing special really. You could have this with any other man if you want to."

"Well, I don't want to. I want to spend time with you Jacob if that is what you want. We don't have to do everything at a hundred miles an hour, do we? We can take time to get to know each other properly. I would really like that."

"So would I, you are one very special lady Ella, and I could fall for you big style."

"And I, you Jacob. Let's spend time together then, shall we? Enjoying each other".

"Yes, please. Now, have you finished using my body or should we try once more?"

"Well, as you are asking me so nicely. I think I could manage once more."

Jacob pulled me to him and kissed me with so much passion. Why had I never been able to enjoy sex before. Well I suppose I know the answer to that. He was an old man compared to me being just a very young girl. He didn't know how to love me just to take what he wanted from me. It didn't occur to him that I might have needs as well. Well, I didn't have needs then but now things are very different.

Jacob is a lovely caring man who is trying to teach me how to live and love properly. If he is to be my teacher then I will be the perfect pupil.

We kissed and caressed each other. I felt really brave and reached down to take him into my hand. He is a very big man, I love the feel of him. He was soft when I first held him, but he soon began to harden and grow.

"Jacob, I want to do everything with you, I want to make you happy as well as you making me very happy."

"Ella, baby steps I think. Let's just practice what we have learned so far, shall we? It might put you off if we do too much too soon."

"Okay, if you say so, kiss me then make love to me again, please."

He did, he kissed me thoroughly then paid attention to my throbbing breasts. I reached for his hardness. "Please Jacob, I want to feel you inside me, please."

He rose over me and gently slid inside me. He began moving and I joined him in the wonderful movement. We rode together for a while then the pulsing began again. I pushed myself hard against him. I wrapped my legs around him pulling him even further into me. It was as if all the stars in heaven flashed inside my head.

A wonderful feeling swept over me as the pulsing reached a final pitch throwing me over. I felt Jacob explode inside me again and it was the most wonderful feeling. We continued moving together for a while until we were both sated. Finally, we broke apart then lay in each other's arms just gazing into each other's eyes. Jacob stroked my hair then kissed my face.

He kissed my lips and then said, "Ella, you are perfect. You are the sunshine in my otherwise very grey life. Thank you for coming to me."

"Jacob, I feel the same about you. Meeting you today has given me hope for the future. I don't have to be lonely any more."

"No, my love, you don't."

"Now, are you tired? Should we sleep? because I am knackered."

"Sorry Jacob, you should have said before. We could have waited to do this again."

"No, we couldn't, Ella. I want you again now so why should we wait."

My eyes must have opened very wide. *Again?*

"I want you every minute of every day my love. But for now we will sleep."

We cuddled up to each other and drifted off into a wonderful dream-filled sleep.

I woke with a start, sunshine was seeping through the curtains. Where am I? It all came back to me in a rush. Jacob, making love, holding him and kissing him and him kissing me. I moved my head, there he was, lying next to me, still holding me. He was awake and watching me. Those beautiful green eyes looking deep into mine.

"Morning sweetheart," he said. "How are you feeling this morning?"

"I am fine, more than fine actually. I slept really well. How about you my love? How are you feeling this morning?"

"I feel well refreshed, happy and ready to face the world. I want to shout from the rooftops. Here is my love, lying next to me, making me very happy."

"If you do that I think people will think you have lost the plot," I said. He laughed at me. "I don't care," he said, "I am happy, and I think I am falling for you in a very big way."

"I'm so glad you feel that way I said because that is exactly how I feel. Now if only I could get this haircut and out of your face?"

Jacob began playing with my hair then stroking my face. "I am one very lucky guy," he said. "Come here my darling, and kiss me.

I did as he asked. I put my hand over his private parts and felt him begin to grow and harden.

"That is an awfully large swelling you have down there Jacob. Is there anything I can do to help cure it?"

"You naughty little minx," he said. "What did you have in mind?"

Well, let me think now. Last night Jacob had used his mouth to give me pleasure, should I do the same?

Feeling very liberated I slid down the bed and did the best I could. I have no idea what I am supposed to do but Jacob appears to like it.

"Now, it is my turn to please you. Lie back on the pillow and close your eyes," he said.

I did as he asked. The next half an hour was just one magical sensation after another. He used his mouth and tongue on my breasts, then down below bringing me to so much pleasure. His tongue is truly magical, he does some amazing things with it and I love it.

Eventually, he rose up over me and slid inside me bringing even more pleasure with every thrust. We broke together in the most wonderful way. Time and again I could feel him exploding inside me and I did the same around his girth. Finally, we collapsed together, breathing heavily.

"How have I managed to live to be twenty-five years of age and never known such pleasures before? I thank God for allowing me to meet this wonderful man. He has woken my body up and now I feel truly alive."

We rested against each other for a while then Jacob said "I think we should perhaps get up. I think Scott is going to work today. Perhaps you and Caroline would like to go with him and do some shopping."

"But I want to stay with you," I said.

"I would love that too my darling, but I think the whole point of you coming here was to introduce you to the wonderful world of shopping."

"I have to do some work this morning as well then back at it again tonight. If you do go shopping then we could meet up at lunchtime and then spend the afternoon together."

"Okay," I said feeling a little disappointed. I could see what he meant though. I did need to buy some more things.

"Okay," I said reluctantly. Let's go and see what those two have planned."

Jacob showed me how to use the shower, I have only ever had a bath before. This shower is fabulous. He said it was a rain shower and the water felt lovely, washing me clean and leaving my skin feeling invigorated.

As I stepped out of the shower Jacob asked, "What are those scars across your bottom?"

"That is where Will used to beat me with his belt. Not every day, just when the fancy took him."

Jacob came and examined my backside closely.

"Ella, that is awful. How can any man do that to a woman, let alone such a gorgeous, sexy lady such as you."

"Well, Will was a very different sort of man to you. He took everything he wanted from me and if I objected, well, that is the result. Sometimes he would beat me because my period had started. I was very happy when it did start because I knew that he would leave me alone for a few days."

Jacob had gone very quiet. "Please don't worry about it, Jacob," I said, "it is over now, all in the past."

I went into my own room to find fresh clothes, wrapped in a towel. As I came out to return to Jacob's room Caroline came out of Scott's room. We looked at each other and burst out laughing.

She was going back to her room to fetch fresh clothes as well. We arranged to meet down in the kitchen in twenty minutes.

Once ready we all congregated in the kitchen and sat around the island. Scott had made coffee and we all sat with steaming mugs in front of us.

Scott spoke first. "This all seems to be working out rather well for us all. Caroline and I had hoped we would be able to get together eventually but you two are a revelation. You both look very happy, I must say."

Jacob spoke. "Scott, you have no idea how much my life has turned around in the last few hours. Thank you for bringing this wonderful woman into my life."

"Well, I have to say I have been surprised at how quickly you both seem to have fallen for each other. In saying that though things have moved pretty quickly for Caroline and me. We seem to have both found what we have been looking for. Well, if not actually looking for then both needing."

Caroline looked up at Scott and I could see the love in her eyes. She was really happy as well.

"Jacob was looking at me and I could see that same look of love that I could see between Scott and Caroline." I reached for his hand, lifted it to my lips and kissed the back of it. He lifted my other hand to his lips and kissed it tenderly. He was holding my fingers tightly, stroking my fingers and kissing them often.

"We were all feeling very emotional, all four of us finding love at the same time. How wonderful was this!"

"Right," said Scott, "we are all getting a bit soppy. Let's make our plans for the day. Caroline had suggested that the two girls come into town with me so they can shop, then at lunchtime we can perhaps all meet up at the pub."

"Can you live without Ella till then he asked Jacob?"

"I suppose I will have to." I have some stuff I need to do this morning anyway before work. Lunch at the pub sounds good though. What time will you be there?"

"Let's say one thirty, we can have a drink and a spot of lunch then come back here for a bit."

"That works for me," said Jacob. "I will be waiting for you, my love. Are you okay for money? Don't want you having to say no to anything you fancy."

"That is kind of you Jacob, but I have plenty of money, thank you. We found thousands of pounds hidden away in the farmhouse after Will died. Scott said for me to keep some cash then he opened a bank account for me, and he put the rest in there. I am now the proud owner of a cheque book and a bank card. I have no idea how to use either of them, but I am sure Caroline will show me what to do."

"That's good then, just be very careful where you keep your card. There are some very nasty people about. Do you have a mobile phone so I can keep in touch with you?"

I laughed. "A mobile phone. Don't be daft, I hadn't used any sort of phone at all until I found Will collapsed in the lane. I was terrified, stupid really, but I didn't know how to use the phone in the office. Will never let me in there. After what we found in there though I am not surprised he kept it locked."

"Why? What did you find?"

"I will show you later."

I am intrigued said Jacob. "Anyway, come on you three. Are you having breakfast before you go, or will you grab something when you are out?"

Scott said he would take us for breakfast before going into his office. So we went up to the bedroom and I got ready for the big shopping day out. Caroline came and checked that I had everything I needed. She bought me a sort of wallet, it fastened onto my belt then I could tuck it into the waistband of my jeans. It would do till I can find a purse and bag.

Jacob had been watching me closely as I got ready. He stood up and came to put his arms around me. "Be careful my darling, I will be worried till you return." He bent his head and found my lips with his. He kissed me with such a passion it really did take my breath away. I will be waiting in the pub when you return. Can't wait to hold you and kiss you again."

"Is that all I asked? Hold me and kiss me?"

He laughed, "you naughty little minx," he said. "I am trying to be good and then you go and fill my head with sexy thoughts."

We kissed some more then Caroline knocked on the door, "Put her down Jacob, we need to go and spend some money."

"Coming," I called. Jacob held me tight in his arms and then kissed me once more. "Go now woman or you will be back in this bed." I reached up and kissed him on the nose. "Bye, my love," I said, "see you later."

We left the house and climbed into Scott's car. Those two were all loved up as well. Pity Jacob couldn't come with us but not to worry, Scott would be going in to work so it would be just me and Caroline.

As we left the driveway I turned to look at the house, it is a very grand looking place, *imposing* I think is the right word. I looked up to the bedroom windows and saw Jacob standing in the window watching us leave. I blew a kiss to him and he did the same to me.

All this attention is doing me a power of good. I feel on top of the world. *"Now let's go and spend some money".*

I have to admit I was missing Jacob already. We will soon be back I told myself.

As we travelled towards the city centre I tried to take it all in. So many houses and shops, the traffic was really very scary. I doubt I will ever get used to all this. My life has been lived with no neighbours and the little traffic we did see consisted of a tractor and Land Rover up to now. It made my head buzz.

We stopped at a café on the way in and Scott bought us all bacon sandwiches and a mug of tea. It was lovely, just what I needed. I smiled to myself thinking, *"All this sex does make you hungry".*

Once we were on our way again Scott said where he would drop us off and pick us up again. I didn't have a clue but Caroline seemed to know what he was talking about.

He dropped us off in a side street, he and Caroline kissed before we got out of the car. I love seeing them together. Wonder if she feels the same about me and Jacob. Bet she does.

"Right madam," she said, "let's shop."

"Oh, Caroline, where do we start. I have no idea and I really am scared."

"Nothing at all to be scared of," she said. "Just stick close to me and you will be fine."

"Okay, I said but before we set off, I really want to buy a gift for Jacob. If all this ends today then I want him to have something to remember me by."

"This won't end you fool, he is mad about you. I wish you could see what I see. You two are made for each other."

"Maybe for today, but he is so handsome and kind he is bound to meet someone better for him than me. I can't believe he wants to be with me at all."

"Well, he does, he told Scott that he has finally met the woman he wants to spend the rest of his life with. He is besotted with you and I can't see that changing anytime soon. But, if you want to buy him a gift just because you can then we will find something nice but, before that we need to buy something knockout for tomorrow night."

"Sorry, tomorrow night? What is happening tomorrow night?"

"Scott is taking you and me to the theatre, so we need to make a statement. 'The girls have arrived,' so you better get used to it."

"The theatre? What theatre? I can't go to a theatre."

"Yes, you can and you will. Scott has the tickets, and we are going to look fabulous darling, so get used to it, we are going out".

"But I look such a mess, look at my hair. My clothes."

"Ella, calm down, that is why we are here. We are going to find you the most amazing clothes and then we have appointments at the hairdressers. No, you are not having it all chopped off. They will cut a bit off the bottom to even it all up then decide on a style for next Thursday night."

"Next Thursday night? Why? what is happening then."

"It's a secret but you are going to be the belle of the ball and Jacob will be with us so there is absolutely nothing to worry about."

"Right, first off let's find some fabulous clothes for tomorrow."

Caroline obviously knows her way around town. We went from one posh shop to another buying things in everyone. Caroline insists I will need a lot of outfits as we will be going out and about a lot."

"Really, can't we just stay home with our men and have fun that way?"

"No, why would we come to London then stay home? You, my girl have a lot to learn. The fact that the gorgeous Jacob can't leave you alone doesn't mean we have to stay home every night."

I have a fabulous dress for the theatre, it cost a small fortune, but Caroline insists it will be worth every penny. I have new shoes, several pairs, some with heels. I will probably break my neck in those, but she says that everyone should have fabulous shoes, they make the outfit complete."

I have handbags in every colour imaginable and a purse to go with each one.

Later I have an appointment apparently to choose my gown for next Thursday. I feel really nervous about this one. The word gown really doesn't fit with anything I know. Still, let's go with the flow. Caroline says it will all be fine, so I have to trust her.

I'm not the only one with fabulous new clothes and things. Caroline has gone mad as well. Most of these things are going to be delivered to the house later today. We would need a lorry to get all the parcels in.

Next my gift for Jacob. I wanted to buy him something gold. It would make a statement I felt. We looked in several jewellers shop windows before finally finding what I wanted. A beautiful gold bracelet. I could say it is to chain him to me forever. I had it gift wrapped. What a revelation that was. I have never had any gifts, not even at Christmas or birthdays. Nothing, it must be wonderful to receive something beautiful, and wrapped so prettily.

I put the package inside my new bag. I was feeling like a very different woman. Gaining confidence as well, bonus.

We went to a very smart shop to order my 'gown'. Well two gowns as Caroline needed one as well. These gowns were very posh. I wouldn't be able to walk in these things, Very tight some of them and very revealing. The shop did everything, not only gowns but shoes, bags, hair accessories, jackets, coats, wraps (whatever one of those was). Everything would be co-ordinated. I was totally lost.

The lady helping us was kind. She said that we were to have whatever we wanted, just as long as we were comfortable in it and happy with our purchases.

Then she said something that really did take my breath away. "Mr Ryan said that you are to have exactly what you want, and he will settle the bill."
"Sorry I said, which Mr Ryan said that?"
"Why Jacob, of course." He said that you are his partner, and you are to have everything you want."

Jacob, but how, when? He is at home waiting for us I thought.

"He telephoned earlier madam, he has an account with our sister shop and so this one is included with it. He hasn't used us before though, so we need to make sure you are happy with everything."

"I am sure I will be, thank you."

"Right, we have our models ready to show you the gowns we recommend for such an occasion. We sat down on very posh seats and were given champagne, never tasted that before but I like it. There was a succession of skinny girls walking out in fabulous gowns and parading in front of us. I turned to Caroline and said, "Can't I just wear my jeans?" She did laugh.

Finally, we both saw something we liked, Caroline's was black velvet with lots of sparkly stones on it. She went off to try it on to see if it would need altering.

I had gone completely overboard with the one I liked. It is very sheer in a very pale green and pale gold. Quite plain really but the material is gorgeous. It is high at the front but really low in the back. "You won't require undergarments with this one madam," she said. "Well, panties will be required but the bra is fitted in the dress and it is lined so no petticoats." I wondered what a petticoat was but didn't ask.

I was whisked off to try the gown on. An assistant came with me to help put the gown on. It felt amazing, I don't think it will require any alterations, feels perfect to me.

The manager came through to check it out and said what I had thought. "Madam, this gown was made for you and the colour goes so well with your beautiful hair. How does it feel?"

"It feels fabulous actually, these shoes go with it so well and they feel really comfortable."

"Good," she said, "there is a little bag to go with it as well, so you are all fit to go".

"Is it okay if my friend comes to check it please?"

"Certainly madam, she is just next door.

Caroline was summoned and arrived still in her gown. She looked stunning.

She just stood staring at me, "Ella, you look a million dollars. That gown was made for you. Wait till Jacob sees you in it. He will fall in love with you all over again."

"Oh, Caroline, do you really think so? I hope he likes it as much as I do."

"He will, he will have his socks knocked off for certain. Try to keep it hidden till the night then surprise him."

"I will," I said.

"You don't look too bad yourself," I said. She did look amazing. She had chosen her shoes and bag, so it looked like it was all sorted.

"We will have all these things packed away for you ladies, then our courier will deliver them tomorrow. I understand they are all to be delivered to the same address. The home of Mr Scott Ryan, is that correct?"

We looked at each other and said, "yes, that is correct. We are all staying with Scott for the time being." said Caroline.

"Right, leave it all to us. The delivery should be around ten o'clock tomorrow morning. If there is anything else we can help you with then please let us know."

"We will, thank you so much for your help," we both chorused.

At last it was time to go to the hairdressers. I was really very nervous about this. I shouldn't have worried, the stylist, Henri, was very good and very French. He put me at ease straight away. He was lovely if a little over the top. He said my hair was amazing, he has never seen hair so thick and long.

He was going to cut two or three inches off the bottom and was then going to think about what to do with it for next Thursday.

"There it was again, next Thursday. Whatever this thing is will be something big, very big. No point worrying about it yet. Got tomorrow to get over first".

Caroline said, "Right, we just about have time to sort a mobile phone out for you."

"Why would I need a mobile phone?" I asked.

Caroline just looked at me.

"Can we just go home," I asked, plenty of time to get a phone?".

"Okay, I will ring Scott to see what time he will be finished".

He was ready now, so we didn't have to wait long. We had made our way back to the side street where Scott had dropped us off what seemed liked two days ago. I just wanted to get back to see Jacob. Wonder if he has missed me as much as I have missed him.

Scott pulled up and jumped out of the car. He put his arm around Caroline and kissed her lips. Fabulous I thought. He took all our packages from us and placed them in the boot of his vehicle. We all climbed in then we were off.

"Is that all you pair have bought," he asked.

"Err, no," said Caroline. "Got deliveries for the rest. You might need to build an extension."

"That's fine just so long as you lovely ladies have everything you need."

I giggled, "what we need and so much more," I said. "I hope I live long enough to wear it all."

"Caroline had taken me to a very posh lingerie shop, and I was forced to purchase several saucy sets. She said that Jacob would probably appreciate them more than the bracelet."

God, I hope he likes it. It has cost almost a thousand pounds. I must really like him.

As we sped towards the pub where we would be meeting Jacob I thought, will he be embarrassed with his gift. I have only known him a bit over a day and here I am spending a fortune on him. No I thought, he will appreciate it I am sure. Will soon find out.

We pulled up outside a beautiful looking building which I am told is their local pub. Never been in one of these before.

As we parked up I spotted Jacob, he was talking to three women. They were all taking it in turn to have a photograph taken with him.

Strange I thought, wonder if that is a London thing?

Oh well, he is a very handsome man, so I expect he draws women in, he has certainly drawn me in.

We parked the car then got out. As we reached where Jacob was standing he said to the women, "Thank you ladies but my partner is here now with my brother and his lady, we have a table booked so I will have to go."

One of the women said, "Can we have a kiss Jacob before you go?"

"Sure," he said then leaned over and kissed them all on the cheek.

"Okay then, thank you ladies and bye."

Caroline was watching me and could see I didn't know what to make of it.

"Don't worry about that Ella, women do tend to push themselves onto handsome men. Jacob will be courteous with them, but he won't do any more than that. It is you that has his heart, and he won't do anything to upset you."

The women moved away then stood watching us as we greeted Jacob. He shook Scott's hand then kissed Caroline on the cheek. He then put both arms around me and pulled me into the most amazing kiss in full view of everyone. He pulled back and looked into my eyes, then he took my face in his hands and kissed me again. "God Ella, where have you been all my life? I have missed you so much my darling."

I was speechless, probably just waiting for you my love. I have missed you too. I then realised that several faces were watching us from the pub windows. Perhaps we shouldn't do that in the street I thought but then Jacob kissed me again so maybe these people are just nosey.

"You have lipstick on your cheek," I said, "as I got a tissue from my pocket and wiped it off."

"Sorry about that," he said, "have to keep up appearances." I didn't really understand what he was talking about, but he seemed embarrassed, so I let it drop.

"Did you have a good days shopping?"

"We did," I said. "Got more stuff than I know what to do with, but Caroline insists I will need it all."

"And thank you so much for paying for our outfits for next Thursday." I have no idea where we are going or what we are doing but Caroline insists I will enjoy it. The gowns have cost a small fortune, you didn't have to do that though, Jacob. I do have money of my own now."

"Am I not allowed to buy my beautiful lady a gift? Anyway, it is all for my benefit so don't say anything else about it. Can't wait to see you in it though."

"You can wait till next Thursday the same as everyone else, but I do have one or two things you might enjoy seeing me in later."

Jacob's eyes grew big as he looked at me. "I am intrigued, do we have to eat, can't we just go home?"

"I'm game," I said. "But I think your brother might have something to say about it."

"Come on then, let's go and fuel up. I want to take you to my bed and soon".

"You're on a promise," I said.

He gave me one more long passionate kiss then took hold of my hand and escorted me into the pub. What a lovely place. Very old fashioned I guessed. The place was very busy, and everyone turned to look at us as we walked in. Jacob put his arm around my waist and guided me through the people standing and just watching us.

The man behind the bar called across. "Hi, Jacob, your usual table is ready for you. Scott, nice to see you again. Ladies welcome."

This felt very unusual to me. We said hello to the man then Jacob took us through to another room that was set further back. The dining room I guessed. All the tables looked to be full, but a lady came over to us and said, "hello, this way Mr Ryan, well two Mr Ryans I guess."

Jacob said, "two for the price of one. Mary, can you please just call us Scott and Jacob, Mr Ryan sounds so formal. We followed her through the tables to an alcove towards the back of the room.

"Your usual table gents."

Jacob said, "Mary can I introduce you to my partner Ella, Ella this is Mary – the landlady of this fine establishment. She always looks after us well. And Mary, this is Caroline, she is Scott's partner. You will probably be seeing a fair bit of us from now on."

"That is lovely Jacob, pleased for you both. She winked at me and said, 'You have a real diamond in this man Ella, he is one of a kind."

"Thank you, Mary," I said, "I think I know that. He is a truly wonderful man".

Mary said, "he has been unhappy for a very long time, it is good to see him with a smile on his gorgeous face."

"I will treat him with only love and kindness, I promise."

"Good girl," she said, "You look lovely together. Very nice indeed. Now come on, take your seats and I will fetch the menus. Then decide what you want to drink".

We sat around the table in the alcove, and it felt quite private. No prying eyes, I like that.

She soon came back with four menus and passed them around the table. "Right, what are you all having to drink?" she asked.

"Just a fruit juice for me Mary, got to drive this precious cargo home once we have eaten" said Scott.

"What about you ladies?" We looked at each other and grinned. "Wine I think," said Caroline, "that will suit me too," I said.

"Jacob, usual?"

"Yes please Mary, a pint of your very finest ale. Which of the wines do you ladies want?" she asked.

"Jacob, choose something nice for us please?" I asked.

"Okay, let's think. I know Mary, do you have any of the Malbec left?"

"I do, saved a few bottles for when you came in."

"Great he said, well a bottle of the Malbec and two glasses please."

Mary went off to sort our drinks out. She was soon back and asked if we had decided on our meals yet.

"Just give us five minutes Mary," said Jacob. He had her eating out of his hand I thought. She is smitten with him. Well, so am I, so I can understand how she feels.

We looked at the menu and I for one couldn't decide what I wanted. "Do you like burgers, asked Jacob?"

" What are burgers?" I asked.

"This is going to be a very long process, bringing you into the real world. I will enjoy every second of it though," he said.

"So will I. I tell you what Jacob, just order what you want, and I will have the same".

"Okay then, two burgers with chips and all the trimmings."

Scott looked up and said, make that three, Caroline? Make it four. Love a good burger. Mary took our order and scurried off.

A few minutes later, a woman came round the corner of the alcove. "Excuse me, Mr Ryan, I don't want to be a nuisance but wondered if you would have a photograph with my daughter. She has been ill for a long time and has just got the all clear from her cancer. She has loved you for a very long time".

"Of course, What is her name?"

"Marie, we are sitting just over there."

I looked at Caroline, "what is that all about," I asked.

Jacob said, "Excuse me a minute, won't be long". He left the table and headed towards the table round the corner where Marie was sitting.

Caroline said, "Don't worry about it Ella, Jacob is a very kind, handsome man. It is only to be expected he will attract interest."

"I suppose you're right, you usually are."

I leaned forward to watch what was happening. Jacob was there chatting away as if he knew these people. Caroline is right. He is just a very kind and handsome man. How lucky am I?

Once his photo had been taken with the young girl he kissed her cheek then came back to us.

I took hold of his hand and kissed it. "You are a very kind man," I said. "Hope it's just your kind heart that she has stolen."

"Never," he said, "it's you that has stolen my heart, all of it. Now kiss me before our food arrives. I did, and then I kissed him again.

"Is your wine okay?" he asked.? "It is," I said, "it's lovely."

"I thought it would be one you would like".

"Is it okay for you, Caroline?

"It is she said, very nice".

Our food arrived then. I have never seen so much food on one plate before. I could see a bun and salad and chips. I doubt I will be able to eat all that.

The men began to tuck into their meal. They must have been hungry because they were making short work of their 'burgers'.

Jacob looked at me and said, "Well, what do you think?"

" Very nice," I said, and it was, but I wouldn't be able to eat it all.

Caroline looked as if she was struggling as well. "I think if we come here again, we can have one between us, or a kiddie's meal what say you, Ella?"

"I agree. It's a pity we don't have a dog, then we could have taken it back with us."

We were all laughing and having a really good time. Caroline and I were getting down the bottle of wine and we were both in a warm fuzzy state. "If this is my new life then I will love it."

"Jacob was holding my hand and then kissing the palm. He ran his tongue over the skin in the centre of my hand. That was very erotic and was making me feel that I needed Jacob on his own.

It is lovely being with Scott and Caroline, but I think it's almost time for us to have some alone time. I need to show Jacob some of my new undies.

"I thought about the gift I had in my bag. Should I give it to him now or later? He might be embarrassed if I give it to him in front of people. I will save it till later."

The men had eaten almost all of their meals and Caroline and myself had eaten as much as we could manage. The drinks were about finished, and I was feeling very warm and comfy. Jacob was paying me an awful lot of attention. He said, I'll just go and settle the bill then we can get off home."

"I can't wait to show you my purchases. I hope you like them."

"Bloody hell Ella, what are you trying to do to me?"

I whispered in his ear, "I want you to take me to bed and make love to me, please".

"That I can do," he said. "It will be my pleasure. *Give me a minute." he stood up and went to the bar speaking to people as he passed them.*

This man of mine is very popular. Seems like everyone knows him. As we all formed a line to leave the pub, Scott going first and holding Caroline's hand then Jacob holding my hand as we made our way through the crowd, everyone seemed to be slapping Jacob on the back and saying things to him.

He stopped just before we reached the door. "Okay you lot, I know you are all interested in meeting this beautiful young woman. Just don't crowd her. She is not up for going out with any of you lot, she is mine, got it? All mine."

"Right, may I introduce my beautiful partner, yes you heard correctly, my beautiful partner, Ella. Hopefully, we will be seeing you all regularly from now on so stop speculating and just be happy for us."

There was a chorus of hello Ella, when you get fed up with poster boy here we will always look after you.

"Thank you all very much, I will remember that if I do ever fancy a change".

There was a great shout from all these lads. Seems like it's not only the woman that like my man.

We finally managed to get out of the pub, and all piled into Scott's car. The house is just a five-minute drive from the pub, so we were soon home.

Mrs Harris, the housekeeper was just leaving as we pulled up. She waited for us to get out of the car then came over to us.

"Scott, I have done all the washing and got it dried, I will iron it tomorrow, unless you need any of it before then. If you do you will have to do it yourself."

"There's a nice fresh loaf on the side so you can have sandwiches. I guess you won't want a hot meal after eating at the pub."

"What did you girls think of our local? Not bad is it?"

"We both said it is a lovely place and the food is amazing. Will definitely be going there again."

"Ella caused quite a storm, all the men were falling over themselves to speak to her" said Caroline.

"I looked at her, what are you on about?" I said. They were interested in both of us but it's just because we are strangers," I said.

"Of course, it is," said Caroline. "Jacob will have a job on his hands trying to hold on to her she said".

"Don't talk daft I replied. They all know I am with Jacob after the speech he made. Made me feel very proud, happy and special."

"Right," said Scott "if that's all, Mrs H we are going to have a nice quiet afternoon. Thanks for everything. See you tomorrow."

"Bye all, see you in the morning. Enjoy your afternoon."

"We will," we all called.

The men folk came and took all the packages from the boot and carried them indoors.

We sorted out which ones were mine and which were Caroline's then took them all upstairs to our respective rooms.

Jacob pulled me in for a full-on snog as we closed the bedroom door behind us. "God Ella, you are driving me nuts. I just want to be with you all the time, holding you, loving you. Say you feel the same, please."

"I do Jacob, I can't imagine my life without you in it now."

"Anyway, whilst I go and try one of these new outfits on in the bathroom, you can sit there and open this. I handed the gift to him.

"What's this Ella?"

"A gift from me to you. Don't go soppy on me, please. I just wanted to give you something special so that whenever we are apart you will have something to remember me by."

He sat on the edge of his bed and turned the package over in his hands. I quickly picked up my bags and disappeared into the bathroom.

God, I hope he likes these things, they were so expensive.

I quickly got out of the clothes I have been in all day then slipped on the bra and panties that Caroline says will knock Jacobs socks off.

I waited a moment then opened the door. I stood behind it hiding myself and looked over to the bed where Jacob was still sitting. He was looking at the open box that I had given him. He looked up when he realised I was there.

"Jacob, whatever is wrong," I said, I rushed over to his side. "Are you crying, my darling?" Tears were trickling down his cheeks, damp and salty as I put my cheek against his.

"What's wrong my darling, don't you like it?"

"Like it," he said, "no, I don't like it, I love it. But why did you buy it for me, Ella?

"Because I want you to think of me each time you see it or feel it on your wrist."

Now, what do you think of your other gift? I stood in front of him. He dried his eyes then looked at me.

"Bloody hell Ella, you are going to kill me. You look amazing and very sexy. Come here and sit on my knee". I did as he asked. He didn't take his eyes off me. As I sat on his knee he began to caress my body. "Ella, you are so beautiful. Whatever have I done to deserve such a wonderful woman?"

He caressed my breasts in their new covering. "Mmm, that feels nice he said".

"It certainly does," I replied.

He was feeling my body all over and I was getting very needy. Can we lie down, please? I asked. "I really can't wait any longer for you my love."

"We moved to lie on the bed side by side. We were kissing and caressing each other. My wanting for him was very strong so I asked him to make love to me now. He lay me back on the bed and removed my panties then rose above me. Slowly he pressed himself into me, moving inside me and bringing me to a state of absolute passion.

The pulsing began, strong, powerful. I could feel myself pulsing around his girth. Such a very strong sensation. Jacob could feel it too. I couldn't hold back, and neither could he. We exploded together, over and over. Finally, we fell apart and lay together breathing heavily.

Jacob lifted himself up onto his elbow and then just looked into my eyes. "Ella he said, you are making me so happy. Stay with me forever, please".

"I will," I said.

He reached over for the box holding his bracelet. "Ella my darling, I love this so much. I will never take it off. Help me fasten it please."

He offered his right wrist and I put the gold chain around it then fastened the clip. "How does it feel I asked?"

"It feels lovely, my darling. It means that you will always be with me, forever. You know I have to work tonight, don't you, my love?"

"I do yes, I will wait up for you to come home though."

"Are you sure? I could be later than last night."

"I will wait for you no matter how late you are. Just come back to me as soon as you can so that I can love you again."

"I haven't gone yet, there is time for more loving before I go you know."

"Don't you need to rest before going to work," I asked.

"No, I need to get as much loving with you, that will sustain me."

"Well, I'm not stopping you," I said.

"Just let me get my breath back first," he said. "Do you want a drink?" he asked.

"Not really, no. I will make a nice pot of tea for us to drink before you slide off to work. Will you want any food?"

"No, I don't think so. That was quite a large meal we had at lunchtime. Did you like the pub he asked?"

" I did, you seem very popular there. Do you know everybody? Seems like everyone wants to speak to you."

"Well, Scott and I have lived around here all our lives and have been going in there since before we were old enough to drink. So, I guess most people know us. I think there was more interest today because you were with me.

It has been a very long time since I have had a lady on my arm and never in there. They all just want to know who you are, and I think most of the men present fancied you."

"Don't talk daft, they don't fancy me. I mean, just look at me."

"I am," he said. "You are a very desirable woman and I love the new things you have bought. More than that though I love this bracelet. I can't believe you have spent such a lot of money on something for me. I will treasure it always. You will always be with me."

"And don't you forget it, Mr Popular. I can't get my head around how everyone wants to talk to you. They are not the same with Scott and he is just as lovely as you."

"Must be my magnetic personality".

"I guess so," I said.

"Okay then my very popular friend. Lie back and think of England. I want to see if this outfit works twice."

Jacob lay back looking up at me. I noticed how the gold of his bracelet shone in the light from the window. I am glad I chose that one, it really suits him. As he lay on his back I climbed across him. He reached for my breasts and began to tease my nipples. "*Wow*," I said, that is nice, very nice."

I leaned over him and pressed my breast to his mouth. Instantly I began to pulse low in my tummy. "*This won't take long* I thought. *I could feel his hardness beneath me. Here goes. I don't know if this is a thing, but I am going to try it anyway*".

I reached down and took him in my hand, leading him to my entrance. He felt so hard as I pressed down onto him. He slid into me easily. All this time he had been fondling my breasts, I loved the feel of his hands on my body and my breasts in his mouth.

I leaned forward and offered myself to him. First one side, then the other. I was lifting myself up and then pressing down onto him and it was wonderful. That beautiful pulsing sensation began, and I moved harder, he was still sucking gently on my breasts and it was driving me wild. I moved faster and faster till I burst with him in a glorious sensation.

In that moment it felt as if we two were one. We were so in tune with each other and so sensitive to every touch. The explosion when it came was epic. Riding together in joint pleasure, each one of us giving everything to the other.

I collapsed on top of Jacob, my hair all over his face. "I think I am now knackered," I said.

Jacob moved my hair away from his face and grinned. "Are you sure?" he asked.

"For now," I replied.

"How long till you have to leave," I asked. He looked at his watch. "Bugger, less than an hour. I need to shower, will you join me?"

"I will," I said.

We showered together washing each other. It was a very intimate thing to do. I got out first and dried myself then said, "I will go and make tea."

"Okay, darling," he said. "Will be down in a minute."

I put on a very skimpy nightie that I had bought and then put my new dressing gown on over the top just in case Caroline or Scott put in a show.

I went down to the kitchen and they were both there looking very smug I thought. "I am making tea, would you like some?" I asked.

"Yes, please," they both said. "Will Jacob want food before work? What did he say?" Scott asked.

He said "Not but I reckon if there is any cake left or biscuits he might manage that".

"Same here, ate too much at the pub to want anything big."

"What do you fancy doing tonight?" they asked.

"Don't mind at all," was my reply.

Jacob came through to the kitchen then already to leave. He looked fabulous. He had on a lovely shortsleeved white shirt with black jeans. "God Jacob, you look good enough to eat," I said.

They all laughed at me. "You are funny. Ella," said Caroline. "If you think it you say it. No filter."

"Don't know what you mean?" I said.

As I was pouring the tea Scott noticed Jacob's bracelet. "That is a very nice piece of jewellery you have on there, bro. Is it new?"

"It is," he said. It's a present from Ella and I love it. She will be with me always now, even if we are apart."

Scott held his wrist whilst looking at the bracelet. "You lucky bastard, he said, "that is gorgeous. I think you have hit the jackpot with this young lady, and you seem to have fallen for each other just as Caroline and I have. I haven't felt this happy and content for years."

Jacob said, "You are right there Scott, I can't get Ella out of my head. I know it's early days, but I feel so certain of her and of our feelings for each other. I am going to take her to see my house next week. See if she would be happy living in it once the renovations are done. I have a renewed thirst for getting it finished now."

I looked at Jacob, "What house? I thought you lived here with Scott."

"Don't worry about it, sweetheart. I will explain everything to you over the coming days and if you decide it's not for you then we can sell it and buy it somewhere else. It's only five minutes down the road. We can go and look at it when you're ready."

I am very confused I said. "I really don't know anything about you, do I?" But then, again I suppose you don't know too much about me. Not that there is much to know. I haven't been anywhere or done anything."

Jacob looked at me, "Ella, from now on things are going to change for you, I promise. We can travel anywhere in the world together if you want to my love, but we do need to take some time to get to know each other properly. That is why I am loving these few, early days. You amaze me every moment I am with you."

I blushed spotting Scott and Caroline watching us.

"You both seem to be very happy and contented in each other's company," said Caroline.

"Ella, you have really begun to blossom. I don't know where that shy, quiet girl has gone. I have to say though I think Jacob has been the reason for this change in you."

I looked at her, "you need to talk, look at you two all loved up. I think that phone call you made to Scott was the best day's work you have ever done. Tell me, will you leave Marchpool and move down here to be with Scott?"

"I think that is the ultimate goal if Scott will have me, but we have a lot of hoops to jump through first. There are Scott's two children to take into consideration for a start. They have to come first. We are going to take them out on Sunday, just the four of us. See if we like each other. They are both very young and have been through a lot with Scott's ex-wife taking them away from their family home and all their friends".

"Then there is everything of mine that I have up in Marchpool. I have my own house for a start. True, I don't have a partner or children to consider but there is my job. I have worked hard to get where I am today, but Scott would want me to be at home, not working. He thinks my job is dangerous and I suppose it is in part, but I would miss it".

"Also, Scott says he would love to have more children. Of course, I want a family as well but when do we start that process? Like you two we don't know each other properly yet but if we leave it too long I will be too old. I'm thirty-four now and wouldn't want to leave it much longer".

"We think the first thing to do is get the girls on our side. If they are happy for their dad to move on then we can begin to make proper plans."

"What about you two, any thoughts on where you go from here?"

"Jacob said that he needs to get the next couple of weeks out of the way, but he definitely wants me to be with him wherever we end up".

I said, "I wanted to be with him too. I have never known such happiness or contentment. I really think I love him although it has only been a couple of days."

Jacob drew in a deep breathe, "Ella, do you really mean that?"

"I do," I said, "I can't imagine my life without you in it now."

Jacob said, "Ella, I love you too, so very much. God, I wish I didn't have to work tonight. I just want to be with you always, my darling."

There was a car hooting out the front. "Shit," he said, "I have to go now. Will you be up when I get back? He asked.

"I will I said. I can't wait for you to get home."

He reached over and kissed me with such a passion then kissed me again. I was totally breathless with love and with wanting.

"I have to go, I'm going to be late again."

"Just go Jacob, the sooner you go, the sooner you will be back." He kissed me again then left.

I felt bereft again once he had gone. I wanted to cry. Caroline must have noticed the tears and rushed to my side.

"Ella, don't cry, Jacob will be back soon."

I dried my eyes and took a big gulp. "I don't know what is wrong with me. It just swept over me when he left."

"Look, let's go and make a sarnie and another pot of tea. We can sit and talk about tomorrow night. I am so looking forward to going to the theatre, are you?"

"I don't know, Caroline, I have never been to a theatre and don't really know what happens."

"Well, I can tell you one thing for sure, you will love it."

"You really think I will?" I asked.

"Believe me, you will be over the moon then afterwards we are meeting up with Jacob and we can either do something or just come home".

"Okay," I said. "I will look forward to it if you are sure it's something I will enjoy. I just wish Jacob could come with us. Still, it will be nice to see him later on."

"Plus we have all our lovely new clothes to wear. I love getting dressed up and going out on the town, you will love it too, I promise," said Caroline.

"I tell you what, let's go and sort all our bags and packages out. The other stuff arrived when you two were playing tiddly winks in the bedroom."

"What's tiddlywinks?" I asked.

"Oh, Ella, I love you, you are like a sister to me. Just imagine if we both end up living down here with these gorgeous men of ours and having families of our own. Do you think that is something you would want with Jacob?"

"To be honest I haven't thought about it, but yes, I would love to have children with him. I just hope I haven't done any damage to myself with all the pregnancies I ended with Will. I don't think he ever cottoned on to why I never had a kid. He could be a bit thick about some things."

"I am sure you won't have caused any damage but if you couldn't get pregnant there are so many ways to help you these days. It might be worth talking to Jacob about it though. He might not want children."

"You are right," I said, "I guess these things are usually spoken about when you start going out with men, get it sorted before committing to something that's not right for you."

Just a thought Ella, are you and Jacob taking precautions?

"What do you mean I asked?"

"Well, I know you are not on the pill, but does Jacob use a condom?"

"Sorry, pill, condom? What do you mean?"

"Sorry Ella, my fault, I should have thought about it before. Been so wrapped up in being with Scott it never entered my head. They are both to stop you from getting pregnant. I take it he isn't using a condom then."

"I don't think so," I said, "we have been so wrapped up in each other and I have to admit I have been so desperate to have him inside me. I will have a proper talk with him tomorrow. He will be tired tonight."

"Can I ask you something, Caroline? You know when your man is inside you and that feeling starts between your legs. It is so overwhelming, it has never happened to me before, but I love it. What is it called, you know when you both lose yourselves?"

"Ella you poor thing, your life has been awful for so long. It is called a climax or orgasm. "It is one of the best things you can experience with your man. Beautiful for you both."

"Well, Jacob and I manage to have whatever you call it time after time. I think maybe I manage it more than him, but I really love it."

"Also, is it okay to use your mouth on your man and him on you? We have been experimenting and we both like it but I'm not sure if it's okay to do it".

"Ella, if it is what you both want, and it gives you both satisfaction then it is fine. That is called oral sex by the way."

"I am learning a lot today aren't I?"

"You certainly are my friend, and I am really pleased for you both."
"You really do look the perfect couple. We just need to talk to Jacob about birth control to see if he wants children or not. If you use these things then you can plan when to have children, not just leave it to fate.

Scott had left the room when he realised which way this conversation was going but he came back in now."

"Have you ladies finished your heart-to-heart?"

"We have," said Caroline. "We just need to speak with your brother about one or two things. Ella thinks tomorrow will be soon enough."

"Right then, come on let's make food and drink then have a look at what's on the box. If there is something good to watch then time will fly by and Jacob will be home before we know it".

Mrs Harris had left some sliced chicken in the fridge for us and there were another couple of fresh loaves, so Scott sliced the bread, I buttered, and Caroline put the chicken and pickle onto the sandwiches.

We cut some for Jacob for his return and wrapped them in cling film. This was something else new to me. So many things to make life easier, I will need to try them all. Jacob will help me though, I have no doubt about that.

Scott was looking through a menu on the TV, he turned and asked us, "have you two ever heard of Outlander?"

I said no, but Caroline said she had heard of it but never seen it.

"Okay then, fancy giving it a go?"

"We both said, Yes, fine by us."

He found what he was looking for and pressed a button on the remote.

What a revelation that show is for me. I love it. We watched five episodes before Jacob arrived home. The leading man is gorgeous and has the look of my Jacob about him, except his hair is red. Jamie Fraser's not Jacob. It is set in Scotland. Might be on the moon for all I know of different places. I do remember some things from history at school though. They taught us stuff about Scotland's history, and I found it fascinating at the time. I had forgotten about it till now though.The countryside looked amazing, somewhere I would like to visit I thought.

When I heard Jacob come through the door, "I ran to meet him and flung my arms around him kissing him all over his beautiful face."

"Now that is a welcome I appreciate. What have you been doing in my absence?"

"Watching Outlander, will you take me to Scotland one day?" I asked.

"Yes. I will, just so long as you don't go rushing around looking for Jamie Fraser and then ditching me."

"I would never ditch you, my darling," I said. "I love you too much. Have you had a good night?"

"Not bad, busy but the time soon passed so I could come home to you my darling. Is that all you have done, watch that sexy Scot?"

"Well, no, actually. I have learned that the lovely feeling I get when we make love is called an orgasm or climax and when we use our mouths it's called oral sex."

I thought he would choke, "Blimey! you have been busy. I hadn't realised you didn't know what they are called. Will need to do some explaining along the way I guess."

"I want you to teach me everything."

"Caroline and I talked about other stuff as well. I was going to wait until tomorrow, but no time like the present I suppose."

"Okay my darling, go for it."

"Well, Caroline and I were talking about her and Scott moving in together and they want to have a family of their own, then she asked me if we were taking precautions."

"I didn't know what she was on about. I thought if you had sex and a baby happened then that was it. I didn't know you could plan these things."

Jacob said, "I think I should go out and come back in again. You have gone through a few subjects, but can we talk about this upstairs".

"Yes, we can," I said. "We have saved you a chicken sarnie if you are hungry."

"I am a bit now, come on. Let me eat and have a drink, then we can go upstairs. I guess those two have gone up already."

"Yes, they have, just before you came in. We are all alone".

"Just let me catch my breath first he said".

He went to the tap and poured himself a big glass of water then downed the lot. "That's better," he said. "Now, would you like a glass of wine?

"Only if you do," I said.

"Okay, let's leave the wine, I will eat this then we can go up."

I sat next to him whilst he ate and played with the fingers of his left hand. He has beautiful hands. Obviously, doesn't work on a farm.

It only then occurred to me that I have no idea what he does. He will tell me when he's ready.

Once his sandwich was finished we put the plate in the dishwasher, another revelation, and then we moved upstairs. As soon as we were through the door he put his arms around me, pulling me to him for a lovely kiss. We kissed for a while then his hands began to wander underneath my jumper. He found my breasts and took them in both hands.

"I have been wanting to do that all night" he said. He teased my breasts and then began to undress me. I was soon naked and wanting. I removed his clothes swiftly and we were very quickly making wonderful love. I love this man so much.

I could feel his bracelet on my skin. He does like it I thought, so glad I bought it for him.

We climaxed together, it was wonderful. The pulsing sensation went on and on. My body was so alive, so in tune with this wonderful man. Finally we stilled and lay together in each other's arms until our breathing returned to normal.

We lay still for an age just breathing each other in.

"You smell divine I said. I could lie here just breathing the scent of you forever".

"My darling I love you so. I have loved wearing this gift tonight. Each time I felt it move on my wrist I could feel you next to me. Had several compliments on it too. Told everyone who asked that it was a gift from my gorgeous girlfriend. They were all jealous. They all want to meet the woman that has made me smile again".

"Really," I said, "how can I meet them, "I don't even know where you work or what you do."

"Can I keep you in the dark till tomorrow night, please?"

"Okay, if that's what you want."

"I do," he said.

He pulled me to him and began kissing me thoroughly, playing with my nipples again and making me squirm. "Now who is getting a sexy feeling then?" he asked.

"I am," I said, will you make love to me again? please."

"I certainly will my darling girl".

And he did, taking me to new heights of passion.

We lay together in each other's arms loving each other. How wonderful is this man? I love him so much.

I had a sudden thought, "Jacob, what is a condom?"

"Well, it's something a man uses to stop a pregnancy from happening."

"That's what Caroline said, she also asked if I was on the pill. I didn't know what she was talking about."

Jacob swallowed hard. "Ella, he said, what have we been doing? A massive sex fest and neither of us thinking about birth control. What if you are pregnant?"

I thought for a moment then said, "well, I guess if I am we will have a baby. How do you feel about that Jacob?"

"I would love it, my darling. I have always wanted a family of my own. I love Scott's two girls, but they are his not mine."

"How would you feel about it, Ella?"

'Well, I would love to have your children, Jacob. I can't think of anything I would like more to be honest. There is just one problem I need to tell you about."

"Okay, this sounds serious. What is it, my love?'

"Well, as you know as soon as I was sixteen, I was forced to marry that awful old man. He forced me to have sex with him almost every night. I had no idea about being pregnant and what that meant apart from bits I remembered from school, which wasn't much."

"Anyway, my period was late not long after we were married, and Will was over the moon. I was terrified, I couldn't bring a child into the world in that toxic house, so I set about trying to get rid of it. I went all around the farm lifting heavy things, jumping off high chairs and throwing myself on the hard floor. Eventually,

I had the most awful period, so I guessed I had managed to get rid of the child. The same thing happened many times over the next nine years. A child would have been amazing, but I couldn't allow anyone else to suffer the way I did."

'Ella, that must have been awful for you. I do understand why you did what you did. A child would have made everything so much worse.'

"Has Scott told you what happened to me?"

"No, he hasn't. I know you had a bad break-up that was difficult to handle, but I don't know any of the details.

"Do you want to know?" he asked.

"Only if you feel able to talk about it, my darling."

"Well, almost two years ago now, I met a model called Cleo Roberts. She was nice enough and we went out a few times. Then she discovered she was pregnant. I didn't love her, but she was okay, and we'd had some good times together. I promised to stand by her and support her and the child. I bought the house down the road, got the architects in to re-design it all then employed builders to do the work. I thought it would all be okay but unbeknown to me she had an abortion. Do you know what that is?"

"Not really," I said, "but I guess it meant getting rid of the child."

"Yes, that is the outcome. It is done medically though. She had done it without even mentioning it to me. She didn't ask what I thought, nothing. I couldn't be with her any more, so I finished it."

It was only after I had finished it that she informed me that she had been having an affair with my best mate, Arlo. She didn't know whose baby it was, so she got rid of it. She thought at first she could pass it off as mine but then realised that as Arlo is Jamaican she was dicing with the truth. Whatever, she got rid of it and I got rid of her.

I had used protection the few times we had sex so I guess if I had looked at it sensibly I would have realised the truth of it earlier."

"It was very hard for a long time. I didn't think I would ever find anyone to really love, who would love me, to build a brilliant future with. Then I met you."

"Look, if you are already pregnant then so what? We intend to be together anyway, so pregnancy would just bring that all forward."

"If you're not pregnant then we can use contraception till we decide the time is right." Are you okay with that my love?"

"Oh, Jacob, I am. I just hope that I haven't done any damage with the way I dealt with my problem."

"I shouldn't think there will be any danger. It would seem that you do get pregnant easily. I would be so happy, Ella. You, me and our own special baby".

"When is your next period due?"

"Not sure," I said, I will have to look back at a calendar and see if I can work it out. Can't be much more than a week though I wouldn't think."

"*Wow,* a baby of our own," Jacob was excited. "I know we have only just met really, but I know we are the real deal and will be together forever. We have a beautiful house in the making, I hope you like it, Ella. We could go and look at it tomorrow if you want?"

"Slow down Jacob, let's find out first if there is a baby or not."

"Baby or no I want to be with you, my sweet girl. If not now then surely it won't be too long before we have our own little miracle on the way."

"If Caroline moves here and they have children, and our house is just up the road it would be fantastic. You would have a best friend on the doorstep. Just imagine it. Sorry, I know I'm running at a hundred miles an hour again, but this is what I want, and I want it with you."

"Oh, Jacob, how the hell did we get to this point? From you not wanting to spend time with the weird widow that was coming stay to now talking about houses and babies and forever after. My head is in a spin."

"I know, my darling, but I am so excited about our future together."

"So am I Jacob but I think we do need to slow down just a bit, don't you?"

"I guess you're right, but I like thinking about our future together."

"So do I my love, it all sounds so amazing, but we really do need to take a reality check. Slow down just until we know what we are dealing with."

"I know you are right my love, but I am still excited at the prospect. Let's try and sleep now we both have a busy day tomorrow."

"I lay in Jacob's arms and finally fell asleep, dreaming of houses and babies and fun-filled days with Caroline."

We woke early the next day, "morning darling, how are you feeling today? asked Jacob."

"I feel fine actually, my love. Slept well, did you?"

"I did, a few little dreams but generally slept well."

"He cuddled up to me, kissing my neck once he managed to get my hair out of the way."

"I could feel his wanting of me pressing into my buttocks.

You have a tidy swelling there. Mr Ryan," I said.

"I do, don't I?" he whispered into my hair. What are you going to do about it?"

"Well, I could turn over and slide down the bed and see if a little mouth action might help or I could lie on my back and let you enter my body, or we could just lie here and pretend it's not there."

"Ha! Ha!" he said, "very funny. I have news for you my lovely. It is there and it wants to be inside you right now."

"Okay," I said. "Well, we hadn't better disappoint then, had we?"

"Our love-making" was becoming so comfortable between us. Neither of us shy any more. We know each other's wants and needs instinctively. A very comfortable place to be. I love being in this man's arms.

If I think back to just a week ago, I was terrified. Hadn't a clue what would happen to me in the future but now look at me. Madly in love with this gorgeous, handsome man who loves me too.

We decided we would get up early, have some breakfast then walk down to see Jacob's house. He is really keen for me to see it, so I had better go and see what all the fuss is about. Surely, it can't be any better than this house. I love it."

We showered together and I loved the feel of it. Never had someone to wash me all over before. I love it. Jacob is so gentle "with me. If this keeps happening we will be back in bed. Very erotic.

We did manage to get out of the house fairly early and we walked down the pretty tree-lined street. There are some lovely houses on this street. Very posh I thought.

We walked along hand in hand. A few people passed us and said good morning to Jacob and nodded to me. Looked like they had been to a shop was my best guess. Most were carrying a newspaper. Everyone seemed friendly. We stopped outside an enormous house that was obviously having work done to it. A lot of work.

There was a lot of equipment, machines, stacks of bricks all sorts of stuff.

I looked at Jacob,"Are you telling me that this is your house?"

"It is, do you like it he asked?"

"Jacob it is massive, how can two people live in a house this size?"

"Well, it might not be just the two of us for long. We could fill it with our children. Wouldn't that be something?"

"I think you need to hold your horses mate. Sounds like you want me pregnant for the rest of my days."

"Only joking but two or three of our own would be wonderful, don't you think?"

"I do but would we really need a house this big?"

"Let's not worry too much about the size of the house. Wait till I show you the plans and see what you think then."

"Okay Jacob, it is a lovely place to live, and the house does look amazing, it's just not what I am used to."

"Nor me if I'm honest, I lived in an apartment before moving in with Scott, but we will study the plans and then see what we think after."

"Now, back home, well Scott's home. Let's go and spend some time with those two." Do you think we should buy a pregnancy test whilst we are out?"

"Pregnancy test? What is one of those?"

"Well, it's a thing that you pee on and it tells you if you are pregnant or not."

"How clever, I don't know if we should do that yet though. Do you want to know that desperately?"

"I do, I love you more than life itself and I want to marry you and have a family with you, and I want it now. I have never been very good at waiting."

"I quite like the not knowing, if it says no you will be disappointed but if we don't know then it could still be a maybe. Does that make sense? Whether I am or not we will still be heading in the same direction. We will still be together and building a home together. If I'm not then it won't be long before I am. All the practising we do."

"Okay, leave it for now. Let's get home and I will show you the plans for the house."

We walked back to Scott's house hand-in-hand. Jacob kept kissing my hand. There were a few more people around now and they all seemed to be interested in us. Not being used to living in or around other people I wasn't sure if this was a thing or not.

"Do people always speak to you when you are out Jacob? Is it just you they are interested in or do people always speak to each other? I have lived on a remote farm all my life so am not used to mixing with people."

"Like I said before Scott and I have lived around here all our lives, so I guess most people know us." It's good to be friendly, don't you think?"

"I guess so," I said, "I'm just not used to it."

We had reached the house and made our way inside. I could hear Scott and Caroline talking in the kitchen. Jacob said for me to go through to them and he would fetch his plans.

The love birds were sitting at the kitchen island side by side and feeding each other with pieces of toast. They jumped apart as I walked in.

"Please don't stop on my account," I said. "It's lovely seeing you two so happy together."

Scott jumped up, "tea or coffee Ella?"

"Tea, please. Jacob just took me to see his house. It's massive, we won't need something that size, will we? This house is big enough but that one, well it frightened me when I saw it. I am not used to all this luxury."

Scott laughed, "Just because you are not used to it doesn't mean you won't get used to it. If you and Jacob are going to make a life together then you will need something special, believe me."

"Okay, he is fetching the plans for me to see so we can all have a look at them. See what they reveal." Jacob arrived then with huge sheets of rolled-up-paper. Apparently, these are 'the plans'.

We cleared the pots away from the island surface and Jacob unrolled his 'plans'.

I didn't understand most of it but along with the technical drawings were some coloured drawings of what the finished thing should look like, inside and out.

"Tea all right for you Jacob?"

"Yes, please. Now what do you think of these my darling?"

"Well, it all looks fabulous, but it's not something I know. It looks a bit clinical if that makes sense. The farmhouse where I lived was like something out of the Dark Ages. All this is so different. Will I get used to it Jacob?"

"You will my love. It won't be down to you to do all the cooking and cleaning. We will employ staff so that will leave you free to travel with me or whatever we decide to do."

"If we are lucky enough to have a family then you can have a nanny or at least help with the children."

Scott said, "Jacob, you are selling it to me and Caroline, but you are scaring the life out of Ella."

"I think you two need to take baby steps. Let Ella get used to one thing before you bamboozle her with everything all at once."

"I am sorry Ella, I keep forgetting all this is so new for you, but I am so excited to be finally finding my forever after."

Scott said, "I think the best thing you can do is get on and finish the house, get it how you want it. Then if you want to try living there, give it a go. If you decide in the end it's not for you then get it on the market and find something that does suit you."

"Mr Sensible is always right," said Jacob. "Sorry if I rushed you my darling. Right, tea, is there enough bread for more toast?"

"There certainly is."

I jumped down from my seat and went to help Scott with the tea and toast. I whispered a thank you to him. He understands. He has seen where I come from.

We enjoyed a lovely day together. Scott showed me around the rest of his house. I hadn't seen half of it. *A really nice place. I could live in a place like this* I thought.

Scott said that the actual size is very similar to Jacob's home, but the internal design is very different. If you don't like the design then tell him, let him know what you really want. After all it will be the two of you living there. He will see the sense in it I'm sure."

"Thanks, Scott, I love him to bits, but he is very impulsive."

"He has always been the same I'm afraid. But to be honest with you, Ella I have never seen him so in love as he is with you. I know he was planning a future with Cleo, but he didn't love her, never had but he wanted to do the honourable thing."

"With you, it is the real deal, I can see it a mile off. He will be good for you and you for him. You will make a great team."

"Now, come and have a look round my garden. It has taken me years to get it how I want it but finally, I'm there."

"It is stunning Scott, have you done it all yourself?"

"Well, not all of it. I had the experts in to do the really big stuff then Jacob helped me with the rest."

"The garden at Jacobs place is a lot bigger than this one, more than twice the size, but if you want it to be a certain way tell him then you can do the work yourselves. My girls love coming here when the weather is fit so they can play outside. Jacob and I built them their own little house at the bottom of the garden. They play in there for hours."

"I will talk to him and tell him my views if you think it is the right thing to do."

"I do and you will both be happier for it, believe me."

"I do and thank you. You have done so much to help me."

"It is Will's cremation tomorrow, you know, I said?"

"Yes, I did know, he was a very odd man. Fancy not allowing anyone to be at his funeral."

"I am glad to be honest with you. I wouldn't be able to force myself to cry for him. The life he gave me was little more than torture."

"Jacob is showing me there is another way. I really do love him, you know."

"I know you do Ella, it shows on your face when you look at him. He loves that bracelet you bought him you know. He told me he cried when you gave it to him."

"He did, yes. He was really overcome. I am so glad I got it for him. After all, he has saved me and look at all the lovely clothes he has paid for. I can't imagine what I will wear them for though."

Scott smiled, "All will be revealed Ella, just don't push him. He will tell you all about it in his own good time."

"And of course, we have our theatre trip tonight to look forward to. Caroline tells me you have a special dress for that as well."

"Caroline is a one-woman shopping machine," I said. "My head was in a spin, first this shop then that one. She knows exactly what she wants and goes for it. She will look amazing. We won't let either of you see us though until the night or day, whenever it is."

"Definitely the night. Caroline says you look amazing in your gown as well. Hope us boys scrub up well enough to be able to escort you both."

"I am sure you will both be fine. I just hope I enjoy it, whatever it is."

"Oh, you will, that is one thing I am certain of."

"Come on, let's get back indoors. I think we should have a late lunch today then go on to a restaurant after the show tonight. Jacob will be with us so it will be nice for the four of us to have a lovely time together."

"I can go with that," I said, "I am still full of toast. We had some before we had our walk then came back and had some more."

"Do you want me to cook later?" I asked.?

"Heavens no, Mrs H will be here soon, and she will sort something out for us. She tells me she really likes you and is so happy to see Jacob smiling at last. She worries about us both. She thinks that Caroline is just perfect for me as well and I have to say I agree with her entirely."

"Since I first met her my head has been so full of her. She is a lovely woman and has definitely put a smile on my face as well."

"Now we have to leave here by six-thirty to get to the theatre on time, so make sure you are ready. Jacob will have already left but we will meet up with him after the show has finished."

"Right, I said. I am quite excited about going to a theatre. No idea what I will see or what a theatre looks like inside, or outside come to that. Another first for me."

"Come on, let's go back inside, you will be getting cold."

"Jacob had gone upstairs when we returned. Caroline said, I am to ask you to pop up when you came in. Can't imagine what for."

I felt myself blush.

"Don't worry," Caroline said, "we will be right behind you.

Won't Mrs H wonder where we all are?" I asked.

Scott said, "I have a feeling she might guess."

I went up to find Jacob, he was sitting on the edge of the bed just looking at his bracelet. He looked up as I entered. He had tears in his eyes again.

"Jacob, are you okay my darling?"

He took a deep breath. "I am," he said, "I was just thinking what a wonderful person you are. I really love this he said, it means the world to me."

"Well, I love you, so no more tears.'

"Scott and I have been discussing the housing problem. Well, not a problem as such. He said I should tell you exactly my thoughts so here goes."

"I love where the house is, and I love the look of the outside if I'm honest but I'm not so sure about the inside. It all looks so impersonal. All white and modern. Nothing wrong with that at all but it's just not me. I'm not sure it's you either if I'm honest."

"Well, it can all be changed to whatever you decide he said. They haven't done that much to the inside yet so it shouldn't be too difficult to alter. I can arrange for the architect to come and talk with us next week, see what he can do."

"Are you sure Jacob, it is your home so it should be what you want first and foremost.?"

"Correction, it is our home, and it has to be what we are both comfortable with. I know what you mean about the all-white. It does look a bit like a clinic. I'll call him later, see if he can come over and meet us at the house. We should be able to come up with something that suits us all."

"Now, come here future wife, I need to be loved before I have to scurry off."

"I wish you were coming with us, Jacob. I know you have to work but I will miss you."

"I will miss you too, my darling but I will be able to meet you after the show and Scott said we are going for a meal together so that will be nice. I like being out with you, showing you off.'

I went to stand in front of him and he put his arms around my waist, pulling me into him. I bent my head and kissed him.

He pulled me onto the bed and made love to me in a mad frenzy. "*Wow,* I said, what did I do to deserve that?"

"Sorry," he said, I just couldn't help myself. I wanted you so badly.

"Don't be sorry Jacob, I wanted you just as badly". What a wonderful way for us to show our love for each other.

He had to go to work earlier than usual, so we showered, Jacob put on his clean jeans and a beautiful dark blue shirt. I slipped my dressing gown on as I would be dressing a little later for our trip to the theatre.

Jacob opened his arms for me to walk in to. He enveloped me in a beautiful hug then held there tightly in his arms. "My God Ella, you have made me the happiest man alive. I promise to love you always, my darling."

"Jacob, it is less than a week since we met but like you, I know this is where I want to be, where I need to be, by your side."

"I wish I could marry you today my sweet girl."

"And I, you."

Let's do it as soon as we possibly can. I want you to be my wife, say yes, Ella."

"Is this a proposal?"

"It is my darling, will you marry me, please?"

"Yes, Jacob I will, as soon as is decently possible. After all, today was Will's cremation."

"I suppose we will have to wait a few weeks to make it look seemly, but not too long my beautiful darling."

We left the room and went downstairs. Scott and Caroline were already there. They had made up some plates of sandwiches thinking that will sustain us till we eat later on.

Jacob seems a little nervous tonight I thought. Perhaps it's just me reading something that isn't there. He says that he loves me, and I believe him, no reason not to. I love him too with all my heart.

His car collected him about an hour earlier than usual and I felt the loss of his body by mine. It will be a long night at the theatre without my love.

Caroline came to help me dress and she applied a little make-up for me. She put some product through my hair to help stop it flying about making me look like a mad witch.

I put on the lovely dress that I had bought for this occasion. It fits really well, and I feel really grown up in it for a change. I put the silver sandals on, again bought for this occasion, and then finished it off with the little silver bag bought to match the sandals.

I stood in front of the mirror and saw a stranger staring back at me. Caroline came and stood by my side and we looked in the mirror together.

"Blimey! I said, just look at us two imposters. We do scrub up well, don't we?"

"I should say so," said Caroline. "I think we look fabulous, darling. Now let's go and show Scott how amazing we look."

We went off down the stairs and found Scott in the kitchen. He turned when he heard us enter. "My God, who are these two beautiful women and what have you done with my girlfriend?"

We laughed, "You don't look half bad yourself, Scott. It will be an honour to be by your side this evening my darling," said Caroline.

He did look very handsome in dark grey slacks and a light grey shirt.

A car piped out the front. "Come on then ladies, let's go show the world how fabulous we are."

"Are you ready for this Ella?"

"I think so"? I replied. "Still don't know what to expect but let's go and find out".

Scott checked he had the tickets, we all slipped our jackets on and left the house.

There was a very nice car waiting for us. No idea what make it is, but it is wonderful. We sat on leather seats, I knew that much. A whole lot better than the battered old Land Rover or the tractor that I sometimes drove around the farm.

Scott sat in front with the driver and Caroline sat in the rear with me. She reached over and squeezed my hand. "You will enjoy tonight Ella, I promise."

"Okay, if you say so. I will enjoy myself."

We set off for what Caroline called the West End. I guess that is a part of London.

We were soon driving through streets flooded with lights. Loads of people were rushing about going goodness knows where. I didn't think I would ever get used to all the rush and hurry that is London but for tonight I will give it a go.

Eventually, the car came to a halt. The driver jumped out and came to open the doors for us. Caroline held on to me one side and Scott the other. We hurried up a few steps then into a foyer that was heaving with people.

"Do you want a drink before the show?" he asked.? We both said, "No, we would be fine."

"Right then, shall we take our seats?"

What a sight greeted me. I don't know what I was expecting but it wasn't this. There seemed to be hundreds of rows of seats. How the hell would we find where we were sitting.

Scott didn't seem troubled by it, he showed the tickets to a woman at the door, and she directed him.

Caroline and I followed him down the centre aisle, right to the front row. How the hell had he got these I wondered.

We were the last three seats next to another aisle. Scott said, "I was lucky to get these. Someone had just cancelled when I rang so I snapped them up." I noticed Caroline give him a sly look.

I sat on the end then Caroline next to me then Scott. I didn't fancy sitting next to someone I didn't know.

Scott said these tickets are like gold dust, so we are very lucky. "Enjoy it all Ella, we could be up there next time."

He pointed up and behind us, there were people sitting right up near the ceiling and there was another layer between us and those in the roof. It looked to me that all the seats were full.

We sat talking for about ten minutes or so when the lights went down.

A man walked onto the stage from the side. Apparently, he is a well-known comedian. I have never heard or seen him before obviously. He was very funny though. We all laughed a lot. I thought that was it when the lights came back on. Men and women walked down the aisles and were selling ice creams, people were getting up and leaving. Caroline said, they will be back, they are going to the loo or to the bar to fetch drinks. Won't be long now till the main act comes on.

There was sound and movement in front of us. Huge curtains were right across the stage, but we could still hear movement behind them. Caroline said it was the orchestra warming up.

"Okay," I said.

Finally, the lights went down again, and the curtains opened. The orchestra began playing what appeared to be a selection of different tunes. Then they stopped playing and a man I couldn't see began singing. Beautiful, what a voice, Caroline leant over and whispered, "Isn't it wonderful?"

"It's beautiful," I said, "but who's singing it?" Just then I noticed movement from the side of the stage and a man walked on, singing. I looked at him and then looked again, it was Jacob, dressed in a fabulous evening suit. The audience was all on their feet screaming and shouting *"Jacob" "Jacob"*

I couldn't move, I just sat there staring at my man, the love of my life. This is his job, he's a singer? I looked at Caroline and Scott and they were both grinning like the cat that got the cream. I just sat with my mouth open. I couldn't believe it. He has the most amazing voice. The orchestra had joined in with the song now and then it came to an end. How on earth can he sing like that. Amazing.

He was looking down to where we were sitting. He blew me a kiss. I looked at Caroline again, "Is it really Jacob?" I asked.

"It is," she said, "Isn't he wonderful?"

"He is," I managed to say.

He went from one beautiful song to another, some really strong, powerful, serious stuff then some were faster, with a jolly tune. I have never heard any of them before but each and every one of them was fabulous and beautifully sung by this wonderful, amazing man. I was getting into it now the initial shock has worn off.

The crowd seem to love him. Caroline whispered, "Ella, he is a world-famous singer and actor. Didn't you have any idea?"

"I did not," I said. *It never entered my head. I glanced behind at all the women in the audience and they were all in love with him too. I could see it on their faces. "What does he want with me? He could have any of these women?. They adore him."*

"That's as maybe," she said, "but it's you he loves and wants to be with".

I looked back up at that beautiful face and he was watching me again.

He was talking to the audience now, thanking them all for coming to see the show, he hopes they are enjoying it so far. Once more they went mad. He looks adorable, so very handsome. Surely, he won't want me for much longer, just look at these beautiful girls and women all lusting after him.

He was still talking when he began to walk down the steps at the side of the stage. He was walking along the front of the seats and heading towards where we were sitting.

"I have some very special guests of my own here tonight," he said. "This fine gentleman here is my big brother, Scott, take a bow Scott, let all these lovely ladies get an eyeful of the other Ryan."

Scott stood up, turned to face the crowd and did a bow.   "This beautiful young woman here at his side is Caroline, his partner." He held his hand out to her and she took it as he pulled her to her feet. A bow from her too.

"Next is Ella, she is my partner and the love of my life". He held his hands out for me to hold. I was trembling from head to foot. He lifted me from my seat. "I am the luckiest man in the world, and I love this woman with all my heart. I must apologies, she is very shy. She didn't know till tonight who I am or what I do so she has had quite a shock."

He looked into my eyes, "do you still love me my darling even though I have kept you in the dark till now?".

"Yes, I do Jacob, with all my heart." He leaned into me and kissed me full on the mouth right in front of everyone. There was a huge round of applause, he kissed me once more then let me sit back down. "See you later, my darling," he said.

"This next song is a new one for me to sing. We only learnt it this afternoon, so I hope it goes well. I want to dedicate it to Ella, my love."

As he began to walk back to the steps the orchestra started playing. "This song is called *Making Memories*' and I sing it for you, Ella. Hope you like it."

He began singing.

I couldn't take all the words in, my head was buzzing.

Once the song ended the audience went wild. I guess they do like the new song. So every night when he said he was going to work this is what he does.

I can't get my head round it. This wonderful man that has been making love to me several times each day is actually a famous singer. Any wonder he can afford that fabulous house.

He will soon get fed up of me surely. Look at all these beautiful looking women, some young, some not so much. But all of them would take Jacob at the drop of a hat.

I looked at Caroline, "Why does he want me? He can't really love me, can he?"

"I think he does Ella, he just told about fifteen hundred people in here that you are the love of his life".

"He did, didn't he?"

"What do you think of his voice?" she asked.

"Oh, Caroline I think it's amazing. I could listen to him sing all night long."

"Well, my friend, sit back and enjoy the rest of the show. I am going to and so is Scott."

I did, I relaxed back in my seat and just lost myself in the wonderful voice and fabulous song choices, I didn't know any of them, but I enjoyed every single one.

He chatted to the audience in between songs, had a laugh with the members of the band and continually looked at me. He is one amazing man and how I love him.

All too soon the show came to a close. As the last song ended loads of women got up and made their way to the stage. Jacob went first to one side and held his hand out to touch their fingers, then the other side and did the same.

They didn't want him to leave the stage. "Okay then, one more. What do you want? They all started shouting, *'The Impossible Dream'*. All right then, give me a second." He walked over to the piano, the man who had been sitting there got up and Jacob sat down.

He began playing beautifully, then he started to sing. What a voice, what a man. He looks ten feet tall on the stage and he dominates the whole space.

Halfway through he stood up and the other man sat back at the piano. Jacobs voice just got stronger the more the song went on. Finally finishing with a note I didn't think it was possible to reach.

I stood up with everyone else and clapped until my hands hurt.

Some of the women spoke to me as they made their way back to their seats.

"You are a very lucky girl, look after him, he is a diamond. Throw him my way when you've had enough." All good-natured though.

Even Scott was getting some longing looks. Caroline hung on to his arm, laying claim to her man.

Scott said we were to stay in our seats until the audience had left then we would be going backstage to meet up with Jacob.

"Sorry for the deception Ella, Jacob was so worried that if you knew who he was it would frighten you off. Now though he feels confident enough in your relationship to let you know the real him. That is why he was so jumpy earlier. The reason he had to leave an hour sooner than normal was so that they could rehearse that song. I like it, do you?"

"Oh, Scott I do, it was all wonderful. I still can't get my head around it all though."

"You will get used to it eventually. I'm his brother, and it took me a while to figure it all out. At the end of the day though, he is just a man."

"Not just any man Scott, he is my man."

Caroline was hanging on to me. *She said she had been so worried when we arrived at the theatre. Jacob's name is written in lights all across the front and there were huge pictures of him either side of the doors, she had visions of me fainting if I had spotted them.*

I hadn't noticed a thing.

Once most of the audience had left a man came over to us and shook Scott's hand then said for us to follow him. He climbed up the steps to the stage and we followed. He took us through the gap in the curtains. The orchestra were still there, talking and laughing. They were packing their instruments away and putting it all tidy. We walked past them all, Scott spoke to some of them, he obviously knows them well.

Before long we were taken to a door that was closed. The man knocked and Jacob called, *come in*. The man, Scott said his name is Sam and he is

Jacob's assistant, opened the door and poked his head around it saying, your brother and guests are here Jacob. *"Great, send them in."*

The door opened wide and there he stood, still in his evening suit and looking gorgeous. He held out his arms and I walked into them.

"Jacob, I don't know what to say. You have the most amazing voice and I have loved watching you perform but why on earth do you want me when you can have your pick of any of those women out there?"

"Why, because you are the most amazing woman I have ever met. You have a heart of gold, you are gorgeous to look at, and you make my heart sing."

"I didn't let on who I was before because I thought it would frighten you off. Forgive me, please?"

"Of course I forgive you but if you had told me before I wouldn't have known who you were anyway. Honestly, I had never heard of you."

He pulled me to him and then kissed me with so much passion. "I love you, my darling and I want to be with you forever more."

He kissed me again and then let me go. "I had better have a quick shower and get out of these clothes so we can go and eat. Are you sure you can cope now you know the truth?"

"I'll give it a go," I said.

Scott and Caroline were stood watching this. "We are here as well, you know bro".

"Sorry, just needed to check that Ella is okay with all this."

"I know," said Scott, I don't think you need to worry about this young woman. She is in it for the long haul."

"Thank goodness for that," he said, "I really couldn't cope if she left me."

"I am going nowhere, my love. You're stuck with me I'm afraid."

One more kiss then he went off to shower and change. Shortly after he came back looking refreshed and gorgeous.

He picked me up and swung me round. Then he kissed me again. In that moment I knew without doubt we would be together forever.

Once we were ready to leave a couple of men who Scott said are Jacob's security led us out to the stage door. There were quite a few fans there waiting for Jacob. He got too signing autographs, having photos taken and also I noticed receiving a fare few kisses. We stood and watched as all this was happening.

I received a few unbelieving stares. *I guess these are the hard-core fans that don't want him to be happy with anyone but them. Tough I thought, he is mine.*

Finally, we were able to get into the car. A different car to the one we had arrived in. This one was big enough to take all four of us plus the driver and a security man. We sped off into the night and soon arrived outside a restaurant, somewhere, I have no idea where.

We all piled out of the car, Jacob had rung and booked for us all in the afternoon apparently.

We were met at the door by the manager, Emile. He obviously knew both Jacob and Scott. They introduced Caroline and I as their partners. He made a fuss of us all.

He walked us through the restaurant where other diners were eating their meals. They were all looking up at us as we walked past, then we could hear them whispering to one another. He took us to the back of the room and showed us to a table kept especially for us. It was out of sight of the other diners and quite discreet.

We took our seats and Jacob asked that we have drinks first. He must be really thirsty after all that singing. He ordered a pint of water to start then a couple of bottles of wine.

I didn't understand the menu as it was in French so I just said I would have the same as Jacob. No idea what it was.

We had a lovely couple of hours. Jacob was able to unwind after his evenings work.

I asked him, "Do you do this every night?"

"No, six out of seven, they give me Sunday off."

"Is it that full every night?"

"It is," he said. "I have been doing this show for eight weeks now. Just two more to go then I can have a bit of a break."

"Do the same people go every night?"

"Not really, a few of them do, the real hardcore fans, but mostly it's different ones each night. A lot are people that are in London for just a night or two. Some come to London especially to see the show. Some of them live here and just want a night out. Some are business people taking clients out for the night. A real mixture."

"Well, I see why they want to come and see you. You are amazing, I love you."

"I love you too, my darling. You'll keep me on the straight and narrow."

"I will, will I?"

"Yes, you will. We are real. Not this existence I have been living for years, made of magic and fairy dust. I just want a nice quiet life with the love of my life. That's you."

"How did you enjoy your first trip to the theatre anyway?"

"I loved it then when you began singing. I couldn't see who it was at first, and then you walked on stage. I couldn't get my breath. It was such a shock. I will forgive you. No more surprises though."

"Okay, no more surprises I promise."

"First thing you need to know though is that next Thursday night we are all going to an awards thing. That is what you need your gown for. It is very posh, but I will be by your side all night. Scott and Caroline will be there as well so nothing to worry about."

'Someone will come around in the afternoon to do your make-up and nails, and Caroline's then Henri will come and do both your hairs".

"Scott and I will be preened and trimmed and made to look decent and worthy to have you two gorgeous ladies on our arms."

'Now, does anyone want dessert?"

We all declined, *I just wanted to go home with this wonderful man so that I could love him.*

Jacob made a phone call from his mobile, then the car appeared like magic. The manager came to tell us the car was outside. He thanked Jacob for gracing his restaurant once again.

"That's fine," replied Jacob, "you always look after us well and the food is always good so why would we go anywhere else?"

He thanked Jacob once more then said that some fans must have heard where he was and were gathered on the pavement. "Do you want me to move them away before you leave?"

129

Jacob said not to worry, "We will speak with them before we get off home. They are a bit curios I expect, seeing me with my beautiful partner. Not something they see every day."

"If you would just ask my security man to keep an eye on things."

"Of course Jacob, there are still a few customers in the restaurant as well, I guess they are curios as well."

"Not to worry my dear friend. If you will let me settle the bill first then we will be out of your hair."

The manager came back with a card machine and Jacob did whatever you do with these things. It was soon sorted, and we began to get ourselves ready for the great escape.

I thanked all the staff as we walked through the other tables. It felt like everyone was watching us. Of course it was Jacob they were interested in mostly, but some did speak to me and wished us luck, which was nice.

A few people seemed to know Scott as well. They greeted him like old friends then eyed Caroline up. I guess this is a novelty for them as well. Two very handsome men out and about with two strange women.

As we reached the door the manager appeared again and shook hands with Jacob and Scott then said goodnight to Caroline and me.

"Blimey! I feel like the Queen," I said to Jacob as we walked outside.

"Just wait my love," he said, "this is nothing." There were loads of flashes as people took photographs then Jacob spoke.

"Thank you all for waiting so long for us. We needed food before we go home, and it had been a really nice evening for us. Have you tried the food here, it's amazing?"

Most said no, they hadn't tried the food but would give it a go. I said, "You must, my first time here but I loved the food, and the staff are great."

I felt Jacob squeeze my hand, "good girl," he whispered. "Getting brave at last."

He then spoke to the waiting fans again. "Most of you know my brother Scott, but maybe not his partner Caroline. You will be seeing a lot more of them from now on, also, have you all met my own lovely partner, Ella. She is usually shy but I'm sure if you treat her gently she will speak with you. This beautiful woman has made me very happy by agreeing to be by my side from now on.

She didn't even know who I was until tonight, so she has had quite a shock. Thankfully, she rather liked the show. Don't know what I would have done if she had said I am rubbish."

"I have never been in love before, but I rather like the feeling."

"Now if you want photographs or autographs I am happy to do that then we must get home. It's way past our bedtime."

They all laughed at him. "Might be bedtime, Jacob, but I reckon it will be a while before you sleep, having this lovely lady of yours keeping you awake," said one of the men.

I felt myself blush. Whatever do you mean I managed?

Jacob was squeezing my fingers and rubbing the back of my hand. "That's my girl, give as good as you get. They will love you for it."

Some took photos of Jacob on his own then they asked that we stand together so they could get pictures of the two of us. Why they would want a picture of me was beyond me. Never mind, give them what they want is what Jacob said.

Some were taking pictures of Scott and Caroline as well, I thought that was lovely. They were intrigued by all the attention.

Once we arrived home we all piled into the kitchen. "Who would like a nice cup of tea," asked Jacob. Everyone said, "Yes, please." He went to put the kettle on, but I beat him to it.

"Go sit yourself down," I said, you have been working your socks off tonight, let me spoil you now."

I quickly made the tea and assembled the tray. They had all moved into the lounge by the time it was ready. Jacob came back into the kitchen to carry the tray for me.

Before he did that though he came and put his arms around me. "Ella, my beautiful girl. I really do love you so very much."

"And I love you, Mr Singing Superstar. Will you sing for me, Jacob?"

"Always, my darling just not tonight, I think I have sung enough for one day."

"There are some CD's and DVD's of the films I have been in. They are all in the music/cinema room I think. I will show you tomorrow and teach you how they work. You can listen and watch them whenever you want then."

"Thank you, Jacob, I am sure I will love them, but I think having you sing next to me will be amazing."

"Okay, tomorrow, I promise I will sing for you."

"I will have to work again tomorrow night though then I have a night off on Sunday. We can do something together or just do nothing at all."

"As long as I am with you Jacob, I don't mind what we do. Can I go with you to the theatre again? I asked?"

"Of course you can, you can come every night if you want."

"Really, do you mean it?"

"I do my darling, I will love having you there, but you may have to stay backstage. Not too many seats available for the remaining shows."

"I don't mind, just as long as I can be with you and hear your amazing voice."

"What happens once the show is finished at the theatre?" I asked.

"Not sure yet, there's a film in the offing but that isn't set in stone yet. I thought we might take a holiday first. Somewhere warm where we can relax together. Let's take the tea things through to the lounge then we can see if those two want to come with us. Where do you fancy going my love?"

"Anywhere with you, Jacob."

"Come on, let's take these things through before they both die from thirst."

We took the tea tray into the lounge. It looked as if they had been kissing rather a lot when we opened the door. They sprang apart like kids in the playground caught doing something wrong.

We both smiled at them.

Jacob sat down then began pouring the tea.

"Right you two, I think that you are both as loved up as we are. Can't stand to be apart I guess."

Scott said, "You could say that, yes. Why?"

"Well, after this run of shows I was planning on taking a break anyway, now that I have Ella with me that is even more important. Can you both take some time away from work?"

They both said, "Yes, why?"

"Well, I want to take Ella to the house in France for a few weeks, we wondered if you would like to come with us."

They looked at each other and smiled. *"Yes, please," they both managed. Caroline said she would be able to take a couple of weeks if she can sort her diary out. Scott said the same for him. He has a couple of high-profile things to sort out but should be able to take a couple of weeks.*

"Right, let's have our drinks then get some sleep, then tomorrow we will have a look at our diaries and see if we can manage at least a couple of weeks in the sun," said Jacob.

"Sorry," I asked, "whose house will we be staying in?"

Jacob smiled, "My house, my love. Well once we are married it will be our house."

"Married, are you proposing to me again?"

"Yes, I am Ella. Why do we need to wait? We both want the same thing, don't we?"

"It would appear that we do. So I guess I agree, why wait? So yes, I will marry you, Mr Ryan."

Scott and Caroline were looking at each other. "Well, said Scott, it would appear that we all have the same thing in mind. Whilst you two were making tea I asked Caroline to marry me, and she said yes."

"We still have the girls to get on side, but I'm sure they will love her as much as I do."

Jacob said, "Well, congratulations to you both, you make a fabulous couple, and I am sure you will both be very happy."

"The same from me, I am so happy for you both," I said. "I could see this was going to happen right from the first day you laid eyes on each other. We are all so very lucky."

We drank our tea then carried the tray through to the kitchen. Scott said, "We are off to bed, goodnight".

"Goodnight Jacob and I said, "We will be up shortly."

"How many houses do you have Jacob?" I asked.

"Just the two, why? How many would you like?"

I laughed at him. "You do realise I don't have a passport, don't you?"

"If we get on to it tomorrow they should be able to rush it through. You will love it in France. The house is on the edge of a lovely old village and the people there are great. They know who I am, but they don't make a fuss. Just treat me like another villager. It's not in the tourist areas, I like that, just being one of them."

The people around here are generally pretty good on the whole, well you've seen some of them, but It's not easy to go shopping in town. Everyone watching me feels like I'm under a microscope."

"Don't worry about it though my love. We will survive it all. Just this award ceremony on Thursday to get through. Are you looking forward to it Ella?"

"To be honest Jacob, I have no idea what will happen, what is expected of me, any of it. I was worried about tonight though, but that worked out fine so I am sure Thursday will be okay."

"You will be on display, everyone will want to know who you are and what you are doing with me. The best thing is just keep your head down and keep walking. Leave me to answer any questions."

"I can do that I said. Now, will you shut up, come here and make love to me, please?

"I thought you would never ask," he said.

"We made love, twice, Jacob knows exactly what to do to make me happy and contented." It would appear that I make him feel the same. Feeling him inside me, moving together is the most wonderful feeling. He really is my heart and my soul, my everything.

We eventually slept really well. We woke late but still managed to make love again before we got up.

We showered and dressed then went down to breakfast. Scott and Caroline were already up. They were discussing what they would do the next day when they picked the girls up. Scott said, "It would be good to go somewhere quiet so they can tell them that their dad and Caroline are going to get married."

It would seem that they didn't want to wait either.

Jacob began asking Scott about getting a passport for me quickly and he was able to reassure us that it could be done.

Jacob was wondering if we could get married in France, but I said, "Wouldn't it be easier to do it here and then go to France for our honeymoon."

"Okay, that works for me. Once this show is finished, we should set about organising it. I don't want to wait any longer than I have to he said. I want to be your husband and have you my wife."

"Oh, Jacob, I want that too."

"I want to buy you an engagement ring so that everyone will know that you belong to me. It won't be easy, if anyone sees us shopping in jewellery stores they will all know what we are doing."

"I can sort that problem out for us. Scott, where did you put the stuff from the farmhouse?"

"In the safe, why do you ask?"

"You'll see," I said. "Can you get it for me, please?"

"Certainly, hang on here a minute."

He went off to get the jewellery from his safe. He was soon back and put the bag on the island top in front of me.

I opened the bag and took the boxes out first then a smaller bag that contained the rings.

"There you are, take your pick. Jacob was looking at the rings with interest. Wherever did you get these from?"

"Well, we found them all hidden in the farmhouse along with loads of money. Why bother buying a new ring when we have all these here."

"Don't you want a new ring, Ella?"

"No," I said. "These are beautiful, why spend money on a new one when we have these to choose from?"

"I think they must have belonged to Will's grandmother if not his great-grandmother. Now they belong to me. They are obviously very old."

"They are, definitely antique I would say," said Jacob. "Is there one you like in particular?"

"I don't know, I have never tried them on, except that one. It was my wedding ring. Don't want that anywhere near my finger ever again.

Jacob was picking them up and looking at them. "These are very beautiful, Ella, are you certain you don't want a new ring?"

"No, I will be very happy to wear any one of these rings. No one else need know where it came from," I said.

"See, I'm a thrifty woman, I will save you a small fortune."

We all laughed but Jacob could see the sense in what I was saying. "Which one do you like Jacob, I asked?'

He was looking through them, picking each one up and studying the stones and the settings.

Eventually he said, "This one I think. A single diamond in a beautiful setting. Simple yet stunning.'

"It is my favourite too," I said.

"Okay, then if you are sure you are happy with it".

"I am," I said.

"Jacob took the ring, checked it once more then got down on one knee in front of me. Ella, my beautiful, amazing girl. Will you marry me, please?"

"I will," I said, just as soon as we can possibly arrange it."

He slipped the ring on my finger and I instantly knew it was the right one. It fits perfectly and feels just right.

Jacob threw his arms around me and kissed me with such passion. "My fiancée" he said. "That sounds amazing. Never take it off, my love."

"I won't, darling."

"Now, Scott, please choose one of these to give to Caroline with all my love and thanks for everything."

"Ella, that is very generous of you, but I can't do that."

"Why can't you? Do they not belong to me?"

"Yes, of course they belong to you but that would be too much."

"Stop talking, I said and start choosing". "The sooner you decide which one then the sooner you two will be engaged as well."

Scott looked at Jacob who just lifted his shoulders then pointed to the rings.

"I should do as she says if I were you, bro. She doesn't take kindly to people that disagree with her."

Scott looked at Caroline. "What do you think my darling? Will one of these beauties suit you?"

"Most definitely, but are you really sure Ella? These rings will be worth a small fortune."

"Caroline, if you like any one of these rings then I will be delighted for you to have one. You have been the best of friends to me. I wouldn't be here now if it wasn't for you."

"Please, just choose the one that you like the best. Try them on, see how they feel.

"Well, if you are sure and Scott are you really sure about it all?."

"My darling, Caroline, I love you and want you to be my wife. For you to wear one of these rings signifying our love for each other I will be honoured."

"Right then you two, just get on and choose one please. My belly thinks my throats been cut".

"Jacob, you are always thinking of food."

"Not always," he said as he looked at me with longing.

"Just wait a while please fiancée," I said. I want to join in the celebration with these two first.

Scott and Caroline were looking through the remaining rings, trying them on then looking at them   longingly.

"Can't you decide Caroline," I asked?

"I think I like this one the best, it's a sapphire and two diamonds. I think it suits my hand don't you?"

I looked at the ring nestling on her finger. She was right, it did suit her hand.

"I like that one too," said Scott, "it's really lovely.
Are you absolutely certain Ella? I will pay you for it".

"Don't insult me Scott, it is my gift to you both, Now get down on one knee and do the business."

He did, his proposal was as lovely as Jacobs had been. I had tears rolling down my cheeks, I was so happy for them both. Scott put the remaining rings and the boxes back in the safe. Then we all sat around the kitchen island drinking tea and eating toast. Caroline and I kept looking at our rings and smiling. We were both so happy. For ourselves and for each other. We are two very lucky girls, finding love in the most unusual of times and places.

Mrs H arrived as we were finishing our breakfasts. We all chorused 'Hello Mrs H'.

"Blimey! "You lot are very cheery this morning."

"We are," I said. "These wonderful menfolk of ours surprised us both with these this morning." We both flashed our left hands in front of her.

"My   goodness,   you   are   both   engaged,   how   wonderful. Congratulations, I couldn't be more happy for you. You make lovely couples. Have you set wedding dates yet?"

"No," said Jacob, "not yet but it won't be long. You will be the first to know".

"I should think so too."

"Have you seen the morning papers by the way?"

"No, why? What's happened?"

"You my lad and your fiancée, that's what's happened". "What do you mean?" asked Jacob.

She reached into her bag and pulled out several newspapers putting them on the island. Jacob picked up one and Scott another.

I could feel my heart beating faster and faster.

"Blimey! what's going on?" I asked.

Jacob had opened the paper and found what he was looking for.

Staring back at me was a picture of Jacob and I from the night before. Jacob looking as handsome as ever and me looking lovingly up into his face.

Written across the top of the page were the words, *'Actor and singer Jacob Ryan out on the town with a mystery woman'. Anyone know who the lovely lady is? We will pay good money for this information.*

"Shit," I said, "why can't they leave you alone?"

"Me," he said, "I am used to all this crap but now they are going after you."

"There's more in this paper Jacob" said Scott, "and I reckon the rest will all be the same."

"Well," I said, "there's not a lot we can do about it now. It's out there. Why don't we just come clean, tell them the truth."

"We could I suppose, after all we are not doing anything wrong. It would work well if the story of our engagement were to come out on Thursday, the same day as the awards. Get it all over with in one day, well two days I suppose. Thursday and Friday. There is bound to be a lot of press coverage of the awards."

"Let's think it all through first before we go all out and tell them everything. It won't hurt to keep them hanging for a few days more. We won't be able to go out and about though like we have been doing. I bet there are press out the front now."

"Did you see anyone when you came in Mrs H?"

"Yes, three guy's hanging around the gates. I told them to bugger off. They were asking if Jacob's bird was staying here? I told them I didn't know what they were on about. I said he's foot loose and fancy-free as far as I know."

"Always got my side haven't you, Mrs H?"

"I sure have, lad, she said." "Now you are all official though it might be as well to come clean."

"We will just need a couple of days to ourselves first, said Jacob".

"Anyway, can I have a look at these rings, please?" she asked.?

We both held out our hands.

"My oh my, they are beautiful. Antique by the looks of things. You are two very lucky ladies bagging these two adorable men. Looks like they intend to spoil you both rotten."

"At least that's one person who thinks the men have bought our rings. Will I still be able to come with you to the theatre tonight?"

"I don't see why not. Don't get dressed up though. Jeans and a jumper perhaps. When the car comes to pick me up get in the back and lie down so they can't see you. You can stay backstage during the show then we can come straight back here afterwards."

"I blame myself for this newspaper frenzy. If I had just kept quiet last night then they wouldn't have been any the wiser. I am just so happy to be with you, my darling I want to shout it from the rooftops but also keep you out of the limelight, I know how it scares you."

"I am getting better at it Jacob, I will get there eventually. Just stop worrying about it. We are together and happy to be so and intend staying that way so what does it matter if they know now or next week."

"You are very pragmatic all of a sudden, my love."

"I know, if I don't start and get brave with these things then I will be a coward all my life. I mean, last night you introduced me to the world in front of all those people and I lived."

"You did, didn't you".

Let's try and forget those morons for now. I said I would show you how the CD and DVD players work, didn't I?"

"You did, I can't wait to hear you sing again and I have only seen one film in my life, that was 'Love Actually' that we watched the other night. What sort of films are you in Jacob?"

"Well, nothing like '*Love Actually*'. I should warn you, there are a few sex scenes in them. It might look like we are really having sex, but we are not I can promise you. There's usually about twenty other people in the room when it happens. You won't get upset will you?"

"Not sure, I might do. I am the only woman you are allowed to make love to."

"I promise you, my darling girl, you are the only one for me from now on. There is nothing to compare with what we have."

We went into the music/cinema room. There is a massive screen on the wall and comfy seats all facing one way.

"Why is the room set out like this I asked?"

"Well, we can all come in here to watch a movie or music video, so it's set out like a cinema. I have a big cinema room planned for the new house. That is something that we can change though if you're not happy with it."

"No, don't change it, we could have some lovely nights watching films, particularly ones with a certain handsome man that I am quite fond of."

"Fond, is that all you feel for me?'

"You know I am joking, I love you so much and all after just a few days. How will I feel about you when we have been married for forty years?'

"Forty years sounds a bit scary, but I'm sure if anyone can do it we can. I love you Ella, don't ever leave me."

"I won't you daft thing."

"Daft am I? You will need to be punished for that, my darling".

"Really, and how will you punish me?"

'Not sure yet, leave it with me."

"Jacob showed me how to operate the CD player. I asked him to put one of his albums on. He chose the very first one he had done. We sat down on one of the sofa's, me curled into him and his voice filled the room. So many beautiful songs, one after another.

Scott put his head round the door. "We are off out for a while," he said. "Will you be okay when Jacob goes to work, Ella?"

"I should say so, I am going with him."

Scott looked a bit surprised, "are you sure that's wise, bro, after this morning's headlines?"

"It will be fine, said Jacob. Ella is going to lie down in the car till we get going then once we reach the theatre we can drive into the back entrance if need be."

"If anyone spots her then we will just have to play it by ear. I would prefer it if we could keep in on the low-down till Thursday but if we can't then we will cope."

Scott said, "So long as you are aware of what is going on. Don't get into any arguments with any of them, you know how they love all that stuff".

"Don't worry Scott, we have this. I won't let anyone spoil it for us".

"Okay, see you later then."

"Right, enjoy your trip out."

"We will, bye."

"Have a good day," we both said.

Jacob had stopped the music when Scott had come in but now he pressed play once more and we spent a lovely hour listening to the album.

Once it had finished he asked me, did I want any more? "Not at the moment," I said, What I really want is to go upstairs and make wonderful love with you."

He was on his feet in a second, "I can manage that," he said. He held out his hands to me, I took them, and he pulled me to my feet. He enveloped me in a wonderful embrace then kissed me with so much passion it took my breath away.

Mrs H knocked on the door, "I am off now Jacob, do you need me back later to make some food for you?"

No Mrs H, you take the rest of the day off and enjoy yourself for a change".

!I can sort the food out I said, I can cook you know?"

She laughed, "I'm sure you can chuck. Jacob will need to move away from your side whilst you do it though. He doesn't look as if he can bear to be more than six inches away from you."

"That is true, Mrs H, but we can always cook together, can't we?

She laughed, "you cook. Never seen that happen before".

"You might be surprised," he said.

"I would to be sure. You will have to let me know how that goes, Ella."

"I will, I want to see this for myself as well."

"No faith in us men," he said. We all laughed then she left for the day.

Jacob locked up and we went upstairs. Spending the next two hours making love and talking, it was a lovely time, did us both good. Just the two of us being comfortable and honest with each other.

He told me all about the problems he had suffered with Cleo and how he came to be living here with Scott then I filled him in on a bit more of my story. He was shocked by some of the things I told him.

"Ella, I promise I will never do anything to hurt or harm you".

"I know you won't Jacob. Can we make love again, please?" I asked.

"I should think that might just about be possible."

"We did, each time we came together in love was amazing. We both have so much love to give."

Once we had finished we decided to shower, Jacob said, "Ella, I know I haven't mentioned it for a few days, but have you thought any more about being pregnant? I didn't want to put you under any pressure, but I will be so excited if you are."

"Yes, I have thought about it and I too will be over the moon if I am. I know the timing could be better, but we can cope with anything, can't we?''

"We certainly can," he said. "I know, what about if I ring Scott and ask him to pick up a pregnancy test".

"Would he do that for you I asked?"

"Of course, he will. Hopefully, no one will be watching him. Can you imagine what would happen if I went into Boots or even Tesco's to pick one up. Talk about 'Breaking News'. They would have us expecting triplets before the day was done."

I laughed at him, he can be so funny. Is it any wonder I love him so much?

"Well, if you think he won't mind, and you can't possibly wait any longer then go for it."

He reached for his phone and rang Scott, it was Caroline that answered, she said Scott was driving. Can I ask you to do something for me Caroline?"

"Yes of course, what is it?"

"Will you pick a pregnancy test up for me please?"

A little pause then she said "yes, of course I will, need to get one for myself anyway".

"Really" he said. "That's amazing. I am pleased for you both. You will make great parents. When I heard him say that my mouth dropped open. "Really?" I asked.

Jacob finished his call then turned to me. "It would appear that the Ryan bothers really do everything together."

"How fabulous for them, I do hope she is," I said. And I also hope that I am. I have wanted a family of my own for such a long time but there was no way I could bring a child into that toxic place. Now giving you a child will be wonderful. Oh God, Jacob I am so excited."

"So am I, my darling girl? We will be a really happy family I just know we will. God, I feel so excited I could burst."

"Don't do that Jacob, I need you with me, always."

We went into the kitchen and I set about sorting out what we would eat. I was so excited I didn't think I would be able to eat anything.

I rummaged through the fridge and found what I was looking for. "Right my love, how do you fancy lasagne?"

"That would be lovely," he said. There must be some frozen ones in the freezer."

"No, I will make one myself. For all you know, I might be a dreadful cook."

"You might be I suppose but do you know what, I don't care. Feed me cat food and I will be happy."

"Well, that's not going to happen my love. Sit down and be prepared to be amazed."

He did, he fetched a bottle of white wine and opened it pouring a generous glass for me.

"Are you not joining me? I asked?"

"I will have just a small glass with my meal. Don't forget I have to go and entertain the masses tonight. Alcohol doesn't do the old vocal chords much good. Now after I finish, well that might be different. You should enjoy that glass whilst you can. If you are pregnant then no drinking until after the birth. If you are pregnant though I will cut out the alcohol with you. We don't actually need it do we?"

"I suppose not. I had never tried it till meeting you and Scott, so I guess if I got to be twenty-five years old without it then another few months won't hurt. Do you think It's okay to drink this one?"

"I am sure it will be fine," he said. We will know one way or another by tonight so there is time then to do all the right things."

All the while we were talking I was preparing everything for the lasagne. This was the one 'foreign' thing that Will would eat so I have made it many times before. I had found an old recipe book that must have belonged to Dot and this was in there.

Jacob was watching everything I did with interest. "You really are clever, aren't you?" he said.

"Jacob, it's a lasagne, not a five-course Sunday lunch."

"I still think you are brilliant," he said.

"Tell me that after you taste it," I said.

It was soon assembled and ready to go in the oven. I had made a big one so if Scott and Caroline were hungry when then got back they could warm some up. Whilst it was in the oven we went back upstairs and made love again.

That wonderful sensation when we both lose ourselves, I love it, can't happen often enough for me. My body feels so alive, tingling all over.

A quick shower then dressed and ready for our exit from the house. We went back down to the kitchen and I served up our meal.

"If I do say so myself the lasagne had turned out well. I served it with a green salad, and I sipped at my wine, still sitting on the worktop where I had left it earlier.

I watched Jacob as he took his first bite from his meal. "Ella, this is lovely, you really are clever, a revelation to me." I have never had a girlfriend that could cook. Not that I have had that many girlfriends. Girls and women tend to want to be with me to further their own careers, not just to be with me. It has been quite hurtful over the years".

"But now I have you and I feel really loved for me, not for anything else. We are going to have a wonderful life together my darling and if you continue to cook meals like this for me then I won't even need to go out to eat."

I tapped his arm playfully, "Jacob, I love you for you not for anything you have or can give me. Plus I will have plenty of money of my own soon once the sale of the farm has gone through and all the insurances have been sorted. Then there is all the money we found hidden around the place. I have no idea what we will do with that. I have never been allowed to have any money of my own before. I had never even been in a shop to buy a pair of slippers or anything really. I was scared stiff when I went shopping with Caroline."

Jacob was looking at his bracelet, turning the links around in his fingers. "So when you bought this for me it was a bit of a trauma for you."

"A bit yes, but I really wanted to buy it for you, so I manned up as Caroline says, went in and did the business."

"This bracelet means more to me than anything else I have, because it has come from you and I can feel all the love from you to me."

"I really wanted to buy you an engagement ring, I can see the logic in this one, he held my hand and looked at the beautiful diamond ring I was wearing. Really Jacob I am more than happy with this ring. After all it is not the ring that counts but the man that put it there."

"Oh, Ella, I love you so much."

"And I love you, my darling".

"Now come on, let's get moving. I hear there a fabulous singer on at the theatre tonight and I really want to hear and see him".

Jacob kissed me then, holding me so tight in his arms. "Okay, he said, let's get moving. The sooner we get there the sooner we get back then it's test time."

"Jacob will you be really disappointed if I'm not pregnant?"

"I guess I will but then we can spend more time trying, that could be fun".

"I hadn't thought of that" I said.

The car had arrived and pulled through the gates, then closed behind it. Jacob opened the front door, his security man shielding me from prying eyes. While Jacob was locking the door I slipped into the rear of the car and lay down. There was plenty of room in the foot well, so I got down on the floor.

Jacob was soon in the car next to me and dropped a car blanket over my head. As soon as we were on the road he pulled the blanket off me and I sat on the seat next to him. He reached over and fastened the seat belt for me. He held my hand and kept kissing the back of it.

"You might have to get back down there once we arrive. There is a rear entrance where they unload all the equipment and stuff. We don't usually go in that way but if security think there are too many people around then that will be the best option."

The security man sitting in the front seat spoke to Jacob. "Apparently there is a mad frenzy by the stage door, it will be best all round I think if we go the back way".

Jacob said, "Okay, whatever you think. Just as long as Ella is kept safe. If needs be then I will go and speak to them through the second-floor window. Don't suppose they will be happy but it's the best they will get tonight."

"I have caused you so much bother Jacob, would it be easier to just get rid of me."

"No chance," he said. "Don't even think about it."

I did feel guilty though. His life must have been so much easier before.

I bet all his female fans are not happy. I can understand that. Some of them have been following him for many years then I walk through the door and 'bingo' as Caroline would say.

I could feel my ring on my left hand. It feels so good knowing that Jacob put it there making it obvious that no one else need bother looking. I am spoken for. I smiled at the thought.

"What is so funny? he asked.?"

"Nothing really, I was just thinking how this ring will be a warning to anyone hoping to step in."

"It will be he said, "I can't wait to put a wedding ring on your finger and also you put one on mine. There will be no doubt then. Both of us spoken for".

The security man spoke to Jacob, "Sorry mate, we are almost there. The crowd has got even bigger now. It will have to be the back entrance."

"No worries," he said, "Ella get back down my love. I will lie down as well. Hopefully, they will think the car is empty."

"The car drove into the rear space at speed and then came to a sudden halt. "Before we could sit up the big gates had been shut keeping prying eyes away."

"Okay my love," he said, "we are here and safe I think."

The car door was opened, and the security man held out his hand for me, it made it a bit easier to exit the vehicle. Jacob was up and out of the car in seconds. He came round to my side and put a protective arm around me, pulling me in close to him. He kissed me before we were escorted through the corridors till we reached Jacobs dressing room.

The room was empty apart from rails of clothes and a dressing table covered in pots of creams and things. Not sure who uses those. There were rather a lot of flowers in vases and some arrangements. They were all beautiful.

"Who's are the flowers I asked?"

"Mine of course," he said. "Some of the fans send them to me to wish me luck. Kind of them isn't it?"

"You are one very lucky man, all those women lusting after you".

He sat down in front of the dressing table. "Come here and sit on my knee". I did, he put his arms around me then pulled me in for a long, sexy kiss.

"I like that I said, more please". Before he could kiss me again though someone knocked on the door. Jacob called out, 'come in'.

A man came in and looked over to where we sat. "Evening," he said, "so this is the young lady that is causing all the interest. You are one very lucky bastard he said to Jacob. Do you have any sisters at home he asked me?"

"I laughed, sorry no. Just me and I'm spoken for."

"Ella, meet my manager Eddie, this is Ella, the love of my life. Our lives are going to change very quickly mate. I won't be hanging around for years before making an honest woman of her. We will be getting married very soon."

Eddie held out his hand and shook mine. "Very pleased to meet you, Ella. My phone and office has been under siege since yesterday. You might have given me the heads-up pal before announcing to the world that you are in love."

"Sorry about that Eddie, I obviously hadn't thought it through before going for it. You know what I'm like."

"The thing is since we met our lives have been running at a hundred miles an hour. I just wanted the whole world to know how happy we are."

"I get it, Jacob, I really do, she is adorable, and I hope you will have many happy years together. You just need to think about your next move. You don't want to lose all this do you?"

"I'm not that fussed if I'm honest. We just want to be together, happy in our little bubble." Of course, I love my job and all that it brings but I love Ella more."

"I really think that once they get used to us being together it will all blow over".

"You're probably right but these things need handling properly." Try to keep out of the public eye for the next few days. I know you have to come here but other than that keep a lid on it."

"I suspect you are taking Ella with you on Thursday".

"Too true I am. We will come out to the world then and put them out of their misery."

"No talking you out of this is there he asked".

"No chance Eddie, we are both very committed to each other and we can't see why we should have to live under these conditions. If the fans don't like it then that will be the end of my career, if that happens then so be it. I am sure though that the majority of fans will be happy for us. Most of the ones last night were okay with it so we will just have to wait and see. Ella is my top priority though. So long as she is safe and happy we can work round the rest of it."

"Okay mate, I hope you are right. I am sure you are. Will just take a bit of getting used to that's all. Now young lady, where will you be sitting during the show?"

"I don't know, I said, I just want to be able to see and hear Jacob. I didn't know who he was or what he did for a living until last night. I have led a very sheltered life up until now."

"When Jacob walked on stage last night singing his heart out I was flabbergasted. I really couldn't get my breath. He is amazing though".

"I fell in love with him before knowing any of this side of his life. If he ends up sweeping the streets I will still love him".

"As for the lavish lifestyle he leads, well if it all ends tomorrow then so be it but I am a wealthy woman in my own right. He will have to be a kept man for a change".

"Well, that told me, didn't it?" "I can see that you are both genuine and love each other. Good luck to you both."

"Now Jacob are you going on stage looking like that or will you manage to change?"

"If you bugger off Eddie, I will change. Ella can sit at the side of the stage tonight. She can keep an eye on me from there."

"Okay Jacob, I am off, good luck for tonight. The natives seem in a hurry to see you so be good".

"It will all be fine, you will see."

With that Eddie left and Jacob resumed kissing me. "How long have you got I asked?" He looked at his watch.

"Not long, the first act is just closing so I had better get dressed."

"He got up from his seat and I sat down in it to watch him transform into the superstar that he is."

He had a clean white shirt ready for him, his evening suit was immaculate. He then had to put his bow tie on. I have never seen one before, but he made short work of tying it in place. Black socks and shiny black shoes completed his outfit.

"Right," I said, "let me look at you". I stepped back and took a long hard look at this gorgeous man. "Fabulous," I said, "you look good enough to eat."

"I may hold you to that later on," he said.

"Right then, hair okay, clothes okay, let's go," He kissed me once more with passion. "I love you, Ella," he said

"And I love you, Jacob. Now go and entertain those adoring ladies."

He held my hand as we walked from the dressing room, along corridors then up some stairs. We were finally there. "Here he said, Sit yourself there then I can keep an eye on you."

I laughed at him. "I will be keeping an eye on you."

"Good," he said.

With that he stood just to the side of the stage, the curtains hiding him from view.

The orchestra were playing their intro, someone handed Jacob a microphone. The band stopped playing and Jacob began to sing.

I was mesmerised.

He sang without music for a while then slowly walked onto the stage. A huge spotlight was on him as he made his way to the centre of the stage. His voice just got stronger and stronger. I could feel the strength of it beating in my chest. So beautiful. I could cry just listening to him.

Finally, the band joined in and they finished the song together. He then did as he had done the night before and just went from one lovely song to the next. He is just amazing, every chance he got to look to the side of the stage he did. He would wink or blow a kiss. I could just go and grab him off the stage, strip him naked and make love to him right there. Perhaps not the best idea though.

He then began talking to the audience as he had done the previous night. Some shouted asking him to sing certain songs. Others were just in raptures watching and listening to him. Then someone called out, "Jacob where is Ella tonight?"

He smiled at whoever it was and then said, "She is right here in my heart, where she belongs" There were lots of shouts and whistles. They seemed happy that Jacob had a girl.

The show continued much the same as the previous night until finally, it was time for his last song.

He said, "A change for tonight. Last night I sang a song especially for Ella, it was the first time I had sung it. The audience seemed to like it and Ella definitely liked it. I would like to finish with it tonight if I may."

Again lots of shouts and whistles.

The music began and he started singing, such beautiful words, I had a lump in my throat as it was obvious to everyone that he was singing it to me.

The crowd loved it and shouted for more as he finished singing.

He went to both sides of the stage touching the hands of those lucky enough to get close then walked off, straight into my arms and kissed me.

The audience was going mad. "One more he said then I am all yours".

He walked back on stage and sang *'The Impossible Dream'*, the closing song from last night. Finally, he left the stage, the curtains closed and he went to speak with the orchestra guys then came over to me.

He gathered me up in his arms and kissed me right there in front of the whole orchestra.

"Come on, he said, let me get out of these clothes. I am wet with sweat. It was warm out there tonight."

"Who washes your clothes?" I asked?.

"The people from the wardrobe department look after it all. The suits go for cleaning and the shirts get washed along with other stuff".

"I don't have to wear the same thing every night," he said. "I think there are five or six suits and must be at least ten shirts ready for me. The ladies look after me well. I have performed in this theatre many times over the years and so I know a lot of the staff. Some of them have been here since my career began."

"You're a good man Jacob, everyone seems to be in love with you."

"Well, I am in love with just one woman, you."

"Nearly time for the test," he said.

I hadn't given it a thought, I was too wrapped up in watching and listening to him singing. Now, thinking about it my tummy gave a little flutter of excitement.

Getting out of the theatre would be more difficult than getting in had been. The street outside the stage door was rammed.

Jacob said, "I will have to go and speak to them, they will just stay there all night if I don't."

"You go and wait in the car my darling, it is still in the space round the back. I will get someone to walk around with you. I will go and speak with the crowd, at least get rid of some of them, then I will come back this way and join you for the journey home".

"Are you sure you will be okay?" I asked him.

"Sure," he said, "we get this almost every night. Security will be with me, don't worry."

He was right, he had called a young stagehand over and asked him to escort me to the car then he had gone out of the stage door to speak with as many people as he could.

He made a swift job of it as before long he appeared at my side, he kissed me then we both got down in the back of the car. He pulled the blanket over our heads and there we stayed until a voice from the front said, "okay Jacob, all good, we are on our way".

We both sat up and looked at each other. He reached over and kissed me. I felt happy and safe in this man's arms. He held me tightly as we winged our way back to Scott's house.

"I wonder if they have done their test,"yet I asked.

"I reckon if they have we will know by the look on their faces," he replied.

We were soon having to get back down in the back of the car as we approached the house. The gates swung open, and the car entered. The gates closed behind us and we were able to get out and walk into the house.

Scott came into the kitchen to see how the show had gone. He shook Jacob by the hand and said "thank goodness you are back so soon. We are beside ourselves waiting to do the test. Caroline wants to do it with Ella, it must be a girl thing" he said.

"We called round to see the girls for half an hour before picking them up tomorrow," said Scott.

"How were they?"Jacob asked.

"Oh, they were fine, happy to see daddy with a girlfriend."

"Flora was her usual happy self, she could curdle milk with the look she had on her face when she saw me. I don't know why, it was her choice to leave and live with someone else".

"Anyway, we have all moved on. Come on, let's get these tests done." I will explode soon if I don't find out".

Caroline came in just then and was carrying the two boxes containing the tests. "I think we should go to our respective rooms and do the tests then meet up on the landing" said Caroline.

"Okay," I said, "are you taking Scott with you?"

"Of course, Jacob can be with you then once we know we can party, one way or the other".

"You are so funny Caroline," I said. "Come on, let's go and find out how these things work?"

Caroline said, "I can tell you if you want".

"It's okay," I said, "we will figure it out."

We all piled up the stairs and went to our respective rooms.

"Jacob asked me how I was feeling?

"Nervous," I said. Do you know what I have to do?"

"Not really, give it here and I will have a quick read".

He took the instructions out of the box and read. "Well, it all looks easy enough," he said. "Just pee on that piece then leave it for a few minutes,"

"Come into the bathroom with me, Jacob?"

"Well I have been asked to do a good many things in my life, but this is a first."

He came with me into the bathroom. I did as requested then set the test down on the side of the bath. We both looked at it, nothing happened.

"I know I said, let's go into the bedroom, you can kiss me several times then we can come back."

"Okay, he said, so we went through to the bedroom and stood kissing, enjoying being together again."

"Right," he said, "are we ready"

"No," I said. "What if I'm not pregnant?"

"Well, if you're not, then we had better put in a better effort."

"You fetch it, Jacob, I don't want to look at it."

"If you are sure."

"I am," I said.

He went back into the bathroom and came out a few seconds later, beaming from ear to ear.

"You are pregnant, Ella. I am so happy, we are going to be parents."

"Are you sure?" I asked.

"I am, just look what it says." He passed the test over to me and I looked at it? There it was, plain as day, pregnant.

"I began to shake, is it real, Jacob?"

"It is," he said. "I'm going to be a dad and you a mum, I couldn't be happier." He picked me up and swung me around.

"Let's go and see how Scott and Caroline have got on." He picked the test up and took it with him. Scott and Caroline had just come out of their room, they were both grinning from ear to ear.?"I guess we both have the result we were hoping for" Jacob said. "Looking at you two I take it you are both happy."

"We are, Jacob. I know like you that it hasn't been very long but this all just feels so right," said Scott.

"Two pregnant women in the house, blimey! However, will we cope? replied Jacob.

"What do we do now? I asked.

Scott said, "Well, I would like to go and get drunk to celebrate, but I promised Caroline that I would give up the booze along with her."

Jacob laughed: "That is what I told Ella. I know, let's go and have a cup of tea instead."

So that is what we did, Jacob made the tea and Scott set the tray, "come on ladies, let's go through to the lounge."

We followed him and watched as the two of them poured out mugs of tea, both of them with big grins on their faces.

"How do you feel?" I asked Caroline.

"Fine," was her reply.

"I feel different somehow," I said, "I have thought for a few days that I was pregnant, you know just tingling breasts and wanting Jacob to make love to me constantly. I don't suppose that is a sign but ever since I met him all I want to do is take him to bed."

"I think that is part of falling in love, Ella, not being pregnant."

"I know you are right but all this, I know it is really fast, but I couldn't be happier."

"I know how you feel," she said, "I feel exactly the same. You do realise that we will be sisters-in-law once we get married?"

"I never thought of that, but you are right. When we first met I wanted you to be my friend forever and now you will be."

"You will move down here, won't you? I asked.

"Of course, I will," she said. "I will have to go back up to Marchpool to put my house on the market and then work my notice, but I will be up and down anyway. Once everything is sorted I will be down here permanently. There is nothing really keeping me in Marchpool. "Will you and Jacob get married do you think?

"Definitely, it is all he has talked about for days. "Will you and Scott get married?"

"Yes we will, Scott has been talking about nothing else but wedding bells and babies for days." "We will be able to help each other through it all, won't we?"

"We certainly will" I said.

"I asked Caroline if she was hungry?"

"Not at all."

"We found a lasagne in the fridge that Mrs H must have made before she left. It was to die for".

"It wasn't Mrs H." I said "I made it for our dinner before we went to the theatre."

"Really Ella, it was very nice indeed. In fact, Scott had two pieces."

"I laughed, what is so funny asked Jacob?

"Scott is eating for two I said. He rather liked my lasagne."

"Did you make that Ella? It was very nice indeed?"asked Scott.

"I did, I'm not completely useless, you know."

We all sat around talking and drinking tea, then Jacob said, "Well, guys, I am going to have to leave you, I am dead on my feet. Are you coming up, Ella?"

"Yes, I called to his retreating back? Just going to put these pots in the dishwasher first."

By the time I got upstairs Jacob was in bed, he looked adorable. He hasn't had much sleep at all since we met, and his job must be very draining. I went into the bathroom to clean my teeth and pop a nightie on. I crept back into the room and slid into bed next to my wonderful husband to be.

We both slept well and woke refreshed. Today is Sunday I thought, no work for my man. We can have a lie in as well. Never been done before by me. I cuddled up to Jacob and felt him move. His eyes opened and he beamed when he saw me.

"Morning, my very pregnant and soon to be wife – I love you."

"Well thank you sir I said, I love you too."

We lay there wrapped in each other's arms, feeling very happy and contented.

Jacob lifted his head and rested on his elbow, "do you think it is okay to carry on having sex like we have been whilst our baby is growing in there.?"

"Well, I don't know for certain, but I bet Caroline will know. I will ask her later. I feel sure it will be fine though. Should we find out first do you think?"

"What I think is that you think too much. Come here, kiss me and then make love to me, please, I really need to feel you inside me." "Then once you have done that, what do you think we should do for the rest of the day. It's your day off right?"

"It is he said, do you have something in mind?"

"No, not at all, I wondered what you normally do on a Sunday".

"Bugger all usually. Sometimes we go down the pub for a drink with the lads. We often stay there and have Sunday lunch. Don't know if that will be possible now though."

"What should we do instead then? I asked.'

"Well, we could go over the plans for the house, make sure we have everything there that our child will need." Then we could start and make plans for our wedding. Do you want all the white dress and stuff?"

"Not really, I would like to get married in church but not with all the posh stuff that people do."

"Should we talk to Scott and Caroline about it? We could do both together on the same day said Jacob".

"Could do I suppose, save inviting the same people to two weddings?"

"First things first young man I said, my body is desperate for your attention."

"Is it now he said? He pushed my nightie up exposing my breasts. I could feel his breath on my skin and began to tremble. He reached down and sucked very gently on one nipple then moved to the other side and did the same.

My wanting of him inside me was so strong. "Jacob, please make love to me now." He slid inside me and began to move. My feelings were so powerful. I raised my legs and hips wrapping my legs around him, pulling him further into me. We rode against each other in a mad frenzy finally exploding in the most amazing climax. It went on and on and I loved it.

We lay together, breathless and sweating, "*Wow*" he said finally able to speak. Where did that come from?"

"From my love for you I guess" was my answer. I really cannot get enough of this wonderful man. He has made my life complete.

Eventually we got up, showered and dressed. We made our way downstairs finding Scott in the kitchen making tea.

"Is Caroline still in bed I asked?"

"No, I'm not cheeky," she had followed us into the kitchen. "I was just getting dressed. Did you two sleep well?"

"We did I said, Jacob was so tired last night, he has had a very busy week. I think we are just going to chill for the rest of the day."

"What time are you collecting the girls?"

"Picking them up at eleven, then we are going to have lunch. Thought we might just take them for a walk through the park first. They can't be too long as they both have stuff to complete for school. Then I thought we might start making plans for the wedding."

"Same here," I said, "if we are going to do it soon we will need to get our fingers out. I have never planned a wedding before."

"Really" asked Jacob, "who planned your first one then?"

I laughed, "that farce you mean. It was on my sixteenth birthday, what a present. I didn't know anything about it till I had cooked breakfast.

Will came in from sorting the cows out and just announced that today we were getting married. Before this I had lived alone in the cottage that had been my mum and dads place.

I lived there alone from the age of eleven when my dad had died. There was no inside toilet, the outside one was disgusting but I couldn't get it clean no matter how hard I tried. I was allowed to use the bathroom in the main farmhouse once a week but apart from that I had to make do with the poor conditions in the cottage. I was terrified, he had been through the old clothes that had once belonged to my mother and found something for me to wear."

"He drove me into Marchpool in his battered old Land Rover, it was filthy and stank of sheep. He had done all that needed to be done without telling me a thing about it."

"He ushered me into the building and introduced me to the woman dealing with whatever. He then went and grabbed two people off the street to come and be witnesses. Not a clue who they were. The ceremony, if that is what you called it took place, I was just in a daze."

"Afterwards we went back to the farm in time for me to cook his lunch."

"I thought that was it, we would just carry on as we had done before. How wrong was I?"

"Bedtime was awful, he suddenly announced that it was time for me to go upstairs, take my clothes off and lie on the bed and wait for him to come up. What he did to me that day was horrendous, he just took his stinking clothes off, climbed on top of me and rammed himself into me. I screamed out with the pain and got a hard smack across the face for my trouble."

"That is what happened almost every night, except when I had my period. I hated it and I hated him. He was just a cruel, wicked, vicious person. That is why I have no doubts about spending all his money. He kept me living on little more than the animals had. It was up to me to make the basic food we ate taste of something."

"He didn't like me reading books, wasn't allowed any newspapers or magazines. I really did hate him, I still do."

"I didn't begin to live until the day Caroline arrived to help me then Scott arrived and then finally I met you my darling Jacob."

"I must have been saving all my love up for all those years so that I can give it all to you, my precious man, my life saver."

"I had wanted to kill myself many times over those years, just didn't know how to really. So pleased that I didn't manage it now."

I turned and leant into Jacob, he had his arms around me and then kissed me. As we pulled apart I could see that he had been crying. "Jacob, don't cry please. We have each other now so all is well with the world."

He held me tightly and wouldn't let go. "Ella, I am so sorry for all that you have suffered but from now on you will have all the love you need. I will never hurt you my darling."

I smiled at him, "that is all in the past now, onward and upward from now on." "I looked at Caroline and Scott and they too had been silently weeping."

"I am so sorry, I have upset you all".

"Don't be sorry, Ella, said Scott. You have led an awful existence until now. If only I had realised what was going on before I could have maybe done something to help. Will was always very rough and ready whenever I met him but just assumed that was being a farmer. He always seemed quite clever and always wanted everything done 'right and proper' is how he put it."

"He has at least managed to leave you without any money worries. I am still ploughing through all his paperwork and my friend who is clearing all the house stuff up has found a few more interesting things. We will wait until he has finished his work before going through everything."

"The sale of the land and buildings is going through quickly." "You will need to sign some paperwork soon so that we can get that finalised. Nothing for you to worry about though, Ella. I will get everything in order, all the money side of things sorted and all the other stuff, if you don't want it then it can go to auction. I have made claims on all the insurance policies that we found, just waiting for the cheques to arrive from them."

"There will be considerable death duties to be paid I'm afraid. There is nothing we can do about that, but I will make it all as painless as I can. I

have a small team of people working on it as we speak. It will all take another few months but once that is sorted out then there will be nothing left for you to do except enjoy the rest of your life with this brother of mine and the little bundle of joy that this baby will be. I still can't get my breath over how quickly all this has happened and how happy you two are making me and my brother."

"Once we have everything cleared up, we can all enjoy our lives. We all get on amazingly well, don't we? Then once these new little Ryan children are born we will all have a great life."

"I have told our sister Ingrid that I will be taking a backseat with the business as well. She has suggested that we sell up and enjoy our lives instead of working ourselves into the ground. All to be thought about but I really like the sound of that."

"Will just leave Jacob working to bring the money in."

"Jacob laughed at his brother. Don't worry bro, he said. "As soon as all my commitments are completed, I will also be taking stock and will only do what we really feel comfortable doing."

"I want to spend as much time with Ella as possible and once this baby arrives I fully intend to do my bit. This baby will be ours, not just Ella's. Now, weddings, said Jacob. How shall we do this?"

"Two separate weddings on two separate days or should we do them together?" seems to me we are doing everything else together." Scott and Caroline looked at each other and then nodded.

Scott spoke first, "funny you should say that Jacob we were talking about it this morning and Caroline said it would make more sense to do it together. We don't want to take any of the limelight away from you though. This will undoubtedly bring fresh interest in you and your life. Having us there might not work."

"We all seem to be travelling this road in one direction. Let's see if we can get it sorted out and then do it together as quickly as we can said, Jacob." "As for the limelight, you are very welcome to it."

"Firstly, we need to speak with Gerald," said Jacob.

"Who is Gerald?" I asked?"

"He is our local vicar and also a distant cousin. We should be able to do it all in three weeks I think,'' said Jacob. "Would that suit everyone here?"

"Well, I have nothing else on," I said. Caroline said she thinks she will be able to sort it with work. As she would be leaving work anyway she thinks they will work something out.

"Scott said he would be able to sort his work stuff out so that he would be free."

"Jacob said that's it then, I will be finished with the show. I was planning on having some down time before the next project. That should give me a good few weeks off."

"If we can get married in three weeks then we can all go to France and have a joint honeymoon. How does that sound?"

"It sounds amazing I said, but I still don't have a passport."

"Right Scott, can you help Ella sort a passport out please. I know you always manage to perform miracles on a daily basis."

"Leave it with me Jacob, I take it you do have a passport Caroline and it is in date."

"I do," she said.

"Right, are we all happy to sort all this out for three-weeks time? Jacob asked. "I nodded, Caroline said yes, please, Scott said just as soon as humanly possible.

"Okay, then, we had better make a list of things we need to do then a list of guests to invite. Of course, the ladies will be kept busy with choosing dresses and flowers. What about bridesmaids?"

"That's easy for me. I said I don't know anyone. If I had to choose one then it would be Caroline, but as she will be getting married at the same time that won't work."What about you Caroline?"

"Same here really, I have people at work, but they are colleagues. As for proper friends, it would have to be Ella."

Jacob asked, "What about we have your girls Scott, and they can be for both. We can ask Ingrid if her little one can do it, but I think she might be a bit young." We all said that was a great idea, they would be thrilled. "What happens about best men?" Jacob asked obviously, we would have each other but that can't happen. I could ask Eddie I suppose."

Scott said he would ask his friend Gregg from the pub. "What about a reception?"

"Well, first we need to see how many guests we will be talking about then see if we can find a venue big enough at such short notice. Or we just keep it really small. That might work better. Fewer people to be involved, less chance of nosey photographers."

Caroline and I both said we would prefer to keep it small. After all, neither of us have any family or friends to invite anyway. Neither of us is interested in trying to outdo everyone on the planet.

The next few days flew by in a whirlwind of appointments, visiting the vicar, fittings, talks with the architect and builders, time spent with Scott sorting out my passport, shopping for weddings and holidays, talks with the hotel that was going to cater for the reception, loving and lots of sex.

Mrs. H was all of a flurry. She was so excited. Of course she would be coming to the double wedding as a guest of both parties. Jacob told her to go to a specific boutique in town and choose whatever she wanted. He would pay the bill. She was so full of excitement. When we told her that two babies were on the way I thought she would burst.

I gave her one of the rings still left in the safe. I gave her the choice.

"Oh, my," she said, "why would you want to give me one of these? They are gorgeous. You should keep them all for yourself."

"I was looking at the ring I wore on my engagement finger. I have all I want, Mrs H. All wrapped up in a parcel called Jacob. He makes me so happy."

"I know he does lass, anyone seeing you together can see how well-matched you are. And you are making him very happy too you know."

"I know, it's like you fell out of the sky one day and landed right here with the love of your life. You pair have never been so happy. It shows all over your faces as well," she said.

"I am so happy that both my boys have found what they needed."

We had kept the invitation list to the bare minimum but that still came to over a hundred people. Scott's two girls were so excited. They seemed to love Caroline which was a good sign.

We took them with us when we shopped for their dresses. We let them choose which ones they wanted themselves. They looked gorgeous but very different. Couldn't be seen wearing the same outfits could they? Just not done.

A jeweller friend of Jacobs came to the house with a selection of wedding rings so we could decide what we wanted without running the daily gauntlet of press that insisted on following us wherever we went. Of course they soon put two and two together and realised that Jacob and I would be getting married. Caroline and Scott managed to keep under the radar though, so it was a bit easier for them. No one had worked out that it would be a double wedding though. Good to keep something secret.

He looked at my engagement ring and said how beautiful it was then asked, is it a family heirloom? "I guess you could say that" was my reply.

Jacob continued to do his shows every night and I went with him, marvelling at just how talented this man is. I had the car routine worked out well by now and we managed to get in and out of the theatre without incident.

Thursday night was this award thing that we needed the posh gowns for. Hope I still fit in it, it is very fitted and slinky. The wedding planning had to be put on hold for that day as there was so much preparation to be done.

A different show was being put on at the theatre for the one night so that Jacob's Musical Director and some of the orchestra could go along to this award ceremony. I really didn't know what to expect, I have never seen or heard about such a thing before. Hope I enjoy it.

Thursday arrived as did an army of people to get us all ready. We were too excited to eat a proper meal so made do with sandwiches throughout the day. There was to be a meal later at this 'thing' we were all preparing for.

Once I had been made up, hair and nails done and dressed I looked in the mirror. I was amazed, I looked like a complete stranger.

My hair looked amazing, Henri had done one long plait right down the back, but it started at the top of my head somewhere. It was pulled into a very long and very wide plait. Henri had then threaded long strings of shiny stones through the plait, and they twinkled like stars as the lights caught them. I looked like someone out of one of the films I had managed to see in the cinema room.

Scott and Jacob were being got ready in one of the other bedrooms. I was dying to see what Jacob looked like. I finished my look with the emerald necklace and bracelet. I couldn't use the earrings because they are for pierced ears and mine haven't been done.

Caroline was being done up as she called it in her and Scott's room. She was wearing the ruby necklace, bracelet and earrings. They looked amazing against the black of her gown. We would look proper posh I thought. Hope I don't let Jacob down. He would be mortified.

As soon as our men saw us they were gobsmacked by the looks on their faces. "*Wow!* they both said. "You girls look amazing. We gave them a twirl and received a kiss each. Jacob couldn't take his eyes off me."

"My darling, you look amazing." I am so proud of you."

"You scrub up well yourself, Mr Ryan," I said. They both looked amazing in their evening suits. So excited.

Soon it was time to set off. Two cars arrived for us, Caroline and Scott went in the first one then it was time for Jacob and me to set off.

The car was on the driveway in front of the house, but there appeared to be an awful lot of press people on the other side of the gates.

Jacob said, "How do you feel about giving them an eyeful before we get in the car?"

"Whatever you think Jacob".

"What I think is it's time for the world to see us together as a newly engaged couple. Make sure they see your ring, sweetheart."

"You look a million dollars, do you know that? Listen, if you're not comfortable answering all the questions that will be coming our way then wait for me to answer. Just try to relax and enjoy the evening, then once we get home I will delight in taking you out of that stunning dress and making love to you, maybe more than once."

"I laughed at him, you are such a beautiful man Jacob, both inside and out. I love you, my darling.'

"Now, ready? "

"As I'll ever be" I said. He opened the door and I stepped out. The flashing lights made me blink, there were so many of them. As soon as Jacob joined me there were another load of flashes.

People were shouting questions at us, but I couldn't make out what they were saying. I just smiled and hung onto Jacob.

He walked me over to the gate and introduced me to all these press people.

He said, "I know you are all interested to know who this gorgeous young woman is and what she is doing with an old reprobate like me, so I will introduce her. This is Ella, my fiancée and soon-to-br-wife."

163

"Once all the preparations are complete for the wedding you will be told where and when, until then though I suggest you save your breath. We won't be divulging any of the details until we are ready. Now, can you all please move away from the gates so that we can get the car out safely? I think we have been more than generous with you for now."

We walked back to the car and the driver held open the doors for us to get in. "This car is beautiful," I said, "so comfortable. I love it."

"You did so well back there Ella, I think they all fell in love with you my darling".

"Don't talk daft" I said "It's not me they are interested in, it's you."

" Actually it's us, They are obsessed with any couples in the public eye. They try to push people together then if they succeed in that they then do everything they can to pull them apart. I won't let that happen to us my darling."

"It won't," I said, "I have waited too long to meet you, and I won't be going anywhere".

Our car sped towards the city, thankfully it was quite warm and no rain about. I'd had visions of my beautiful gown dragging in the puddles.

We held hands all the way to the venue. I had quite a shock when I saw the queue of posh cars waiting to unload their passengers. We joined the queue and slowly moved forward as each car emptied. Soon it was our turn. There appeared to be hundreds of people on the street just waiting to see who would be next.

Jacob got out first and there was a huge cheer, he reached in to hold my hand as I got out of the car. Another cheer. They all seem happy to see us together at least.

We began walking down the red carpet, what's all that about I thought? A carpet on the pavement. It looked like we would have a long walk before finally reaching the entrance.

Caroline and Scott were waiting for us and joined the long trail of people. We kept close together, it was obvious that all these people wanted Jacob, but he wouldn't let go of my hand.

As we made our way down the line Jacob was introducing me as his fiancée, we received so many congratulations. It was lovely, scary but lovely.

Halfway down the line a man with a microphone approached from the other side of the red carpet and asked Jacob if he had a few words for the camera. Of course he did, the man's a natural.

The guy asking the questions was saying "you are up for one of the top awards tonight Jacob, what do you think your chances are?'

Jacob just shrugged his shoulders and said, "to be honest I won the best prize ever when Ella agreed to be my wife."

The man said, "I can see that Jacob, may we see the ring, show all our viewers."

"Certainly" he said, he held my hand up so that the ring was prominent, and the camera man zoomed in on it.

"Wow" the man said, "that is some rock, you must love this lovely young woman a lot."

"I do," replied Jacob. "Now if you will excuse us, our dinner will be getting cold."

We left him to speak to the next one in line. We returned to Caroline and Scott then carried on till the end. Jacob turned round and waved to all the people and they gave him one more cheer.

I said to Caroline, "I feel way out of my depth here,"

"She said "don't worry Ella, you are a natural."

"Jacob, what did that man mean when he said you are up for one of the top awards?"

"Just because I am nominated doesn't mean I will win it. There are plenty of others up for the same award."

"Well," I said, "if they don't give you the award they must be mad, you are an amazing singer and I imagine you are an equally good actor. They should give you every award going."

"Well, thank you," he said, "you could take over the job of being my agent and publicist."

"Not likely," I said. "I will have my hands full with dirty nappies and sick before too long."

"Delightful," he said,

"Do you want to do all that stuff yourself Ella?"

"Well, who else will do it, you?"

"Of course I will do it, I'm not frightened of a bit of shit behind my nails," he whispered. "I did wonder though if you would want a nanny?"

"A what?" I asked.

"You know, a nanny, someone that would live in and help look after the children?"

"We're having more than one then are we?"

"At least five or six," he said.

"In which case we may need a nanny or two. Just imagine all those sticky fingers all over your posh white walls and sofa's. "

"I thought we had agreed to change the colours, something more in keeping with a house full of kids he said."

All this talk was going on whilst we ate a very nice meal.   "How long do the awards take I asked?

"Oh God, hours, your bum will be numb by the end. And we're expected to smile all the way through. Then once it is all over there are several parties going on. We could go to any number of them. I never bother though, it all gets a bit much. Once it's done in here I usually go home."

"I don't much like the sound of parties to be honest and you are on a promise, remember?"

"I do remember and I could just get up from here now and take you home to claim my promise."

"Down tiger," I said. You might win tonight after all."

"I doubt it my darling, just here to make up the numbers. But it is a good night usually."

"Have you ever won before Jacob?"

"No, never been nominated before. I have been to a few of these things though as a guest. The trick is not to drink too much then you won't have to keep going to the loo."

"I will remember that, going to the loo is not going to be that easy in this dress."

The ceremony began and we took an interest in all the awards, that is until we got a bit bored, it did go on an awful long time. Not sure when Jacobs category will be announced.

"Do you think I will have time to go to the loo before they start talking about you?"

"Don't think so, we are up next he said. Can you hold on?"

"I will do my best," I said. I have everything crossed for you my darling".

All the nominations for Jacob's category were announced then a short film of them all performing. I was mesmerised by Jacob's voice all over again. He truly is one fantastic singer.

The winner was about to be announced by some young thing wearing next to nothing.

"And the winner is – Jacob Ryan for his one-man show." Jacob looked stunned.

"My darling, you won," I said.

He got to his feet and I could see he was shaking. He shook hands with Scott then kissed Caroline on the cheek, then he pulled me to my feet and kissed me full on the mouth. Then kissed me again.

"Go on, get your award," I said.

He made his way to the stage being congratulated all the way up. His musical director stood up and hugged him, all the band members were cheering him. He sure is a popular guy isn't he?

Scott said "he always has been. He just gets along with everyone, he treats people well and they appreciate him. Of course, it also helps that he is devilishly handsome and loaded."

"He has also been very lonely for a lot of his grown-up years though."
"Women only wanted him for the kudos his name gave them, so he didn't bother with them. Since meeting you Ella he has changed so much and I for one am very grateful.

By this time Jacob had reached the stage and was climbing up the steps. The young actress handed over his award then the compare asked him to say a few words.

"He began by thanking everyone, particularly his musical director and his band members, he said he couldn't do it without them. He also wanted to thank his brother Scott and his fiancée Caroline who supported him always.

"Finally I want to thank my fiancée, Ella, since meeting this beautiful young woman my life has turned full circle. She is the love of my life and I can't wait to make her my wife. Thank you my darling Ella, I love you. This is for you."

I just sat watching and listening, I couldn't believe he was saying all this, and it would be going out on the television. I mouthed back to him, I love you too, then blew him a kiss.

The compare was asking him if he would sing for the audience. I know you sing it mostly without any backing music. Do you think you can do the whole thing without your orchestra?

"I will do my best" he said. The room fell silent. *He moved over to the microphone in the centre of the stage. He took a deep breath then began singing. His voice was so clear, so powerful. As the song went on he got stronger and stronger. The end of the song finishes with one long very powerful note and it goes on and on, seems like it will never end.*

The whole place erupted, everyone standing on their feet clapping and shouting. He put his hand on his heart then blew a kiss to me. I could have cried, his passion shone through tonight and they all appreciated him.

Caroline had told me that a lot of those people in the audience were stars in their own right, naming many of them but of course I didn't know who they were.

All these stars were on their feet clapping Jacob as well. He must be loved by so many. He never took his eyes from me until he reached our table. I was on my feet still clapping him. He put his award down on the table, picked me up in his arms and swung me round then kissed me with such a passion, it really did take my breath away.

The compare was trying to get the audience to sit back down and be calm and quiet, no chance. They would have had Jacob back on the stage for the rest of the night if they could.

Eventually they did calm down and the rest of the awards could be handed out. There was no doubt in my mind, Jacob had been the star of the show.

I said to him, "I will have to go and pee before I wet myself."

" Okay, he said, don't be long."

Caroline came with me. We were both desperate. Sipping water all night, it has to go somewhere.

We went into the ladies and remarkably it was empty apart from the lady handing out towels. We had a cubicle each and the relief was immense. I was finished first then went to wash my hands. *The door opened and a woman came in and marched straight up to me. She looked drunk. She began screaming at me. Telling me that Jacob was hers, I should leave him alone. Once I was out of the way he would take her back. She would never give him up. Never. She then started calling me names, shouting slag, slapper, prostitute.*

By this time Caroline had come out of her cubicle, she moved to come and stand next to me.

She said, "Why don't you go and sober up? You are making a complete fool of yourself. Jacob doesn't want you, never did and never would. I know what you did to him and he will never forgive you."

The woman started kicking off properly then, she lashed out at me, punching me in the side of my head. I staggered and almost fell. Caroline made to grab her, but she pulled free and tried to punch Caroline.

This situation is crazy. Who is this woman? Someone came into the loo, it was the lady that had been handing out towels, she saw what was going on and rushed out. The next minute two security men came in but before they could get hold of the woman she kicked out, catching me hard in the stomach. I grabbed at my stomach, "my baby," I screamed. I fell down onto my knees. I was terrified. Caroline came and put her arms around me." Ella are you okay?"

"Not sure I said, I dare not move. Get Jacob for me please."

The woman was now being held by the two security men, but she was still screaming. She said that she should be wearing that ring, not me. How she managed to work that one out I wasn't sure.

The next minute Jacob came charging through the door. He rushed over to me. "Ella, my darling, what the hell has happened? Please get an ambulance for my fiancée."

" On their way Mr Ryan."

The woman was still shouting, and Jacob looked round to see what was going on. "Caroline, stay with Ella, please" he asked.

"Cleo, what the hell are you doing here and what have you done to my beautiful Ella?"

"She is nothing more than a slag, Jacob. I want you to come back to me. We can sort the other stuff out. I just want to be with you."

Jacob stood up and walked over to Cleo, he looked her straight in the eyes and said, "If you have damaged Ella or my child that she carries I will swing for you."

"I never loved you Cleo, but I would have done the decent thing if you hadn't done what you did."

"I didn't do anything, honestly."

"Cleo, you told me you were pregnant with my child and I believed you, then you had an abortion once you realised that the child could be Arlo's. If you could have got away with it you would have but with Arlo being Jamaican that was impossible. So you did what you did and got rid of the child."

"To be honest it was a relief, I had never loved you or wanted you if I'm honest, but you threw yourself at me and then at Arlo, it has all gone horribly wrong for you because of your selfishness."

"Now hear this and hear it well. I don't want you, never did and never will. I have been lucky enough to meet this amazing woman who loves me for me, not for what I can do to further her own career but for the man that I am. I love her more than life itself. We are engaged and will be married very shortly."

"Get her out of my sight, please. Send for the police, I want her charged with assault."

"On their way sir," the security man said. "We called them immediately we heard what was happening in here."

With that both police and ambulance arrived.

Jacob came back to me and Caroline went to get Scott and to collect our things from the table, including Jacobs award.

The ambulance people were amazing. They checked me all over to see if there was any apparent damage. They then said that I should go to hospital anyway to check that everything is okay with the baby. Of course I agreed instantly.

Jacob was going to come with me in the ambulance and Scott and Caroline would follow in their car. The driver of the car that we had arrived in said he would also follow so he could drive us home once everything was checked. Both of our cars also had a security man sitting beside the driver.

The police had arrested Cleo and a van had arrived to take her to the police station. What an awful person she is, whatever did Jacob see in her? She was still shouting abuse as she was put in the back of the police van.

We were soon at the hospital and I was pushed through to the A & E department. There seemed to be dozens of people waiting around there. I hope I don't have to wait here for hours. For one thing everyone is looking at us and whispering, then the fact that I am still dressed in my beautiful gown with all my glitter on display.

Jacob was at my side and was whispering words of love in my ear. "How much longer will we have to wait he asked the lady in reception."

"I am sorry, Mr Ryan, it is a very busy night as you can see. We will get your fiancée seen just as soon as we can.'

A short time later I was wheeled through to a cubicle. A male nurse came to talk with us, and he filled in a mountain of paperwork.

He took my blood pressure and pulse readings and said they were all good. He then came to take a blood test. "I have never had any of these things done to me before, it was all a bit much really. I was feeling very weepy. Jacob was holding my hand all the time."

"Don't worry my darling, this is all precautionary. *I am sure everything will be fine. I am so angry with that idiot woman and with myself. Can't believe I got involved with her in the first place. She has always been toxic.*"

"How are you feeling now my darling?" he asked,

"I am frightened Jacob, I have never been to a hospital before. Not seen a doctor either that I can remember."

A senior nurse came in to the cubicle then. "Mr. Ryan a pleasure to meet you, just a shame it has to be under these circumstances. Jacob was still looking very worried.

"Thank you nurse" he said, "we have all had such a wonderful evening and then this has to happen. My fiancée and I are really worried about our baby. Ella is only a few weeks pregnant, and we are still getting used to the idea. Is there a test you can do to check if the baby has been damaged?"

"Don't worry, Mr Ryan, we will do all we can. Babies can be quite resilient, even in these early days. I will just go and fetch the equipment I need." She disappeared through the curtain and was back within a few minutes with whatever it was she needed.

"Right now, Ella isn't it?"

"It is," I said.

"Let's have a look to see what is going on.'

She needed to get access to my stomach area which was impossible whilst wearing my gown.

"*Wow*" she said, what a beautiful gown. It was quite the occasion, I believe."

"It was," I said, "Jacob won an award and then he sang for the whole audience. He is amazing."

She smiled over to where Jacob was sitting, still holding my hand. "So, I heard," she said, "your performance has been quite the talking point in here tonight. You will have to serenade all the staff here once your lady gets the all clear."

Jacob smiled at her, "don't feel much like singing at the moment," he said.

"I don't suppose you do. Now can we remove this gown of yours so I can conduct my tests. There is a very flattering hospital gown here for you".

I sat up and Jacob helped me out of the gown and put the hospital gown on me. The nurse was right, very flattering. I handed Jacob my necklace and he popped it into his pocket.

I lay back on the pillow and tried to relax. The nurse put some gel on my tummy then used part of the equipment moving it over the skin. It felt cool. She moved it one way then another. She smiled at us both. "Everything looks fine, just one thing, have you seen a doctor or been to a clinic yet?"

"Not yet," said Jacob. "We have had a lot of change and things to get our heads around recently. A visit to the GP was on the to do list for next week." "I'm not altogether sure that Ella has ever been registered with a doctor, to be honest. She has led a very different life up to now."

"That was going to be my next question," the nurse said. "We are having trouble locating any notes for her."

"Not surprised," said Jacob. He explained my situation briefly, the nurse looked horrified.

"Let's not get bogged down with all that yet," she said. "We can sort you out here then you will need to register with a GP. I suppose you will be using your own doctor, Mr Ryan."

"We will yes, I will ring them tomorrow and make an appointment. Are you sure everything is okay with the baby," he asked?

"More than okay I would say, look here. She was pointing out tiny little things on a monitor. See there, that is one baby, and this is a second one. Both look absolutely fine. Congratulations to you both."

"Sorry," said Jacob, "are you telling me we are expecting twins?"

"I am Mr Ryan, the pictures don't lie."

Jacob was looking at me, "Ella, we are having twins. God, I am so happy."

I looked at the nurse again, " honestly," I asked.

"Let me show you, see, there and there. What you do need to do though is go home now and rest for a couple of days. Get over this horrible attack. Then see your GP next week. He will then refer you to a consultant. They will keep an eye on you then for the remainder of your pregnancy. I will leave you both for a moment to gather your thoughts, I can see this has been a bit of a shock."

"It has, a very happy shock though, neither of us can quite believe it," said Jacob.

"Well, gather your thoughts, get yourself dressed and then I will discharge you once the doctor has checked everything."

She left us sitting there just looking at each other. "Well, this trip started out being awful and now it is amazing," said Jacob.

"Ella, you have made me so happy, all my dreams come true with meeting you and now expecting twins. Life can't get any better."

"Jacob, I can't believe what has happened these last few hours. I was so worried about our baby and now we find out it's two. You are right, life can't get any better."

"Will you help me get back into my gown, please?"

"I will my darling, then when we get home I can help you out of it again."

"Jacob, you are naughty. I have to rest, you heard the nurse."

"Come on, my sweet angel, let's get you dressed. As soon as the doctor gives you the all-clear we can go and find Scott and Caroline. Blimey! they won't believe any of this."

The doctor arrived to check the nurse's findings, he was lovely. He seemed a bit in awe of Jacob. I still can't believe how most people dream of meeting him and here's me living with him and carrying his children. Life is funny.

The doctor checked everything and gave me a clean bill of health. He said, "I hear the news of twins has come as a bit of a surprise."

"It has doctor," said Jacob, "but a very happy surprise at that."

"Just rounded our evening off really."

"So I understand Mr Ryan, I hear you won a big award earlier."

"I did," said Jacob, "but this news is an even bigger award. I am such a lucky man. A wonderful, beautiful partner, twins on the way and a career I enjoy."

"The talk out in the waiting room is that you did an impromptu song at the awards."

"I did," he said, "but they didn't give me much choice. When you are standing on stage in front of hundreds of people and the TV cameras rolling what else can you do but try."

"Well, don't be surprised if they try to get you to perform out there. There is a lot of excitement amongst the staff and patients."

"Okay, thanks for the warning. And thanks for the treatment here tonight. You have all helped us to cope."

"Goodnight then, Mr Ryan, Ella, good luck to you both."

We thanked him once more.

As soon as I was dressed and looking presentable we made our way through to the reception area. It was still packed. As soon as we were spotted a round of applause went up.

I felt myself blush. Jacob put his hand up to quieten them.

"Thank you all so much, it has been a bit of a night and I need to get Ella home but truly, thank you all for your concern."

"Give us a song then Jacob," someone called. Soon the room was full of shouts, "give us a song, come on, make our night."

Jacob looked at me, "What do you think, my darling?"

"Go for it if it keeps them happy. If you are sure."

"Okay," he said, give me a minute. Any requests? "*'Somewhere'* was the overwhelming shout."

"Blimey! you lot don't take any prisoners, do you?"

I spotted Caroline and Scott coming over to us. "Are you okay, Ella they asked?"

" I am," I said, all seems well. Just got to take it easy for a day or two."

Jacob was holding my hand, I squeezed his fingers. "Go on my love, knock their socks off."

The room went quiet, everyone watching Jacob and waiting. Someone said, "He can't do it without a microphone. That's all he knows," I thought.

Jacob began to sing, the words I was beginning to know so well.

A shiver went down my spine and I guessed all these people had the same reaction. Everyone was watching my man and listening to his beautiful voice.

His voice got stronger and stronger the more he got into the song. It built and built till the end when that final note went on and on. Everyone was holding their breath along with him.

Finally, he finished and a huge round of applause began. He did a comedy bow to his audience and then said, "Thank you all. I am going now to take my beautiful Ella home so she can rest."

The applause was still loud as we left the hospital.

"Jacob, you are amazing," I said, "Where do you find the energy to do that song not once but twice in one night?"

He just smiled at me, "Come on, let's get you home. I want to get out of this monkey suit as well and I bet Scott can't wait to get his loungers on."

"Do you think we should give them our news before we leave?"

"Okay, go for it."

"What news?" asked Caroline.

"Well, they did a scan to check all was well with the baby and it was more than okay. Actually, they found two babies."

Caroline and Scott were quiet for a second, then they grabbed us both hugging us. "Bloody marvellous," said Scott.

Caroline was close to tears, "I am so happy for you both. What a brilliant end to a very strange day."

We arrived home in the two cars that had taken us into London earlier that night. So much had happened. Poor Jacob, it should have been his night then that awful woman ruined it for us all.

"I wonder what will happen to her," I asked.

"To be quite honest, Ella, I don't know and I don't care. She is a bloody liability."

"How dare she try to break us up and think she stood half a chance with me. The few times I did go out with her, everything was a big drama and all about her."

"I know I was floored when she had the abortion, but that was thinking she had killed a child of mine. The horror when she told me what she had done, I could have killed her. Then to top it all, eventually she admitted she had been having an affair with my best friend, Arlo. That put all the ducks

in a row as far as I was concerned. Arlo had been my friend since University days then they had both done the dirty across me. True, I didn't want that lunatic Cleo, but to do that with my best mate, she must have really hated me."

"I really think she wanted me for the fame and a 'shoe in' for her to get into acting. Her modelling jobs were drying up and she thought this would be an easy way to stay in the limelight. As soon as she met Arlo she was smitten with him, but I didn't think she would do what she did. I let the abortion take over all my feelings and I sank into an even deeper depression. It was only getting back on the bike so to speak with this gig I'm doing that dragged me out of it. I will never end up in that state again."

"Oh, Jacob, I knew most of it of course, but I hadn't realised just how low you had sunk. We will be okay though won't we?"

"We will, my darling. We have everything we need to make us happy, we have each other and all the love that brings and now two babies. How lucky are we?"

"Very lucky, indeed," I said.

"Go and get comfy on the sofa and I will make us a nice cup of tea. I will shout Scott to see if they want to join us."

Of course they did. A tray of tea and biscuits were delivered into the lounge. I went to get up to pour, but Jacob said, "Sit and don't move. You heard what the doctor said, rest."

Scott and Caroline had been up to change into more comfortable clothes. I was still dressed in my lovely gown. I began to remove the remainder of my jewellery, "will you put this back in the safe for me?" I asked Jacob.

"Of course, I will. Give it here, I have your necklace in my jacket pocket. Let me take all those things out of your hair as well, bet you can't wait to get a brush through it?"

"True I said but I did like the style that Henri created for me. It was all very comfortable, and I still felt like me. It did look good though didn't it?"

All three said, "Yes, it looked amazing."

Jacob said, "You looked fabulous tonight, my darling. You always do but tonight you outdid yourself. You handled all those people brilliantly. I can't believe how much you have changed in the past couple of weeks. Not shy any more, are you?

"I am actually Jacob, but I force myself to do these things for you. I don't want to let you down."

"You could never let me down, my darling. You are the most stunningly beautiful woman I have ever met and now we are going to be a proper family. I can't wait."

"I think you will have to wait, my love. Babies don't grow overnight, even I know that."

Jacob's beautiful face was beaming. It would seem that all he really needs in his life is to have someone to love and to love him back.

Well, I do love him and if we manage to grow these babies both our lives will be complete. "What do you think will happen to Cleo?" I asked.

"To be honest Ella, really I don't care, I would throw away the key. She has been nothing but trouble ever since I first met her. She is very selfish, she wants everything she can't have and then kicks off when it doesn't go her way."

"I saw some of that behaviour when I was with her, but she really seems to have lost the plot now. She and Arlo were an item for a while but when she realised he wouldn't be able to give her the lifestyle she wants, she dropped him. I think he really did love her, he was devastated afterwards. Not only had he lost Cleo but also me, his best friend. I could never trust him again. She caused a lot of heartache to us all."

"That is in the past though now my love. Nothing like that will ever happen to us. We are the real deal."

We sat sipping our drinks and thinking over the nights events.

"Jacob, I am so sorry your special night ended so horribly. I was so proud of you winning that award. You did yourself proud too when you sang for us all. You really do have the most amazing voice."

"I will second that," said Caroline, "you really know how to stir everyone's emotions. Have you always been a singer?"

"Not at all, no, acting was my first love. Then I was asked to audition for the lead in a musical at University. They asked if I could sing obviously before the audition, I said that I could hold a tune, but I was by no means a singer. A music producer was in the audience supporting his daughter who was also in the show. He signed me up straight away, found me a good manager and the rest as they say is history. Following that first show I

auditioned for a part in a musical in the West End, in the theatre where we are now funnily enough."

"When I did the audition they must have seen something in me because they gave me the lead part. They then organised singing lessons for me. Those few weeks leading up to the opening of the show worked wonders. When we did the show for the first time in front of the press it was amazing. They loved everything about the show and gave us all five-star reviews."

Scott interrupted, "Actually they gave Jacob five-star reviews. The whole show was a success, but it opened up a whole new career for him. I think that now he enjoys singing as much if not more than acting."

"You could be right Scott, it certainly gives me a lot of satisfaction."

"Those people at the hospital loved it when you sang for them tonight, I said. Everyone knew who you were and also knew that song. I could listen to you every day of my life," I said.

"We will have to see where we end up in the future," said Jacob. Do I concentrate on singing, go back to acting or try to do some of both? With my growing family I will need to keep bringing the money in."

We were all laughing, growing family indeed.

"How can all this have happened in such a short space of time," I asked.? Before meeting Scott, I was in such a desperate state and now look at me?. I couldn't be happier. I never knew what it felt like to be happy before."

"Well, my darling, from now on each and every day will bring you happiness if I have my way."

"Now, let's check over all the wedding arrangements," said Scott, "have we missed anything?"

I said, "I have no idea because I have never even been to a proper wedding. I am excited to become your wife though, Jacob."

"So am I," he replied.? I just hope the press doesn't spoil it."

"We will just ignore them, we will do everything that we want and if they choose to spend their time following us around then that's up to them. I know they can be a pain in the arse but let's just get on and do it for us four. We could perhaps lay on some food for the press, do you think that would help?"

"It might do," said Scott and Jacob together. "I mean we could have gone down the celebrity magazine route and let them pay for everything, but then they would want to dictate the whole thing. I want it to be about us four, your two beauties and these children that are yet to be born," said Jacob. "Perhaps if we get the hotel to set up a room separate from our reception to give them food and drink they may decide to treat us gently."

We all decided to look into the possibility.

I said, "We could send them all an invitation, that would throw them. After all, we are not doing anything wrong, we are just cementing our love for each other."

It was agreed then that we would definitely look into including the press, see where that leads us.

Jacob and I had decided to lay off our athletic sex life for a few days to make sure everything settled down properly. That didn't mean we didn't satisfy each other's needs, there is always a way apparently. I couldn't wait to feel Jacob inside me once again, though.

Jacob had made an appointment for me to register with his GP. He came with me and explained as best he could about my history then about our journey so far. I had an examination and various tests were done. The doctor said he would be delighted to take me into his practice. He said he would arrange an appointment for me to see a consultant at the hospital. "They will want to keep a careful eye on you as you are expecting twins. You are young and healthy and strong so I doubt you will have any problems, but just to be on the safe side, we will also monitor your progress from here as well. Our midwife Sylvie, will contact you about future appointments. She is very good, you will like her."

"Now, do you have any worries or concerns that I can help you with?"

Jacob began to say, "No, thank you, doctor. You have been very helpful..." I interrupted him, though."

"Can I ask you something, doctor?"

"Certainly," he said, "what can I help you with?"

Well, I began, "Jacob and I have a very active and athletic sex life and I was wondering if we need to alter that?" I caught sight of Jacob, he was actually blushing.

"Carry on as normal," said the doctor, if you are feeling well then that won't be a problem, but as you get further into your pregnancy you may have to adapt. Two babies are going to take up quite a bit of space so new positions may be required."

"Thank you, doctor," I said, "that has put my mind at rest. I really want to keep our sex life active for as long as I can. Jacob is a wonderful lover, I really love that side of our life together so much, I don't want it to end."

"I am pleased to hear that Ella, so many women use pregnancy as an excuse to keep their husbands at bay. There really is no need for that to happen. So long as you are careful and remember your growing babies."

"Thank you, doctor," I said, "I am reassured and so is Jacob, although he does look a bit embarrassed. I tend to just say or ask what is on my mind without thinking. My friend Caroline says I have no filter."

The doctor laughed. "Well, I think that no filter is a good thing. At least, you ask the important questions and get answers."

"Thank you, doctor," I said, "we might just go home and try a little gentle loving if that is okay."

"That is perfectly fine, Ella. Good luck to you both. We will be seeing you regularly from now on."

"Oh," I said, "I just thought. We are getting married in a couple of weeks and we are going to France for our honeymoon, will that be okay?"

"That will be perfectly fine, you are well and this early on in your pregnancy there shouldn't be a problem."

"Now, may I congratulate you on not only your pregnancy but also wish you all the best for your marriage."

"Thank you, doctor," I said. Jacob managed to say the same. He had gone very quiet. "Come on then, my darling," I said, "we are wasting time."

The doctor chuckled as we left the surgery.

"I really like him, Jacob," I said, "he is very easy to talk to."

"So I noticed," said Jacob. "I think you have made his day."

"Come on," I said, "let's not waste another second. Take me home and make love to me Jacob style, before I burst."

He laughed then, "You certainly know how to ask the hard questions, don't you?"

"Well, if I want to know something, how else am I to find out? I want to have sex with you my darling and it just seemed that he would be the best person to ask."

"Of course, you are right my love," he said. "I just wasn't expecting you to announce that we have a very active and athletic sex life to the world."

"Not the world my darling, just the doctor."

Caroline and Scott had an appointment for later that day for the same thing. I wonder if Caroline will ask the same questions?

We had arranged with them to meet up in the pub for lunch. Scott wanted to ask Gregg if he would be his best man and we had decided that sneaking around and trying to lose the press was a waste of time. If we just carry on and do what we want they might get bored and leave us alone. Wasn't likely but we would give it a try.

We arrived at the pub and all seemed quiet. It certainly wasn't as busy as the last time we had been here. Scott and Caroline were already there and were chatting away with Gregg, it looked as if he was happy to be Scott's best man. Jacob had spoken with Eddie and he was delighted as well. Everything was coming together nicely.

Caroline and I had been into London for the day to find our outfits. They were being adjusted and then we would go in once more before the big day for a final fitting. The bridesmaids dresses had been purchased and were now hanging up in their bedroom at Scott's house. All the accessories were in there as well.

We'd had meetings with the hotel to decide on menu's and table layouts. We had also spoken with Gerald, the vicar at the local church and the order of ceremony had been agreed. Jacob has asked the local florist to decorate the church in whatever way they wanted. He gave them full reign to use whatever they thought appropriate. He had also organised for flowers for the hotel to be delivered and arranged. Bouquets for both Caroline and I had been ordered along with baskets of rose petals for Becki and Melisa. They would burst before the day, they were so excited. Buttonholes for all the men had also been ordered. The florist was over the moon. This is the biggest occasion she has done by far she said.

There didn't seem much else to worry about, so we went into the pub and met Caroline and Scott then went to sit in our favourite seats.

Mary came to congratulate us then took our drinks order. She was puzzled when we all ordered a jug of water and a fruit juice each.

Jacob said, "Sit here with us a moment, Mary. We have some news for you. Keep it to yourselves though for now."

"Of course, Jacob," she said, "you know we never indulge in tittle-tattle. What's to do?"

"Well, Scott, first I think," Scott cleared his throat and said, "Well, you know that we are getting married next week?"

"Of course, I know. We are guests after all."

"True," said Scott, "but what you don't know yet is that Caroline and I are pregnant."

"Oh! Scott, that is amazing news. Congratulations to you both. I am so pleased for you. What amazing news."

"That has made me all of a flutter," she said, "now young Jacob, what is your news?"

"Well, not to be outdone by my brother we are also pregnant, with twins."

I thought Mary would do a handstand, she was so excited. "How bloody lovely for you all. That is amazing, you will all make fabulous parents. God, I feel like crying with happiness."

"I will get your drinks and thank you for trusting me with your news. I won't tell a soul," she said. She hurried off to get our drinks then came back with the menus and the drinks on a tray.

She put them down on the table then went all soppy again. "I am so happy for you all. You are such great lads she said and now you have these amazing young women and babies on the way. Brilliant."

She left us again to go to serve some other people that had just arrived. We looked at the menu and I couldn't decide what to have. I have never been so spoilt for such choices of food. Our diet at the farm was very basic to say the least.

Jacob said, "I think I will have the sausages and mash in a giant Yorkie."

"I will go with that as well," I said. Scott decided to have ham, egg and chips and Caroline went for a chicken salad.

Each time Mary caught sight of us she would smile, a very knowing smile. She was happy.

We sat and went through all the arrangements to make sure we had done everything we could do. We could none of us think of anything else. All the invitations had been sent out four days previous and we were starting to get acceptance cards and phone calls. No one has said they can't come yet. I guess it is an honour to be able to witness these two handsome hunks finally tying the knot.

All that remained to do was to hand out the invitations to the press guys. That would surprise them I thought.

We ate our meals in peace and enjoyed being with each other away from the house. It was when we got up to leave that things went a bit silly. Somehow some of the press guys had found us in the pub and were waiting for us to leave.

"Let's tell them to follow us back to the house because we have something for them," I suggested. The others agreed, get it over with or as Caroline put it, rip the plaster off in one go.

"Okay," said Jacob, "if you are sure."

"Go for it," we said.

There were a few people sitting around in the pub and our men spoke to most of them as we passed. Locals, I guessed.

"Do you want to do this?" Jacob asked Scott.?

"God, no mate, it's all yours."

"Thanks for that," said Jacob. "Okay, are you all with me?"

"Go for it," was the reply.

As we stepped outside, the pressmen seemed to appear from nowhere and began clicking away with their cameras.

"Okay guys, can I get you to stop what you are doing for a moment. Thank you."

"Ella and I will be going back to Scott's house and we want you all to accompany us. We have something for you."

"What's that then, Jacob?" asked one guy.

"You will have to wait and see. You all know where he lives. See you there, we will be walking. Scott has an appointment so won't be joining us."

"Right, Scott, Caroline, see you back at the house later." They shook hands and cheeks were kissed. They went off to their appointment with the doctor and we set off walking back to the house.

It must have looked quite the sight, Jacob and I leading the way and all these press guys following behind.

Once we reached the house, Jacob said, "Can I ask you to come into the house two at a time? You will all receive the same thing so there is no need for a rush."

"Okay," they all chorused.

Jacob and I went in first, Mrs H was just getting ready to leave so she said, "I will have to stay to see this. I will man the door. "Two at a time you say, Jacob."

"Yes, please Mrs H and thank you."

We sat at the breakfast bar with the pile of envelopes in front of us. We hadn't put names on them but asked for acceptances so we would know how many to cater for.

"Okay, Mrs H," called Jacob, "let the first ones in."

"This is all very mysterious Jacob, what's going on? Asked the first two men."

Of course, they all knew we were getting married but had no idea about these invitations.

"As you know, we are getting married next week and we wanted to invite you all along to the reception."

"Really?" they both said.

"Yes, really," replied Jacob. "All we ask is that you treat the occasion with respect and have a good time."

"Of course, we will," they said. "This is very kind of you both. Never had this happen before."

Jacob grinned, "You are nearly always kind and respectful to me and Ella thought it would be a way to thank you all."

"Thank you, Jacob. It is very much appreciated."

"Just one more thing. This will be a double wedding. My brother Scott and his partner Caroline will be getting hitched alongside of us. We are all good friends and were both planning to get married at the same time, so this seemed to make sense."

"Fantastic Jacob, good luck to you all. I will definitely be there."

"Please bring your partners along as well if they would like to come, just let us know in plenty of time so that the caterers get plenty of warning."

"Will do Jacob and thanks."

They left happy and the next two were let in.

They all seemed very happy with their invitations and all promised to be respectful of the day. "Let's hope they stick to it," said Jacob.

"I'm sure they will. Like they said, it has never happened before. If they mess it up it won't happen again."

"Trust you to find the positives," he said.

Once they had all left, Mrs H left for home chuckling to herself.

"She seems happy," I said.

"She is," said Jacob, "she treats us like her own kids and is just happy to see us happy."

"How long do you think Scott and Caroline will be?" I asked.?

Jacob looked at his watch, "At least another hour, I should think. They are going over to see the girls after the doctors, could be even longer."

"Good," I said, "get your arse up those stairs, Mr Perfect Superstar. I've had enough of being very gentle, I need some loving, Jacob style."

"Is that right?" he said,

"It certainly is I replied. I think I will explode if I have to wait any longer."

"Right, I will turn the key in the door and by the time I get up those stairs I expect to find you suitably naked and wanting."

"I didn't need to telling twice." I quickly went up the stairs and stripped off all my clothes. By the time Jacob reached the door, I was ready for him.

"Strip off before you come anywhere near me," I said. He did and it was obvious he was more than ready.

He climbed onto the bed and began kissing me with an urgent passion. He kissed my lips, my neck then my breasts, finally taking each nipple into his mouth and gently sucking each one in turn.

I began to squirm on the bed, I wanted Jacob so badly. "Now Jacob, I need you now." He slid inside me and it felt wonderful. He began to move, and I joined him in this wondrous joining of the two of us.

My orgasm was epic, I burst all around him, over and over again. I felt him explode into me and I loved him more and more.

"Thank you, Jacob, I said, I really needed that."

" So did I," he said, "I can't live without you, Ella. You are my heart and my soul and I love you so much, my darling"

"As I love you, my darling," I said.

We stayed in bed for a couple of hours and still Scott and Caroline hadn't returned. "Hope everything is okay with them," said Jacob. "I couldn't stand any more bad luck."

We showered and dressed then went downstairs in search of food. Jacob still had a couple more nights at the theatre before the show finally closed. Poor lamb, he must be knackered. He could do with a rest after that but no such luck. The wedding would only be a week away, so he won't be able to rest until after that. A holiday in France would sort him out I'm sure.

I was getting excited at the prospect of becoming Mrs Ryan and also going to France. What a treat for me. Never travelled more than ten miles from the place I was born before coming to London and now France. Where next I wondered.

We decided on sandwiches again having eaten in the pub earlier. I made enough for when Scott and Caroline returned. I was just putting all the things away that I had been using when I heard a car on the drive. "Jacob, I think they are here?"

Jacob went to open the front door, I heard him ask if everything was okay.

"Yes, fine," they both said.

"I thought you would have been back before now,' said Jacob.

"We would have been, but we had to go to the hospital for a scan before picking the girls up."

"Why did you need a scan?" asked Jacob.

"Come on, let's get inside and we can tell you all about it."

They removed their outdoor clothes in the hallway and then came through to the kitchen. "Tea?" I asked.

"Yes, please," they both said. I busied myself putting the kettle on and laying the tray whilst the others all found seats. Jacob came to carry the tray down to the seating area and I carried the plates of sandwiches.

"Right, it's quite funny really," he said. "We went to see the doctor to get Caroline registered as you know and he decided to send us for a scan. We had been talking about you two expecting twins and I happened to mention that there are a few sets in our family history although my two were born apart."

"Caroline then threw in the fact that she was a twin also, her sister had died when she was baby so she rarely thought about being a twin. She then said that her mother had also been a twin so the doctor thought it would be a good idea to get a scan done early so we know what we are dealing with."

"So, brother you are not the only one expecting twins. It was a bloody shock to start with I can tell you. I hadn't given it a thought before. Quite exciting now the shock has worn off though."

"Anyway, we called into the pub and had a coffee to calm us down before picking the girls up. Of course, we had to tell them the news and they were so excited. I think they are of the opinion they can have one each. You know, like a doll."

Jacob and I sat listening to this story. "Scott, can you slow down a bit? Are you telling us that you are also expecting twins?"

"Yes, we are, didn't I say?"

"Well, yes, you did but it all sounded so unbelievable it didn't quite register. Congratulations to you both. How amazing is this?" said Jacob.

"Truly amazing," I said. "Do you two always do everything together? If so, then Caroline and I will have to keep a check on you both, it might give us prior warning of some great event in the future."

"We all hugged one another then I asked Caroline, how do you feel about it then?

"Shell shocked actually," she said. "I never gave it a thought but now it is sinking in I think it will be amazing."

"The doctor wants to keep an eye on my blood pressure though. It was a bit high when he checked it, so we bought a blood pressure monitor for here. We can all use it. I think mine was high because of the situation. If I sit and relax before taking it I bet it will be lower. Anyway, it will be a good idea for us both to keep a check on our blood pressures then if it does go up we can get it sorted straight away."

"Okay," I said, sounds like a plan. Really though Caroline I am so pleased for you. You too have suffered in the past and it is great that things are going well for you now. Even our men have suffered, look how Scott's wife treated him and poor Jacob having to deal with that raving lunatic, Cleo."

"We have all had bad things happen but not any longer. We have two adorable, dependable and very bloody sexy men by our sides. I for one am more than happy with how my life is going now."

"Let's have a nice cuppa and toast our good luck," said Jacob.

"Yes" let's we all chorused. So that is how we toasted our good fortune. *All meeting because of something dreadful happening but turning it around and finding so much love and happiness between us.*"

It was soon time for Jacob to leave for his penultimate show. He said that if I wanted to stay behind tonight he wouldn't mind.

"Well, I would mind," I said. "If you are let out on your own heaven knows what women will try to snag you. You are mine, Mr Ryan whether you like it or not."

"Well, soon to be Mrs Ryan, I do like it, I like it a lot. Come on then, get your arse into gear woman. You will make me late."

I was ready to go. We both went to shake hands with and kiss Scott and Caroline. "Really are made up for you both," said Jacob.

"So am I, we are going to be able to start our own school at this rate"

We heard the car pull up and we left the house, this time though Jacob said that I was to get in the car and sit down next to him. No need to lie down now.

"The whole world will soon know all there is to know about us and our wedding so we might just as well start now."

"Okay," I said if you say so.

"I do," replied Jacob. "I love you so much, my darling and I want the whole world to know."

We left the house holding hands and then climbed into the back of the car. There were a few flashes as we left the house but nothing like the mad scramble of the previous nights.

The security man asked Jacob what he wanted to do when we reached the theatre. Back entrance again?

"Find out what it is like before we make a decision. If there are not too many people there then we might risk the stage door."

"Okay sir," he said. I will get an update when we are nearer the theatre."

Word must have gone around that Jacob was now using the rear entrance so there wasn't much point in hanging around the stage door.

"Not too bad sir," the security man said.

"Okay then," said Jacob, "let's do this. Just make sure that Ella is kept safe, please."

"I will, sir. Will you be going in together or do you want me to escort her in first?"

"No, she can be by my side, but just be aware of anyone going over the top, please."

"Will do sir, I will be right behind you both."

This will be something new, I thought. Hope I can pull it off. I know some of Jacob's fans can be very protective of him. If they think I am not right for him then they will let me know.

The car drew up next to the stage door where a small crowd of people were waiting. The door was opened for us by the driver, and we stepped out.

I was holding on to Jacob's hand very tightly, but I needn't have worried. They were all fine. All of them wanted to speak to Jacob and he was happy to do so. "Have you all met my fiancée?" he asked?.

"This is Ella and I love her more than life itself." Well, they could be in no doubt about his feelings now I thought.

The crowd were really nice though. They spoke with me as well as Jacob and wished us luck in our futures together. That was really lovely I thought.

"When's the wedding then Jacob?" someone asked. "A week tomorrow, he replied, and I for one can't wait."

"So soon?" someone else asked.

"Yes," he said, "I can't wait to make Ella my wife. She will be by my side for the rest of our days he said. I am one very lucky man."

There was a ripple of applause as we finished speaking with the crowd. Good luck to you both, people were calling.

"Thank you all so much, you are very kind," I said.

Finally, we made it inside and made our way to Jacob's dressing room. Eddie was in there waiting for us.

"Hi, you two," he said as we entered. "All good out there tonight?" he asked.

"Yes, fine," said Jacob. "Not too many waiting, so I thought we would give it a go. They were all very respectful and kind."

"How are you and the family Eddie?" he asked?

"All good, thanks mate, looking forward to your nuptials. Eileen is so excited, it's been a while since we have been to a wedding and now I'm to be your best man, so she thinks it is awesome." "All the plans coming together then?"

"Yes, all sorted we think don't we, my love?"

"Definitely," I said, "can't think of anything else. Just waiting for the clock to tick down now."

"Your plan to invite all the press guys seems to have gone down well. Only heard good things so far. A stroke of genius that."

"Don't thank me for that," Jacob said, "that was Ella's idea. Glad they all like the plan though. It has put the bill up a bit, but it will be worth it, I think."

"I think you are right," said Eddie, "like I said a stroke of genius. If you have any more thoughts about how things should be run Ella then let me know. It would make my life a lot easier."

"Now Jacob, tomorrow night. Have you got everything sorted regarding your guests?

"Yes, of course, I have. I pre-booked forty seats so that will be plenty. Stop worrying."

"One more thing Jacob, have you heard any more about what is happening with Cleo?"

"No, have you?

Eddie looked a bit stunned. "Well, yes, I have. You know she is out on bail but is not allowed anywhere near you or Ella."

"Yes, of course, I know that," he replied. "What else have you heard?"

"She is going around telling anyone who will listen she is going to be here tomorrow night and is going to ruin the night for you and your fiancée."

"Oh, God, I said, not again, please."

"Don't worry darling, I have extra security on the doors. If she tries to get in then they will get her removed and transported to the nearest police station. I can't understand what is wrong with the woman. It is all her own fault in the first place. Now, she can see how happy I am with you and has decided she should be with me. Well, that will never happen."

Eddie said, "I have spoken with the police and told them what she is saying. They have a call out for her. If she makes a move then they will arrest her again. I think she has totally lost the plot. Never could understand what you saw in her. A complete loon as far as I can tell."

"Well, you know I was in a bad place before all that started," said Jacob. I think she picked up on my vulnerable side and just went for it. Of course, when she started seeing Arlo she thought she had it made. Him to provide all the love and affection and me to supply the money and a way into what she really wanted. I can't see any of the theatres or film companies giving her work. She would be a terrible actress anyway."

I sat listening to this but didn't interrupt. I hadn't given a thought as to what had or hadn't happened to her. So long as she kept well away from me and mine I was happy. Maybe I should have taken more of an interest.

I'm not particularly worried for myself but for poor Jacob and our unborn babies. Whatever had he done to deserve this? Once our wedding is over and we can get away to France then we can get on with our lives without having to worry about her and her lunatic ideas.

Once Eddie and Jacob had finished talking Eddie left saying he would see us the next night and not to worry too much.

Then Jacob said, "I had better get ready. They will be starting without me."

"Okay, night both".

"Goodnight Eddie," I called.

Jacob was sitting in the dressing chair. He looked in despair. I went over to him and put my arms around his neck.

Don't worry darling. We will be safe," I said.

He reached for my arms and pulled me round to the front of him then he put me on his knee, wrapping his arms around me.

"Oh God, Ella, what a cow she is proving to be. If she hurts you or our babies I swear I will kill the stupid bitch. As soon as our wedding is over, and we can get over to the house in France then we need to think about our futures. I don't want to be this person who is always out there, doing the next project and then looking for the one after that. I want to be with you and our children, safe and happy together, not on this continual treadmill".

"Don't ever leave me Ella, please. I love you so very much."

"I won't leave you, my darling. We have a brilliant future together all mapped out for us. Now stop worrying, kiss me then get yourself ready to *wow* all those ladies".

He did kiss me with so much love and passion. I knew at that moment that we would be together forever and always happy.

He quickly got ready for his performance. He looked as gorgeous as ever. I kissed him and told him once more how much I loved him. "Now go," I said.

"Okay, come on fiancée, come and give me inspiration."

We held hands as we walked to the side of the stage, ready for Jacob to make his entrance.

The band were already coming to the end of their intro. A microphone was put in Jacob's hand and he began to sing.

Slowly, he walked onto the stage singing his heart out. I really love that song and the emotion he puts into it makes it even more special.

Once that song was over he went into his routine with renewed vigour. All doubts had left him, and he just did the most amazing performance. He had sent some tickets to the hospital that had treated me following the attack and also to the ambulance crew that had looked after me as a thank you and some of those staff were in tonight. They were cheering and shouting along with the rest of the audience. Finally, it was time for his last song. This one, he always dedicated to me. Most nights when he sang this song it made me cry a little but tonight as he was making his dedication he called out for me to join him on stage.

"I can't do that," I said.

One of the stagehands was standing by me. "Go on Ella, he wants you by his side".

Shaking like a leaf I went to join him on stage. He put his arms around me, pulling me to him and kissing me in front of another full house. The audience went wild. Screaming and shouting Ella, Ella, Ella. I felt so emotional. They seemed to have accepted me as part of Jacob's life which is amazing.

Jacob continued to hold me tightly to him then he began to sing, what he referred to as 'our song'.

And so the song went on. Jacob singing this lovely song, especially for me.

As the song finished he pulled me in for another passionate kiss. "Thank you Ella for agreeing to be by my side forever. I love you, my darling."

"And I love you my dear, sweet man. Forever and a day. Until death do us apart". He kissed me once more then walked me back to my seat.

"Sorry about that folks," he said. "I just love that woman so much I want the whole world to know."

I sat there shaking, why did he do that the bugger I thought. Just wait till I get him home. I thought about what he had done then and began to beam. He loves me that much. I am so very lucky.

He had come off the stage and stood by me.

"One more my darling then home to bed".

"Promise" I asked.

"Promise" he said. He walked back on stage then for his final number.

"Okay folks, what's it to be?"

There were shouts of a few songs, but the overwhelming request was for *'The Impossible Dream'*. "Okay, he said, let me get my breath back."

He took a long drink of water from a glass he kept on the piano then the intro began. *Such a hauntingly beautiful song. He started singing and I could feel the beat in my chest. It was the same each time he sang that song. So much power in his voice. I love it. It will be strange after tomorrow's last show. No more listening to this wonderful man singing just for me, or maybe he would sing just for me.*

He left the stage at the end of that song, he was totally drained. It will be good for him once tomorrow is over. He can then rest properly. Then our wedding, then our honeymoon in France. So excited.

Jacob had invited the hospital workers who came tonight to join us in his dressing room for a drink. I thought that was a lovely gesture. There were eight of them. Two were doctors three nurses, two ambulance men and one lady off reception.

They arrived at the dressing room door all of a fluster. I let them in and then explained that Jacob was just having a quick shower before coming to meet them. I poured them all a glass of champagne that Jacob had organised and was just handing them out when the man of the moment came through from his shower, he looked a million dollars. His tired eyes looked better for the shower. He had on black jeans, his favourite and a lovely dark green shirt that matched his eyes. He went over to his guests and shook their hands thanking them for the care we had received on the night of the attack.

"What did you think of the show"he asked?

They were all full of praise. Said it was the best show they had ever seen. They also said it was such a shame it was finishing after tomorrow.

Jacob laughed, "I do need a rest occasionally he said. Also, Ella and I will be getting married next week then we are taking a long honeymoon. I think we deserve that, don't you?"

They all agreed. One of the doctors said that his work ethic was one to be admired. You may not work the hours that some do but my goodness the effort that goes into your shows is epic.

They all agreed. Jacob was so natural with them. He put them at their ease instantly. They finished their drinks then all had photographs taken with Jacob and then with me as well.

The older doctor who was with them said, "Jacob, I want to thank you personally for your impromptu performance the other evening at the hospital. It put everyone in a good mood, and they all appreciated it."

"That's okay," he said, "they didn't give me much option, to be honest. Once everyone realised who I was it was more of a demand. Just glad I was able to put a smile on some faces and that we got a brilliant outcome after Ella's attack."

"We are just there to help," the doctor said.

"I tell you what," said Jacob. "How about we organise a fundraiser for the hospital say nearer Christmas. I can get my agent to rope in some of the other acts he has on his books and I will definitely perform. What do you think?"

"What do we think? We think 'yes please' that will be amazing."

"Okay, give me your details, name, and phone number then I will speak with Eddie, get the wheels in motion. I will be busy myself for the next few weeks, but I will get Eddie to ring you and then we can begin to sort something out. Will that be all right with you all?"

"Mr Ryan, you are wonderful."

"Well, thank you," said Jacob, "but please, my name is Jacob, and I will be pleased if you all call me that."

They were all eating out of his hand. He has such a wonderful, charming way about him. How could anyone not adore him?

"I believe another party from the hospital will be joining us tomorrow evening so if you would tell them that they are all invited back here after the show."

"We will Jacob and thank you so much. It means such a lot to us."

"Well, what you do for all of us means a lot, especially what you did for Ella and me. I won't ever forget that."

It was time for them to leave. Jacob shook hands with the men and kissed the ladies on the cheek making their night complete. I shook all their hands as well, thanking them once more for all their help.

They left the dressing room and the young stagehand escorted them to the stage door and let them out into the night. I could just imagine those left waiting outside wondering who the hell are they that they get invited backstage.

Jacob put his arms around me, "I am knackered," he said.

"I know sweetheart, come on let's get you home. A nice long sleep is what you need."

"I do," he said "but I so want to make love to you as well."

"That would be nice, but I think sleep tonight and then love in the morning when you are feeling refreshed."

"Okay, if you don't mind."

"I don't mind at all," I said. "I love you and want you with me forever more. If you keep performing the way you do then loving me half the night then forever won't be very long and I want you with me till we are old and grey. Understand?"

"I do," he said, "just to sleep with you in my bed is wonderful then when we wake up, Oh, the love we can make."

I laughed at him. "Do you want me to find out if there are many fans waiting? We could just escape through the back way."

"Let's see what security thinks? He picked his mobile up and rang them. I guessed from one side of the conversation I could hear that there were a few people hanging about but not too bad."

"Okay, he said, stage door it is then. Get the car ready to go, please. I don't want to hang around half the night."

He switched his phone off then took me in his arms and kissed me once more.

"Jacob, I could drown in your kisses," I said.

"I know how you feel he said. I just love kissing you too. We really were made for each other don't you think?"

"I do I said." I kissed him again then said, "come on Mr Superstar, let's get you out there making your fans happy and weak at the knees, then home and bed."

" Okay," he said. "Getting quite bossy, aren't you?"

"Only where you are concerned my darling."

We linked arms and walked from the dressing room, along the corridor and out into the fresh air. There was a huge round of applause as we came out. "Blimey!" said Jacob, "what did we do to deserve that?"

"Someone said "you brought Ella out with you. It's great that you share her with us."

I thought that was such a lovely thing for them to say. Jacob said, "Well, I am very proud of her. I want you all to love her as I do."

"We do," they all said. I felt myself blush. They don't know me but are prepared to accept me because of their love for Jacob. Isn't that amazing?

We spoke with all those people waiting, they appeared to want to speak with me as much as Jacob. I was just happy that I could take some of the work off his shoulders. I really needed to get him home.

"Come on tiger," I said, "home time." The crowd all laughed at that, but they made a way through for us and we were soon sat in the car and heading for home.

Jacob was stroking my fingers all the way home, "you are amazing Ella, did you know that?"

"I didn't no but I do now was all I said."

By the time we reached Scott's house, Jacob was almost asleep.

"Come on sweetheart," I said, "we are home."

The driver got out and opened the door for us. Jacob managed a thanks guys before we reached the front door.

Thankfully, Scott and Caroline had gone up to bed. I guided Jacob into the kitchen and then sat him down.

"Do you need food?" I asked?"

"No thanks, I'm all right. What about a drink then?"

"I could murder a mug of tea," he said.

So could I so I put the kettle on and set the mugs ready. Jacob was leaning across the island.

"If you stay there Mr you will be asleep. Come on, upstairs. I will bring the tea up."

I quickly made the tea and then prodded Jacob again. "Come on tiger, bed."

"Okay," he said. He managed to get to his feet and then climbed the stairs. I followed him into the bedroom, putting the tea down on the bedside cabinet.

"Okay, let's get your clothes off."

I helped to strip his clothes off then he just lay back on the pillow. Within seconds he was snoring softly. I lifted his legs and pulled the covers over him. I went to my side of the bed and sat sipping my tea. Just what I needed. *I wish Jacob had managed to drink his, but he was just so tired. I hope he's not sickening for something. He gets tired but never this bad. I will have to keep an eye on him.*

I finished my tea, used the bathroom then climbed into bed next to Jacob. I reached over and felt his forehead. No temperature thank goodness. I put my hand on his chest and kept it there thinking that if there was a change in his breathing then I would feel it.

He slept the night away and was still sleeping at eight the next morning. I got up and put my dressing gown on then went downstairs to make fresh tea.

Caroline and Scott were already up and drinking their own tea. "Where's Jacob?" asked Scott."

"Still sleeping" I said.

"That's not like him, is he okay?"

"I'm not sure, to be honest," I told them how he had been the previous night. He seemed fine then all of a sudden he came over really tired. I just put it down to it being a busy night and a long week. He is in desperate need of a break.

"This doesn't sound right to me, Ella. What did he have to drink say towards the end of the night before he became sleepy?"

I tried to think. "I didn't see him drink anything apart from the water he had on stage."

"Did he sip it or take a big drink?"

"He had a big drink, it was just before his last number and he said he was dry."

Scott said "wait here, I am going to check on him."

197

He flew up the stairs and into our room. He came down again a few minutes later.

"I think someone has drugged him. He won't wake up."

"Ella, get dressed and put some money in your bag. Caroline can you get dressed as well? I am going to ring for an ambulance."

I was in a mad panic. No, how could this happen and why didn't I do something last night? I did as Scott said so by the time the ambulance arrived I was ready to go with Jacob.

He was still asleep. The ambulance men were asking me questions and I answered as best I could. *Scott had been on the phone to the theatre and was asking if the glass of water that Jacob had used the previous night was still there. There was a lull in conversation whilst they went to check I guess. I was so confused, how could this be happening? My poor, beautiful Jacob. God, I hope he doesn't die. I couldn't live without him now.*

Whoever Scott spoke to must have come back to the phone. "Okay thanks, I will come straight round to collect it. Please put it safe and don't let anyone else touch it. No, don't wash it, please. I won't be long."

The ambulance men were doing tests on Jacob.

"I think you are right sir, it looks as if he has been drugged. I don't think it is anything that will be fatal, just put him to sleep. We will take him in though and get him checked out properly."

Scott said that he had spoken with the theatre and the glass that Jacob had used the night before was still there. He was going to collect it and then take it with him to the hospital. It may be useful.

"That's great thank you, sir. It will be very useful." He turned to me, "Did you see who put the water ready for him?

"No, sorry, it was just there. Always is every night, he usually sips it throughout the evening but last night was very warm in the theatre and he had been doing a lot of very powerful songs. I did notice that before he sang his last song. He picked the glass up and drank at least half of it straight off. Do you really think he has been drugged?"

"It looks like it, but they will be able to do tests at the hospital to determine exactly what has happened. I do think the police should be informed though. This is a very dangerous thing to do. Does he have any enemies that you know of?"

"Cleo, but how would she have been able to put something in the water? I began to shake, why hadn't I done something the night before? If Jacob dies it will be my fault."

"Caroline came and put her arms around me. "Now less of that," she said. "How were you to know what had happened? Jacob does get very tired some nights, doesn't he?"

I had to admit that, "Yes, he does get tired, but this is crazy. Thank goodness Scott has his wits about him."

They managed to get Jacob onto a trolley and downstairs. Scott said that he would go to the theatre and then drive straight to the hospital. Caroline was going to stay with me. The ambulance men said that she could come with us as I was pregnant and needed the support. They were very kind.

We collected all the bits and pieces we thought we may need then got on board the ambulance with Jacob. He just looked to be asleep. But this was way too much. He would never sleep this long. I guess Scott is right.

If this is down to Cleo, she wants locking up and the key thrown away.

As we arrived at the hospital Scott pulled up in his car. He had the glass in a brown paper bag. He came over to us and we all piled into A & E. I went with Scott to the reception to give all Jacobs details. Whilst we were doing that Jacob was being taken through to a cubicle. Scott then went with him and was explaining his theory to a doctor. The doctor took the glass and went off with it.

We sat outside in the reception whilst they did various things to Jacob then a nurse came and called us through.

"He is waking up she said. He is just very confused and keeps asking for Ella."

"That's me, I said, I'm his fiancée."

"So he keeps telling anyone who will listen to him. Come on through, he may calm down when he sees you."

I followed her through the doors and then behind a curtain. There he was looking very confused indeed.

"Ella, thank goodness you are here. What the hell is happening? I can't remember anything after we left the theatre last night. The doctor was saying he thinks I have been drugged."

"It looks that way, my darling."

"You fell asleep and we couldn't wake you. Scott was asking me what you had to drink last night, all I could remember was the glass of water you had on stage. Scott rang the theatre, and they found the glass. He has brought it here and they have taken it off somewhere to do tests."

"The ambulance men asked me if you had any enemies. All I can think of is Cleo, she wouldn't do that to you, would she?"

"Probably," he said, "she has a screw loose. But how would she manage to put something in my water glass?"

"We don't know but I think they will call the police in once they find out what it is you have had. How do you feel now, my love?"

"Confused really. I am still a bit groggy, but it is becoming clearer as time goes on. I am bloody hungry though. Will they let me have something to eat, do you think? And something to drink, I am really thirsty."

"Let's just wait and see what they come back with. They may let you home soon if you are feeling better."

"I hope so," he said. "Will I be able to do the show tonight, do you think?"

"Let's hope so but we need to find out what it is you have had and who it is that has done this awful thing to you."

"Well, if it's not Cleo, then I have no idea," he said. "God, why can't she just leave us alone and let us enjoy our lives together? Anyway my darling, how are you and our two little Ryan's doing?"

" We are fine," I said, just so long as you are going to be okay."

"I will be okay once I can eat something and have a nice cup of tea." Just then the curtain opened, and a lady came in with a plate of toast and a cup of tea for the patient.

She looked at Jacob and then said, "It is you, it really is you."

"Yes, it definitely is me," said Jacob. "Thank you so much for this he said. I was desperate for food and a drink, you are a lifesaver. What's your name?"

"Vera, yes Vera. She looked totally gobsmacked."

I put my hand on her shoulder. "He won't bite," I said to her.

She turned and looked at me. "You're Ella, aren't you?"

"Yes, I am," I said. How did you know that?"

"I was in the audience a few weeks ago when he introduced you to everyone. It was such a lovely moment."

"It was I said, I hadn't a clue who he was until that night. When he walked out on stage I could have dropped through the floor."

"I could tell you were shocked she said, I was sitting just behind you."

She turned to Jacob then. "I love your voice, Jacob. I play your music every day. The beautiful songs you sing mean so much to me."

"Why thank you, Vera. I don't suppose you will be there tonight, will you?"

" No, I tried to get a ticket but they were all sold out."

"Well, if you haven't anything better to do, would you come along as one of my special guests and then come backstage afterwards for a glass of something bubbly?"

"She turned and looked at me. Is he joking Ella?"

"No Vera, he is not joking. If you want we can pick you up on the way there and then we can introduce you to the other guests before the show."

"I think I am dreaming," she said.

"No, you're not dreaming," said Jacob. "I know, let's get Scott and Caroline to pick Vera up then she won't feel so alone."

"Brilliant idea," I said. "I will go and fetch them then you can make your arrangements. They are just out in the reception area."

"I know, come with me now, let's introduce you to them."

A very shaky Vera followed me out to find Scott and Caroline, I introduced them and asked if they would be able to pick her up later and take her with them to the theatre. Jacob has asked that she be included in his private party.

"Of course, we will," said Scott, poor Vera, she really did think she was dreaming. Caroline will look after her I know."

"I then said to her that several of the hospital staff would be there tonight as well so you will know a few people."

"Is this really happening to me, Ella?

"It is," I said. "Jacob is a wonderful man, and he likes to treat his fans whenever he can. All we need to do now is get the all-clear from the doctors."

I felt her pull on my arm, "Ella, is that really Jacob's brother."

"Yes, of course, he and Jacob are very close as are Caroline and myself. You do know we are getting married next week?"

"I had heard that 'yes' but didn't know how true it was."

"It is definitely true, we are having a double wedding with Scott and Caroline, that is how close we all are."

"Well, I think you are all amazing. You two will be beautiful brides and the men, well, who could say no to those pair?"

I laughed with her. "Not me, for sure. I love the very bones of him. I just hope all this nonsense stops. It is very worrying how easy it was for someone to drop something into Jacob's water glass."

"At least once we are married we will be taking a few weeks away so that Jacob can really rest. Once the babies arrive he will be doubly busy."

"Did I hear you right, are you pregnant?"

"I am, I said, with twins. Please keep that information to yourself for now, won't you?"

"I will, I promise. I am so happy for you both, what wonderful parents you will make."

"Now Vera, I am going to leave you with Scott so that you can tell him where you live and arrange what time you are to be picked up. I am going back to Jacob to see if he is still improving. See you later," I said.

I went back to Jacob and was pleased to see he now had some colour back in his cheeks. His eyes looked brighter, and he seemed almost back to his normal happy self.

"You have made Vera very happy," I said. "She can't believe what is happening. She seems a really nice lady."

"That's what I thought," he said, "so why not give her a treat."

"I told her about the wedding and the babies, she promised to keep it to herself. The news has made her really happy as well."

"Would it be possible for her to come to the wedding, do you think I asked?"

"I don't see why not, she has been a fan for a long time. I have seen her many times in the audience. Always seems to be on her own, though."

"We can ask her tonight about the wedding," I suggested.

"Good idea he said. "She won't be able to sleep all week she will be that excited."

Jacob said, "I like her, I recognised her as soon as she came through the curtain. She's not a nurse as such but helps wherever she is needed and does jobs like keeping grumpy patients filled up with food."

"Have you seen anybody whilst I was out there?"

"No, not yet hope they don't keep me here for long though. Am I still on that promise from yesterday?"

"I should think I might be persuaded if you promise to be good."

"Why, aren't I always good?" he asked?.

"You are my darling, very good. I do love you so much.

"You really scared me, Jacob. I thought you were just very tired but then when you wouldn't wake up this morning I got really scared. I thought you were going to die." I felt the tears prickle at the side of my eyes and then run down my cheeks. "Do you really think it was Cleo?"

"I can't think of anyone else, to be honest," he said. "I have been wondering if she got one of the theatre staff to do it for her. I can't see any other way."

The curtains opened then and a doctor I hadn't seen before came through.

"Mr Ryan, how are you feeling now?"

"Much better, thank you, doctor. Do you have any explanation as to why this has happened to me?"

"I do, thanks to the quick thinking of your brother I believe, he retrieved the glass you had used last night, and we have done some tests and found significant traces of a drug used to induce sleep. I take it you know nothing of this."

"I don't, doctor, and it is very worrying as to how easy it was for someone to drop something into the glass without anyone seeing. Will there be any after-effects?"

"No, thankfully, once it has passed through your system then it is gone. You should feel fine now. Have you eaten anything?"

"I have, thank you, Vera bought me tea and toast a while ago. I was feeling very hungry and that made me grumpy, but as soon as I had eaten the toast I began to feel normal."

"Good, that's what we like to hear. They tell me you have another show to do tonight."

"I do yes, the last one of a ten-week run. Then next week we get married and will be off on a long honeymoon in France so I will be able to catch up on some sleep."

"That's lovely, Mr Ryan, congratulations. You should be fine by tonight, but I do want you to consider calling the police in on this.

Thankfully we have a good outcome, but it could have been so much worse."

"I will be doing that definitely. Can I give them your name if they need to speak to anyone here?"

"Certainly, I have all the results and findings and with your permission we will co-operate with the police in any way we can."

"Can I ask you doctor, will you be in the party from here tonight that are coming to see the show?

" Regrettably no, they drew the numbers out of a hat and mine wasn't one of them."

"Well, if you would like to come tonight as one of my guests that can be arranged."

"Really? Why thank you very much."

"Do you have a wife?"

"I do yes, she has all of your albums, plays them all the time."

"Well, bring her along too. Jot your names down for me then I will let them know at the stage door to expect you. If you can be there for say six thirty then you can have a drink with us before the show."

"That is exceptionally kind of you Mr Ryan. My wife will be over the moon. I had better ring her and warn her to be ready."

"I will get my houseman to come and discharge you, you can get off home then so you can rest before tonight."

I smiled to myself thinking he has a promise to fulfil before he can rest. I am just so relieved he is okay. I couldn't stand it if he had been really ill or even died.

"Thank you, doctor we both said, see you later."

"Have all your allocation of seats for tonight been filled now? I asked.?

"No, I think there are still a couple left, why?"

"Nothing really, I wasn't sure how many you had and how many were left that's all."

"Did Scott think to bring me some clothes he asked?"

"Not sure, I'll go and ask him. If not I will wrap you in a car blanket. I want you home."

"I went back out to the reception and found Scott, "I don't suppose you thought to bring himself some clothes, did you?"

"I did actually, is he okay to leave then?"

"Yes, just waiting for the houseman to do his discharge forms, then he can go."

"He certainly knows how to cause a storm, doesn't he?" said Scott.

" He does" I replied. The doctor said he should tell the police and they will cooperate with all that they know."

"Someone had put a drug into his water that they use to induce sleep in patients. Thankfully, no further problems are expected but it could have been so much worse. Do you really think it could be Cleo?"

"I can't think of anyone else who would want to harm him. You know what he is like, he puts himself out all the time to help others. Just that stupid cow. If he hadn't been suffering from depression at the time I don't think he would have ever bothered with her. Then, of course, doing what she did just made the depression worse. Thank God, he met you when he did. He certainly fell in love with you very quickly but then so did Caroline and myself. Life's funny sometimes, don't you think?"

"I will nip to the car and get his clothes, won't be long."

I went back to Jacob, the doctor was with him signing his discharge forms. They were having a good old chat. Honestly, that man of mine can talk to anyone. He is such a natural.

He was offering this doctor and his partner the last two seats for tonight's show.

"Are you sure Mr Ryan, that would be awesome? My partner Luke is a big fan of yours and so I know lots of your music. If you are sure I will say yes and thank you very much."

Jacob added his name to the list then explained where to go and who to speak with and also to be there by six thirty.

"There should be quite the contingent from the hospital." "There certainly will be he said. There has been so much talk about it for the past few days, the lucky ones are so excited."

"I will go and ring Luke, he won't believe me when I tell him. Thank you so much."

"No problem" said Jacob, see you later."

Scott arrived with a bag containing clothes for Jacob, I would never have thought of that, thank goodness for Scott.

Jacob was soon dressed, and we were ready to leave.

We entered the reception area and there were dozens of people waiting to be seen. They are so busy all the time. Everyone's heads popped up as we walked in. There were a few open mouths as we passed. I don't think they could believe who was walking past them. Not me of course. Jacob seems to attract attention wherever he goes. He is one very beautiful man though and he is all mine.

We arrived home just before lunchtime, "do you think you should rest for a while? I asked. You have had quite a night."

"I have," he said "and for all of it I was asleep. So no, I don't need to rest."

"I do need to spend a little time with my fiancée though."

"You do I asked?"

"I most certainly do. I think you are on a promise if I remember rightly."

"That is true, I can give you a pass though if you are still a little sleepy."

"Not sleepy at all now, he said."

"Scott, would you two mind very much if I took Ella upstairs? There is something I desperately need to do."

Scott chuckled, "be my guest bro, when needs must? Caroline and I will sort some lunch out. Mrs H has left some stuff in the fridge ready for us. Said she had to leave early so she can make herself beautiful for tonight."

We all laughed, Mrs H is such a sweetie. She will be over the moon once all these babies arrive. Like a proper granny".

Jacob held my hand and took me upstairs. "Come here, my sweet girl he whispered into my hair." He put his arms around me, pulling me into his embrace.

"Jacob, when I realised what had happened last night I was so worried."

"If anything were to happen to you because of me."

"Nothing will happen to me, so long as I have you with me I will be safe and happy."

"What about you though? It would appear that someone won't give up. She certainly wants you badly."

"I am going to ring the police shortly and put them in the picture. They can do what they want with her, lock her up and throw away the key."

"We don't actually know it was Cleo for sure, do we I asked?"

"I would bet my life on it being her. After what she did to you I wouldn't put anything past her. Now come here and love me please."

"Oh, Jacob, I do love you so much. I have been so frightened. I was convinced you were going to die and leave me all alone."

How could you be alone when you will have our two children to love.''

"Two children, I still can't believe it, I said. Just a few weeks ago I was this scared, frightened person, terrified of everything and everyone. Now look at me – Soon-to-be wife to this gorgeous, handsome man and mother of his two babies. It is a bit scary don't you think?"

"Ella, scary it might be, but we are going to do this together and we will be a very happy family. Because of you all my dreams are coming true. Now come and show me just how much you love me."

And so I did, we spent over an hour showing each other how much love we have. Finally we got up, showered, dressed and went downstairs to find some lunch.

"Good to see you are back up to speed bro" said Scott. I rang the police, and they will be round in about an hour."

"Thanks, Scott, this thing needs to be stopped now, before it gets completely out of hand."

They had waited for us before eating themselves, so we all sat around the kitchen island and ate. There was a huge bowl of salad, slices of chicken and ham and fresh bread sliced and ready for buttering.

We had a pot of tea then when that was empty we made a second pot. Scott and Jacob were so far being as good as their word and not drinking any alcohol.

"Scott I need you to add these names to the list of guests for tonight if you don't mind. I will probably forget if its left to me."

"On it Jacob, what about the restaurant? Will all these be coming with us?"

"Yes, they will plus the other guests from the hospital. Can't leave them out, can we? Would you give them a ring at the hospital to let them know what's happening and also they will need to be there by six thirty. Should be quite the party. I must say though I will be glad when it's all over."

"On it, Jacob, we will need a bigger bus as well. Leave it with me."

"One more week then these young ladies will be officially Ryan's. "I can't wait," said Jacob.

"Neither can I Jacob, I can't believe how lucky we have been finding so much love and at the same time with these friends. I really didn't think I would ever find love. We are two very lucky bastards, aren't we?

"We sure are," said Jacob. A life filled with love from now on."

Any news on Ella's passport?"

"Yes, said Scott, "should be here this week. "Taken a bit longer because she has never been on any electoral register or anything, but I have spoken with them myself and explained the situation, they have promised it will be here by Thursday at the latest."

"Have you girls got all you need for your holiday, no more shopping trips needed?"

"No," I said, we're good to go. I am so excited. I have never been out of the country before, well not been anywhere really. How will we get there?"

"By car to the airport, then plane to France and then we have a hire car booked for the rest of the journey to the house."

"Really I said, a plane? Will I like it, Jacob?"

"I really hope you do, you will be flying a lot from now on. We can go anywhere in the world."

"What about once the children are born, what will happen to them?"

Jacob laughed at me, "they will come with us, of course. You don't think I've waited this long to be a father then the first chance I get would leave them behind. No way."

"That's a relief," I said. I don't think I could leave my babies once they are here."

"You won't have to my love, we are going to be a proper family with so much love between us."

"Scott and Caroline will be the same. If he does decide to sell his business, which I hope he does, then he will work for me and we will all travel together. Hopefully, Flora will get over her paddy and allow Becki and Melisa to come with us sometimes."

A knock on the door bought us all back into the here and now. It was a police officer who came to talk about what had happened the night before.

Scott answered the door and brought him through to the kitchen.

He was introduced to everyone and I offered him a drink.

"Tea would go down a treat miss," he said to me.

Whilst I was putting the kettle on and sorting out fresh cups for everyone Scott and Jacob explained what had happened the night before and this morning.

Once the tea was made I joined the conversation and I told him what had happened from my perspective.

I said how Jacob had been really tired, which was unusual. I said how he had fallen asleep in the car home then once here I had taken him up to bed with a cup of tea which he hadn't managed to drink. He just lay on the bed and fell fast asleep. He was spark out and then he slept all through the night. When I tried to wake him this morning I couldn't, so I fetched Scott. Scott finished the story.

We then told him all that had been said at the hospital and gave the Doctor's name for the Police to contact him. Scott said about how he had rung the theatre to find out about the glass that Jacob had used and had been able to collect it then took it to the hospital where they had done some tests. We said what the doctors had told us about there being significant traces of a drug they use to induce sleep.

He knew about the attack on me and all about Cleo. He asked if we had any proof that it was her but of course we didn't. We all said that there simply was nobody else that would want to cause Jacob harm. He is such a lovely man with everyone.

He said to leave it with him, and they would investigate. They have Cleo's details on file and would be speaking to her.

I had a thought, I wonder if she has friends at the theatre or has somehow convinced someone that works there to do this awful thing on her behalf."

"We will look into that possibility as well, miss. I understand that you will be appearing there again tonight, sir."

"Yes, I will, it is the last night of a ten-week run. There will be a lot of influential people in the audience tonight. Film and television people along with other musicians and some civic dignitaries. I am a bit concerned that she might try something else. She loves an audience."

"After the show, we will all be going to a restaurant, she could even show up there."

"Then my real concern is that we are getting married at the weekend, that's all four of us, a double wedding. I am praying she doesn't turn up for that."

"Leave it with us, sir. We will speak with the young lady first then if we do have any concerns we can arrange for extra bodies to be around both tonight, at the theatre and restaurant then also at your weddings. I am sure there will be plenty of people volunteering for those jobs."

"Like I say, leave it with me. We will make a start by speaking to her first then decide what and how much security you will need. We will be in touch later to let you know how far we have got."

"Thank you, officer," said Jacob. "Can I give you my brother's number for contact as well, I will be tied up for a long time tonight."

"Certainly, Mr Ryan, we will do all in our power to sort this out. By for now and good luck for tonight."

"Thank you, officer," said Jacob, "I will leave it all in your hands."

After he left, we sat around for a while talking about all the possibilities.

Jacob asked, "What did we think about increasing our personnel security? I don't like too many heavies around me normally, but it's not only me now, is it? I know we have managed well enough with minimal staff up to now, but the thought of any of you coming to harm because of me, well it terrifies me, to be honest."

Scott said, "Let's leave it to the police for now. Hopefully, they will be able to sort it all out. We can look at the security issue at a later date. We have too much to think about at the moment. Surely, we don't need an army to keep one mad woman at bay." Speak with the company that provides your security, Jacob. See what they recommend. That can be done at a later date though." Once the wedding is done and dusted and we can all relax a bit in France then it might all look different."

"I hope you're right Scott, this has really spooked me," said Jacob.

I suggested that Jacob try to get some rest. He has had a rough few hours and tonight is going to be another very long night.

He readily agreed but said that I should go with him as it would be a long night for me as well.

Scott and Caroline decided a nap in the afternoon would do them both good as well so off we all trouped to our bedrooms.

Of course, Jacob's idea of a rest began with a lot of energy being used first. Not that I objected at all. Feeling my darling Jacob move inside me was just what the doctor ordered.

We did manage a couple of hours, of sleep before Jacob's mobile rang waking us both with a start.

It was the police reporting on their findings. I thought they were supposed to be ringing Scott but never mind, we needed to wake up. Cleo had been interviewed, initially, she had denied all knowledge of the offence but eventually, she admitted that she was in fact behind it claiming that it was all my fault. If I hadn't stollen Jacob from her then she would have been fine.

Of course, the police knew the true story and so she was arrested. They would be keeping her in the cells at least until tomorrow, further questions needed answering.

She admitted that although it wasn't her that put the drug in the glass of water she had got one of the young stage hands to do it for her.

He was also arrested and questioned. It would appear that Cleo had convinced him to do the deed with the promise of hot sex once done.

The lad is only seventeen and quite shy with girls. I knew who they meant and had noticed how he always blushed if a female spoke to him. Cleo had claimed that the drug would just make Jacob appear a bit drunk and would teach him a lesson.

The police left it up to Jacob as to the lad being charged. Of course, he couldn't do that to him. He was suffering enough as it was. Jacob said that he would have a chat with him and give him some friendly advice about certain women.

The police were happy to leave it at that although the lad was given a police warning which would stay on his record. Poor lad, he was going to suffer as well as Jacob at the hands of that mad bitch.

A night in the cells would do her some good I felt, but was still uneasy at the thought of her being out and about before too long. I don't know what we will do if she turns up at the weddings.

Jacob said not to worry, he was going to organise some discrete security for the day. He won't let her ruin it for any of us.

We had to get ready early as the car would be collecting us soon. We quickly drank a mug of tea and ate a piece of Mrs H's Madera cake.

Jacob had ordered a new dress for me to wear tonight as a surprise. It is fabulous. Finishes just below the knee, quite loose fitting so is really comfortable. It has an all over flower design which I love, lots of greens with splashes of red, blue and lemon. Such a lovely surprise, I had been wondering what to wear. This man of mine thinks of everything.

Caroline had come and tamed my hair putting it into a long plait similar to the way Henri had done it for the awards ceremony.

Just before the car arrived, Jacob surprised me once more with a beautiful ring. I will need to grow more fingers at this rate.

He said it is a dress ring so I can wear it on my other hand. It really is beautiful. A stunning square emerald surrounded by tiny diamonds. He slipped it onto my finger, and I loved it instantly.

"Jacob, you are so thoughtful," I said "but you must stop spending so much money on me."

"Rubbish," he said, "this is nothing to the gifts that you are giving me. Not one but two children. I have never been this happy in my entire life before. Now come on, let's get this show on the road."

During the drive to the theatre, Jacob explained that he had ordered gifts for all the theatre staff and his orchestra, everyone who had contributed to making this show such a success. Of course, they had all been gift-wrapped and delivered to the theatre. Jacob couldn't be seen soiling his hands with wrapping paper and sticky tape.

His jeweller friend had provided my ring and also a gift for Mrs H, a lovely heart on a chain. Jacob said, "I hope she likes it."

"Also, said Jacob, I was thinking about Vera. I know we don't know anything about her, but she seems a really nice woman. I was wondering how you felt about asking her if she would be interested in having the same sort of job that Mrs H does for Scott but with us once the house is finished. She would be able to have one of the staff quarters if she wanted. The house is too big for just us to keep clean and with two babies to look after and raise we will have enough to do. What do you think Ella?"

"What do I think? "I think it's a fine idea, Jacob. Do you want to mention it to her, or do you want me to do it?"

"Ella, if you are happy to do it then that is fine by me. She will spend more time with you than me I guess anyway."

"Don't forget to mention that it won't be for another couple of months, but if she wants to come and look around the place this coming week then we can arrange for someone to collect her."

"Jacob, you are wonderful. You think of everything."

"How will this work tonight? I asked. I know we have to be there early but what will happen different from the other nights?"

"To begin with, all of our special guests will be there early as well so we, that is you and me will have to speak with them all. Drinks will be served but there will be waiters laid on to do that job."

"Is that wise Jacob, after what happened last night?"

"Don't worry, Ella, all these people have been security checked. I am sure that little episode is behind us now."

"Are you sure though Jacob, or are you just trying to stop me worrying?"

"Look, what happened last night won't happen again. Everything is being double checked and I will be supplied with sealed bottles of water. Now stop worrying."

"Okay, let's do it," I said.

We were just a few moments away from the theatre. There were only a few people hanging around the stage door, so we decided to go in that way. We were a couple of hours earlier than normal so that at least played into our hands."

As we stepped from the car a few women approached Jacob and asked for photographs. He was more than happy to oblige, and they loved that he spent time with them. A couple of them came over to me and asked how I was, which was lovely. We had a brief conversation then we went through the door and made our way to Jacob's dressing room. It was empty thankfully and gave us a few moments alone. I love these times, just Jacob and me, it feels so right.

There was a tap on the door and Jacob called, come in.

The young lad that had done the deed for Cleo put his head round the door.

"Mr Ryan, you want to see me."

The poor lad looked terrified. "Yes, Lee come in."

He stepped into the room and looked so unhappy and scared.

"Mr Ryan, can I please apologise for what happened last night? I don't know why I agreed to do what I did. That Cleo woman is very persuasive."

"I do know that Lee and I hope that this has taught you a valuable lesson. It could have been a very different outcome. Thankfully, my family realised something was wrong and got me to the hospital. I want you to promise me you will never do anything so stupid again."

"I won't, Mr Ryan, this has really frightened me. I will never step out of line again, I promise. I feel worse because you have always treated me well and been fair with me. I really didn't know what the powder was. I will never trust another woman as long as I live, sorry Ella I don't mean you. You and Mr Ryan are a lovely couple."

"Thank you, Lee, that is kind of you to say so. I only hope you are as lucky as I have been in finding the perfect partner," said Jacob.

"I hope so too, sir, is there anything I can do to make it up to you?"

"Just stay on the straight and narrow from now on, no more nonsense."

"I promise, sir."

"I guess you will be called to give evidence once this gets to court."

"I believe that is right. I will be terrified, but I will do what I have to do. "

"Good lad, we'll say no more about it then. Go on, get back to work."

"Thank you and you too, Ella. I won't mess up again." With that he turned and left the room.

"That was good of you, Jacob. You could have ruined that lads prospects but instead you have probably sorted his future out now."

"I hope so Ella, he is just a kid and he doesn't deserve to be punished for Cleo's actions."

"She, on the other hand, deserves everything that she has coming. What a bitch, not only trying to cause us injury but quite prepared to ruin that young lad's future as well".

"Let's try and forget about it for now," I said. "You need to be Mr Fabulous for the next few hours. Will you get ready first or meet your guests and then come and change?

"I am changing first then if it drags on I will still be ready."

"Are you up for this my love?"

"I am I said, didn't think I would be but with you guiding me I will be fine".

"Right, let me get ready then they should be arriving, I think."

"Scott and Caroline will be here first with Vera so if you want to have that conversation we spoke of it will be fine to do it here."

"Okay, I said, we'll see what she thinks."

Jacob was tying his bow tie when the door opened and in walked Scott, Caroline, Mrs H and Vera. Bless her, she looked lovely.

She looked totally bewildered. "Hi, Vera" I called, "so glad you made it. Come on in. She stepped into the dressing room behind the other three. Scott made straight for Jacob and they began chatting. Caroline and Mrs H were watching, wondering what was being said I guess.

I took Vera by the hand, come on in, don't look so worried. He is only a man you know."

"I know that, Ella, but what a man!"

I had to agree with her. He certainly cuts a very fine figure no matter what he wears but in his evening suit he certainly steps up a gear."

"I need to have a chat with you Vera before the others arrive. Can you pull yourself away from my fiancée for a few minutes?"

"You are funny Ella. What is it you want from me? I pulled her over to the dressing table area. Tell me Vera, are you happy in your job?"

"Happy enough lass, why?"

"Well, Jacob and I have been talking and we wondered if you would be interested in doing the same sort of job for us that Mrs H does for Scott and Caroline?"

"Whatever do you mean? You want me to work for you? Is that what you are asking?"

"I am I said, our house is almost finished, and we will be moving in once we get back from France. It is a very big house and what with that and twins to look after I will be needing help. Jacob came up with this idea. What do you think?"

"Oh, Ella. Why would you want me to work for you?"

"Well, why wouldn't we? We both took to you straight away. Jacob told me he has noticed you in the audience many times at his concerts. It was Jacob who said he wondered if you would like to come and work for us."

"Well, I have worked at the hospital for a very long time. It is long hours, and the work can be hard, but I have never worked anywhere else, never thought about leaving. I would like to find out a bit more about it though."

"All it would be is helping me really to keep everywhere clean, perhaps help to get a meal ready, then once the twins arrive I will need help with them."

"The job comes with living accommodation as well if you want it. I don't know where you live at the moment or any of your circumstances but if you do decide to come and work for us we will look after you. Let's not make any decisions yet, something to think about. Jacob says if you want to come and have a look round the house we can pick you up and bring you over in the week. We can discuss specifics then if you like the idea."

"One more thing, we will be abroad sometimes throughout the year and you could travel with us. Jacob owns a big house in France and we will be spending time there each year."

"Like I say, just something to think about. Have a chat with Mrs H. I'm sure she will tell you what we are like to work for?"

"Also, if you are free on Saturday we would like to invite you to the weddings. It's not going to be a massive affair but just our friends and families. If you would like to come then you will be more than welcome."

Poor Vera, she couldn't speak.

"Now, come on, let's get in amongst these guests". "What do you want to drink Vera, champagne?"

"Well, Ella, I have never tried champagne, but I would like to try it now." I handed her a glass, and she took it with a shaking hand. "Stop that," I said, "you will soon get used to us, I promise." She smiled.

I spoke to Mrs H and asked her if she would have a word with Vera about working for us. Put her at ease will you?

"Of course I will. Us skivvies have to stick together." She winked at me as she spoke.

Other guests were starting to arrive. A very handsome man was in conversation with Jacob, I thought best not to interrupt them, but Jacob spotted me and called me over.

"Andrew, can I introduce you to my fiancée, Ella?" I moved forward and held out my hand. A firm handshake and a smile from Andrew.

216

Jacob said, "By this time next week we will be married, and I can't wait."

Andrew said, "that's lovely but surely that wouldn't stop you taking this show to Broadway."

Jacob laughed, "No, being married would not but the twins we are expecting in December most definitely will."

Andrew looked down at my flat stomach.

"Early days, I said "but they are definitely in there."

"Congratulations to you both. I now realise why you are so against this offer. What about if we put it on the backburner for a while and then look at it again for next year? They will love this show over there you know."

"I do know that Andrew and I am really grateful, but my priorities have changed and all the non-stop working, going from one film to another, one show to another, I feel like a hamster in a wheel, to be honest, and after being so ill last year with my mental health I am not prepared to take that risk again."

"Ella and myself are going to take some time to raise our family. I will look at doing the odd thing, but I will not commit to a long run again. I am just looking forward to being a husband and father. Put a bit of normality back into my life."

Jacob put his arm around my waist and pulled me into his embrace. "This wonderful woman has filled me with so much love Andrew, I want to be with her and our babies every second of every day."

"I can understand that Jacob and I can see how much you two love each other. We will leave it for now, but I will be asking again this time next year."

Andrew left us then and went to speak with Jacob's manager, Eddie. He had been forewarned not to agree to any work projects for a while. He's not happy but Jacob is very determined.

The room was rammed with all sorts of people. Jacob did his best to introduce me to most of them. The names and faces meant nothing to me, but I smiled and nodded in all the right places.

Jacob made a point of having a long conversation with Vera. Bless her, she still thinks she is dreaming. She said to me that she feels very special, Jacob is so kind including me in all this.

I told her that the night wouldn't end with the show finishing. She would be coming with us to the restaurant with everyone else.

She really couldn't believe what was happening to her. All her friends from the hospital had arrived and were watching her 'hob knobbing' with Jacob and his posh guests.

"This will all take some explaining," she said. "They must think I'm a closet posh person".

Jacob said, "Vera, we are not posh. We are just normal people, true we do have advantages in life but that doesn't mean we forget where we came from."

People were moving in and out of the dressing room, hanging about in the corridor then going back into the dressing room.

The doctor who had treated Jacob was there with his wife. She too looked in awe, being in the company of this wonderful man."

I went over and introduced myself to her. Her husband said, "Of course, how rude of me. I hardly recognised you. What a difference a day makes."

"Jacob tells me you are getting married at the weekend. He may have told me that this morning, but it has been a very busy day. Please forgive me."

"Don't worry about it," I said. "I can hardly believe it myself. We just want to get it all sorted now then we are going over to the house in France for a few weeks. Get ourselves ready for when these two babies decide to make an appearance."

The doctor's wife said, "How wonderful, twins. You must be so excited. You two will make beautiful babies. I couldn't believe what my husband was saying when he rang me this morning. To be invited backstage with you all and actually meeting Jacob, well, it has been something I have dreamed about for years. And now, here I am."

"I am so happy you are enjoying it," I said. The staff at the hospital were brilliant this morning. Poor Jacob, I didn't think he would be able to perform tonight but he says he is fine now."

"He certainly seems to be on top form. He is a natural with everybody and they hang on his every word."

Time was pressing on, Scott spoke with Jacob and suggested he take all the guests through to the bar then they could take their seats for the first half of the show.

"Good idea" I heard Jacob say, "I could do with a few moments with just me and Ella. She is really getting into this side of things isn't she."

Scott smiled, "she certainly is. Who would have thought it?"

Jacob clapped his hands to get all their attention. "Right ladies and gentlemen if you wouldn't mind going through to the bar with Scott and Caroline where they will arrange drinks for you all, then you can take your seats for the first half of the show".

"I need a while to get myself ready. After the show we are all going for a meal and you are all invited of course. Those wanting to join us if you can let Scott know then we can tell the restaurant exact numbers. It will help them no end. Oh and transport there and back is arranged."

"Okay, see you all later."

Scott led them all through the theatre to the bar, it was very busy in there, but Jacob had arranged for a couple of barmen to be dedicated to his party, so they were soon served.

The bell rang to announce that the performance was about to begin so they all went through to the auditorium. The front couple of rows were all reserved for our party. I would be joining them for Jacob's spot.

Until then I would be wrapped around him in the dressing room, telling him how much I love him and giving him endless kisses.

Once we were on our own he picked me up and sat me down on his knee.

"Ella, you are amazing he said. Where has my shy lady gone?"

"It is you that is making me brave" I said. "I just don't want to let you down."

"You couldn't do that if you tried my darling" he said.

He had been sipping water all the while everyone else was drinking champagne. "Are you sure you feel okay to do this tonight?" I asked?

"Of course my love, I wouldn't be here if I felt any after effects."

All the while we were talking he was turning the links of his bracelet round. "You really do like that don't you, I asked?"

"I do, I won't ever take it off. You are with me every time I feel it move. I love you Ella, thank you for making my life so happy and me so contented with it."

I kissed him with as much passion as I could muster. "I love you too my darling. I will have to go shortly, almost your time."

"I know, I will be keeping my eyes on you all through the night. Vera seems as if she might be interested he said."

"I know, poor woman thought I was joking when I told her what we wanted."

"I guess you have put her right."

"I have, she seems such a nice woman. I think she will fit in with us and our life don't you?"

"I do," I said, "she is someone I can get along with and someone I can trust."

"Let's keep our fingers crossed then for a positive outcome. I will pick her up on Wednesday lunchtime, it's her day off. We can go to the pub first and then show her around the house."

"Perfect," I replied.

"I am going now, don't like walking in when everyone else is already there." I kissed him once more, then kissed him again before finally wishing him luck and leaving the room. We both had lumps in our throats when we parted.

I made my way to the door that leads straight into the auditorium then waited whilst the comedian finished his act.

Once he had left the stage the audience began their usual exits, loo's, bar. As I pushed the door open a man was just placing a chair by the bottom of the steps leading up to the stage. Jacob had said that there would be increased security tonight. The theatre manager had insisted on it.

The guy smiled at me but let me pass. I made my way across the front of the seats to the far end which is the seat reserved for me. I would be sitting next to Vera, keeping her calm I hoped.

I spoke with all the guests still sitting in their seats then spoke to Scott and Caroline.

"How is he feeling" asked Scott, "he said he was fine, and he certainly looked fine."

"We managed to have a nice amount of time together before having to come out here."

Jacob's manager was sitting behind me and put his hand on my shoulder. "Is Jacob okay?" Ella? "He says he is fine Eddie, and he looks fine. I'm sure we are all worrying unnecessarily. He wouldn't risk it if he had any real concerns."

"That's good then, my dear. He would tell you if he was worried. How are you feeling now anyway? No ill effects from the attack."

"No, I'm fine thank goodness and more importantly the babies are fine."

There had been a press frenzy following both the attack on me and then the attempted poisoning last night. I think we have managed to reassure them though that all is well. Jacob's performance tonight will be the final piece of the jigsaw as far as they are concerned."

Since handing out the wedding invitations to the press crowd they had treated us very kindly so maybe that has worked in our favour. Whatever, they should all enjoy the wedding, I know I certainly will, and Scott and Caroline are looking forward to it. Jacob is more than looking forward to it. He says this is the beginning of his new life. He has given me a new life and now I am returning the favour.

I sat down next to Vera and she reached for my hand.

"Ella, I am so excited. All those from the hospital can't believe how you two treat me. I think the women are jealous."

"Wait till you see the house Vera, it is very special. We hope you love it so much so you will want to come and live with us".

"I'm sure I will Ella, once I get to believe it is all real." I squeezed her hand.

"It is real Vera, and you will love the life we have planned for us all. Also, don't think you will be the only one having to do the work. Jacob is planning on giving you a small staff to do the jobs mainly. That will be part of your job, choosing who you want to work for you. Don't worry about it yet though. We have this fabulous show to see first."

The orchestra were beginning their intro, I could feel my heart starting to thump in my chest. The music stopped and Jacob's beautiful voice came clear and strong:

That was it, me lost in the wonderful song sung by this amazing man. When sitting here, listening and enjoying every moment I am just another fan. The moment we are alone is when I become his and his alone.

The song came to a close, the orchestra had joined in halfway through and then went straight into the next song. I noticed a bottle of water on the piano, no glass. That's good I thought.

Jacob went from one song to the next effortlessly. Eventually taking a break and speaking to the audience. They lap up every word, every little joke he tells. Then it was time for the next song, again so effortless. He is amazing. A couple of upbeat numbers then another chat with the audience and the orchestra.

Someone from further back called out, "Jacob, where's Ella tonight?" That dragged me out of my dream state.

"Oh, she is here, don't worry. I won't let her out of my sight with you randy lot waiting to nab her the minute she is on her own." Laughter rang around the audience.

"Come on mate, let us all see her. Don't keep her to yourself."

"Is that what you all want?" asked Jacob.

"Yes," they all shouted then it began, Ella, Ella, Ella. I could feel my face going redder by the second.

"Okay then, let me see if I can coax her up here with me." Jacob moved to the side of the stage where I was sitting.

He held out his hands and then said, "Ella, my darling. will you join me?"

Vera was pushing me up. "Go on Ella, give them all a treat."

What else could I do? I stood, trembling then walked the few steps to the side of the stage.

Another security man was sitting there, he stood up to let me pass, took my hand then helped me onto the bottom step.

Jacob was there waiting with his arms outstretched. I must have looked like a beetroot. Thank goodness Caroline had managed to tame my hair into a similar plait that had worked so well at the awards.

Jacob pulled me to him, putting his arms around my waist. He kissed me, full on the mouth and with so much passion. The audience was going wild. Apparently, they loved to see Jacob so happy. Thank goodness for that.

When he had finished kissing me he turned to the audience and asked, "well, have I done good or what?" Another round of applause then someone shouted, sing that song to her again about memories.

Still holding my hand Jacob took me over to the piano, he pulled a stool forward that he sometimes uses and sat me down on it then he went to sit at the piano. His musical director had stepped away.

As Jacob sat down a hush came over the audience. I couldn't take my eyes off him. He began to play what I have come to think of as our song. Then he began singing:

He then stood up and his musical director sat back down and continued playing.

Jacob lifted me from the stool, put his arms around me and said, "dance with me my darling."

I have never danced in my life before but with Jacob leading me I managed to keep up with him. He finished the song like this, holding me close and then kissing me once more.

I was holding my breath, the audience was all on their feet, shouting and whistling. We stood together, arms wrapped around each other and waited for the noise to stop.

"Is that what you all wanted then" he asked, more shouting. They seemed very happy and so was I. When the noise stopped a second time Jacob began speaking.

"I am very happy to tell you all that Ella and I will be married before the week is out and I for one can't wait. Not only that but my brother Scott and his lovely fiancée Caroline, will also be married, alongside us in a double ceremony. It should be quite the party."

Again more shouting, when it went quiet once more Jacob said, "I shouldn't be telling you all this yet, but I am so excited. Ella and I are expecting twins and not only that, but so are Scott and Caroline so between the Ryan men we are going to be very busy with dirty nappies and screaming babies every night, but I tell you what, I don't care. Both Scott and myself are just so happy to become fathers. I know you have probably heard about the problems we have had recently but that is not going to rub the shine off our happiness,"

"I love this woman with all my heart, and she tells me that she loves me the same so what more can a man ask for?"

He turned and kissed me once more then led me back to the steps, kissing me again he then handed me over to the security man who walked me back to my seat.

The crowd were still going potty, but Jacob signalled for the orchestra to start playing the next song. Soon all was quiet apart from the lilting voice of my wonderful Jacob.

Several hands reached over and held my hand or patted my shoulder. I couldn't stop shaking. The man that Jacob had introduced me to as Andrew was watching all of this and then looking around at the audience. I don't think he could believe the power this beautiful man has over such an adoring crowd.

Vera had tears in her eyes, she leant forward and said, "I think I will have to come to work for you Ella so that I can continue to witness this beautiful love you two have for each other."

I squeezed her hand and said, "I really hope you do Vera. We can share a beautiful life, all of us together."

All too soon the show was coming to a close. Jacob sang another wonderful song, then said goodnight. The usual crowd were by the steps, handing over flowers and bags containing what was a mystery, and envelopes which he put into his suit pockets.

He left the stage and handed all his gifts over to Sam then came back for one more song.

"Well, what's it to be he asked?

Overwhelmingly the call was for *'The Impossible Dream'* of course. "Okay, he said, you lot don't take any prisoners, do you?"

He picked up his bottle of water, opened it and drank straight from the bottle. I felt a sudden urge to protect him, but I was certain that this water hadn't been tampered with,

He turned to face his audience and began to sing, very softly to begin with then with each line it became more powerful until finally, that last note just went on and on. Wow, that was all I could think.

He left the stage after another walk along the front, reaching over to touch fingers with all these adoring women. Once he had gone and the curtains were closed they all turned to go back to their seats before finally leaving the theatre.

Some of them wanted to touch my hands as well, they were all wishing us luck, some saying you're a lucky bugger, wish it was me. Most were congratulating me on expecting twins. I noticed that a lot of people were also congratulating Scott and Caroline which was lovely.

Once the audience had thinned out we all stood, Scott said that we were all to follow him through the curtains and back to Jacobs dressing room. "Please be careful of trailing cables back here. Don't want any accidents."

I held onto Vera and I noticed that Mrs H was hanging on to Scott, as was Caroline. By the time we had all reached the corridor outside Jacob's dressing room he was already in the shower. I went in to see how long he would be. He was just stepping out of the shower and reaching for his towel, I held it away from him for a second to just take in the sheer beauty of this man. He wiped his hand across his eyes so he could see.

"I should have known it was you, little monkey, come here and kiss me."

"No, you are wet, here dry yourself first then it's kisses time."

He took the towel and dried himself off. "What did you think of it all then?" he asked?.

"Jacob. You know I think you are brilliant whatever you do but when you called me up on stage I could have died."

"Ella, they all love you and the majority of them love that we are together. I wanted to share that with them. You didn't mind really, did you?"

"Not once I got used to being there. Being with you helped. Now come on, the masses are waiting."

"There is a coach out by the stage door waiting to take them all to the restaurant. Scott will get them all on board and then go with them to the restaurant. We will go in the car and should arrive once they are all seated."

"Amazing," I said, when did you arrange all that?

"Well, I didn't to be honest. I asked Scott to sort it out for me."

I went to the door and listened, couldn't hear much so I opened the door an inch. They had all gone. "Right," I said, looks like they are on their way. Time to make yourself look gorgeous once again."

"Can't I just be scruffy for tonight?"

"No, you cannot, there are some very influential people there. Wouldn't do for you to look like a tramp."

"Okay, I give in, I suppose I should scrub up a bit if I'm to sit next to the most beautiful woman in the world.

"Who? Vera?"

"Did she enjoy the show?"

"What do you think?" I asked him? She did and seeing what you did with me up on the stage has more or less convinced her to jump onboard."

"That's great, it is all starting to come together at last. Just our wedding to go. How fabulous is all this turning out to be?"

"Very, now come on husband to be, get your arse into gear and let's go party." One more magical kiss then he started to get dressed.

"I think I may have to deal with that once we get home, I said pointing to his very erect appendage."

"Okay," he said, this is one promise I won't be breaking. Sorry about last night, my darling. I just couldn't understand what was happening."

"Don't think about that now my darling," I said. "Tonight is going to be a very happy night, I've decided."

He quickly dressed in black slacks and a deep maroon shirt. Bloody hell, he looked good enough to eat. He ran a comb through his damp hair and then asked, "Will I do?"

"You will do very nicely for me, Mr Ryan. Will there be a lot of fans waiting do you think?"

"I guess so, but we can soon deal with them, can't we?"

"I'll give it a go I said. What happens to all your stuff that is here?"

"It will all be cleaned then sent over to Scott's in the week. Just need to find somewhere to put it all. It will be a good job once the house is finished. We can get out of Scott and Caroline's hair then, let them have some peace before their own new family arrives."

Jacob had spoken with his security team and they said it was very busy, but all seemed good natured, so we decided to just go for it, get it done as quickly as possible then get on our way. I was beginning to feel a bit peckish.

The waiting crowd were lovely. They were pleased to see us together and took loads of photographs. We chatted to as many as we could then said we would have to go as there were a lot of people waiting for us. They reluctantly let us through and into the car. Once settled we set off for the restaurant.

It was the same French restaurant we had been to before. As we entered everyone stood up and began applauding.

"Please, no more," said Jacob, "let's just have a pleasant evening together and enjoy the wonderful food they serve here."

We were seated at the top of the table, a bit like a wedding really I suppose. At least we were hidden from the street.

The chef had devised a trimmed down menu with there being so many people to be served at the same time. The others had already placed their orders before we arrived, so it was just us they were waiting for.

"Okay, sweetheart," he said, "what would you like?"

"I will have the same as you please, whatever you have will be fine by me."

That didn't take long. Wine was being served to everyone except us four on the top table. We had a big jug of iced water between us. Caroline and I hadn't managed to have a proper talk for a few days, but I could tell she is really happy, so I won't worry about her.

Vera sat next to me, she said she felt like the queen, she had never had such an exciting time in her whole life. Jacob reached over and held her hand. "Well, Vera, if you do decide to come and work for us, this will be just the first of many such occasions." She beamed.

I noticed her colleagues from the hospital were watching her very closely, I don't think they could understand why Vera was being given the star treatment. She would have a tale to tell when next she went into work. The doctors at the party were very jovial, they all seemed to be enjoying themselves very much. The one whose wife is a big fan, well she couldn't take her eyes off Jacob. The doctor's houseman had made it with his partner, Luke. They said they'd had a magical night and couldn't believe how Jacob managed to speak with everyone, including them. He just gets on with everything though as if it is what he does on a daily basis.

The bigwig that Jacob had introduced me to as Andrew was in conversation with Eddie for most of the night. Hope they are not plotting to take him over to America just yet anyway. I need him and will do for a long time.

I am so looking forward to our holiday in France. I have never been on holiday in my life before. This will be something very different. I'm not sure what it is you do when you are on holiday. I must have a chat with

Caroline before we go. Scott has worked his magic and got my passport sorted so there is nothing stopping us now.

The food was excellent as usual and the staff very attentive. We spent a couple of hours with all these people and chatted to most of them throughout the evening.

When it was time to leave I said, "Jacob, how will they all get home? They must all live in lots of different places."

"They do darling, but don't worry. Scott is on it. Most of them will be going on the coach and they will drop people off as they go. A few that live too far out will be supplied with a cab home. The car that Scott and Caroline are using will take Mrs H. and Vera and drop them at their doors. That just leaves you and I to pay the bill then get home. As I recall I am on something of a promise."

"You certainly are my darling and I am really looking forward to it."

Some of the people were making as if to go and pay their bills but Jacob said, "Please, you are all here as my guests. I won't hear of any of you paying. My guests, my bill. Have you all enjoyed your evening though?"

There was a chorus of "Oh, yes, it's been amazing, best night ever." I didn't hear anyone say no, it's been rubbish.

They couldn't thank us enough for everything. The show, the get together beforehand and now this meal then to sort out transport home just made the evening perfect.

I noticed Eddie and Andrew still had their heads together. I expect Eddie's lifestyle is funded by the work that Jacob does. I bet he tries to talk him into going to America. I can see that taking this show over there would be great for them and for Jacob's career, but he does need to take some time for himself and for us.

Once the twins are here and we can get into some sort of a routine then perhaps he could look at doing it then, but they will have to respect his wishes for now. I will put my foot down if they try to convince him otherwise. It's not going to happen. Surely Eddie can remember what happened when he overworked before. We don't want him going back into a depression again.

As the evening drew to a close we made our way to the front of the restaurant and waited for each and every one to take their leave. There were handshakes and kisses for them all.

This was all so new to me, but I did my best, not wanting to let my man down.

Everyone was most thankful for their treat. When it was time for Vera to say goodnight Jacob made a real fuss of her. He had asked for her phone number so that we could arrange a time to collect her on Wednesday. She had written it down on a napkin and handed it to me. I will ring you on Tuesday evening if that's all right. "Definitely she said. I will be home all evening."

She left us with a beaming smile on her face and lots of interested faces watching her.

As soon as everyone had left we went to thank the restaurant staff. It had been a remarkable effort on their behalf. Everything had gone perfectly. The food was tasty and the service second to none. Jacob was speaking to the manager and arranging payment for the whole evening. Goodness knows how much it has all cost. An eyewatering amount I would guess, but Jacob says it is worth spending a little to keep everyone happy. He had even arranged for little gifts to be delivered for all the restaurant staff as a thank you.

A few of the guests had used their own transport but the majority had taken advantage of the coach being provided. No one would be drink driving that was for sure.

As soon as we had finished our chat with the staff our car pulled up ready to take us home.

We thanked them all once more then left. As per usual there were a couple of press guys waiting by the door. "Evening Jacob," one of them said. "Have you had a good night?"

"We have indeed Mike, thank you for asking. Been a good end to a very good run of shows. Going to have a rest now before the wedding. Have you guys received your invitations by the way?"

One said yes he had but this Mike bloke said no, he had been away for several days and missed the invites.

"Not to worry, do you have a spare one on you, my love?" he asked me.

"I do yes," opening my bag I removed one of the invitations and handed it over. "Just let them know at the hotel if you will be there, just so they have a good idea of numbers. It wouldn't be too bad if it was a buffet but with it being a sit-down meal they really do need to know numbers."

"Thank you so much, Ella, Jacob. This is most kind of you. I know we give you a rough ride at times and you really don't have to do any of this, but I know those that have had invitations are very appreciative."

"To be honest I hadn't given it a thought, it was all Ella's idea. Glad you all like it though. This is a very special time for us and also for Scott and Caroline, it will be nice to have you all enjoying the occasion with us".

"We will certainly do that they replied. Any chance of some photo's tonight? Why not" said Jacob.

We stood by the car and they snapped away for a few minutes then thanked us once more before allowing us to climb into the car. We both let out a long breath we didn't know we had been holding. At least that is over now. "We can hide away now for a few days. "Get our heads back in the right place," said Jacob.

"How are you feeling my darling?" I asked.?

"Better than this time last night that's for sure. Don't think there is any long-term damage he said. As the Doctor said, once it was out of my system I was back to normal, whatever normal is."

"I like your normal," I said.

"Thank goodness for that," he replied. "Be a bit difficult if you suddenly decided you are not so keen on me."

We laughed as we headed towards home.

By the time we reached Scott's house we had begun to unwind. "Are you tired now?" I asked him.?

"Not too bad, been a long day and night and I was buzzing earlier but I just feel mellow now. Looking forward to having a few days of just us to be honest."

I had to agree, just us two and Scott and Caroline relaxing together. Sounds good to me.

As we reached the house we noticed that the lights were on so Scott and Caroline were in. "They must have had a good run dropping Vera and Mrs H off. Hope she likes the house and us," he said. "I think she will fit in great."

I laughed, "once she gets over being in awe of you," I said.

" What do you mean?"

"Jacob I will be forever in awe of you, you are one very special man and I love you so much."

"That's all right then," he said, "I need to keep some fans, don't I?" Good for my image".

"Now, let's get out of this car and relax for a while indoors. I could murder a nice, strong cuppa."

"Your wish is my command," I said. "Come on, let's get in. I need to take these shoes off, my feet feel a bit swollen."

"A worried look passed over Jacob's face. Is that normal he asked?"

"I guess so, I said, I have been in these shoes for hours and they are not the most comfortable. I can make the tea then lie on the sofa with my feet on your lap so you can massage them for me."

"I can do that," he said but you do realise though that I am the only one that has been working tonight."

" I do," I replied "but my feet need a rub, and you are the best person I know to do that for me".

"Come on then, let's get in." We said goodnight and thanks to the driver and the security man that had travelled with us. They left and we moved into the house.

Scott and Caroline were cuddled up on one of the sofa's in the lounge. I'm making tea, do you two want some.

"Yes, please they both called. Jacob came with me to give me a hand and to carry the tray back for me."

Once it was all done we took the drinks into the lounge and took our seats. We all picked up our mugs and began to sip appreciatively. "Nothing like a good cuppa," said Jacob.

I relaxed back on the sofa and then put my feet into Jacob's lap. He began to massage them, and it felt lovely. I would soon be back to normal, just the busy night. Think I might stick to flat shoes for a while though. I'm not used to wearing heels anyway.

Caroline said she was the same, her feet had been throbbing for the last hour or two."

Once revived by the tea we began talking about the nights work. "You are very good at all this stuff Scott, do you enjoy it?" I asked.?

"I do actually, I have always played a part in Jacob's career to a lesser degree, but I do know how it all works. If I do decide to sell the practice Jacob has asked me to take on a bigger role with him. That would suit us all I guess. If we are all travelling together or if you ladies and babies are staying

231

at home when Jacob needs to work then we would all have each other to rely on. Keep it in the family so to speak."

"I have always seen the legal side of Jacob's career so that needn't change. I just need to decide if it is what I really want to do. It would give me much more time to spend with Caroline and the children once they arrive. I think I will explore the possibility a bit more this week. I will have to go into the office on Monday anyway, I can speak with an agent that is way up with selling a business. Not straightforward I know that. I need to have a serious chat with Ingrid as well. We should have her and her brood over this week before the weddings. I think she is feeling a bit out of things. She hasn't even met your intended yet Jacob."

"I know, there just hasn't been time up to now, but now the show is over I can take Ella over or like you say we could invite them all over here sometime this week. Any day should suit me except Wednesday or Thursday morning said Jacob."

"We are picking Vera up in the afternoon on Wednesday and taking her to see the new house. We are hoping she will be our Mrs H."

"That's a great idea, said Scott, she seems a really nice person. She and Mrs H got on like a house on fire. Hope it works out for you."

"I guess you spotted Eddie and Andrew with their heads together? Andrew is trying to convince Eddie to try to convince you to do this America thing."

"Just be aware Jacob, what they are talking about is massive. It would take you over there for months and I know it's not what you want. Particularly at the moment."

"I won't do a long run like that Scott, it would not be good for me. I will not allow myself to sink into that black hole again. I really thought I would never recover the last time. I was really in a desperate state and that mad bitch Cleo only made it worse."

"I hope they manage to deal with her swiftly. Do you think we will have to appear in court he asked?"

Scott was thinking, "I hope not Jacob, if she admits what she did and accepts any punishments they dish out then probably not. It could all be dealt with in the magistrates court. But, if she pleads not guilty then it is likely you will both have to appear."

"I drew in a deep breath. I can't do that I said. No, impossible."

"Scott said you may not have any say in it, Ella. The law is a strange thing at times. Let's not get too bogged down yet though. She may decide to do the sensible thing and admit everything. There really is nothing for her to gain by arguing the case. Everyone that witnessed what happened to you Ella will have made a statement and there is no getting away from it, also, that young lad, Lee from the theatre has made a statement telling the police everything she did and how she got him to do the deed."

"I hope and pray we don't have to go to court. I will just die."

"Right said Jacob, enough of the negative. We four have something very exciting to look forward to and I can't wait."

"Scott said you and I bro, who would have thought it?"

Caroline and myself were listening to them, really, men getting excited about tying themselves to women for the rest of their lives.

"I asked, "are you two really so happy about making this commitment?"

"Definitely," said Jacob. "And I will second that, said Scott."

We were all feeling very tired by this time so decided it was time for bed.

"Scott checked we were all locked up then we made our way up the stairs to our rooms." "Goodnight" we all chorused.

"My feet were feeling a lot better after my foot massage. Jacob asked how I was feeling?"

"Fine now," I replied. "Feet restored, so I'm floating on air."

"Good," he said, are you feeling energetic?"

"Could be I said, how about you? Feeling more energetic than I was last night that's for sure."

"He walked over to me and picked me up in his strong arms. He whirled me around then lay me down on the bed."

"Do you think you could manage a little loving, my darling?"

"Oh, I think I could manage that." Come here and kiss me." He did, his kisses are wonderful. I love being close to this man.

"We made love, very gentle and tender but still reaching a magical climax". We lay in each other's arms for a long time, just being with each other and loving each other. So very special.

Finally, we fell asleep and woke at eight-thirty the next morning. We reached for each other. Jacob stroked my arms, and my face and then tried to push my hair back off my face. It really does get everywhere. I get trapped by it when I sit down and lean back in a chair.

"Jacob, would it upset you a lot if I had some of this hair chopped off."

He looked horrified, "please don't Ella, I love your hair so much. I won't mind if you have a bit cut off, but please keep it as long as you can."

"Okay, I said, I was just thinking that all this hair will be difficult to manage once I have two babies to feed. Not sure how that will happen, do I feed one at a time or have one in each arm? Could be tricky."

"Can't you just tie it back for those occasions? I could live with that, and I have no idea how you feed twins. I bet Caroline will know though said Jacob."

"I will have to ask her," I said. It is just that it has always been the one thing that I always wanted to change about me, don't get me wrong, I love that you love it but it's just so hard to keep out of the way."

"I won't do anything with it yet though. We will have to see how I cope with it once my life gets busier with two babies to look after. I can always plait it I suppose. Makes me look like an old granny though."

"You could never look like an old granny he said. You will always be my beautiful Ella."

"Should we get up do you think?"

"Maybe in half an hour or so. I think I need a re-run of last night first."

"Funny you should say that," I said. *Jacob pulled me to him and began kissing me thoroughly. I felt his tongue push between my lips, so I opened my mouth slightly giving him access. I love what this man manages to do with his tongue. I reciprocated giving him my tongue. All this exploring of my body and Jacobs is still so new to me. My whole life has been lived without affection or love of any kind but now I am receiving more than my fair share. I hope we manage to love each other this way forever, even when we have been married for fifty years.*

Finding each other every time we are together this way is wonderful. So much love for each other and so much fulfilment each time we make love.

Very soon Jacob began to move his head down my body and found my breasts with his mouth. Then we began to make beautiful love and it lasted for quite some time before we were both sated and spent. We lay next to each other just drinking in the sight of us.

"Once we were two now are two parts of one whole."I said to Jacob,

"My wonderful darling," he said. "What a fabulous thing to say to me. I do know what you mean though, it is exactly how I feel about us. We fit so well together don't we?"

We got up then, showering together. I don't think I could shower alone now, knowing how brilliant this is. We wash each other paying attention to various parts of our bodies. It is such a lovely, special thing for us to do for each other. Once showered, dried and dressed we ventured downstairs. Scott and Caroline were sitting in the kitchen side by side. They were whispering to each other. I love how these two are together. Different from Jacob and I but still with so much love for each other.

"Morning" we chorused as we walked into the kitchen. "How are you both today?"

"We are just fine, thank you," they said. "Not been up long ourselves. Are you fully rested now, Jacob?"

"I am Caroline, thanks for asking. I feel so much better knowing we don't have to rush about now. Do you have plans for today?"

Scott said, "We are picking the girls up, going for a walk over the park then taking them to the pub for Sunday lunch, what about you two?"

"Nothing much. Might just slob about for a bit then we could join you for lunch if you don't mind."

"Of course, we don't mind, the girls will be thrilled to see you both. We thought we could run over what they will have to do as bridesmaids, they are so excited."

"I have been thinking, we have sorted out who is going to be our best men, but who is going to give our girls away," asked Jacob. Usually, the bride's father but as they don't have one of those, who could they choose?"

I shrugged, "I don't know a soul so I will have to give myself away, what about you Caroline?"

"Same here" she replied. I hadn't given it a thought, to be honest. What about asking Mrs H. She is the closest person we know apart from Scott and Jacob and they can do it."

I looked surprised, "Is that possible? I always thought it had to be a man."

Scott said, "Well, there is no law to say it has to be a man and Mrs H would be over the moon. Why don't you ask her in the morning?"

Caroline said, "I will, I can't think of anyone else I would want to do the job. What say you Ella?"

"That would work but what if I were to ask Vera, it would welcome her to the family, wouldn't it? You could have Mrs H and me have Vera."

"What do you men think?"

They both nodded, "sounds like a plan to me said Jacob. Vera will really think she has joined Royalty. Bless her. I think she is going to fit in perfectly with us all, did you like her Scott?"

"I did Jacob, she is lovely and seems to know what she is doing. I could hear her and Mrs H talking away in the back of the car, I think they will become good friends anyway."

I asked Jacob, "Can I use your phone, please? I will call her now."

"Certainly my love. If she doesn't want to do it then Mrs H can give you both away."

Jacob handed me his phone. "Can you show me how to use it please, Jacob?"

"What are you like?" he said.? Here give it to me. Are you happy to speak to her?"

"Yes, I can manage that, just don't know which buttons to press on your phone."

Jacob called Vera's number and listened. "Morning Vera, Jacob here. How are you feeling this morning?"

"Good, thank you, how are you all?"

"We are all fine as well, thank you, Vera. Ella is here and wants to ask you something, I will pass her over. I took the phone from Jacob,

"Hi Vera, I have a really big favour to ask you."

"You do? What's that then?"

"Well, as you know our wedding is on Saturday and I wondered if you would do me the honour of giving me away?" I had my fingers crossed.

"Me? Why on earth do you want me to play such a big role on your special day?"

"Because I like you, a lot. I don't have any family at all, and I would deem it an honour if you would do this for me?"

"Are you serious Ella?"

"Of course, I wouldn't joke about such a thing. Please, will you do this for me?"

"Of course I will Ella, it will be a real honour and a pleasure, I won't have to make a speech, will I?"

"No, of course not. We can leave the menfolk to do that. Right, you said you are off work on Wednesday, is that right?"

"Yes, it is, why?"

"Well, we will have to alter our plans slightly, we can take you into town to get your outfit in the morning then we will take you for lunch at our local pub, then take you along to see the house. The workmen will still be there but they are on the final bits now so you should get a good idea of how it will all look. Will that be okay with you?"

"Yes, of course, it will but it seems to me that you are really spoiling me, and I don't know why?"

"I told you, we like you, a lot."

Okay, then I will call you on Tuesday evening to let you know what time we will pick you up. See you on Wednesday. Bye till then."

"Bye Ella and thank you."

Sorted, now if you ask Mrs H and she needs to go dress shopping we can all go together. I know Jacob told her to go to a certain place and he will pay the bill, but I bet she hasn't been yet.

The other three were all watching me open mouthed.

"What?" I asked.

"Who is this confident, bossy woman and what have you done with my Ella, asked Jacob?"

"Well, it's about time I learned to speak up for myself. No time like the present."

"Hi five to that," said Caroline. "Now, let me ring Mrs H."

She did and Mrs H was gobsmacked to say the least. "I was right, she still hadn't been to get her outfit so it was arranged that we would take both her and Vera into town on Wednesday morning. She told Caroline that she was really pleased for Vera, such a lovely woman. We intended to be friends after meeting last night anyway so being able to share the duties on Saturday with her will be great.

Scott said that he needed to go into the office on Wednesday anyway so he could pick the ladies up and then drop us off in town the same as before.

We could shop then he would pick us up and meet up with Jacob back at the pub. He would drop us all off at the house after we had eaten then walk back to meet us. He said he hadn't been to see the house since we had altered the plans. He will be interested to see how it is coming along.

Scott and Caroline went up to their bedroom to get ready for their day out with the girls.

"What should we do? I asked Jacob. We won't need to go to the pub till lunchtime so that gives us some free time together."

"How about we stay in bed all morning, replied Jacob?"

"We could I suppose, I replied." We do need to double-check everything is okay for Saturday as well. I think we could probably do that in bed though."

"Now that sounds like a plan," he said. "Breakfast first though. I am starving."

"Mr Ryan, you are always hungry."

"I am," he said, "always hungry for you, my darling."

"So that is what we did, just had toast and tea, doing some for Scott and Caroline as well. Didn't want too much if we were eating in the pub at lunchtime."

Scott and Caroline went off to pick up the girls ready for their walk in the park then arranged to meet us back in the pub at one thirty.

We on the other hand spent the morning getting our exercise in bed. We spent time just exploring each other, finding little things that made us who we are.

Jacob was counting all the little scars on my hands, arms and legs from when the blasted farm dog had bitten me when I was a baby. Just because I ate his food. Horrid dog. There had been three different dogs that I could remember, all of them were bullies towards me and all called Dog. Still, I suppose I did eat their food.

Jacob did a thorough examination of the strap marks across my backside, some of them have been there for years. A couple of them reached as far as my lower back. I remember them happening, they did hurt but I refused to cry, wouldn't give him the satisfaction.

I found a few scars on Jacob that I hadn't noticed before. One was on his stomach where he'd had his appendix out when he was a teenager. Another one on his left arm I noticed was quite big.

"What happened here?" I asked.

"Well, that is where Cleo stabbed me after I broke up with her. Should have gone to the police back then. All this crap might not have happened then."

"Well, my darling, I said, it is what it is, and we will just have to deal with it now."

"Get you he said, Miss Logic. I think someone crept in during the night and stole my Ella away then left you in her place."

"Are you complaining?"

"Not at all, I am thrilled you are beginning to come out of your shell. Now come here and let me count your scars again. I might just get a pen and play at joining the dots."

"Fabulous, I said. "That should look amazing with my wedding dress."

We laughed a lot, played around a lot and loved a lot. I really enjoy being with Jacob in this relaxed and happy place.

At twelve-thirty Jacob said, "*I suppose we had better get up and ready. By the time we reach the pub Scott, and his ladies will already be there. You will love the girls seeing them in a relaxed setting. I know you have met them a few times, but it was all to do with the wedding plans. They are very funny when you get them to relax and just enjoy their time away from their bitch of a mother. Flora thinks that children should be seen and not heard. Apparently, if she does take them anywhere they are not allowed to join in with adult conversations. They are expected to just sit and behave. I ask you, they are kids for God's sake. Scott would love it if they came to live with him and Caroline permanently. Flora could then do what Flora does best. Float around town spending money like water, having the most expensive treatments she can find then complain when nothing works.*"

"I take it you are not her biggest fan."

"God, no, I have never liked her that much and the way she treated Scott has been appalling. It is great to see him so happy with Caroline."

"They do make a fabulous couple, don't they?" I said.

"I think they do, and they obviously love the bones of each other. I think that once the new babies arrive the girls will want to come to live here. If Scott does sell up and just works for me it will free him up to spend more time with them as well as be around for Caroline and the babies."

"Listen, Ella, I have something to tell you. Hope you like what me and Scott have done."

"What have you done?" I asked?.

"Nothing bad, my darling. Just an extra little treat for you and Caroline."

"Okay," I said, tell me.

"Well, after the wedding on Saturday, we will come here to spend the first night then on Sunday we are flying to Paris, that's in France if you wondered.''

I laughed at him, I seem to remember that from my school days. It's the capital isn't it? Like London is to England."

"Yes, that's right. It is a beautiful city. Lots of amazing things to see and the food is fabulous. Anyway, we thought we would spend a few days sightseeing there before driving to the house. Once there we will be staying for at least a month, you and me."

"Scott and Caroline will stay for two weeks then fly back home. Caroline has to go up to the Midlands to sort out her house, put it on the market probably or she may decide to rent it out. Whatever, it's up to them to decide."

"Scott still has a big case that he needs to be here for. It will keep him busy for at least a month, probably more like six weeks. It is then that he has to finally decide about selling. I think he will, since Ingrid took a back seat to bring up her family all the work has landed on Scott. He is a very clever lawyer and is in big demand, but he needs to get his priorities right."

"I think he will sell, that is my advice to him anyway. He can earn a good wage working for me. As well as sorting out anything legal he is really good at organising stuff. Most of the people that I deal with know him anyway so it would be an easy transition for him. I am convinced he will be happier doing that."

"I know I have said I will be more picky with the work that I take on and I will, but I do still need to work. Now I have this growing family to support. I will not take anything on until after the babies are born and we have a good routine sorted with them. Once I do decide to take on some jobs then I don't want to be away overnight if I can help it."

"This thing in America would be huge and would be a very good payday for us but there is no way I will leave you or them and I definitely won't take on that much work that it sends me into depression again. I know things are different now that I have you, but I need to have you and the children with me not separated by an ocean."

"That would really upset the apple cart, so I won't do it. I need stability in my life, and you give me that, my love. We have enough to give us a good standard of living and we will be able to take holidays and just have time to be together. I don't need anything else."

"Whatever is put on the table regarding work we will sit down and sort out what it will mean for us all, if it works then I will consider it but if not then they can forget it."

"There is nothing on the cards for me to do at the moment apart from a TV thing on Thursday, they want to interview me about the show, or so they say, I think more of the questions will be about you though my darling. You'll come with me, won't you?"

"Of course I will my love, you won't have to face anything else alone. I will be by your side from now until we leave this world. Even if you turn into a grumpy old man I will still love you."

"I promise not to be grumpy in my old age he said."

"Now come on, we have spent enough time being idle. Let's take a walk to the pub and have a fabulous lunch. I am starting to feel a bit peckish," he said.

"Again, you do love your food, don't you?"

"I'm a growing boy," he said. "I can't be hungry, that really does make me grumpy."

We were soon showered and dressed. We took a leisurely walk down to the pub and arrived just as Scott pulled into the car park. The girls looked so excited to see Jacob. He spoils them rotten.

We waited for them to unload then they ran over to us. They were so full of chatter, obviously excited that they are going to be bridesmaids and will wear their pretty dresses. Apparently, Flora has been giving them lessons on what they can and can't do. They are not to keep talking when adults are speaking. They are there purely for decoration is what she has told them. We'll see about that I thought.

Once they were over their excitement at seeing us we all trooped into the pub. It was packed, loads of people eating and it smelt divine.

Jacob said, "We will be round the corner in our usual seats I guess. Let's just go around and save some time. Mary will be rushed off her feet poor woman."

There were a few young girls waiting on tables today. They were all looking at Jacob and giggling. Sorry girls, already spoken for I thought.

We found our table and Jacob said he would go to the bar and order our drinks. "Water and tea," is it? He asked.

"Lovely," we all said. I touched his arm,

"Jacob, if you want a pint or wine then I don't mind, really I don't."

"I know you don't, my love but I think it will do me good to lay off it for a while. Might have to have the odd glass of wine in France though. Are you looking forward to it my darling?" he asked.?

"Oh, Jacob I am. Paris sounds so posh, so exotic. I am still pinching myself. You really do spoil me."

"And I intend to spoil you forever more, my love. Now girls, what would you like to drink? Wine, beer, vodka?"

They went into fits of giggles. "Uncle Jacob, you are so funny."

"How about a fruit drink then?"

"Yes, please" they chorused.

I touched Caroline's arm to get her attention. "Well, what do you think about going to Paris then?"

"Brilliant," she said. She has been once when she was still at school but to go now with Scott will be very special.

Jacob went off to the bar, it could be a while. I noticed people kept touching his arm, wanting a word with him.

Scott said, "we picked up the Sunday papers whilst we were out. Seems that last night was a huge success. Lots of photos and good write-ups. I think the wedding invitations for the press was a stroke of genius. Well done, Ella for thinking of it."

"Well, if you can't beat them, join them is my theory," I said.

Jacob returned with juice for the girls, they will bring the rest over in a minute. All the lads want to know if we are having a stag do. I said not likely, we need to be sober on Saturday.

"I don't think I would enjoy that one bit said Scott."

"Me neither said Jacob. What I have done though is put a grand behind the bar so they can all get bladdered without us. They seem happy enough with that."

"I will give you half towards it, Jacob."

"No, you won't, my treat. Treat the girls with it if you want. I don't want your money. After all, you have been looking after me for months then the other night thinking about the glass. I told you then I owed you one."

"Talking about owing you one. When Caroline and me take Mrs H and Vera to town I will pay for their outfits, no arguments."

Scott looked at Jacob, "That's told us then."

"It has, now shut up and tell me what's for dinner?"

A waitress came over with a tray of cups and saucers, a teapot, a milk jug and a sugar bowl. She was followed by another girl carrying a jug of water, "I will fetch your glasses now, Mr Ryan," she said, looking at Jacob and blushing as red as I had when he had got me up on stage."

"Thank you, Belle," he said.

"Belle is it, and how may I ask do you know her name?"

"She is the daughter of one of the lads we used to knock about with. She's a sweet kid but very shy."

"Shy she might be, but she has the hots for you, Mr Ryan, I said."

"Don't talk daft, she's only fourteen."

"Fourteen or not I'm telling you she fancies you."

"Tough," he said, "I am well and truly spoken for." He put his arms around me and pulled me in for a long passionate kiss.

Becki and Melisa both said, "Yuk! Uncle Jacob, how can you do that? It is so dirty."

He turned round to them and said, "Well, I don't care if it's dirty or not because Ella is going to be my wife and I love her to the moon and back."

They set off giggling again. "Uncle Jacob loves Ella," they started singing. "Well, I love Uncle Jacob as well and I don't care if it's dirty either."

"Jacob loves Ella and Ella loves Jacob," they started singing.

"They really are lovely girls, I hope they can live with Scott and Caroline eventually. Flora sounds a right cow."

Mary eventually made it over to take our order. It was easy, four roast beef and two children's roast chicken.

Off she scurried to the kitchen. It wasn't long before the waitresses came with our meals.

"God," I said, "these are enormous, where will we put it all?"

Jacob was laughing at me. "Wait till you taste it, you won't be able to leave it alone. Best pub food in London," he said.

We all sat and ate in silence. He was right, everything was so tasty. Caroline and I did manage to eat most of it, of course Scott and Jacob cleared their plates. I really don't know where they put it. The girls did very well with their meals too. Very little left on the plates.

Mary eventually managed to come and speak with us. The poor woman looked exhausted.

"I am knackered," she said.

Jacob said, "The problem is Mary, everything here is so damn good everybody and their dog wants to eat here. Really though, you should look at taking on some extra help. You deserve a life as well you know."

I know Jacob, we are seriously thinking about it. "We are not getting any younger, are we? Anyway, enough about us, how are your plans coming along?"

"Just about there I think Mary, going to have a rest this week apart from Thursday, they want an interview on **'This Morning'**, I think it's actually Ella they want to speak to, not me."

I nearly choked on my water. "Don't you dare drag me into your interview, I wouldn't have a clue what to say."

"Oh, I'm sure you would manage just fine. Do what you always do, listen to the question then give them your answer. It might not be the answer they were hoping for, but it would be the truth."

They all laughed at me, but I would have to make Jacob promise not to put me on the TV. I would be mortified.

Us girls have a bit of shopping to do on Wednesday then I think we are good to go.

Mary said, "Gregg was looking through the papers this morning and he said the write-ups are brilliant from last night. It's a pity we never managed to see the show."

"You know I wanted you both to come along, said Jacob. This is what I mean about getting help in. Who is going to run the place on Saturday?"

"Gregg's sister and her husband are coming over and seeing to everything for us." They will stay a couple of days so their help will be great. I might ask her if she would like to come on board permanently. Having someone we know would be good."

"Yes, I have met her a few times and she seems a good sort. It would allow you to take a bit of time for yourselves, wouldn't it? It's about time you two had a holiday."

"I will think about it, Jacob, I know we can't get any busier without help. And thank you for putting that money behind the bar for the lads. They are all well chuffed."

"We let her get back to her other customers and we gathered all our bits and pieces together before leaving for home."

Scott said, "Come and say bye to Uncle Jacob and Ella, you two. We have got to get you back to your mum."

"Oh, Dad, do we have to? It's boring there. We only have fun when we are with you and Caroline and Uncle Jacob and Ella. We love being with you all."

"Well girls, next week you will be with us for a lot longer won't you? Are you looking forward to being bridesmaids asked Scott".

"Yes Daddy we are but mum say's it's all for show and we shouldn't believe everything you say. She said that once the babies are born you won't want us. It's not true is it Daddy?"

Scott looked over at us, what could he say to that?.

Caroline called them over to her, she stooped down and spoke with them in a very grown-up way, eye to eye.

"Right girls, what I am about to tell you both is the honest truth. Neither me nor your dad will go back on anything that I tell you now. Is that understood?" They both nodded.

"Right, until I met your dad I was very lonely then he came into my life through work really. As soon as I met him I knew that he was very special. We both felt the same and before long I realised that I loved your dad very much and he told me that he loves me as well, so we decided to get married."

"The only thing he worried about was you two. If you had said that you didn't want him to get married then he wouldn't or if you decided that you didn't like me then he would have to finish with me. Your happiness means more to him than anything else. Do you understand?"

They both nodded. "So when your dad got us together so we could meet, and we got on really well he was so pleased. Then when he asked you both if he could marry me and you said yes it made us both very happy indeed."

"I don't know why your mum has told you those things but none of them are true. Your dad and now me being his wife shortly will do everything in our power to keep you both safe and happy. Once these new babies are born they will be your brothers or sisters so you will always be part of one family. We will love you all equally, do you understand what I am saying? They both said yes they did understand."

They then both put their arms around Caroline's neck. "We love you, Caroline, you are so kind to us, and you make our daddy very happy. We wish we could live with you instead of Mum and that horrible man. He won't let us play in the house in case we make a mess. We have to stay in our room when he is there. We don't think he likes us very much."

Scott looked aghast, "Why have you never told me any of this before?"

Mum said, "We shouldn't tell you things that happen at his house. She said you will be angry."

"Well, she is right about that. How dare she allow these two beautiful girls to be treated so appallingly? Caroline, what can we do?

"I think we need to find out everything that is happening there for a start. Do you want to do this before the wedding?"

"I don't know of course, I don't want anything to spoil our day, but I can't allow this to go on unchecked, can I?"

"Look, ring Flora and tell her we are keeping the girls till later. Say we are all having such a fun day that they don't want it to end. We can take them home then and see what else we can find out".

"Right,' said Scott, just give me a second. I need to compose myself first."

Scott looked so angry and upset, any wonder. What an awful woman. How can she claim to be a good mother? Her idea of good parenting is definitely different from mine.

Scott finally felt he could make the call. He went outside to speak with Flora, didn't trust himself not to start a shouting match.

A while later he returned to the pub and sat down.

"What a cow she is he said. "She started off by trying to blame me for firstly the marriage failing and then turning the kids into little brats. Eventually though she has admitted that her partner is not a child sort of person. He never wanted kids at all and only puts up with Becki and Melisa because Flora keeps them away from him when he is home."

"I have told her in no uncertain terms that this is unacceptable. She can either hand over the children to me so that Caroline and I can care for them or she can look forward to her day in court."

"I hope I have done right. Caroline, you didn't sign up for this."

"My darling Scott, of course, you have done right. Those poor girls have been made to suffer enough. What will happen now?"

"Well, I told her she has twenty-four hours to get everything of the girls packed up. I will send a van over tomorrow afternoon to collect all their things. I told her to include the girls passports as well as they will be coming on honeymoon with us. Please forgive me Caroline, and you two, this impacts on us all."

"You daft thing, of course, they will come with us. Can you increase the booking for Paris?"

"Yes, I should think so. They will enjoy that, I think," he said.

"Your house in France, Jacob, will it take us all?"

"It sure will he said. We have plenty of rooms. The girls have been there before, they love it."

Scott said, "Are you sure Jacob, this has put a spanner right in the works. You were hoping to have a lovely quiet time with you and Ella and us two, now it looks like it might be a school party."

"Scott, you do what you have to do to keep those beautiful girls safe and happy. We will all have a rare old time, won't we Ella?"

"We certainly will," I said.

"Then, once you come back home we can have our quiet time then. We have plenty of time to be on our own, mate. You know how much those girls mean to me. I can't get my head around that stupid bitch. Fancy letting that go on right under her nose. It seems to me that she is the main one laying down these rules. If she had wanted to keep the girls with her then she should have put his lordship in his place long before now."

"I had better let the girls know what's happening." All the time this had been going on Becki and Melisa were being entertained by two of the waitresses. The pub was thinning out now, so they had a bit of time on their hands.

Scott called them over to where we still sat.

"Right, my beauties, I have been speaking to your mother and she has kindly agreed to let you both come and live with Caroline and me, and of course Uncle Jacob and Ella for the next couple of months. Then, once their house is ready they will move just down the road and we will all be at our house together."

The girls were listening open mouthed. "Really Daddy, will she really let us live with you and Caroline?"

"Well, if I am honest I didn't give her much choice. I told her you are both coming to live with us, and she has had to accept that."

"Caroline and myself will not allow anyone to treat you two badly any more. How do you feel about that then?"

"Is it true Daddy? Are we really going to live with you and Caroline?"

"Yes, you are and what's more you will be coming on honeymoon with us. Really Daddy, really Caroline?

"Yes, it is true. We will have to go and see your teachers at school tomorrow and tell them of the new arrangements" said Caroline. We will have to arrange for you to have time away from school to come with us."

"It's the wedding next Saturday, then on Sunday we are all flying to Paris for a few days. We can do some sightseeing, might even manage a day in Euro Disney if you are good. Then we will be driving to Uncle Jacob's house in France. Do you remember going there before?"

"I do, I do. We spent all the time in the pool. I learnt to swim there said Melisa. Didn't I, Daddy?"

"Yes, you did. Are you both happy then with the new arrangement?"

"Yes, Daddy, thank you so much. We promise to be good, don't we Becki?" "Definitely" came the reply.

"Well, I think you should be thanking Uncle Jacob and Ella, they have agreed that you can come, and it is their honeymoon as well."

"Thank you, thank you, came the chant as they threw themselves onto Jacob. Thank you, Ella, we love you as well. You have made Uncle Jacob happy again. He was really sad for ages and ages, then he met you and he is happy again."

"Caroline, are you sure you don't mind us coming to live with you and coming on your honeymoon as well?" asked Becki.

"I couldn't be happier," she said, "I always wanted two daughters and now I have your pair."

"Does that mean we can call you mummy?"

"Well, I will be delighted if you do, but perhaps we should ask Daddy first if that is okay."

"Daddy, can we please?"

"Of course, you can. After all, she will be taking the place of your mummy won't she? You will still be able to see Mum though. We can take you there or you can meet her somewhere else."

"Not there," they both said. We can meet her in the park for a bit then come home to you Mum and Dad. We were all sitting there with tears in our eyes. They all look a very happy family all of a sudden."

"Well, I have gone from no children at all to two and soon to be four in the blink of an eye. Hope, I can cope," Caroline said.

"Caroline, if anyone can cope then it's you," I said.

"Right you lot, better get you home. Do you two want to squeeze in or have a walk?" Scott said.

"Oh, I think we will walk," said Jacob. Stretch our legs after that delicious meal. I feel fit to bursting."

As we walked back towards Scott's house, we called in at our new home.

We looked through the railings.

It looks to be coming on well now, doesn't it?" I said.

"It is, replied Jacob. "I am getting rather excited about it now. I will speak with the builder tomorrow and see how long he thinks it will be before we can start putting furniture in. When I came down the other day they were just finishing laying the wooden floors. They look fabulous."

"I bet they do," I said. "Are you happy that Scott is getting his girls back?"

"I am," he said, "you don't know how happy. I think they will all be all right, don't you?. "Caroline seems to love them every bit as much as Scott does."

"She does,"I said. She is very good with them as well. The way she spoke with them when it all came out, she was magic I thought. I expect her job has helped her to understand children and how to deal with their problems."

"I guess you are right, she is a natural. You don't mind them tagging along on honeymoon with us, do you?"

"No, not at all. They will enjoy it and so will we. What is that place that Caroline said they could go for the day?"

"Euro Disney, never heard of it?"

"No, what is it?"

"I tell you what, we can go with them, it will be easier to show you than try to explain it."

" Okay," I said, "I can go with that."

"Right," said Jacob, "back to this house. Do you think you will be happy here now we have made the alterations?"

"I am sure we will all be very happy once it is all sorted. Furniture in and the garden tidied up."

I gazed at the building that was going to be my new home, it was very imposing, very grand. With Jacob's help though I am sure I will get used to it. Then if he has his way and we fill all the rooms with our children we will definitely need a big house.

We left the house and walked the short distance back to Scott's beautiful home. They too would be filling all these rooms with their children. They have a head start over us with Scott's two lovely children moving in with them.

We are going to be bursting at the seams until our house is finished. Mrs H will wonder what has happened to her lovely, peaceful place of work. She will love having the girls there though. She told me that she is very fond of them.

As we entered the house it was very quiet. "They are here, aren't they?" I asked.

"I bet I know where they are, come on out into the garden. Let's see if they are playing hide and seek."

"Sorry," I asked, "what's that?"

"Oh, dear," he said, "I can see I have an awful lot to teach you. Come on, I will explain as we go."

We found them all sitting in the girls' house at the bottom of the garden. Scott had heard us come in so had rushed them all outdoors to surprise us.

"This is an amazing house," I said, I could live in there. It really was fabulous. How lucky are these girls?

They said that they love playing in there, but there are always spiders hiding and making them jump.

"I am not afraid of spiders, after all, I was brought up on a farm."

"Show me," I said. They were pointing here and there, some were tiny little things others were quite big. I said, "Give me a minute and I will put them all outside to play."

They watched me open mouthed as I let the spiders climb onto my hands then took them out and let them crawl onto the plants surrounding the garden. The house was soon spider free, and they went in, closing the door on us grown-ups.

Jacob put his arms around me, pulling me into him for a big kiss. "My brave darling," he said, "now I know who to call when I find a spider in the bath."

I looked at him, "You're not afraid of spiders are you?"

"No, not really, it's Scott that has a fear of them."

"Really?" I asked?

"God, yes," said Scott, can't stand them. I laughed.

"You should have spent more time on the farm, that would cure you."

"I dare say it would, but I think I will just send for you when I am being threatened by a huge foot-wide beast."

We all laughed at him. I said, *"The little things didn't worry me, but the beasts and things used to scare me. I think they knew I was frightened. Even the blasted chickens would run at me sometimes. The sheep were not too bad, especially when the lambs were born. They were cute. Sometimes I would have to take a lamb into the house to bottle feed it if the Mum couldn't cope. They are not so good if they have twins or triplets. They seem to manage one okay, but any more and they struggle. God, I hope I don't struggle with two."*

Jacob said, "I was not to worry, he would be with me all the time and although he couldn't actually feed a baby unless it was with a bottle he would have a go at everything else."

"I know you will, my darling. We will manage between us, I'm sure."

We left the girls playing happily in their house and went back into the kitchen to make some tea. We said that we had stopped and looked at the house on the way past. "It is looking so much better now," said Jacob. "I think all the exterior stuff is finished and I know all the wooden floors are down, the bathrooms are in and the last time I spoke with the builders they said the kitchen and utility would be done this week. The staff flats are all but finished so I think it's just the inside painting and finishing bits to go now. Once that is done the landscapers can get in and work their magic. We are keeping it quite simple to begin with. We can always alter stuff then once we are in and see how it will all work."

I laughed, "I don't know about how the garden will work, I need to learn how the kitchen stuff works. I have used an Aga, of course, we had a very old one in the farm kitchen, but all the rest looks very complicated to me."

Jacob says, "I am not too worry about it as he will be able to teach me. Apart from watching Scott cook steaks for us that day, I have never seen a man cook. I wait to be amazed and if all else fails we can live on takeaway."

They all fell about laughing at me.

"Right said," Scott, let's work out what we have to do this coming week now things have changed somewhat."

The brother's both fetched their diaries, something else I have never used. I wrote everything down on bits of paper and hoped Will didn't move them or use them for his own purpose.

So, Monday Scott was going to go into the girls school to put them in the picture, Caroline was going with him so the girls would stay with us. Scott also needed to pop into work for an hour, but Caroline said she would just sit and wait for him. She was dying to see where he actually works.

We said we would take the girls out for a walk, perhaps pop into the house and show them around. Other than that we would be free to do as we wanted, which was not a lot. Caroline and I needed to get all our wedding stuff out of the girls' bedrooms and put it in the guest room otherwise, I could see we would be having a fashion show with them.

Jacob said he needed to speak with the photographer and also check with the florist that she was happy with everything.

Gerald, the local vicar and distant cousin of Scott and Jacob would be coming round Monday evening to go through it all with us. He thought going through the plan here would be better than in the church. He said he knows how the press like to follow Jacob around, best not to give them too much too soon.

Caroline said that the girls things would be delivered later on Monday so they could sort through it all and get it put away.

Scott said he was going to start proceedings to have the girls live with them officially. He said he has pandered to Flora's requests and demands for far too long but now he has had enough and that is one other thing he needs to go into work for. Start the ball rolling.

"Also, he said. I need to find out how far things have gone with the farm sale and all the other stuff that needs sorting. Need to get it all tied up quickly so you can really move on then Ella."

A firm of accountants were sorting all the financial side of things out and Scott's friend Ed would be coming round on Tuesday to explain all that they have found. Also, what will happen to all the furniture, farm machinery, all sorts of stuff that I had just left behind.

Don't care really what happens to any of it.

First thing to be sorted would be the girls bedrooms so Caroline and I set off up the stairs ready to get everything away and sorted before they came in.

All our wedding things were taken into the guest bedroom and hidden in a wardrobe. Caroline checked in the girls wardrobes and drawers to make sure they would have clean night clothes and also clean clothes for the following day. Scott had said he always kept some clothes at his house just in case. They would be fine until their own things arrived from Flora's the following day.

Caroline said, "I bet Flora is spitting feathers, what a horrid woman treating her own children that_way. I am pleased really, they will be much better off living with us."

Once their rooms were sorted we went back down and found everyone in the kitchen. The girls were drinking squash and Jacob went to make a pot of tea.

"You must have read my mind," I said.

"Ladies, please take a seat over in the posh area," he said. "I have found a sponge cake in the cupboard. I think we all deserve a slice."

"Blimey" That man and his stomach.

We all found seats in the family end of the kitchen. Jacob poured us all mugs of tea and gave us all a slice of cake. I noticed he had the biggest piece.

I said, "You my darling will be getting a fat tummy if you keep eating like that."

" Don't care," he replied, "I will need to fuel up regularly so I can take care of my children when they arrive."

Becki and Melisa said, "Uncle Jacob, are you really going to have babies like Daddy and Caroline?"

"We most certainly are," he said. "Daddy's babies and our babies should all arrive about the same time. Just before Christmas. Blimey! we will have some expensive birthdays and Christmases from now on, won't we?"

The girls were laughing, "Poor Uncle Jacob, got to look after his babies. Will you still be able to go and sing?" they asked.

"Eventually, yes, but not whilst the babies are tiny, I am going to stay home with them and Ella and spoil them all."

"Like you spoil us, do you mean?"

"I do," he replied, "I think it is very important to be around for your wife and children as much as you can."

"That's what daddy says. He said he is going to sell his business and work for you Uncle Jacob so that he can spend more time with all his children."

"I think your daddy is a very wise man. We can all spend lots of time with each other as well. Would you like that?"

"Oh, yes, we will love that, won't we, Melisa?"

"Oh, yes. I am so happy. Are you happy, Becki?"

"I am very happy."

"Does this mean you have made your decision about selling?" Jacob asked.

"Yes, I have, it won't happen overnight I know, but I will have to make time for all the kids and lots of time to be with Caroline. I won't allow what happened with Flora to happen again. I can't believe how selfish she has been with her own flesh and blood. Unbelievable."

Soon Sunday was over, and we all retired to our beds. The girls had gone up at seven-thirty, very excited about their new living arrangements.

Jacob and I were huddled together in bed, kissing and loving and generally enjoying each other.

"I am so glad the girls' story finally came out so that now they can be happy. How awful for them to have to live like that because of two very selfish people. They will be fine now they are with Scott and Caroline. She will be a great mother to them all."

"I can see that" said Jacob, "she is a natural, but you will be an amazing mother too you know."

"How do you know that?" I asked?

"Well, I have watched how you are with the girls and it is obvious they adore you, as do I.

Oh Ella, I can't believe how you have changed my life around in just a few short weeks? I love you so much."

"It is you that is changing things for me Jacob. Until I met you my life had been a complete nightmare. When Will died I was determined to spend the rest of my life alone? I didn't want or need another man and I certainly wouldn't let another man do that to me, then I met you. You have changed everything for me, and I love you more than life itself. Once these babies arrive my life will be complete."

We made love in the big bed that has become ours very quickly. So much loving has happened in this bed. Jacob was so gentle but also very careful in making sure both of us got all the fulfilment we needed from our joining."

"Just a few more days and I would become Mrs Ryan."

I had a little giggle and Jacob asked what was so funny.

"I was just thinking that in a few days I will be Mrs Ryan and then I realised Caroline will also be Mrs Ryan. It gave me a lovely feeling all over. We began as friends and now we are going to be sharing the same name. Life can be funny."

We needed to be up fairly early on Monday morning. We were going to be taking charge of Becki and Melisa for the morning. We had promised them a walk in the park and then said we would show them our new house. They were very excited to see inside it. Even asking if they would have a bedroom in this house as well as their own home.

I couldn't see a problem, there are so many rooms in the house losing one to Jacob's nieces wouldn't make a difference.

Scott and Caroline first went to the school to sort things out there. They explained all that had happened and all that was going to happen, and the school were fine about it. The time away from school to accompany us on honeymoon was a bit more difficult. It would be a chunk out of their school term, but Scott assured them that once they were home he would sort a teacher to home school them in all that they had missed. Of course, there was a fine to pay but Scott said that wouldn't be a problem. He just feels that the girls need to get used to their new living arrangements and extra family.

They left the school feeling happy with the result. They then went into the city and to Scott's offices. He was able to introduce all his staff to the woman that has turned his life around. Everyone seemed to like Scott and seemed happy for him.

He left Caroline sitting in his office with a cup of coffee whilst he went to find the lawyer that deals with family law for the company. He filled him in on the details of what had been happening along with all the other bits of information he needed. He told Scott not to worry, he thought that it would be a simple job to get full custody of his children.

He then went to see the people that have been handling the sale of the farm to see how far things had progressed.

All seemed good there as well. Everything was moving along at the speed with which they would expect. It looked like I would have a final figure by the time we returned from France.

Scott then rang his friend from the auction house to confirm he would be coming out to see us the following day.

"Yes, Scott, got everything sorted and the stuff that needs to be sold will be ready for the next auction in a couple of weeks." He suggested that all the farm machinery and such be sold at the farm on a date to be arranged. He said there is an awful lot of stuff there and it needs to be disposed of properly, so they agreed to hold a farm sale within six weeks.

Scott thinks it will all be done and dusted before the twins arrive.

He then spoke with the senior people that work for him. He informed them that his intention was to sell the business and that he would in effect retire, although he would still work for Jacob. They were all surprised, after

all Scott is only thirty five, but fully understood his reasons once Scott had
revealed everything to them.

He said that the reason he was telling them this now was so that if any
or all of them decide to buy him out then obviously all their jobs would be
safeguarded. It would save him having to sell through an agent as well. He
wanted to get it all sorted out before his babies arrive so if any or all of
them decide to go for it then once they return from honeymoon the wheels
can be set in motion. He said he really hoped that they would step up and
buy because it is such a good team that works there.

He and Caroline left the building feeling much happier. So far it has
been a productive day.

We all met up in the pub for lunch and Mrs H joined us. We had waited
to tell her the news of the children moving in permanently, after all it is
Scott and Caroline's news to tell, not ours.

Mrs H was over the moon. She said the children should have never
gone with their mother in the first place. The girls seem to love her, and they
call her nanny H. How lovely is that?

We had a lovely lunch in the pub, it wasn't nearly as busy as the Sunday
lunch had been, and it was just nice to be able to sit and eat and talk, have
proper conversations. Scott drove Mrs H and the girls as far as our new
house then waited for the rest of us to arrive.

Jacob spoke with the builder and asked if it would be okay to show the
family around.

"Of course, it is Jacob, got some small hard hats for them to wear." He
went off to find the safety wear for us all. The girls thought it was great,
wearing workmen's hats as they called them.

Jacob got busy taking photographs of them with not only the hard hats
but also yellow safety vests. They were made to promise not to touch
anything, especially machinery and they promised to be good. And they
were.

It was amazing how much had changed since our last visit. The wooden
floors look fabulous. Colour was being put on lots of the walls. The kitchen
units have all arrived and are gradually being fitted along with the cooker,
refrigerator and goodness knows what else. The Aga will be fitted by
specialists. It was there but not fitted yet.

The downstairs bathroom was all but finished as were the en suites to the bedrooms. There was still some work going on in the family bathroom but most of the bedrooms were finished. The girls were running around deciding which ones they would have.

Our bedroom is enormous, there is a full-size bathroom with a separate shower, a walk-in wardrobe and a dressing area, something I have never even heard of. A balcony was being constructed leading from double doors. That will be nice on warm days I thought. The room off our bedroom was going to be the nursery and Jacob says he wants to decorate it himself. Should be interesting.

The landscape gardeners would be starting work the next day. Most of the builders' machinery has been moved so they can make a start at least.

There had been some outbuildings that had included stables, storage areas and a workshop. These have been extended and turned into what will become the staff quarters.

Jacob has plans to add a swimming pool at a later date but that can wait for now. I can't swim anyway. Everyone was in awe of the place. Mrs H said it is fit for a Queen.

I still can't believe that I will be living there with this man of mine and a good many other women's dreams and will then be giving birth to his twins.

How my life has changed. The previous life I led is fast becoming a distant memory.

Once they had all seen enough Jacob went and spoke with the builder again and told him how pleased we are with the standard of work. If we decide to do anything else in the future we will definitely be using them again.

The new security fencing and electronic gates would be installed at the same time that the gardeners were working. They needed to work together to make sure it all fits and works. One of the last jobs was to be the block paving of the enormous driveway at the front. There would also be some patios around the back. Not sure if I know exactly what a patio is but I am sure Jacob will tell me.

Once satisfied we all left and went back to Scott's. Mrs H came with us for a while. She wanted to spend a bit of time with the girls. As we all arrived there a big van pulled up with all of the girls' things. "My God," said Caroline, "where the hell are all these things going?"

Scott said not to worry, what wouldn't fit in the house would have to go into the garages. He said, "I think some of this stuff can go to the charity shop as well. I think Flora has used it as an excuse to get rid of a load of rubbish."

The men who had arrived with the van soon had it unloaded and boxes that needed to be upstairs were carried up there for us.

Caroline and I set about emptying the clothes boxes and soon found homes for all that stuff. As for the toys, well I think that the men should sort that lot out.

Gerald the vicar was due at six o'clock, so we quickly tidied up the kitchen and set about cutting slices of cake, a plate of biscuits and laying out all the tea things.

Scott drove Mrs H home and arrived back just as Gerald pulled up. He is a very nice man and explained everything to us so we could all understand what was required of us. The girls sat listening very intently.

Once Gerald finished his talk Melisa chimed up, "Mr Vicar, we are all going on honeymoon together, aren't we mum?"

Caroline looked so pleased, it was a lovely thing for the girls to say and they must really be happy with this arrangement. They obviously adore Caroline and she them.

"Yes, that is right, should be a very unique honeymoon but we are all looking forward to it."

Tuesday was a bit easier, only Scott's friend coming in the afternoon to tell me about what else had been found at the farm.

We slept late, all of us. Even the girls were tired. Once we were up though things began to happen. It was decided that both Scott and Jacob would sort through all the toys that had come to live at the house, with the help of Becki and Melisa.

Scott had a word with them before heading for the garages where the toys had all been put. He needed them to keep just what they really wanted to keep, and the rest could be given to a charity.

They said that most of the things could go really. Their mum had refused to let them give anything away when they had wanted to make a shoebox donation the previous Christmas. Melisa said that mummy had told them that if the children's parents couldn't afford to get them toys then that was their fault, not hers.

Scott was seething, "What is wrong with that woman? She grew up having everything and now it seemed that she wanted to keep it all." Whatever had made him marry her? She has turned into a right cow he said.

Still, onward and upward. "Let's go sort toys" he said, and they all trouped out to the garages.

That would keep them busy for a good while. "Anyway, once I have made my calls, we can do whatever you fancy," said Caroline.

Well, I think everything that can be done towards Saturday has been done so "how about if we go and relax in the cinema room and watch something good."

That is a great idea. It will let us relax for a while. "What do you fancy seeing?"

"No idea," I said. "You know I have never seen anything before. I really enjoyed 'Love Actually' and that thing we started watching on the television, that was really good."

"Oh! You mean Outlander, that is great. I hadn't seen any of it before, heard of it of course. We could put that on again if you like, there are loads of episodes of that to catch up on, or we can watch something that Jacob has been in."

Blimey! choices all the time. I leave it to you Caroline. I am sure whatever we put on will be great.

"I'll think on it while I make these calls. She needed to ring the estate agent handling her house sale. If there isn't any interest she might just rent it out, it could be rented furnished as she won't need any of her furniture down here. Will just have to wait and see.

She went off to fetch her phone then returned about twenty minutes later.

"Right, come on, let's go find some of the sexy Jacob movies." We can start on the first one he made then work our way up to the latest one."

"Okay," I said, not sure I would enjoy seeing him performing with pretty young things, but I guess I will have to see them sooner or later.

We made a pot of tea, poured mugs for Scott and Jacob and squash for Becki and Melisa. Caroline said, "I'll take these over to them if you take ours through to the cinema room. Won't be long."

I did as she asked then sat waiting for her to return. She was back quickly and then set up the machine that would play the movie. I would never get my head around all these things.

Right, she passed me the case that the DVD came in. There on the front was my Jacob, shirtless and gorgeous with his arms around a beautiful blonde girl with her boobs on display. They looked a stunning couple. How can I get my head around this? To me it looked very real.

I looked over to where Caroline was setting up the machine. "Caroline, I don't think I can do this."

She came over to me and put her arm around me. "We don't have to watch this if you will be uncomfortable. I can see where you are coming from, though."

"The whole world knows you are the only girl for him after his very public declarations of love but seeing him acting with pretty girls could be unnerving, I get that. The thing is Ella, all this has happened long before he met you. He won't stray from your side, ever."

"Scott has told me that Jacob has always been rather shy with women. He can act with them and that's not a problem but over the years women have treated him badly. They wanted him to get them into films or plays, not to have a proper relationship with him."

"The business has been very kind to him in lots of ways but on a personal level, it left him a little soulless. You can't live your life by continually giving, sometimes you need to receive as well. That is why he is so happy with you."

"That idiot Cleo really did a number on him. He had worked himself into a right state and became very depressed then she really went for it. He was in a very bad place for nearly a year and then he was convinced by his manager to take on this latest show. That helped him so much, but it is you that has put him back together again."

"Scott can't believe how much he has changed since meeting you. You do need to make sure that he never works so much again though Ella. It was working so much that ran him into the ground. He was exhausted but still kept pushing himself. Look after him Ella, he is a very special man."

I could barely speak I felt so emotional. That poor man. "I will look after him forever and won't allow him to overdo it ever again."

"Caroline, I knew some of it of course I did. We have had long conversations about the problems he suffered but listening to you spell it out like that has made me realise just how fragile he can be."

"I won't ever do anything to hurt him. Looks like we have saved each other."

We gave up on watching a film after that and instead played Jacobs CD's. Hearing his amazing voice so clear and strong come through the speakers. It made the hairs stand up on my arms. He is wonderful.

'Somewhere' was playing and I could feel the tears forming in the corners of my eyes. Whatever is wrong with me. I looked over at Caroline and could see she was close to tears as well. "What is it with this man's voice? Just listening to him fills me with so much emotion."

A noise behind me made me jump. I turned to see Jacob standing in the doorway watching me.

"Whatever is wrong, my love?" he said as he rushed over to me.

"Nothing, my darling, really. We were just listening to your beautiful voice and it filled me with so much emotion, I love listening to you." You mean every word, don't you?"

"If it is words of love then yes I do and every one of them is for you my darling."

He put his arms around me, pulling me into his embrace then kissed me with so much passion. I knew without a doubt that this man truly loves me. I am so lucky to have met him. I really cannot wait until Saturday when we will make promises to each other and I will become his wife.

"Are you feeling better now? he asked?

"I am my love, now you are here. Sorry, it was just listening to that beautiful song and your stunning voice. Promise you will always sing for me."

"I will my darling, whenever you want me to."

He held me close for a few moments then said, "tell me I don't have to cuddle you as well Caroline. You look a little teary."

"I am, Jacob, you have such a gift with your voice. It certainly stirs something in me, I'm okay now though."

"Good," said Jacob,

"Ed is here to tell you all about his finds. We have finished out in the garage now. Scott is making tea so when you have gathered yourselves come on through and find out what other goodies he has found."

"I have got to set up a movie for the girls to keep them happy whilst we do business."

Caroline and I got up and went to leave the room, giving Jacob chance to sort his movie out. He held my hand then pulled me to him.

"I need kisses before you leave me, my darling."

I turned into him and hugged him to me kissing him as passionately as I could. "I feel a promise being made," he whispered.

"Definitely a promise," I said." Let's see what this guy has to say then we will have to eat before I fulfil my promise to you."

"Be there in a minute, my love and send the girls through then. Tell them all is ready for their entertainment."

Caroline and I walked through to the kitchen and met with the very handsome Ed. I don't know why but I was expecting a crusty elderly man but no, Ed is film star gorgeous but not quite got the edge that my Jacob has.

He was lovely and very easy to speak to. He said that he has never had such a job before. Yes they do often go into properties to empty and sometimes find things that turn out to be valuable, but the farmhouse was something very different.

Scott had told him about all the money, jewellery and watches we had found, and he thought that would be it but no, there was so much more.

He had sheets of paper with him with everything listed. Right down to a box of nails found in a drawer.

One page listed everything that had been destroyed. The next one was all the things that were too good to burn but not particularly valuable. Ed suggested that all these things should be donated to one of the charities that had a furniture department. I agreed with that, might do someone some good.

Next came the furniture that had been restored because it was actually valuable. I struggled to believe that any of the stuff could be worth anything. Ed suggested it all be put in their next auction and see what it would achieve. He had hopes of at least one hundred thousand pounds, probably more. This I did not believe. It all looked like rubbish to me. Ed said that there were some ornaments, vases, glass and porcelain objects. Loads of things that in his opinion would be worth selling.

Finally all the other stuff that they had uncovered. First there was a lot of very old bank notes, no longer in circulation. Ed was in talks with the powers that be at the Bank of England to see if these notes could be redeemed, still waiting to hear back from them. These had all been found in drawers in the loft.

There were a lot of collections of military medals, all very old. There were books of rare postage stamps. Collections of all sorts of stuff, why save all this rubbish is what I thought but then found out they were worth thousands. Ed thinks these all must have belonged to Will's great grandfather and mother or maybe even their parents. His family has owned the farm and land for a very long time.

The whole thing was blowing my mind. I really could not get my head around any of it.

"Jacob, help me please. I don't want any of this. The money from the sale of the farmland will more than cover anything we are likely to need."

Jacob was thinking, "You are right Ella, there is no way we need or want any of this money. How would you feel about giving it to charity?"

"Oh, Jacob, that would be the ideal answer. Let Ed do whatever he wants with all this stuff then once he has a final figure we can decide who should have it."

Jacob said, "Well, I am happy with that, but the final decision is yours, my love."

"No, I said, ours. We are a team you and I. Everything we do we will do together."

We gave Ed free reign to do what he wanted with all the things he had uncovered. Once it was all disposed of then he would give us the final figure and we would then decide who would benefit from it.

Ed left happy and we all gathered around the kitchen island to decide what takeaway we would eat tonight.

It had been a strange day and none of us felt like cooking.

Chinese was favourite again, so we all gave Jacob a list of what we wanted, well my order was the same as Jacob's. This way of handling food decisions hadn't failed me yet.

He got out his mobile then rang through to whoever and gave a list of numbers. It seemed a strange way of going about things to me, but it seemed to work so who am I to throw a spanner in the works.

Once again our meal was delivered very quickly, and we all ate together, again gathered around the kitchen island. All the dishes were opened and placed in the centre with plates and cutlery for us all. It struck me that this is a very civilized way to eat. Very friendly I thought. The girls were loving it. They said that they were never allowed takeaway at 'his' house. He said it made the place smell disgusting.

Jacob said, "Well! I think he smells disgusting so there." Of course, the girls were in fits of giggles.

Once we had eaten our fill the girls went off to relax for half-an-hour before having their baths and then bed.

We all had another pot of tea and sat around having a really pleasant time. We are such a tight family now. We all get along brilliantly and can talk about anything.

Once the girls had gone to bed, happy and smiling we discussed Ed's lists. I still cannot believe that all those years we were living hand to mouth there was such riches all around me. We decided that Will was definitely a very strange character.

We all said we would have an early night. We had another busy day on Wednesday. Jacob had rung Vera to check she was still okay for shopping with me and Caroline.

"You bet," she said. We arranged to pick her up at ten o'clock then Jacob would drop us in town, we would shop till we couldn't shop any more then ring Jacob and he would come and collect us then take us to the house so Vera could decide if it was what she wanted then we would meet Scott and the girls in the pub.

Our early night was wonderful. We showered together, washing each other all over, then we spent an age drying every little nook we could find, finally falling onto the bed and finding each other in a wonderful, magical wave of love and lust.

Finally we fell asleep in each other's arms.

I woke as the early morning sun streamed through the curtains. I lay there watching Jacob sleep. I had an overwhelming desire to kiss him but didn't want to wake him. He looked so peaceful. Before long his eyes opened and I did kiss him, as thoroughly as I could. We lay gazing into each other's eyes for a long time, eventually moving together for some early morning loving.

By the time we had concluded our morning exercise we needed another shower. We dressed and went down to find the rest of the family all up and eating their breakfast. We just had tea and toast, I was beginning to feel a bit queasy first thing and didn't fancy anything more. Hope this doesn't last too long I thought.

We were discussing our morning shopping when Jacob said, "Here, my darling I had a debit card ordered for you. It is to pay for all the things that Mrs H and Vera will require. Also, if you see anything you fancy for yourself then just get it."

I put my arms around his waist and said, "Well, thank you, my darling, but you won't be paying for any of these things. I will buy them myself."

He held me tight and said, "You don't have to do that sweetheart, use this card. It is our money after all." I took the card and said "Thank you very much", but I won't be using it today. This will be my treat so stop trying to pay for everything".

"Okay," he said, I give in."

Scott was trying to give Caroline the money to pay for Mrs H's outfit, but she refused to take it. I will get it so keep your money safe.

I said, "No, you won't, Caroline. Today is on me, well to be precise today is on Will." Everyone laughed at that then said, "Well, thank you, Will, most kind of you."

Jacob had ordered a car to pick us all up, us first then Mrs H and finally Vera.

She was looking out of the window as the car pulled up. She couldn't believe her eyes. She lived in a little terrace of houses. They all looked nice and neat but small. Whatever will she make of our house when she sees it.

She came out of the front door and looked about her. I thought, she is checking to see if any of her neighbours are watching.

Jacob jumped out of the front seat and went to meet her. He planted a kiss on her cheek then took her arm and walked her to the car, opening the door and helping her inside.

I had noticed a few net curtains twitching, I bet the street would know before diner time that Vera had been picked up by Jacob Ryan no less. I could just imagine the conversations.

We all greeted her warmly as Jacob got into the front seat again.

Bless her, she was blushing. "I bet your neighbours got an eyeful then," I said.

"You can be sure they did.

I have only told a couple of people about my wonderful night with you folks, but I am sure they didn't believe me. They will now though won't they?"

"They sure will," I said.

"Are you all ready for this shopping trip?"

"I am yes, I saw a lovely little suit in 'M & S last' week. I think I might buy that for the wedding."

I just smiled at her. We'll see I thought.

Jacob's driver dropped us in the same side street as before. We all clambered out then I noticed several people had stopped to see who was getting out of this big posh car. Jacob had got out and opened the door for us. Yes, I thought 'and there is the star of the show'. Before leaving us he pulled me into a big hug and kissed me thoroughly. "Ring me when you're finished," he said. He then kissed the other three ladies on the cheek before finally kissing me once more.

He climbed quickly into the front seat of the car and they sped off leaving us with an audience still watching the proceedings.

I could feel the colour rising in my cheeks but thought no, he is my future husband, and I am allowed to be kissed by him no matter who is watching.

Caroline took hold of Mrs H and I took control of Vera. "Right ladies, let's shop" and we set off for the first of several shops we would visit this morning.

Caroline and I had decided we didn't need anything else for ourselves but we both wanted to treat our menfolk and also get a little jewellery gift for the girls as they were going to be bridesmaids.

Caroline was hoping to find a bracelet similar to the one I had bought Jacob, and I would buy the gold chain that would match Jacob's bracelet. I was torn between the two when I got his first gift. He loves that bracelet so much. I often catch him just looking at it, turning the links around in his fingers. The matching necklace will be a lovely wedding gift for him to remember the day. I have all this money doing nothing and will shortly have a whole lot more that I don't need so to spend some of it on this wonderful man that is making me so happy will be money well spent.

First, though we need to get our ladies kitted out. After checking out a few other shops we finally went to the bridal shop where we had both found our wedding dresses. I noticed Vera and Mrs H looking at each other. "Come on ladies, let's see what wonderful outfits we can find for you both in here."

As soon as we entered the shop the owner recognised us and came over. "Good morning, ladies, and how can we help you today?"

"I should say that your gowns are both ready and will be delivered tomorrow."

"That's lovely thank you. Today, we would like to find something special for these two glamourous ladies. They will be giving us away so will need something really special"

"Of course, madam, come this way."

We followed her through to the area where the mother of the bride outfits were kept. Poor Vera, she thought she was going to M & S and now she finds herself in this very posh shop.

I suddenly thought, I bet they both think they will have to pay for them themselves. They were both being measured and looked terrified.

As soon as the assistants had gone off to find what they had in the correct sizes I pulled them both to me.

"Please don't look so worried. You won't have to pay, it is my treat. You are both doing us a real favour by agreeing to do this and we certainly wouldn't dream of asking you to pay for your clothes."

Vera looked at me, "Ella are you sure? You and Jacob have been so kind to me ever since we met. You don't have to do this, you know. I would give you away without any of this."

"I know you would Vera, but it is something I want to do. Jacob wanted to pay for everything, but I wouldn't let him. He is so generous with his money and his time with everyone that he meets so I put my foot down and said no, I am doing this."

"He didn't like it though. I can be just as generous as he can."

Mrs H had been listening to the conversation then leaned over and said, "Thank you, Ella so much. You and Jacob make the perfect couple as do Scott and Caroline and now they have those two gorgeous little girls, all in the world seems right."

"I agree Mrs H, they are a wonderful family and once their twins arrive everything will be perfect. I am so excited for us all."

An hour later we left the shop with everything they could possibly need. Dresses, jackets, under garments, hats, shoes and bags. I was a few thousand pounds lighter, but I don't care. They are happy and they do look the bee's knees when dressed in their finest. They were chattering together discussing how grand everything was. They both said they had never had such fine clothes before. They and I were very happy.

We then went to the jewellers I had used before. I spoke with the same man that had served me last time and he said that he remembered me and the piece that I had bought. When I said, "I now wanted the necklace to match the bracelet I could see the pound signs going around in his eyes." He quickly found the one I wanted and set too gift wrapping it. I then said that I also wanted two bracelets for young girls that are going to be bridesmaids.

"Of course madam, gold or silver?"

"Why gold of course," I said. He fetched a tray with several designs, I called Caroline over to help me chose. She pointed two out saying that she thought they would be ideal. They were different but similar enough so that one wouldn't think she had something better than the other. "Good choice," I said. "I will take those two then please, but can you write Becki on that box and Melisa on the other one? Thank you."

"Certainly madam." "Is it yourself that is the bride he asked,

"Yes," I said, one of them, Caroline is the other one?. My fiancée and hers are brothers and we are having a double wedding on Saturday."

"How wonderful," he said. "It is," I replied.

Then he said, "Your fiancees wouldn't be Scott and Jacob, would they?"

"Well, yes they are," but how did you know?"

"Well, my fiancée and I were in the audience for Jacob's last show. When he called you up on stage I thought I recognised you then I caught sight of the bracelet you bought from me. Of course, I know Scott from school, we were in different years, but everyone knew Scott Ryan. I don't expect he would remember me, but I never forgot him. He was always the one all the other boys wanted to be. Very clever man I recall."

"Yes, indeed," I said, "This lady here is his fiancée Caroline. These two fine ladies are going to be giving us away. We neither of us have any family of our own so our dear friends here have stepped into those shoes. So kind of them don't you think."

"Yes, indeed," he said. "Is that all for today then Miss Adams?" I had dropped the Mrs as soon as I left the farm.

"For me, yes, but Caroline is hoping to find a wedding gift for Scott as a memento of the day. Let me settle my bill first then you can help my future sister-in-law out."

I saw Caroline smile, I bet she is thinking, get her, talking to people, how brave is she.

I did feel brave though, after twenty-five years at last I could stand on my own two feet.

"Right madam, how can I help you today?"

"I was hoping to buy a bracelet for Scott, not the same as Jacobs obviously, but something similar."

"That shouldn't be a problem, madam."

"Can I stop you there a moment," said Caroline.

"Please drop the madam and just call me Caroline, when you call me madam I feel about ninety."

"Right then Caroline, we have a new selection in actually, let me show you those then if there is nothing to take your eye I can get others from the window display."

He placed the tray in front of Caroline, and I could see that instantly she had found the one she wanted. It stood out from the others being chunkier links and had a really nice clasp.

"This one," she said, "definitely this one." As he handed it over to her, he noticed her engagement ring.

"What a beautiful ring he said, antique if I'm not mistaken as is yours, madam."

"Why thank, you, I said but my name is Ella, all this madam business doesn't really suit us, does it Caroline?"

"It does not, my ring and Ella's for that matter, are both family heirlooms. We felt that using the family jewels, so to speak, was much better than buying new ones."

"Absolutely," he replied, "my fiancée has done the same. She said that it wouldn't seem right buying new when her families jewellery stood gathering dust.

"Sensible lady," I said. "Would you do something for me once Caroline has finished her purchases?"

"Certainly Ella, what can I do for you?"

"I would like you to value both of these rings for me if you can."

"Why certainly," he said. Let's finish these sales first then I can take a proper look at them both."

Caroline jumped in then and said, "For insurance purposes, can't be too careful, can we? "Certainly," he said.

Caroline also bought two necklaces with a heart pendant for the girls for being bridesmaids for her as well. She quickly paid her bill then we handed our rings over to him.

"I will just take them through to the back so I can do a proper inspection of the stones. Won't be long."

He went through the door and into the rear workshop. Mrs H and Vera were watching all this with open mouths. "You young girls certainly know how to spend your money, don't you?

I said, "Don't worry about it, I have considerable funds of my own as does Caroline, so we don't need Scott and Jacob's money. I imagine people think that we are only in it for what we can get but that is far from the truth."

"My farm and land is in the process of being sold to building developers and once that goes through I will be very wealthy, but don't think I am bragging, please. I came from nothing. This is all my reward for living a very sad and lonely life until I met and fell in love with Jacob."

"I really had no idea who he was when I met him. I've still not watched any of his films. Too jealous, can't bear thinking about him drooling over pretty young things."

"I can tell you one thing though, I love that man with all my heart and will do everything I can to make him happy."

Mrs H said, "I know you do Chuck, and he loves you. It's there for all the world to see."

Caroline said, "I too have my own money, I have had a very successful career and have given it all up to be with Scott and his two girls. It is all because of Ella that we all met in the first place. This has been a memorable year for us all in one way or another. I have my own house up in the midlands, it is up for sale at the moment, so you see I don't need Scott's money, just his love. And those two girls of his are amazing. Do you know they asked if they can call me mum, isn't that wonderful?"

Before anyone else could speak the salesman returned with our rings. "Well, ladies, you certainly have some very valuable rings here, so I think having them valued is a good idea. You may need to have a separate policy for each of them though. I should check with whoever looks after your insurance business, be guided by them."

"Okay," I said. I'm intrigued. "How much is mine worth?"

I have valued it myself then got my assistant to do the same to be certain. We value your ring Ella at one hundred and sixty to one hundred and eighty thousand pounds, for insurance purposes we suggest a figure in excess of two hundred thousand pounds."

I couldn't speak, are you sure I asked,"

Yes definitely, it is a very rare and special piece".

"Be careful with it, don't drop it down the sink."

"I won't," I said.

He handed me a piece of paper, it was written on headed notepaper and gave all the details. If you decide to insure it separately then give the agent this paper.

"I will," I said. Good God in heaven above I thought, I was wearing it the other day when I was catching spiders in the garden. I quickly slipped it back onto my finger.

"Now, Caroline, yours too is of similar value. The stones individually are less expensive but there are three of them, so we have put the same value on yours, here is your valuation certificate and it comes with the same advice."

"Mrs H, do you have your ring with you?"

"I do lass, why?"

"I think that this gentleman should value that one as well, just to be on the safe side." She pulled it from her finger and handed it over.

"Would you mind?" I asked?

"Not at all, better to be safe than sorry I always say."

He was soon back. "Again Ella, this is very valuable. Not as much as those two, but we have put a value of eighty thousand pounds on it but for insurance purposes, we have suggested one hundred thousand pounds." He handed the ring back with the certificate.

I turned to Mrs H, "I think we had better insure that one as well, don't you?"

"Ella, I can't keep it now I know how much it's worth."

"Of course you can, it was a gift. I will ask Scott to sort it out for you when he does ours."

"Vera, I have one for you too back at the house. I think we had better try to get it valued as well, along with the others."

Vera said, "Don't be daft Ella, you can't give me such a thing. I don't deserve all that you have done for me without giving me an expensive ring."

"Please Vera, it gives me a lot of pleasure being able to spread some of my wealth around. We will have to sort out this insurance business, though now we know."

"Is that it then, ladies, nothing else I can interest you in?"

"No, I think we are done. How much do I owe you for these valuations?"

"Please, Ella, you have spent a small fortune with us today, the valuations are my gift to you with our thanks."

"That is very kind of you. Write your name and number down for me and I will ask Scott if he remembers you."

"Well, thank you, I have a business card here with both name and number. Thank you ladies so much for your custom and I hope to see you all again soon. And good luck for the weddings, I will be looking in the papers for the pictures."

We thanked him once more then left the shop. We were all in a daze with the news we had just received.

"If these rings are worth that much how much will the necklaces be worth?" I said to Caroline.

"God alone knows," she said, "really I can't thank you enough. I love the ring so much."

"As I love mine, we had better get on this insurance stuff though before too long don't you think?"

"Will get Scott on it as soon as we get back."

We all four decided we had shopped enough for one day, we should ring Jacob and then get back to the pub for some lunch before going on to the house to see what Vera thinks.

I borrowed Caroline's mobile and rang Jacob,

"All done, my sweet girl?" he asked.

"We are, can't wait to get back now to my man."

"Glad to hear it," he said. "We should be there in about thirty minutes, go and get a drink whilst you wait. Meet you where we dropped you off."

"Love you. Ella.

"And I love you too my darling, Jacob."

We went into a posh coffee shop and all had tea, doesn't make sense I know, but it was what we fancied.

As soon as we had finished we collected all our parcels up and made our way back to where Jacob would be picking us up.

Just in time, we had literally just walked round the corner and the car pulled up.

Jacob jumped out of the front and came to take the parcels from us and stowed them in the boot. He held the door for us ladies to get in. I was last and he pulled me to him and gave me the longest kiss, full of so much love and passion. He handed me into the car then got into the front with the driver and we began to move off.

I looked around as we were leaving the narrow street and saw several people standing and watching. Some had their mobiles in their hands. I thought God, I bet they have all taken photos. Who cares was my next thought.?

The car made swift progress once we left the city streets behind us. As we pulled into the pub car park I spotted Scott with the girls. They had arrived in Scott's car, so we quickly took the parcels from our cars boot and stored them away in Scott's boot. Vera would be taking her things home with her but that wouldn't be till later.

Once done we all piled into the pub. Of course our table was ready for us. Jacob had rung earlier and told Mary how many we would be. We introduced Vera to Mary and Gregg, she says she feels really special. We told her it is because she is special.

As usual our meals were lovely. Being mid-week they weren't as busy as the weekends but still a good trade. I heard Jacob ask Mary if they had talked any more about getting more help in and she said yes, they will be speaking with Gregg's sister over the weekend. They can't go on as they are.

Once we had finished Scott drove Mrs H and Vera up to the house and the rest of us walked. As we reached them I could hear Vera saying, "This house is amazing, why do they want me here, they could have anyone."

Scott said, "Vera, for whatever reason, they want you, and to be honest I can see why. If you do take them up on the offer they will look after you."

"I know that" she said, "they are so kind to me."

Jacob had walked all the way with his arm around me but now he moved over to the gateway and asked if it was okay for us all to come in. Of course it was and now most of the work is complete there was no need for the hard hats except that Becki and Melisa wanted to wear them.

Firstly we took Vera over to the staff quarters. The main two flats are two bedroomed with everything that Vera would need. The kitchen/diner was lovely. All the appliances were fitted so she wouldn't need to worry about any of that. There is a nice size lounge area then the two bedrooms, one ensuite, and a family bathroom. There is a nice seating area outside with room for a washing line if she wanted one.

Vera was gobsmacked to say the least. "Ella, Jacob, this is beautiful, would it all be for me?"

"Of course Vera, you will need to have somewhere nice to relax when not working. There will be one for the gardener above yours if he wants it then another for anyone that works in the house and needs somewhere to live."

"What would I do with my little house?" asked Vera?.

"Well, that is up to you," said Jacob. "Do you own the house?"

"I do yes. I was married many years ago and we bought the house as soon as we could." My Nigel died though before he could enjoy what he had worked so hard for."

We all said how sorry we were. Jacob said, "If you don't want to sell it then you could always rent it out. Cottages like yours fetch a good rent being so close to the city. Something for you to think about."

"So Vera, do you think you would be happy here?"

"Oh, Jacob, of course, I would be happy. It is beautiful and all on one level which I like."

"If you decide to rent your home out then you could rent it furnished which would bring in more money. If you do decide to do that then we can take you shopping for new stuff for the flat. We are still choosing stuff for the house so it could all be delivered together."

"I am overwhelmed by all this. A fortnight ago, I was just plain Vera working at the hospital to bring in a few pounds, now look at me."

We then took the party into the main house. It is now almost finished. The walls have all been painted and what a difference that makes. It is looking more homely now. No stark white walls staring at us. There is just the nursery to be decorated but Jacob still insists he is doing that himself. Say's he has some great ideas.

Vera and Mrs H are very impressed with it all. We showed them everything. It does look very impressive now even if I do say so myself.

Vera was really taken with the kitchen and all the appliances. She said it looks like something out of a magazine.

The landscapers have begun working at the back. They have a couple of mini diggers there moving soil around. The fencing people are there as well making sure they have everything on site that they will need starting the following day.

Jacob was telling Mrs H and Vera where he wants the pool to go. *He says it won't be this year, want to see how it all works before making a final decision. He wants it to be an indoor pool so it can be used all year round. He will need planning permission for it so they can't begin building it until that is sorted anyway. He said once it is done though Scott's girls will want to move in with us. They both love swimming and would live in the water if they could.*

I said to Jacob, "I can't swim, never been in a pool either. When I was at school and the other kids had lessons I wasn't allowed to go with them. Never did find out why."

"Don't worry, my darling he said, I will teach you." We can start when we are out in France. The pool there is amazing. You will love it."

I said, "Yes, but will these two like it do you think, pointing to my tummy area."

"I bet they will love it," said Jacob. It is very relaxing just being in the water, so you don't have to do anything too excessive. Just a bit of gentle floating. I will be there to help you."

"Right, have you all seen enough? "Yes, they all said."

"Vera, do you want to have another look at the flat?"

"Would you mind? I can't take everything in. Want to make sure I haven't missed anything."

Jacob went back over with her and I could see them chatting away happily together. I said we would start to walk back to Scott's house. He could wait for Jacob and Vera to drive them back. I enjoy this walk. Not far but it helps to stretch the legs. Since leaving the farm I have done very little as regards exercise, well apart from lots of sex. Not sure if that counts as exercise though. Gentle walking would be good for me and for the growing babies in my tummy. Caroline said the same thing. She thinks we should work out a nice little route to walk in France otherwise we will both be like a couple of elephants by the time we come home.

Once we were all back in the house I made tea. Jacob came with me to carry everything.

I said, "You and Vera were having a good old chat when you left us.

"We were" he said, "she is over the moon with it all, she loves the flat and our house and says she has made her mind up, she is definitely going to be working for us. He had advised her about time scales with us going over to France. He has told her we will probably be over there for six weeks then once we get back another two weeks should see us all moved in. She says she is happy with that. It gives her time to sort out what she will do with her house and then get the wheels in motion."

She said she can start packing the things she doesn't use often then nearer the time all her other things can be packed. She asked if he knew of a furniture removers or someone with a van to move all her things. She has decided to leave most of the furniture there and buy new stuff for the move. He has told her we will be buying whatever she needs, all she has to do is choose what she wants. She thinks her furniture will be too old fashioned for the modern flat.

Becki and Melisa wanted to take Vera up the garden to see their own house. The three of them trundled up there hand in hand. I turned to Jacob and said, "She is perfect, this is all going to turn out well."

"It is," he said, and you are right, she is perfect. Like a proper nanny."

Once they were back in the house we all had our cups of tea and homemade biscuits curtesy of Mrs H. I sat in one of the squishy chairs and Jacob sat on the floor, holding my legs and feet rubbing them gently.

Vera smiled, just look at the superstar, sat on the floor like a regular guy. We all laughed at her.

"I told you Vera, he is just a man."

Once it was time for the girls to go to bed, Mrs H and Vera both said they should go, they had taken up enough of our day.

Vera said, "Ella, thank you once again for all the beautiful clothes and things you have bought me. You are all so kind. I am so excited about Saturday. What time do you want me here?"

Jacob said that he will send a car to pick her up at eight forty-five am. "You can come here and have breakfast with us all, then Scott and I will be whisked away to meet up with Gregg and Eddie. We are all going to be polished to within an inch of our lives then we may break our promise not to drink and just have the one for Dutch courage. Then we will be driven to the church to wait for all you gorgeous ladies. Whilst all that is happening to us you will all be made up, hair and nails done then dressed to impress."

Scott and myself will be waiting at the alter to meet you all at one o'clock. Please don't be late.

Caroline and myself both said, "God we are so excited. It can't come soon enough."

Becki and Melisa can't sleep, they are so excited. They haven't even asked if they can speak to their mother. That tells you something about the woman, doesn't it.

It was decided in the end that all the parcels from today's shopping trip should stay here, this is where they will be needed. Once the day is over their things can then go back with the ladies. There is a small room upstairs which is almost empty so we can hang the clothes up in there along with our wedding gowns that will be delivered the next day.

Soon the day was over, the girls were in bed, Mrs H and Vera had been taken home by limo and the four of us were just sitting around enjoying the peace and quiet.

I suddenly thought about the rings and the valuations.

"Right you two, listen up. Whilst we were in town we called into the jewellers where I had bought your bracelet from. We wanted to pick some gifts up for the girls as a thank to them for being bridesmaids. The guy who either works there or owns the place, not sure which remembered us. We got chatting and he said he knows you both from school. Here's his card, thought you might want to speak to him when I tell you what happened next."

He was admiring our engagement rings so we asked him if he would do a valuation for insurance purposes. He took them away then came back with these. I handed mine over to Jacob and Caroline had fetched hers and gave it to Scott.

"Bloody hell" was the reply from Jacob followed by a low whistle and another "bloody hell from Scott." "These will definitely need insurance," said Scott. Ella are you sure about giving this one to us?"

"Of course I'm sure, just get it insured asap, likewise Jacob we should do the same. "The one I gave to Mrs H also needs to be added and the one I intend giving to Vera. Also, I was thinking seriously about the other jewels in the safe. We need to get them valued."

Scott had gone quite pale, "are you okay bro asked Jacob?"

"Yes, I'm fine, it is just such a shock to see these amounts written down, unbelievable."

"You're busy in the morning, aren't you Jacob?"

"I am, yes, got that interview to do, why?"

"I thought I might take all the other stuff of Ella's into this guy, see if I can remember him for one thing then get him to do a valuation on it all."

"Good idea, you don't need me for that though do you?"

"No, of course, not. I think it may be wise if you can get me a car with a driver and one of your security men, though. Don't want hitting over the head on my way into the jewellers."

"Of course I can do that, think we might have to look at home security as well. If those sets we have here are as valuable as the rings it might pay us to get the bank to look after them."

Scott said, "Let's wait and see what this guy comes up with. We can't do anything tonight, can we?

"I am ready for my bed so we will sort it tomorrow."

"We will need to be in town by ten at the latest tomorrow. The interview is scheduled for ten forty-five. Shouldn't be there long once it is done then we can all relax for a while. I guess Friday will be a bit mad then Saturday, roll on. Let's tie ourselves to these two gorgeous women for the rest of our days as soon as we can."

Scott said, "Just a thought Jacob, we are all waiting for appointments for the hospital, if we are in France then that can't happen."

"Thought of that Scott, we have medical cover for France anyway, but I have upped it to include two very pregnant women and all their needs plus two lovely young ladies that will accompany us."

"I can't believe all this has been arranged in such a short space of time. I keep waiting for something to go wrong," Jacob said.

"Stop that Jacob, don't put the kybosh on it. We have made meticulous plans so nothing can go wrong. Come on, bed. Our heads will all be full of possible problems and we won't be able to sleep," I said.

Finally, we made it upstairs and began our loving of each other. Each time we come together I am filled with such a passion for this wonderful man."

Thursday morning, this was going to be another busy day. Caroline was staying at the house with the girls. I was going to the TV studios with Jacob and Scott was on a mission. He was going into London, to the jewellers taking with him the three jewellery sets and the remaining rings from the safe. As an afterthought he also put the three watches into the bag. Might not be able to get a value on those but he thought it might be worth trying.

Caroline was going to be doing some craft things with the girls. She says all little girls like making things. Anyway, they all appeared happy as we left for the TV Studios. Jacob had booked a limo for us to travel in and also booked a car for Scott, together with a driver and a security man who would accompany him into the jewellers.

Jacob looked a dream as usual, he wore his black jeans with another dark green shirt. I think this is my favourite look. I had decided to wear the pretty dress that Jacob had bought for me for his last show at the theatre. It is very comfortable, and I love all the colours. Caroline had done one of the big plaits with my hair. She is getting very good at doing this style.

Our journey was uneventful until we reached the studios. Apparently, it had been announced on the previous day's show that Jacob would be with the presenters in the studio. As we approached the dropping off point it was obvious there would be a problem. Crowds of mainly women were blocking the road in.

"What now?" asked the security man travelling with us.? "Not really sure, was Jacob's reply. I will ring them and ask if there is another entrance."

He took out his phone and rang the security for the studio. A brief conversation and we were directed to another entrance.

Thankfully, we managed to get in there without a problem. This was obviously where stuff was dropped off and not usually people.

We jumped out of the car along with the security man. The car drove off to park up somewhere and we walked into the building. A man was waiting for us and walked us through the building till we reached a room where we were asked to wait. A few moments later a lady came through and took Jacob off to be made up. Not his favourite thing but it had to be done. A little while later he returned. Close up he looked different, still Jacob but with the make-up it made him look unreal.

About ten minutes later we were called through to the studio, Jacob had been fitted with a small microphone. At least I think that is what it is. Something else was fastened to the belt on his trousers at the back. I was fascinated watching all the action taking place. We left our security man in the room with a cup of coffee.

They had gone to an 'ad' break, whatever one of those is, Jacob was taken over to the sofa, first he shook hands with a man named Philip then kissed a very pretty woman on the cheek before he sat down on the sofa facing them.

They were chatting briefly before it was time for Jacob's interview. Suddenly it all looked very professional, the chat had stopped, and the man named Philip was talking to the camera then it went to the woman and she introduced Jacob.

I could see a screen that was showing the picture that was going out on live TV. My God, Jacob looks so handsome, well he is handsome but seeing him on the screen like that was unreal. He looked every inch the star he is.

The talk was mainly about the show that had just finished and about how successful it has been. Then they congratulated him on winning his award. He was very gracious in what he was saying about it not only being him that had won but the whole team that helped put it together. He praised his musical director and several other people.

He was then asked about the incident that had resulted in his fiancée being taken to hospital. Jacob said he was sorry but as this was an ongoing police investigation also linked to the other incident at the theatre he was unable to elaborate further. He just wanted to reassure people, both he and his fiancée, are fine now and looking forward to their wedding on Saturday.

The woman said, "You have your fiancée here with you today Jacob, will she come and say hello?"

Jacob looked over to where I was standing. "You can ask her, but she is very shy."

The man named Philip came over to me and took hold of my hand. "Hello Ella, very pleased to meet you. Come and sit by Jacob and let the viewers have a look at the woman that has stolen Jacob's heart."

"I thought, bloody hell, now what do I do?"

I wasn't given much choice, he held my hand and pulled me over to where Jacob was sitting. Jacob stood up and kissed me. "Come and sit here, next to me my darling."

Someone rushed on and fastened a mic onto my dress at the neck then also fastened something to the belt at the back. God, it all happened so quickly, I didn't have time to think.

"Right then," said Philip, "Ella, it's lovely to meet you."

"Thank you," I said, Jacob squeezed my hand. Then the woman said, you two seem to have had a whirlwind romance.

Jacob spoke, "We have, the minute I met Ella I knew she was the one for me. She didn't know who I was or what I did for a living."

The woman laughed, "Have you been living on the moon Ella, everyone knows who Jacob Ryan is."

Jacob was going to answer for me, but I felt that was not right, so I said. "Well, I have lived all my life on a very remote farm in the Midlands. We didn't have a TV or radio, well not one that I was allowed to listen to."

"My parents lived and worked on the farm, my mother died before I was a month old and so it was left to my dad to bring me up. He was only twenty one and he was out of his depth and so the farmer's wife looked out for me. I don't think she liked me very much but there wasn't much anyone could do. I grew up being scared of everything. My dad died when I was eleven, so I had to do his work as well as go to school and do my homework."

"The farmer's wife died when I was fifteen and on my sixteenth birthday I was forced to marry the farmer. I had an awful life. Scared of the animals and scared of my husband. He was a dirty old man who abused me for nine years."

"Earlier this year he died, I was so scared, I didn't have a clue what to do. I had never used a phone before although there was one in his office. Eventually, I managed to work out how to ring for an ambulance."

"During all this the local GP organised for a social worker to come and help me. She is wonderful. Over the next few days and weeks she rang everyone that needed to be rung, sorted everything really.

One of the people she had to ring was the lawyer that looked after the farms business. That lawyer is Jacob's brother Scott."

"Long story short, Caroline and Scott fell in love. They took me down to Scott's house and it was there that I met and fell in love with this wonderful man."

Philip said, "You poor girl, how awful for you. But, and I am glad to say this, you now have a man you love and who loves you, with a bright future ahead of you."

"I do," I said, "I had never been happy before in all my twenty-five years, but Jacob has taught me how to live and to love. Yes, it has been a whirlwind but we both know, without any doubt that what we have is the real deal."

"The woman said you should write a book about your life, it would be a fascinating read."

"I might do that one day," I said "but just at the moment we have other things to do. We get married on Saturday along with Jacob's brother Scott and his fiancée Caroline, it is to be a double wedding."

"Well congratulations to you all"

"Jacob said thank-you but the wedding is not the only thing we have going on in our lives".

"Really" said Philip, "what can possibly top that?"

Jacob smiled, picked up my hand and kissed it. "Both Ella and myself and Scott and Caroline are expecting twins in December. I know, we couldn't believe it at first, but it is definitely true. We are all so happy and looking forward to the coming months and years. The Ryan brothers do everything together it appears."

Philip said, "Well, folks, how about that for a first. Can't ever remember an announcement like that on the programme before."

The woman said, "I think you are right Philip, I don't ever remember anything like this before."

"This is truly a wonderful end to your story, and we wish you both and your brother and his fiancée all the luck in the world."

We both thanked her.

Jacob then said, "This is not the end to our story though, this is just the beginning."

The woman said, "I feel so happy for you all, I could cry."

Jacob was holding my hand, he lifted it to his lips and kissed it once more.

Philip then said, "What is next for you then Jacob, any more projects we need to know about?"

Jacob smiled. "Nothing for the foreseeable Philip, we will be married on Saturday then we are having a long honeymoon. When we get back we will move into our new home and prepare for the arrival of the next batch of Ryan's. I will be a stay-at-home dad for a long time. I have dreamed of having a family of my own and now that it is happening I intend to enjoy it. I will be a proper hands-on dad and help with everything."

"Once we have all that side sorted I will then look at doing something else, but I don't intend doing another long run of shows for a very long time."

"I am organising a charity show for the hospital that treated us both recently, that should happen in early December but after that then I will just be plain daddy."

Philip said, "Well, from us all here we wish you every happiness. You look a lovely couple, and I am sure you will be a very happy family."

"Thank you Jacob and Ella, this has been a remarkable interview. We look forward to seeing you back here again in the near future, perhaps when you have more details for your charity show. We will both buy tickets for that."

The woman said, "We most definitely will. Thank you both and all the best for the future."

They then went to another ad break and Philip and the woman came over to thank us for taking the time to speak with them.

The woman said to me, Ella, "You have had a dreadful life up until now, but I meant what I said, you should write a book."

I thanked her then apologised. "I am sorry for going on, Caroline says I have no filter. I think it then say it."

"Please Ella, don't be sorry. It has been an enlightening interview and I am so glad you joined Jacob to give us your story. We really do wish you all the best."

"She kissed my cheek then Jacob's, Philip shook hands with Jacob then kissed my cheek.

He said, "Ella, you are a lovely young woman, enjoy your life from now on."

"I will." I said. "Jacob has been the most wonderful person. We just met and fell in love, it was crazy really but when it's right, you know, don't you?" He kissed my cheek again. "We will see you again soon I hope, good luck for the wedding and for your twins."

They went back to their seats and Jacob and I were led back to the room we had been in earlier. Our security man was still sitting in there nursing his coffee cup. He left the room to go for a comfort break.

As soon as we were on our own Jacob kissed me, "Ella you are amazing."

"Me? Why?"

"You came here today just to keep me company then get hauled in front of live TV cameras and you just *Wow* everyone with your honesty, your beauty, everything about you is just magic. They loved you."

"Really," I said, "I thought I had said too much, you know, my usual think it, say it." "Whatever you call it Ella, it works. I bet they want you back again before long."

"Don't talk daft, why would they want me again?"

"Because you tell it how it is. Now, let me get this shite of my face."

He went to find the make-up woman to get something to clean his face with and soon came back looking like my Jacob once more.

"Are you ready, my love?

"I am," I said. "Will we have to get out the way we came in?"

"Not sure, will check. He got his phone out and rang someone to find out the situation." Thinned out a bit out front, do you fancy trying it?"

"Whatever you think Jacob, you know more about these situations than I do."

"Okay, he rang for his car to be brought round to the main entrance. Our security man had been shadowing us all the time we were in the studio. We made our way to the main entrance with an escort. Before we had gone too far, though a man came hurrying towards us.

"Jacob, so sorry, thought I had missed you. Been in a meeting that overran. How are you my friend?"

"I am great, thank you," said Jacob. Let me introduce my fiancée, Ella."

"Ella, this is Jack Watling, the producer of the programme we have just been on." I shook his hand, "pleased to meet you," I said.

"So, this is the young lady that has stollen your heart."

"It certainly is Jack. Philip just got her to join me for the interview and I think she stole the show."

"No, I didn't," I said. "It is only you that anyone wants to see. I am just a novelty."

Jack said, "I don't think so, Ella. As I came out of my meeting, I heard a conversation going on up in the office and you were receiving some very good marks. They were all very positive about you so take some of the glory, this boy gets enough."

I felt a bit awkward, but I thanked him for his kindness.

Jacob said, "We have to go I'm afraid Jack, Scott will be waiting for us."

"Okay then Jacob, all the best, I hear you are getting married soon."

"Yes, we are, Saturday as it happens. We won't be around for a few months after that. We are having a long honeymoon then moving into our new home and then in December our twins will be born."

"Bloody hell Jacob, you don't waste much time do you?"

"What is there to wait for?" he said. "We are in love, we both want a family, why should we wait?"

"True, good luck to you both.'

"Thanks Jack, just got to get out to the car in one piece then we will be on our way."

"They shook hands and Jack kissed my cheek. Look after him Ella, he is a grand lad."

"I will," I promised.

With that we were escorted the rest of the way to the main entrance. Our car was there and I couldn't see any fans.

The man escorting us said that they had moved everyone back and put barriers up as they feared someone would get hurt.

As we stepped outside we heard a huge cheer. I looked to the right and the security man was correct, there were a lot of people waiting.

"This is not right," Jacob said. "These folk have been waiting hours. Let's just go and have a brief word with them before we go. Fair's fair," he said.

"Okay," I said, "if you are sure."

"I am he said, come on, let's stay together."

As soon as we began walking towards them there were shouts of 'Jacob, we love you', 'give us a song' along with several other things that I thought were a bit rude. Not that I am a prude."

We started at one side of the barrier and spoke with all the mainly women there, we then moved along the front of it speaking to all those we could. It didn't take long really, and they all seemed to appreciate it.

There were still calls for Jacob to sing to them. "What do you think he asked me?'

"Jacob, if you feel like singing to them, then go for it."

"Okay," he said, just one. What's it to be? Of course *'Somewhere'* was the overwhelming favourite. Blimey! not sung for a few days, the vocal chords might have seized up."

He stepped back a few paces and began to get himself ready. He began very softly then with each line the intensity went up. Building and building till that very long last note.

I was just standing watching and listening with the rest of the crowd. I could feel my heart beating fast in my chest. I would never tire of listening to this beautiful man. He is amazing.

As he finished there was a huge round of applause. "Brilliant Jacob, they were all shouting."

Unbeknown to us they had been filming us from the building speaking to the crowd and then Jacob singing.

This film was played on the TV at the end of the programme we had been on. Apparently, that and our interview received more emails and phone calls than any other artist has had. All of them saying wonderful things about us both".

"How can Jacob say he won't be performing for a long time, this man is born to entertain?" I will have to monitor him over the coming weeks. If I find that he is missing the limelight then I will suggest that he does some more shows. Not the mad ten-week stint but a few here and there won't hurt. It will give me a chance to watch him perform as well. I would love that."

Scott had a very interesting visit with the jeweller. Once he saw the man he did recognise him. "Julian Moore, of course, I remember you. My fiancée Caroline and Jacob's fiancée Ella have told us some good things about you and your business."

Julian was well impressed to think that Scott Ryan had remembered him. Scott, what an honour. I never expected to see you grace my shop."

To be honest, it was our ladies that found you. We have been bowled over with the valuations you put on their rings. We knew they would be valuable but the actual value you have put on them, well it took our breath away to be honest. Tell me Julian, is this your own business?"

"Yes, it is," Scott, it was my parents' business for over thirty years then when they decided to retire it was handed over to me. I have made a few changes to the place but still try to keep the same atmosphere and values that they created. It seems to work."

"Scott said it certainly does, it is a very nice place."

"Following our ladies visit to you we have decided to get you to put a value on a few more pieces we have if you will. We suddenly realised that separate insurance for these things is something that we need to sort out sooner rather than later."

"Always a good idea," said Julian. What have you bought for me to look at today?"

"Well, if I am honest they don't actually belong to me, they are Ella's family heirlooms but as we all live together at the moment she has asked me to bring them along. Jacob and Ella have had to go into the TV studios this morning for an interview, so she asked that I bring them in for her."

Julian said, "Yes, I saw the interview actually, very good. Ella is amazing, so confident in front of the camera."

Scott looked a little surprised, "Did they manage to convince her to speak on live TV?"

"They certainly did. She looked a little scared when they dragged her onto the sofa but once she started speaking she was amazing. She told a little of the life she had before meeting Jacob, how awful for her. She certainly seems to be coming out of her shell now."

"You could say that," said Scott. "She is a lovely woman, and she has been so good for my brother. It was love at first sight for them both. They have been together ever since. I was worried about Jacob before meeting Ella but now I am happy he is with the person he should be with. We are having a joint wedding on Saturday. Should be quite a do."

"So I hear from your ladies, they are very excited."

"As are we all. It's a fresh start for us. If you can get time away from here on Saturday would you like to join us? Jacob would like to meet you again I'm sure."

"Are you serious Scott, my fiancée is a huge fan of Jacob's? She would be over the moon."

"Of course, I wouldn't joke about a thing like that. I have a spare invitation here, that gives you all the details. Be sure to ring the hotel to let them know that you will be coming. Need to keep a tight grip on guests. Would be awful if you turned up and there wasn't a seat for you."

"I will Scott, I will ring Abbie shortly and tell her. She won't believe me."

"We intend having a good time and we want everyone there to enjoy it."

"Unbelievable," said Julian. "She will think I'm joking."

"We will look forward to seeing you there. Just one thing, no gifts. We are very lucky and have all we need. All we want from you is to have a good time.

Now back to business, this gentleman is one of Jacob's security team. After learning the value of their rings we thought it best to take some precautions with these. He handed the bag over to Julian. "Prepare to be dazzled."

"Very carefully, Julian took the boxes from the bag and lined them up on the counter. This is all very scary," he said.

"Please, we are just interested to know the value so we can take appropriate action regarding insurance and storage if I'm honest."

"Julian picked up the first box and carefully opened it. "Bloody hell," he said, this is amazing. I am going to lock the doors and we can go through to the back workshop. This is very valuable indeed. I can tell you that without looking further."

He came from behind the counter and locked the doors. "Scott, please follow me through to the office. Your security can take a seat in the workshop whilst we do this."

"Okay," said Scott, "I am beginning to feel a bit scared about what you will say next.'

"They followed Julian through to the rear of the shop. Two other men were in the back of the shop working on pieces of jewellery.

Julian asked one young man if he would mind watching the front of the shop for a while. The man got up and went through the door.

"Right Scott, this gentleman here is George. He worked for my parents for years and now works for me. What he doesn't know about precious stones and particularly antique ones you could write on a stamp."

"George can I introduce you to Scott Ryan, he has bought some items in to be valued for insurance purposes. They shook hands. Julian then said, you remember the two ladies that bought those beautiful rings in for valuation well they are the fiancée's of Scott and his brother Jacob. Yes, the Jacob Ryan."

Blimey! said George, pleased to meet you, Scott. You have one very talented brother."

Scott smiled, I certainly do."

George said, "We were watching him only this morning on the TV in the office. His young lady is a gem."

"She certainly is, all this jewellery belongs to her, family heirlooms. She has never had them valued before but after the rings that Julian valued we thought it best to get these sorted."

They took the boxes through to the office and Julian began opening them. Scott thought blimey! these things must be worth a fortune by the look on Julian's face.

"Right," said George, "let's have a proper look at these. They are exquisite, all of them. He began looking at them through a magnifying glass, then passing them over to Julian to do the same.

He was writing figures down on a piece of paper then crossing some out and writing something else. Once they had both examined all the items he put his pen down and let out a deep breath.

"Scott, you might want to get these valued by the insurance companies own valuers. It might be a stipulation of their companies that they get independent valuations. We can tell you what we think but to be absolutely sure you need to be guided by them."

"Okay," said Scott, "let's hear what you two think first."

"The remaining rings were all valued at between thirty-five thousand pounds and eighty thousand pounds. The platinum wedding ring was valued at two thousand pounds."

"Okay," said Scott, "now onto these, first was the ruby set, George said he estimated at least five hundred thousand pounds, then the emerald set, again about five hundred thousand pounds. Scott was beginning to sweat. Caroline and Ella had worn these to the awards ceremony, none of them aware of their value.

Finally the black diamonds. This one is more difficult to value because these stones are so rare. I would value the whole set at nearer a million." Julian said,

"That is what I was thinking George replied." Scott had gone very pale.

"Are you sure he asked?"

"Well," said Julian, this is only our opinion. "The insurance companies might easily double what we think." Scott said, "Can I sit down please? I feel quite faint."

Julian sat him down on the chair behind the desk. "I will fetch a drink of water for you Scott. You look very pale."

Once Scott had drunk some cold water and managed to get his breathing back to normal he said, "That has been the biggest shock of my life. I knew they were valuable obviously, but those figures are out of this world."

"Okay," he said, what do I need to do now? They have been living in the safe at my family home. Yes, it is a good safe but if the news gets out about how valuable these things are, well it doesn't bare thinking about."

Julian said, "Well, Scott, I don't know what to tell you, really. The bank could keep them for you but if the ladies want to wear them it could prove a problem. I suppose you could update your home security and safe but that doesn't really help with your concerns. Would Ella want to keep them or sell them?"

"I have no idea, Julian, I will speak with her later today and see what she thinks. I can't imagine her just keeping them without wanting to wear them. Will she sell them, not sure? She certainly doesn't need the money."

"Well, I suppose we had better get them back home then hide them away until she does decide what to do with them. She won't want to believe me."

"Right, at least I have security with me so that makes me feel safer. We also have a driver so I can sit in the back and nurse these babies all the way home. To think I was going to drive myself in and just carry them in a carrier bag. Madness."

"We also have three watches that need valuing, any ideas who would be able to do that?"

"Again, if you are going to speak with the insurance company ask them about the watches, I can't imagine they will be cheap ones."

"No, they're not. Scott was scratching his head. He thought to himself, Will was definitely a very weird man."

"Well Julian, thanks for all the advice. How much do I owe you?"

"You don't owe me anything Scott, just get them sorted and safe is my advice."

"Thank you again, my friend. See you on Saturday then. I look forward to meeting your fiancée."

"Thanks again, Scott, this really means a lot to me, and it will mean an awful lot to Abbie. She won't believe it till she sees it. See you on Saturday and if there is ever anything else I can help you with please let me know."

"I will Julian, thanks again. See you Saturday."

He quickly put all the boxes back into the bag then he and the security man made a swift exit and headed for the car.

Scott felt tense all the way back home and was very thankful once they turned into the gates of his home.

As he left the car he thanked the driver and security man and then went into the house.

Scott walked into the kitchen to find his beautiful Caroline working hard with his daughters. They were very busy creating something wonderful by the looks of things. There was a strong smell of vanilla and the kitchen side was covered in pieces of cake and icing in several different colours.

Caroline looked up as he entered the room. "Hello, my darling." she said, I hope you are hungry for cake?

His daughters both looked up to see their father looking very interested in what they were creating. "Well, he said, this all looks very tasty and very pretty. Have you been having a good time?"

Becki said, "We have had a lovely time, Daddy. Mum let us bake cakes. We are making them very special, some for you, some for Mum and some for us. We have also made some for Uncle Jacob and Aunty Ella."

"You have been very busy then. I think that once Jacob and Ella get home we should all have a nice cup of tea and then make a start on eating some of these amazing cakes."

"Yes, please, Daddy, we have tasted some of them and they are the best."

"I am sure they are, they look wonderful, and I can't wait to taste them."

As they were talking about all things cake the front door opened and Jacob and Ella came in. They were laughing together as they came into the kitchen.

Jacob stopped and held Ella back. "What is that I can smell? Smells like cakes to me. Who has been baking?"

The girls were giggling, "We have Uncle Jacob, we have made lots of cakes for everybody."

Melisa said, "I saw you and Aunty Ella on the TV today. I liked it when you sang to the fans outside. You sing lovely, Uncle Jacob, I want you to sing especially for me when it's my birthday."

"Okay," said Jacob, "I can do that. How did you hear me singing outside? he asked?.

Caroline said that they had watched the programme when we were on and had left the TV playing whilst they got all the cake-making things out. The programme was just coming to an end when they said that they had filmed you leaving the building and talking to the fans. They said it was a very special moment and so would be playing it for the end of the show. As the credits were rolling you were singing to all those waiting fans. "Honestly, Jacob it really was so special. We have recorded it so you can see for yourself."

Jacob said, "I didn't notice anyone filming, did you, Ella?"

"No, I didn't," I replied. "I was too busy listening to your wonderful voice to notice anything."

Jacob asked Caroline, "What did you think of my beautiful Ella being interviewed? Wasn't she just the best?"

She really was Jacob, I couldn't believe my ears. So confident. It would seem that everyone loved her. I think that one day she should write that book that they were talking about. I think it would be a best seller.

"Don't talk daft," Caroline, "I couldn't write a book, it would take all my time to read one."

"You could get someone to help you, you wouldn't actually write it all yourself. Just tell your story and then they would turn it into a written work. Something for you to think about for the future."

"I couldn't even think about doing something like that. I will have my hands full with babies and nappies, how could I even think about doing anything like that?"

Whilst Caroline and I had been talking, Jacob had put the kettle on and Scott was getting everything ready for our cake feast."

The girls had put loads of cakes onto a big plate and carried it through to the lounge. Meanwhile, I helped Caroline to clear up the debris left on the kitchen island. Blimey! They'd had fun. There was cake and icing everywhere.

I heard Jacob ask Scott how he had got on at the jewellers.

"Wait till we all sit down, you won't believe what they said. By the way, I have invited Julian and his fiancée Abbie to the weddings. I think that will be about it now though. He was really chuffed, and said his fiancée is a big fan."

"That's okay Scott, it is your wedding as well as mine you know. You can invite who you want. Caroline began pouring the tea and Becki and Melisa gave out small plates to us all.

They had to carry the big plate of cakes between them. We all took one and then had to make a big fuss of their baking skills. They were very nice though I have to say.

Having all eaten one, we then had to have a second one. I said, if I keep eating all these cakes I won't fit in my wedding dress. The girls were laughing, they were so excited.

Caroline said they had been really good and enjoyed making the cakes. She had enjoyed her morning with them as well. I guess they have never been allowed to make cakes before. They had certainly had a lovely time.

Jacob asked the girls if they wanted to watch a video in the cinema room. "Oh, yes please, Uncle Jacob. Will you set it up for us, please?"

"I will come on let's find a good one for you." Off they went holding Jacob's hands. "They do love their uncle, don't they?" I said.

Scott said, "He has always been a big part of their lives. We have spent a lot of time together, even before he came to live here. He was a lonely soul, very popular but still lonely. You have made such a difference to him Ella."

"Well, he has made a bigger difference to me. We really are so in tune with each other. I am so happy."

"I know that Ella. We are the same aren't we, my darling Caroline?" She leant into him and kissed him, "We are, my love," she said. "Never been this happy before in all my life."

Jacob came back then and said, "Right that's them sorted. Now, Scott what news do you have for us."

"Well," he said, "I think we should all sit down for this."

We did, Jacob joined me on one of the squishy sofa and Scott and Caroline took the other one. "Okay," I said, "I'm ready, I think."

Scott proceeded to tell us what had happened when he went to the jewellers. He told us everything, right from when he had entered the shop and recognised Julian.

He then told us about the valuations that both Julian and his assistant George had put on the sets of jewellery.

We all went very quiet, I couldn't believe what he was saying. I had found these things in a safe that wasn't even locked.

"I don't want them, Scott. I would be frightened to wear them and what's the point of having them and not wearing them?

Jacob was holding me tight. "Ella, you can't make a decision straight away, you need to really think about this. *You could deposit them with the bank and just leave them there. They would be an investment even if you don't wear them. Let's see about putting them in the banks vaults tomorrow then just leave them there until we have had our holiday and moved into the house. Once our babies are born we will both be busy. Let's just leave it for now, yes we can get it all insured first but I do think it will be wise not to make a rash decision.*"

"Okay, Jacob," I said. "You are right, I was just getting panicky. Let's get them out of the house for now though. It's not fair on Scott to have them here."

Scott said, "I really think that is the best idea. No rash decisions and no keeping them in here. After all, we will all be away for a while and leaving such valuable jewels in the safe here is perhaps just a bit, well just a bit."

That was all agreed then, Scott and Jacob would take them to the bank in the morning. Jacob would get a car ordered along with a couple of security men. They would be fine and getting these valuables out of here was the best thing to do. They would go in early and get it all done before the streets got too busy. Scott said he would ring the bank manager on the way so that they wouldn't have to hang around.

Once the decision had been made we all felt better.

"Okay," I said, now what would you all like for dinner? "I will cook." Three heads turned and looked at me, "Why do you want to cook?

Because it will stop me from worrying about Scott's safe."

"What do you all fancy?"

A chorus of "lasagne" rang out. "Okay then, I will check to see if we have everything I need. Do the girls like it? I asked Scott.?

"I should say so, well they love the bland frozen ones I usually feed them. Just go for it Ella, they eat most things."

"So that is what I did." Jacob came with me and watched everything I did. Thankfully Mrs H keeps a very well-stocked fridge and I found everything I needed.

I set to making the lasagne and still Jacob sat watching me. "What?" I asked.

"Nothing, just watching my darling fiancée cooking. I love you so much Ella. *You know that this morning you were nothing short of amazing. I really thought you would run off when Philip went to fetch you. But, no, you just got on with it. I was so proud of you. Looking back just a few weeks ago you would have died at the thought of doing such a thing. You have changed so much my darling, so brave. I am so in love with you and with our growing babies."*

"Have you remembered we have appointments with the doctor tomorrow afternoon? Need to check all is well with you and with those two before we fly off on Sunday."

"I remembered" Yes, I am sure all is well though. I had a few days where I felt a bit sicky first thing but that seems to have passed. Other than that I feel really well. Caroline keeps a check on my blood pressure as well as her own, all is fine there."

"I am so looking forward to the wedding and then to our honeymoon. It will all be real then, won't it? I will be Mrs Jacob Ryan and I can't wait."

"Do you think we will be able to sneak upstairs once this lasagne is in the oven? I am feeling neglected."

"Well my darling, if you are so neglected then I had better pull my socks up and do something about it. What about the girls? I asked.?

Jacob said, I will have a word with Scott and advise him to keep them down here for half an hour or so. We can lock the bedroom door as well just to be certain. Don't want any interruptions.

"I am looking forward to that my love. Thirty minutes with my darling, uninterrupted as well. Magic."

I quickly finished assembling the lasagne and put it in the oven. The salad was already made, and Mrs H had left a fresh loaf. I would slice it when we came down, rub it with garlic then toast it. That will go nice with the meal I thought.

That was the plan and that is what happened. We spent a good half hour enjoying each other. Our lovemaking is so wonderful. I am so looking forward to enjoying this man and his wonderful body for many years to come.

We came downstairs full of beans and laughter. Jacob was kissing me in the kitchen when the girls came in to see if their dinner was ready. Uncle Jacob, you are always kissing Aunty Ella. Mummy says it is dirty to kiss someone.

"Which mummy?" I asked?

"Mummy Flora, of course, Daddy is always kissing Mummy Caroline, so he doesn't think it's dirty."

I asked, "Doesn't Mummy Flora kiss the nasty man then."

"No, she says it is very dirty and if you kiss someone on the mouth you can catch something."

"Really," I said, "I think she has got that wrong. When you love someone like Daddy loves Mummy Caroline and like I love Uncle Jacob then it is really lovely to share kisses, especially on the mouth. When you get older and have boyfriends you will enjoy kissing as well. They both broke out in fits of giggles."

Once everyone was in the kitchen and sitting around the island I served up the lasagne. The girls first. "Right," I asked, who wanted salad with their lasagne and who wanted garlic bread? They both called out, me, me.

I thought that I had maybe put too much on their plates, but they were soon tucking in and cleared their plates. "Aunty Ella, that was lovely. Did you make it all yourself asked Becki?."

"I did, I don't like frozen meals really, they are a bit tasteless."

Melisa said, "We only had frozen food at Mummy Flora's house. She doesn't like cooking, that horrid man says it makes the whole house smell."

"Well, I don't care if the house does smell, if I cook a meal and it is tasty then so what?" I said.

"We really love this" don't we Becki?"

" Yes we do, it is soo nice. Will you make it for us again, Aunty Ella?"

"Of course, I will. I think that Mummy Caroline is a good cook as well. I wonder what her favourite meal is to make.

"What do you cook nice, Mummy asked Melisa?" "Well, I can cook a very nice Cottage Pie if I do say so myself".

"I don't think we have had one of those have we, Becki? No, I don't think so. We mostly had frozen Pizza or Chicken Nuggets and chips, sometimes we had fish fingers and baked beans. I like the food here best, we have takeaway and lasagne, they are the best."

"I know, when we get to the house in France how about if we have something different every day for dinner, then we won't get bored, will we?"

"Oh, yes please, we like trying new things, don't we Becki?

We do yes," said Becki with a big smile on her face.

"That all right with you folks?" I asked?.

"You bet they said."

We woke early on Friday morning, Jacob was watching me as I opened my eyes. "Morning gorgeous," he said,

"Morning, my darling," I replied. He pulled me into a big hug and kissed me with a passion, I was left breathless.

"What time is it" I asked,

"Almost time to get up," he replied.

"That's a shame," I said, "I was hoping for a little loving before you leave me."

He didn't need any more encouragement. I said, "Almost time to get up, come here, my beautiful darling and let me love you."

I did, we made love and it was wonderful. My climax lasted for an age, pulsing over and over. Jacob exploding inside me and I loved it. We are so good together, one more day to go then I will be tied to Jacob forever.

We got up once we could breathe again. We showered together and then dried each other. I love this intimate thing we do for each other.

Finally, we dressed for the day. Scott and Jacob would be heading to their bank as soon as it opened. Jacob had ordered a car and two security men to accompany them on the journey. I felt happier knowing my man would be safe.

I had kept one of the rings back for Vera. She says she won't be able to accept such a gift, but I really want her to have one. I think she will like this one the best, an emerald surrounded by tiny diamonds, similar to the one Jacob had bought me but a lot older.

We had a simple breakfast of cereal, toast and juice then said we would go to the pub at lunchtime. This would be our last visit there as single people. The girls were excited to go, they feel very grown up when they come out with us. I have to say they are always very well behaved.

As soon as breakfast was over our menfolk got the jewels and the watches from the safe, placing them in a leather bag that Jacob had used when going to the theatre. He put a couple of shirts over the top of the boxes just in case he said. In case of what I didn't ask.

The car arrived promptly and after kissing us all they jumped in the vehicle and it sped off. I would be on tenterhooks till they returned. I just didn't want those jewels anywhere in the house.

All was well on the journey to the bank, Scott had rung the bank manager informing him of what they wanted to do once they arrived. Everything was ready for them as they entered the building and so they hurried off to the bank manager's office.

They told him the story of the jewels and he quickly arranged for it all to be locked away in the banks vaults. He was also able to arrange insurance for everything.

They were both relieved once that job was done. No one had realised just how valuable it all was and then thinking how it had all been stored in the past.

Scott told Jacob how the jewels and all the money had just been shoved in the safe at the farm and the door wasn't even locked. Then since it has been with us at Scott's house it was all just stored in his own safe. Yes it is a safe but not the right place for safe keeping of such valuable items. They have even taken the watches along for safe keeping.

Once they reached the house everyone could breathe more easily. Thank God for that I said. I still can't believe how we had worn them to the awards ceremony.

Once we were all back home and safe we sat for a while just relaxing. Mrs H had been in making everywhere look presentable. She wanted to get a meal ready for us all, but we said for her to get off home and rest before tomorrow. We would probably walk down to the pub.

As twelve o'clock arrived that is just what we did. The weather was good, so we didn't need to wrap up too much. A walk would do us all good.

The girls came with us. They are so excited about tomorrow. I told them if they keep jumping around they will be too tired to enjoy themselves at the weddings. They just laughed at me.

The pub was quite busy, and we attracted lots of looks as we entered. Of course, half the people there wanted to speak to Jacob. He insisted on introducing me to everyone. I am really getting into this socialising. People can be really nice.

Eventually, we made it to our table and Mary appeared as if by magic. We just had plates of sandwiches and bowls of chips, none of us could stomach a cooked meal. Mary said that her sister-in-law had arrived and was clear about everything she needed to know. They had also managed to have a good talk with both her and her husband. They put a proposition to them about joining the pub business so that she and Gregg would be able to take some time for themselves. They liked what had been put forward and would give it some serious thought then let them know their answer before leaving to go back home. Mary said she is hopeful they will come on board.

We convinced our menfolk to have a pint of beer each with their meals. They have both been so good, one won't hurt them. The looks on their faces as the first swallow slipped down their throats. They really appreciated the beer and felt better for it. Caroline and myself had another pot of tea. We will look like the teapot before these babies are born.

We both had appointments at the doctors in the afternoon just to check all is well, so we suggested that Caroline and I go for the appointments and the two men take control of the girls till we get back. Jacob wanted to come with me, but he could see the sense in what we said.

We went along to the surgery straight from the pub and left the men to sort the girls out.

"Jacob was making such a fuss of me," I said, "we are only going down the road, not on a trip to the moon."

"I know he said but "I will miss you. I had to leave you this morning as well."

"Not to worry," I said, "by this time tomorrow we will be married."

"I know," he said, "soppy of me but I just love being with you."

"Okay," I said, "how about if you two take the girls home and set up a good video for them to watch then once we get back we could perhaps take a nap. His eyes lit up. Now that is a plan I can go with," he said.

And so that is what we did, our trip to the surgery was fine. Everything progressing as it should be. We explained about being in France, Caroline for about three weeks and me at least six weeks. We said we have excellent health cover for France as we have a house there. The midwife was happy for us to be away for that length of time just as long as if we have any problems at all we go straight to the nearest hospital. We will we both said.

She said she had heard about the weddings and wanted to wish us all the best, which was lovely of her. Caroline has an appointment for when she returns then as soon as we get back I have to ring up to make my appointment.

We had a nice walk back, it is good to be able to chat without continually being interrupted by the girls chatter. We love them to bits but they do go on a bit.

Caroline asked me if I was still sure we were doing the right thing.

"Why, do you think we are wrong?"

"Not at all," she said "but all this has happened so fast. I can't catch my breath some days. The girls are amazing, and I already love them like my own and Scott is so loving. We seem to be made for each other."

"I know what you mean, Caroline. Just a few weeks back I was terrified of what the next day would bring and now look at me. Giving an interview on live TV. Still can't believe I did that. But Jacob is amazing, I really do love him so much. Not only the way he has brought me into this new life but for all the other things. The way we are when we are together, I know it's all about sex at the moment, but I have never known such joy and freedom before.

Jacob has made me into the woman I always should have been. He is so loving, generous and gorgeous. I know he is this fabulous superstar but honestly, when we are together it is just all about us. I think that once these holidays are over and we can move into the house then you and I will be even closer. We seem to be doing everything together anyway don't we?"

"We certainly do,"she said. You couldn't make it up, could you?" We both agreed that tomorrow would be an amazing day for us all.

We soon reached Scott's home and went in to find the pace in an uproar. "What is going on?" called Caroline. The girls were in fits of giggles. "Where's Daddy?" she asked,

"Hiding mum, come and help us find him." "He is a monster and Uncle Jacob is a cat."

I was a bit puzzled as to why Jacob was just a cat but apparently that is what the girls had decided he should be. We went on a hunt for the monster and the cat finding them both hiding in the cupboard under the stairs. They flew out and chased the girls along the hallway and into the kitchen.

Jacob said, "Thank goodness you two are back. These pair have worn us out."

The girls were still in fits of giggles. They won't sleep tonight," Caroline said. Then they will sleep all through the festivities tomorrow."

"We won't mum, honestly. We will stay awake all day." "We'll see said Caroline.

"Right," I said, "I am making tea, who's with me?"

A chorus of "I am" came from the other three adults. I put the kettle on, and Jacob came up behind me and wrapped his arms around my waist. I turned into his embrace, he kissed me so passionately. What did I do to deserve that? I asked?

Nothing was his reply.

"How did you get on at the surgery? he asked.?

"Fine," I said, "all good. Everything happening as it should. The same for Caroline." We told them about being out of the country for a while and they said that should be fine. I told them about the extra-medical cover we have, and she was pleased with that.

He placed his hand over my tummy, "are they growing as they should? he asked.?

She says so, everything is as it should be. I have to make an appointment to see her again once we get home."

"That's good then," said Jacob, "I do worry about you three you know.

I know that I said but really we are all good. I have made up my mind that this is all going to be fine. Now have you finished playing with the girls?"

Definitely, they are exhausting once they get excited.

Of course, you had nothing whatsoever to do with making them excited, I suppose."

"Who Me? Never. We have had a good time though. Wait till there are six of them running around and causing havoc."

"I think you will find that the two eldest will be too old to play your sorts of games by the time the youngest is old enough to play."

"Oh, well, he said, four will still be good."

"Anyway," I said, "I thought we were having a houseful of kids."

"I'm game if you are" was his reply.

"We'll see," was my answer.

"I think your brother has taken his offspring into the cinema room to try and calm them down if you feel like a nap yourself."

"Funny you should say that," said Jacob, "I have come over all sleepy."

He took my hand and pulled me up the stairs, tea forgotten. We fell through our bedroom door and spent a long time just kissing, lovely Jacob kisses.

We slowly made our way over to the bed discarding clothes as we went. Before long we were joined once more in our wonderful love making. This man is just so perfect for me. We both enjoy this side of our life so much but also just love being together. I am so lucky to have found my forever after, following so many years of pain and misery.

After our lovemaking was finished we showered, dressed then went downstairs to see what everyone else was doing. The girls were still engrossed in their film, Scott and Caroline were loved up on the sofa, kissing and cuddling.

"Right," said Jacob, tea for four.

"Yes, please" we all chorused. I went with him to help. "Is there anything else we need to do before tomorrow? I asked.

"Don't think so," he said, "I rang Vera earlier and told her a car would collect her at eight forty-five. She is so excited, bless her. They will pick Mrs H up on the way here so all you ladies should all be in one place with everything you need."

Henri will be here at nine to start on the hair do's. His staff will be with him to do nails and make-up. Your cars will pick you all up at twelve-thirty. One for you and Vera another for Caroline, Mrs H and the girls. Your flowers will be delivered at eleven.

The photographers will be floating about all morning filming and taking photos wherever they go. If they start annoying you just ask them to give you a minute. They are nice blokes but can be a bit full-on. Just tell them, knowing you that is exactly what you will do.

Scott and I will be leaving here at nine-fifteen and going to the pub. Mary has allocated a bedroom for us to get ready in. Think we will have time for breakfast there before they begin preening us to within an inch of our lives. Our buttonholes will be dropped off at the pub first then they will come to you.

All the cars are booked and know where they have to be and what time. Security will be checking the church over in the morning and also the hotel. Not taking any chances."

"Jacob," I said, "have you spoken with the police about Cleo?"

"I have of course. She is still in custody, they consider her crimes too serious for her to get bail. I will stay in touch with them whilst we are away. They are hoping she will plead guilty then it will be easier, not only for us but also for her. She would likely get a lesser sentence. Chances are she will plead diminished responsibility. Would be the best thing all round I think. At least then she will get treatment, helping her to deal with her issues."

"That's good then, I said. I just want it all sorting out and her letting us get on with our lives."

"All will be well my darling he said. I won't let anything happen to you or our babies."

"There will be extra security at both the church and the hotel making sure things run smoothly."

"We are going to have a brilliant day and night then a wonderful honeymoon. Once we get back and sort the house out so we can move in the rest of our lives will be fantastic. I promise. We have everything we need to give us and our families a good life."

"I know Jacob, you are amazing. When did you sort all this stuff out?"

"Well, to be honest I roped in Sam, you know my assistant when I'm working. He works with Eddie for the rest of the time. He has been great. I have told him what we wanted, and he has sorted it."

"Cheating, getting all the glory when poor Sam has done all the work."

"Don't worry about Sam, he has been paid well."

"Scott and Caroline appeared, where's this tea then?"

"Sorry, I was just putting Ella's mind at rest. She was asking about tomorrow, wondering if we had missed anything. I told her I got Sam on the job and he has sorted everything. Certainly wouldn't have had time to do it all ourselves. He has actually done an amazing job and he tells me he has enjoyed doing it."

"Scott said that he just left it all to Jacob to sort and he passed it on to Sam."

"Thank God for Sam", I said.

"Right, tea, I am parched," said Jacob. Are mugs okay for everyone?"

"Yes please, we are all thirsty."

"Will the girls want anything?"

"Just squash, I think," said Caroline. I will make them a sarnie, some crisps and a drink. They can have it whilst they finish watching their film. I think a bath and bed will be the order of the day then for those two."

We sat drinking our tea feeling all aglow with happy thoughts.

"Jacob had rung Vera and Scott had spoken to Mrs H so they will be here early. I keep getting a flutter in my tummy with excitement."

Jacob asked, "You don't think it's the babies moving, do you?"

Caroline replied, "It's a bit early for that Jacob, once they start though you will be able to spend days just feeling them move."

"I know," I said "Caroline if you sort the girls out then I will do some sarnies for us, God, we will look like a loaf of bread before long." They all laughed at me."

"Once tomorrow is over we can think about eating something else," said Jacob. "I for one, couldn't eat anything but sarnies at the moment."

Scott asked, "Right folks, are your cases all packed?"

"Yes" was the resounding reply.

"Okay, then, passports, money, sun cream and everything else we need, is that all handy?"

"Yes" again.

Caroline had been to help me pack because I didn't have a clue what to pack and what to leave. *It all looked a bit strange to me. After all, when I had been brought down to Scott's house all those weeks ago all I had were the clothes that Caroline had bought for me from Tesco. She had even provided the suitcase. That was the only time I had ever needed a suitcase. I would just follow Caroline's lead.*

So, the girls had their baths then Caroline and Scott took them to bed and read them a story. Thankfully, they were really tired and were soon sound asleep.

Whilst they were busy with the girls I had finished making the sandwiches, cut slices of cake and made a fresh pot of tea. We carried everything into the lounge and waited for them to join us. They were soon back downstairs and we sat around just chatting, eating and sipping tea. We all relaxed and began thinking about the next day, our wedding day.

We were all so ready for this, the first day of the rest of our lives.

We were all sitting in a warm glow of happiness. I don't think any of us could believe that this was actually happening.

Food eaten and conversation over we all made for our beds. The last night we would spend as single people. By this time tomorrow, we will be two married couples.

The men locked up the house and we all went to our beds. Jacob was so loving and tender. We joined together as we had done so many times before and would do many more times throughout our lives, it was wonderful. So much love between us and soon we will have two more little people to share in this love.

We fell asleep in each other's arms and slept remarkably well, dreaming of weddings and babies.

The whole house was awake early, today's the day. The girls were running around and squealing with excitement. They wanted to put their bridesmaid's dresses on to eat their breakfast in.

They will be exhausted by lunchtime at this rate.

Jacob had ordered breakfast food to be delivered at eight thirty so that none of us would have to worry about food preparation and serving. I'm not sure how much of this feast will be eaten but it's here and if we feel like having something there is plenty of choice.

The girls did calm down a bit and eventually ate some of the delicious food.

Jacob and I had made love before getting up. The last time as two single people, the next time we will be married. Each time I thought of it a little flutter started in my tummy.

We had both showered and dressed, we did manage to eat a little of the breakfast food and felt better for it.

Scott and Caroline were up and supervising the girls, making sure they ate enough to keep them going till we ate at the hotel.

We all seemed a little jittery. Nerves I expect.

Jacob and Scott would be going down to the pub and getting ready there along with Eddie and Gregg. They would go from there straight to the church and then wait for us to arrive.

I hope we have thought of everything. All this has been arranged in three weeks. Caroline said we should have had a wedding planner, whatever one of those is, but the menfolk said that we would be able to do it ourselves and it would mean much more to us if it was all our own work, with the help of Sam of course. I could see the sense in that.

As soon as our menfolk had left people began arriving. We had all showered, so the experts had a blank canvas to work on.

First, we all had our nails done. Becki and Melisa thought it was the coolest thing to have happened to them. Apparently, Flora wouldn't allow them to wear nail varnish or play around with make-up.

Mrs H and Vera were just as excited as the girls were.

Once my nails were dry I took Vera into the lounge and gave her the ring that I had picked out for her. A very pretty emerald surrounded by tiny diamonds. She began crying, "Ella, you can't give this to me, it is too precious."

"Look Vera" I said, "this is my jewellery, and I can give it to whoever I want. I want you to have it. It has been insured along with all the other things we have so no need for you to take insurance out. Now, are you happy with it?"

"Oh, Ella, I am more than happy, it is beautiful. I have never had such a beautiful piece of jewellery in all my life. I can never thank you enough."

"No thanks required, you are doing me a big favour today and the ring will be something to remember the day with."

"I will treasure it always Ella."

"Right, hair next I think or is it make-up? Let's go and find out."

Becki and Melisa were being made up as we entered, just delicate colours but they were so thrilled. Once they were finished, it was onto Vera and Mrs H, it was a proper production line Caroline said.

Hair first for me and Caroline. These styles would take a little longer. Mine in particular because it is so thick and long. I had decided to stick with the long plait but in place of the shiny stones I'd had for the awards, there would be tiny flowers.

Caroline was having her hair put up in curls and she would have flowers in each of the curls.

Whilst all this was happening the girls and Vera and Mrs H were having their hair styled. The two ladies were wearing hats as well.

Finally, we were all ready to put our wedding clothes on. The children looked adorable. So grown up. They sat waiting for the rest of us holding onto their baskets of rose petals. I think they were a little overwhelmed because they sat very quietly, all traces of the frenzy of this morning gone.

Mrs H and Vera came through to see if they would do. Honestly, they looked spectacular. Mrs H was dressed in shades of blue and Vera in shades of green. Their dresses were very floaty. They had matching jackets as well. Amazing. They took their seats next to the girls and waited for Caroline and me to finally put on the dresses we had chosen.

We had both decided on oyster satin for our dresses. Didn't fancy white at all. Caroline's dress was floor length, off the shoulder and decorated with tiny pearls. She looked fabulous.

Mine was floor length as well but mine had long lacey sleeves, buttons up the front from below the waist and had a deep V-neck but with a collar that stood up. I felt very regal in it for some reason.

We walked down the hallway and then paraded in front of the others. They all said we both looked fabulous.

I said, "Well, we will have to do now, no time to change things before our weddings."

Mrs H and Vera both had a lovely corsage pined to their jackets curtesy of Jacob. The girls were still carrying their baskets and they had tiny flowers in their hair. Caroline and I both had a bouquet. Caroline had gone for pink roses and I had cream and pale lemon roses. Lots of other stuff in them but not being a florist I had no idea what it all was.

Finally, we were all ready, the time was right, and our cars were waiting on the drive.

Caroline and Mrs H would be going in the first car with Becki and Melisa then I would be in the second car with Vera.

There was the official photographer who had been in the house all morning with us recording everything. Even someone doing a video. The menfolk had also had people with them all morning so we could watch what they had been up to.

Once outside on the drive, there was a flurry of photos being taken by the press. We guessed that would happen. Jacob had suggested that we invite them onto the drive to get the pictures they want so that is what we did. Much better than trying to rush and hide ourselves from them. They will take snaps whether we want them to or not. This way it gives us some control over what they take.

Ten minutes later we were allowed to get into our cars, and we set off for the church. Caroline had reached for my hand before we climbed into the cars, giving it a squeeze. Can you believe we are really doing this?" she said?. I just looked and smiled at her, not really but I'm sure reality will hit once we see those beautiful men of ours.

"Okay, then," I said, let's do this.

Just a ten-minute drive and we were at the church. There seemed to be an awful lot of people waiting outside. As we stepped from the cars a loud cheer went up then applause.

The vicar was waiting for us by the doors. "My goodness, ladies you do look fine," he said. Your men are waiting for you and they are both very nervous so shall we get this show on the road, put them out of their misery?

We both nodded. The vicar led the party followed by Becki and Melisa who began spreading their rose petals in front of them. They were followed by Caroline and Mrs H then Vera and I brought up the rear.

The church was packed, and all eyes were on us as we made our way up the aisle to the front of the church. The church choir were singing as we walked up the aisle, lovely.

Scott stepped forward as Caroline reached him and Mrs H moved over to the left-hand side. He had tears in his eyes as he took Caroline's hands in his. They moved over to allow Jacob to stand waiting for me. He had tears streaming down his face. He reached for my hands then took them in his holding them to his lips. He kissed each one in turn. He seemed really choked with emotion. I mouthed to him, I love you my darling, he smiled and then dried his face with a handkerchief. Finally, we were all assembled, the bridesmaids sitting on a front pew watching everything with interest.

Mrs H and Vera stood side by side waiting for their own little bit when the vicar would ask who gives these women to these men.

The service was lovely, someone was doing a video of the whole thing so we would be able to watch it all when we got back from France. I don't think any of us would be remembering it all.

The service went without a hitch. Mrs H and Vera played their parts to perfection. The girls were brilliant, sitting still and watching the rest of the service with interest.

When it was time for us to sign the register it was a bit of a squeeze, a small room with twice the normal amount of people in there. We managed though.

Jacob was so proud when he held the marriage certificate. I thought, he will want that framed.

Their best men had been brilliant as well. Keeping them calm before going to the church. We were all a little teary as we walked back down the aisle, the two Mr and Mrs Ryan's. We walked out of the church to more cheers and applause. All these people had stayed outside waiting whilst the ceremony had taken place. They all seemed interested to see the photographs being taken.

Finally, we were allowed to leave the church and climb back into the cars. Becki and Melissa went with Scott and Caroline and Mrs H and Vera came in with us. We had huge limo's so there was plenty of room. Eddie and Gregg would be in a third car with their own wives.

Once at the hotel, we had to stand in line to greet all the guests as they arrived. Our friends from the press were very well-behaved. They had all fished their best suits out for the occasion. It seemed that everyone had a camera, press or regular guests.

We had requested that no one bring presents. If they wanted to do something then we asked for donations for the church and the local hospice. The pots were filling up nicely so they should get a nice amount each.

Once everyone was in the hotel and seated we were able to have the meal. I hadn't realised just how hungry I was. Certainly felt better after the food. Jacob kept looking at me, holding my hand and kissing it. He looked wonderful in his morning suit as did Scott, in fact, they all looked great including the best men.

Mrs H and Vera were stuck together the whole day. They were having a wonderful time.

Becki and Melisa were really good throughout the meal, they ate everything and continued to look adorable.

There had been wine served with the meals but now the champagne was coming out for the toasts.

Caroline and I had been sticking with fizzy water as had Scott and Jacob but we insisted that they have champagne along with everyone else for the toasts.

First up it was Eddie and Gregg. Of course, they had got together and worked out a double act. They were hilarious. They should turn professional.

Not to be outdone, Scott and Jacob had also worked out a double act. They were both funny and sincere. They spoke so lovingly about Caroline and myself. Everyone there to witness the event would be in no doubt as to the love those two brothers have for me and my friend.

Someone called out, "Jacob, why don't you give us a song?"

I reached for his hand, he didn't want this whole thing to be about him. "Maybe later," he said. Of course, that set everyone off calling for him to give us a song.

I saw him look towards Scott, what should I do he asked?

If you feel up to it then go for it, bro. You know we can always listen to your golden voice.

He then looked down at me with a pleading look in his eyes. Jacob, if you feel you want to sing then sing. If you don't feel like it then don't.

Caroline reached over and touched his arm. Jacob, please, just sing for Ella and myself. We will really appreciate it.

That didn't give him much choice. "Okay, okay, I haven't sung much for over a week so it will probably sound crap but if you insist. Here goes:

Any requests?" he asked. Of course *'Somewhere'* was the overwhelming choice.

He looked down at me again. "Hold my hand, my darling," he asked. "Of course" I will. Take your time. "He had a drink of water and then composed himself. "Here goes," he said.

He needn't have worried, his voice was and is perfect. He had his eyes closed but was holding onto my hand with a tight grip.

Halfway through this amazing song he pulled me up to stand by his side. He opened his eyes and looked deep into mine. Singing his heart out once again.

The whole place was silent, and the song went on, more and more intensity. His voice just grew stronger with each line. He turned me to face him and was looking into my eyes telling me how much he loves me with just that look. He held both my hands as the song reached its crescendo. Such power, I had tears streaming down my face. How I love this man.

As the song finished Jacob gathered me into his arms and kissed me with so much passion. I think everyone in the room had tears in their eyes if not on their cheeks.

A huge round of applause broke out and everyone was on their feet. Cheering, clapping and whistling, even Gerald, the vicar and his wife were there. "There is no way I can take this man away from his millions of adoring fans. We will have to work out something that allows him to still perform but also gives him quality time with his family. Surely, we can do that."

As the noise abated I noticed Eddie watching his prize asset, Jacob doing what he loves and comes so naturally to him. I think Eddie had the same thoughts as me. He would love to take Jacobs show over to America and I know they would love his live shows. That could be difficult though. It will all take some thinking about.

Jacob turned to his audience and said, for goodness sake, get on and finish your food, we have a ton of cake to eat as well. Once we have finished in here we will be going through to the dance hall where there will be entertainment until you've all had enough.

Thank you again, from not only me and my wife but also from Scott, my dear brother and his wife. We mustn't forget the other Ryan, our beloved sister Ingrid and her lovely family. She blew him a kiss then turned to her children telling them something, probably to behave.

As the room went back to the general chatter of a large gathering Jacob pulled me to him once again. "My darling Ella, thank you, you have made me the happiest of men and I love you with all my heart."

"I know you do Jacob, as I love you. You are my everything. Now, let's get this party going. The sooner it starts the sooner it finishes, and then I can get you home and in bed. He put his face into my neck and his warm breath sent a shiver all through me.

The press guys had been very good and said how much they had enjoyed the wedding and the reception. Jacob said, "Please don't leave now. You are all invited to the party in the dance hall. There is a free bar, and more food will be available later.

"Are you sure Jacob?" one asked,

"Of course, I'm sure, I wouldn't ask if I wasn't sure?. You guys deserve a night off."

"Well, thank you very much, Jacob. This has been a great day for us all. So pleased to see you so happy with the lovely Ella. You make a fabulous couple."

"Thanks, Mike, I know you lot are usually all over the place but as today you are all in one place you might just as well stay here and have some fun."

"Give the 'celebrities' a break for a change. Let them have a night out without you lot following them around."

"Hey Jacob, we still have to make a living, you know. We do try to be fair most of the time."

"I know you do guys. It does get a bit much at times though. Remember, we are all human as well."

"After today, Jacob we all know just how human you are. I know you say it was all Ella's idea, but it is you who will be footing the bill."

"Don't be so sure about that boys, Ella has her own money as do Scott and Caroline so I think you will find it is all of us. We have done this whole thing between us so it's not just me you should be thanking. We are a family team and that is the way we like to do things, together."

"Got it, Jacob I will make sure that you all get equal thanks. It has been a great day and hopefully night. This is the first and probably only time we have been treated so well. I know I speak for all the guys when I say, thank you, sincerely."

With that everyone made their way into the dance hall. A disco was playing a lot of eighties music and people were beginning to dance. The dancefloor was getting crowded, but the brides and their grooms were still sitting together along with the best men and their ladies plus Mrs H and Vera and the two adorable bridesmaids.

Jacobs orchestra began setting up their equipment and tuning their instruments. Jacob had reluctantly agreed to do half an hour from his show. Ella thought, right I can see that happening. Once he started he would just carry on, not that I would mind. I could listen to his dulcet tones every minute of every day and I know without a doubt that the guests would all want him to carry on all night. Let's wait and see how it goes I thought.

The disco played until eight o'clock and would start again once Jacob's spot finished. Jacob was holding my hand, "are you sure you want me to do this Ella?" he asked.

"Of course, I do my darling, y o u couldn't deprive all these people now, could you?"

"But it is our day my love, we are a married couple now and I want to be by your side."

Jacob you will be by my side as well as singing to all these friends and relatives. I will love hearing you sing my love. It is almost my greatest joy."

"Okay," said Jacob, "what is your greatest joy then?"

I leant forward and whispered in his ear. "Being in bed with you, my precious husband."

"Oh, Ella, I wish we were there right this minute. I want you so much, my darling."

"And I want you but, this is our wedding day and I really want to hear you sing before you take me to your bed and make wonderful love to me."

"Okay, I hear you. I will sing like a bird just for you my wonderful wife."

The disco music stopped and then the orchestra began playing their intro. The music faded and Jacob's voice rang out clear and true for the second time today. Then he began singing.

That was it, he was back there singing for all his adoring fans and they were loving him. What a treat for all those guests. They were lapping it up, so was I.

He did his routine from the show, from one beautiful song to the next. He then had a break and was speaking to all our guests. Thanking them for making our wedding day such a beautiful, memorable day for us all. Scott and Caroline had told him they'd had the most amazing day as well.

"I want you all to indulge me for a moment. I had only known Ella a few days and she hadn't a clue who I was, but I knew without a doubt that I loved her more than life itself. It's a long story but the top and tail of it is that through my dear brother Scott who met Caroline at the same time, well we all got together, to help each other, and that is exactly what we have done. So much love between us. I, for one, have never been so happy.

"This next song is one that I learnt to sing for Ella the first night she found out who I was. I was scared she would be frightened off once she found out, but not Ella, she is made of strong stuff. Anyway, my song to Ella, *Making Memories as sung by Frankie Laine.* Come up here with me my darling.

315

I stood up and walked over to my wonderful husband, he held out his hands to me. His musical director began playing the piano and Jacob began to sing 'our song'.

Dance with me, Ella, my love.

I was right back there in the theatre where Jacob first sang that song to me. It was a truly wonderful moment and one I will never forget. He held me close and danced with me whilst still singing.

I will remember these moments all my life, the moments that Jacob sings only for me.

As the song ended Jacob walked me back to my seat, returned to the makeshift stage and sang four more songs. He then thanked everyone once more and was about to leave the stage when the shout went up, "More, more."

"Okay, just one, what's it to be?

We all knew what they wanted, *'The Impossible Dream'*. "All right you lot, give me a minute." He had a long drink of water and then began to sing.

Such a wonderful song and sung with so much passion.

Those last notes just go on and on, so effortless for Jacob so amazing for all those listening to him. He finished the song, bowed to his audience that were going nuts. That included his brother and his wife and also his own new wife. I was clapping like crazy along with everyone else.

Jacob left the stage and headed straight for me. He wrapped his arms around me and kissed me with so much passion. The love of my life.

The disco began again, and everyone was up dancing. That was everyone except Jacob and I, Scott and Caroline, Mrs H and Vera and the girls who had come over all sleepy. We just sat around talking, holding hands and loving.

I asked Jacob if he had enjoyed his wedding day,

"Ella, it has been the most incredible day. Finally, I have you all to myself, well for the next few months anyway. I guess I will have to share you then."

"It really has been the most fabulous day don't you all think?"

Mrs H and Vera were still in that lovely stupor that Jacobs concerts leave you in. All you can hear is his amazing voice going on and on in your head.

Caroline said, "I think that this has been the best day of my entire life. I have loved every second of it then for Jacob to round it all off with that wonderful mini-concert, well it just made it absolutely perfect."

Some of the press guys approached us before leaving for the night. "Jacob, everyone, thank you all so much for this amazing day and night. It has meant so much to us all. A fabulous day and a truly wonderful night. Jacob, that mini concert you performed was faultless, you are one fabulous singer. We all really appreciate it. Good luck to you all. Fantastic."

Jacob and Scott got up and went to shake all their hands. Caroline and I went to kiss their cheeks. I thanked them all for coming and helping to make it the success it has been. "I know it was a risk asking you all, but we just felt that you all have been a big part of Jacob's career for good or bad but mostly have been fair, so we have taken the risk and I think it has all worked out well. You never know what the future might hold I said. I think we may have started a whole new way of dealing with you press guys, treating you as friends and not as enemies. Time will tell."

Lots of them were staying in the smaller hotel within walking distance of our venue so there wouldn't be any drink driving going on. Some of the wives had driven and so they would be heading home.

Most of the other guests were staying here in the hotel including Vera and Mrs H. Jacob's treat he said. He thought they wouldn't want to go home after having such a lovely day, so he extended it for them.

Jacob called for our car to take us back to Scott's home. He went up to the microphone and spoke to the remaining guests. He thanked everyone for making this the most memorable of days. "Continue enjoying yourselves as long as you want he told them all. We are off home now. Got a flight in the morning so don't want to miss that."

Everyone trooped outside to wave us all off. Melisa was almost asleep, so Scott carried her, and Becki was hanging on to Caroline for all she was worth.

We all piled into the car and relaxed back in our seats for the short journey home. I leant against Jacob and reached for his hands.

"Thank you for today, my darling I said, it has been wonderful right from the moment I opened my eyes this morning. I have loved every second of it".

Jacob whispered in my ear "It's not over yet my sweet girl."

We were soon home and piling into the house. Caroline and Scott took the girls up to their rooms and got them changed and into bed quickly. By the time they came back downstairs we had a pot of tea made and ready to pour.

Caroline dropped onto the sofa and said, what a wonderful day this had been. Scott sat beside her putting his arm around her shoulders. "It certainly has," he said, "and the best bit is my brother and I have won the first prizes. Thank you Jacob for everything. You didn't have to pay for it all you know."

"Scott, you have looked after me for the past year and I really appreciate all that you have done for me. I don't know what I would have done without you. But now you can step back and enjoy your life with your lovely Caroline and your expanding family.

Now I have Ella by my side and our future is secure and looking rosy. You and I will always be close and there for each other, I know that, but I just wanted to give something back for all the care you have given me."

"Well, you know I did what I did because I love you and not for any other reason."

"With us doing it all together it hadn't made that much difference to the cost anyway," said Jacob.

"I know that isn't true Jacob, but just know that we both appreciate it. We are also very appreciative of you allowing us to be married side by side with you both. I know that if you had done it on your own it would have all been paid for by some magazine."

"That is where you are wrong Scott, there is no way we would have gone down that route. I would just as soon get married in a registry office and had fish and chips for the wedding feast than do that. Now forget about it please. Let's all just look forward to this holiday. I can't wait to show Ella the house in France."

"I think we should finish our drinks and then head upstairs, tomorrow will be another busy day," said Scott.

"I think you are right bro, come on, let's take our brides to bed."

We all began to laugh, "I for one" will second that", I said. "Come on husband, I need you between the sheets."

Our wedding night was bliss. We made love often throughout the night and again in the morning. We were both too wired to sleep much. "We can catch up on that in France," I said.

We were all up by nine the next morning and were too excited to eat much so just had a slice of toast and a cuppa. Jacob said we could eat at the airport if we were hungry. I was still in that dreamy state, thinking of all the wonderful things that had happened the day and night before. Such a magical day for us all.

Mrs H was coming to stay in Scott's house whilst we were away. I'm sure she will be giving the place a good 'bottoming' before Scott and Caroline returned from France. Vera was going to stay with her for a few days as well. She has a few days holiday to use up, so they have been plotting what to do.

It will be good for Vera to see just how easy we will be to work for. She has finally made her decision and will be joining us in the new house once we return. They had both enjoyed their day in the limelight yesterday, and they had revelled in Jacob's impromptu show. Vera loves him for his music anyway and Mrs H just loves him no matter what but the two of them watching him perform was magical.

We quickly got everyone sorted with their luggage, put all the pots in the dishwasher. Caroline was checking that the girls were all dressed properly, washed and teeth cleaned. They had been too tired for a bath the previous night so she said that could wait until we reach the hotel in France. They still had their nail varnish on and that could stay for a few days, they loved it. They asked if they could wear make-up in France. Caroline said she would have to think about that. She would speak to Scott, see what he thought first. She thought it wouldn't hurt but she will be guided by Scott. So far they hadn't heard a word from Flora. Lovely mother.

We were soon ready, all our baggage was in the hall ready for when the car arrived. The men were checking they had all the paperwork required plus all the passports. I was beginning to feel very excited. I hope I enjoy this flying malarky.

The car drew up on the drive, it was the big one. Needed to be with all of us lot plus luggage. It will be a squeeze I thought.

Shouldn't have worried, we all fit in along with the driver and security man. Plenty of room for the luggage as well. We set off and were all full of chatter. The girls were very excited. They couldn't believe that this was my first time flying. Melisa said, "but Aunty Ella you are old, you must have been on an aeroplane before."

"Well, I am very old of course but up until now I haven't been able to go abroad, there wasn't anyone to take me. You two are very lucky to have been able to travel abroad. When I was a young girl I wasn't as lucky as you two."

"That's so sad Aunty Ella, we go on an aeroplane lots don't we Becki."

"Yes we do and we must remember that we are lucky and remember to say thank you."

"I will Becki. We have only been on a plane with daddy, we weren't allowed to go with mummy and the horrid man. He said we would drive him mad. We came to stay with you didn't we daddy when they went on holiday."

"Yes you did Melisa, we had a good time then though didn't we."

"We did daddy, we always have fun with you, and we love having fun with our new mummy. She is amazing."

"I think we all love your new mummy don't we?" said Scott. A chorus of we do, we do. I think that is one blended family that is going to work very well and be very happy.

Before long we were pulling up at the airport.

"Jacob, don't leave me. I won't know where to go or what to do."

"I won't leave you my darling. Just hold my hand and follow me."

As the car came to a halt two men in uniform approached the car with a trolley each. They quickly emptied the boot and stacked the cases on the trollies. "Mr Ryan, follow us please." They had spoken to Jacob, obviously they knew him and were expecting him. We all followed the men through the doors and made for the VIP lounge. Jacob told me that is where we were heading.

I'm sure this is not normal, people were watching us as we made our way to wherever this place is situated. I guess seeing Jacob walk amongst them is something special, well he is very special, but he is also my husband.

We were soon in the VIP lounge and found comfy seats. I was in a dream, never seen anything like this before. Waiters were serving drinks to some other people. One very smart young man approached Jacob, "may I serve you drinks Mr Ryan."

"Thank you, yes. Can we have tea for four then for the two young ladies, what do you want to drink girls?"

"Please may we have squash please Uncle Jacob?"

"Of course, two glasses of orange squash as well please." He went off to fetch our drinks. Jacob was reaching into his pocket to get some money for a tip. He is such a generous man. I had noticed him slip some notes to the men that had helped with the luggage as well.

I was getting very jittery, God, I hope I enjoy this. Paris is not a long flight according to Jacob, but he has spoken about taking me to places that would mean a twenty-four-hour flight. We will have to see about that. Won't be for a while though. Two babies to sort out first.

We sat in companiable silence as we drank our tea. The girls were taking it all in their stride. Caroline kept looking at me and smiling. She too is used to flying, just me being the newbie.

All our paperwork had been checked and all we had to do now was wait. We were going to be allowed on the plane first then everyone else would follow. It was soon time for us to move. A very smart lady came to escort us through to the plane. My legs felt like jelly.

"Come on, my love," said Jacob. Almost time, we will soon be there. Once we get there you will have a wonderful time, I promise. Do you want to sit by the window or by the aisle?"

"Oh God Jacob, I have no idea. Not keen on heights so perhaps the aisle."

"I guess that will work. The rows of seats are in three's so I think that Melisa will want the window seat then either me or you, see how you feel once you are on. Perhaps if you sit in the middle then we can both hold your hands. Scott and Caroline will have Becki with them. It will soon all be over then the party can begin."

We were escorted onto the plane and then shown to our seats. I went with Jacob's plan. Melisa by the window then me then Jacob by the aisle. They could have a hand each. Jacob kept kissing me, trying to distract me. It was working for now. Scott, Caroline and Becki were sitting in the seats opposite us across the aisle.

I put my head back on the seat and closed my eyes. The next thing I knew Jacob was kissing me again.

"You have the most kissable lips he said. I can't leave them alone."

"I had noticed" I said.

The rest of the passengers had boarded and found their seats. It seemed to me that everything was happening all at once. Jacob was holding my hand and kissing the back of it. We were moving, I gripped his hand tightly. He began talking to me, telling me about this amazing hotel we would be staying in. It's right in the centre of all the action he said. We can get up whenever we want and have breakfast then take a leisurely walk along the river. I could feel things happening with this plane, strange things but I forced myself to listen to all that Jacob was saying to me. It was definitely taking my mind off what was happening around me. Before I realised what was happening we were flying. Climbing high into the air. Keep talking to me, Jacob. He was still holding my hand, he turned it over and kissed my palm, he then used his tongue, my mind was racing with thoughts of what we would soon be able to do in this posh hotel in Paris. He manages to turn my mind to sexy thoughts very quickly. I leaned into him and then whispered in his ear.

"*Is there anywhere on this plane where we could get very close and personal?*"

"Ella, you naughty girl" he said, "don't you ever think of anything else?"

"Err, no." How could I being married to the sexiest man on the planet?

"Blimey Ella" he said, "I have quite a lot to live up to don't I?"

There was a lot of moving around in the aisle. The very smartly dressed air hostesses were going up and down, speaking with people. Checking all was well. Jacob said that they wouldn't serve drinks or food as the flight time was so short. Wouldn't be time to do anything. No sooner up than we are down again. I suddenly realised that we were actually flying, and I felt okay. It was a bit bumpy at times, but Jacob said it's just turbulence, nothing to worry about.

He was right, we were no sooner up than we were going down. I felt really excited. We will soon be in Paris and our honeymoon can start.

We landed safely, Melisa turned to me and said, "see Aunty Ella, there's nothing to worry about. I will look after you." "Well thank you very much my dear I said, that is most kind of you."

As soon as we had landed, and the plane stopped there was another flurry of activity. We were going to be let off the plane first, then taken to the French version of our VIP lounge. I have to say this makes me feel very special. I know it is all because of Jacob. He is the only one of us that is really special, and he is very special.

We were escorted from the plane and then taken through to the lounge. We would wait there until our transport was ready. It would appear that we didn't have to do anything really. Because it is Jacob it is all sorted.

Our car was waiting for us. Our luggage appeared as if by magic. Once more it was loaded onto a trolley then pushed through the crowds of people and stacked in the boot of yet another enormous car. We all got in and then we were on our way. I tried looking through the window to see what France looked like, but Melisa was talking to me constantly trying to explain what Euro Disney was. I was totally lost.

From what I could see it didn't look that different to England except we were driving on the wrong side of the road. We had been moving for a while then Jacob began pointing things out to me. He could have been speaking Chinese for all I knew.

Our car pulled up outside a very smart looking building, I guess this is the hotel. Jacob had held my hand all the way. The car doors were opened by men dressed in some sort of costume. Jacob got out first then held his hand out for me then for Melisa. It would appear that the young lady wants everything that I have. Another man was helping Caroline and Becki, Scott was already out and holding his hand out for his wife. The men were fussing around, unloading luggage and putting it onto two trolleys. We climbed some steps then entered the most amazing foyer you could imagine.

Our husbands went over to the desk and did whatever they needed to do. We were then escorted to lifts that would take us to our rooms. Jacob and myself had one suite and Scott and Caroline had a two bedroomed affair, one for them and one for the girls. We arranged to meet in an hour so we could have a brief walk then get something to eat. We disappeared into the two suites, Jacob holding my hand. The young man arrived with all our luggage and he asked if there was anything else we required. Jacob assured him we were fine then handed him a note. Not sure how much it was because I don't understand the money they use here. After all, I have only just learned how to use English money. The young lad seemed happy with it, so I guess it was generous.

I began looking around the room, it was furnished lavishly, there were two large sofa's, a huge TV, an area to make drinks and several tables. There was a very elaborate flower decoration on one table, looked very expensive to me. On another was a huge basket of fruit and a selection of chocolates. We shouldn't starve anyway.

Jacob came over to me,

"Are you happy my love?"

"I am very happy," I said. Feeling a little neglected though." That was it, he picked me up and carried me through to the bedroom, laying me down gently on the enormous bed. I think you could sleep six people in it, and they would all be comfortable.

Jacob said they had asked if we would like a maid to come and hang all our clothes up, sort out our toiletries. I said not to bother, my wife liked to do all that sort of thing herself.

"That would just make me lazy Jacob, I do like doing things myself."

"Well, there is that then there is also the fact that I will be needing my wife's body before too long."

"Jacob, you didn't say that did you?"

He laughed at me, "no I didn't but it is true, I do need your body and I need it now."

"Well, I said, I'm not stopping you." And I didn't, in fact I helped him. We were soon naked and enjoying each other's bodies. Jacob was very ready, we joined and made love in a mad frenzy. It felt like a long time since we had last done this when in fact it had only been this morning. I lay in his arms and felt complete happiness. Happy and sated, for now anyway.

"Well, Mr Ryan I am feeling a little peckish now."

"So am I" he said and rose above me once more? He entered me once again and began moving, my God this man knows how to please me. We made love again, this time slowly and passionately. My orgasm began and went on and on until Jacob finally exploded inside me.

"*Wow* I said, that was epic."

"It was pretty good wasn't it" he said.

"Are you sure we need a walk after that I asked?"

"Well, that was the idea, but I think we should perhaps eat first then have a walk afterwards."

" That makes more sense" I said. We showered together then dried each other and finally we dressed.

Jacob said, "I picked up some of this morning's papers at the airport, shall we have a look to see if we have good press today?"

We sat together on the bed and looked through the papers. We were in each one as was Scott and Caroline with Becki and Melisa, which I think is lovely.

We read some of the write ups and they were all good. The press that had been to the weddings were very generous in their praise for what we had done. They all mentioned that they had all been invited to the weddings as guests and were treated very well indeed, then to top it all Jacob had done a mini concert for all the guests which was amazing. The little trick seems to have worked, for now anyway. I wonder if any other 'celebrities' choose to do the same thing in the future, I doubted it.

Jacob rang through to Scott to see if they were ready to eat then have a walk.

"Five minutes" he said, "we are all starving now. Did you manage a kip he asked"

"Well, something like that said Jacob?

I could hear him laughing down the phone.

"Don't let the grass grow Jacob" he said.

Jacob's reply, "don't worry, I won't"

We all met up on the landing. Everyone had showered, the girls looked better for a little nap and at last all the make-up was removed. They were hanging on to their nails though. I had to admit, they do look pretty.

"Have you girls seen your photographs in the newspapers" I asked.

"We have Aunty Ella, don't we all look pretty?"

"You certainly do I said. Did you both really enjoy it?"

"We did Aunty Ella, it was the best day ever. Wait till the girls at school see our pictures in the papers, they will be jealous."

"I should imagine they will be" I said. "It's not every little girl that gets to have their picture in the newspapers."

Scott said, "Ella, you played a blinder. All the write ups are positive, and they all give thanks for the amazing time they all had. I know it cost a bit to include them, but it was definitely worth it. Like I say, you played a blinder."

"They loved Jacob singing as well didn't they? I know I did so they must have done. He is just brilliant. Has he always been so confident?"

"Not at all, he was very shy as a kid and even up to meeting you he wasn't so confident. He was fine on stage but seemed to leave a bit of himself up there and would go very quiet and sit on his own a lot. You have bought him out Ella, he is such a different man these days. I know it has worked both ways, you have been brilliant for each other. Now, come on, food before I have to eat one of these children."

In all our rush and hurry Caroline and I had forgotten to give the girls their gifts and also the gifts we had bought for our menfolk. We all sat at a table in the restaurant in the hotel. Caroline and I ordered tea, the girls juice and the men decided to have one glass of wine, and who could blame them.

I had asked Jacob to order for me as I didn't have a clue what any of it said. Whilst waiting for the food we took out the girls gifts and told them they were because they had been the best bridesmaids we could have wished for. They were so excited. They loved their bracelets and put them on straight away then when they undid their necklaces I thought they would cry. "But they are so grown up" said Becki,

"Well, said Caroline, "Ella and I think that you are both very grown up. You both behaved brilliantly yesterday, so thank you." We had to fasten the chains around their necks for them. Caroline said "They mustn't keep playing with them as the chains would break and they are real gold, so you don't want to lose them do you?

"Oh, Mummy, we will take care of them, we love them, don't we Melisa?" "Thank you both so much."

Whilst the girls were happy comparing their gifts Caroline and I gave the menfolk their own gifts. They both looked open-mouthed.

"Just open them," we said together, "just a little memento of our wonderful day yesterday." I could tell that Jacob was shaking as he undid the paper then the box that held his necklace. He looked up at me with tears streaming down his face. "Ella, this is so beautiful. It matches my bracelet perfectly."

"I know it does," I said, "bought it from the same shop. Julian had it there when I bought the bracelet, and I didn't know which one to get but as it happened you now have both."

"I do, don't I? Ella, I love it and I love you."

"I know you do my darling."

All this time Scott had been fumbling with his own gift. His dear face when he opened the box. Bless him, he was sobbing as well as Jacob.

"Caroline this is amazing, I love it but really you didn't have to do that"

"I did," she said "because I love you with all my heart. I know how much you liked the one that Ella bought for Jacob, I wanted to get one for you as soon as I could. I didn't want the exact same one but similar. Do you like it then?"

"No Caroline, I don't like it, I love it. Will you fasten it for me, please?"

As Caroline was fastening Scott's bracelet I was doing the same for Jacob's necklace. He had put an open-neck shirt on, perfect, and the necklace showed as he moved. It did look good, classy I thought, just like my man.

Two big, handsome men crying their eyes out. What will we do with them? Jacob got a hankie from his pocket and dried his eyes and cheeks. "Ella, my darling thank you so much. I love it, love them both. But why did you feel the need to buy me something else. I have everything I need having you by my side as my wife."

"I just wanted to give you something on our wedding day then we both forgot to give them to you in all the rush. I never gave it a thought, the same with the girls gifts. Had too much on my mind I expect."

Caroline was saying the same to Scott who was still overcome with emotion."

Jacob said, "Scott, we have really won the lottery with these two. They are just the most wonderful women ever."

Scott replied, "you're not wrong there, Jacob. We really have to look after them, don't we?"

Thankfully our food arrived just then so it gave the men time to compose themselves.

"This all looks very nice," I said, "so this is what we get in posh hotels is it?"

Jacob held my hand and kissed it. "You will soon get used to all this Ella. This will be our lives from now on. Not every day of course but when we travel abroad or even if we are somewhere else in England this will be how we eat out."

"Really Jacob, can't I cook for you sometimes?"

"Of course you can, Ella. I am talking about when we have to travel for either work or for a holiday. Just enjoy it, my love, I promise you will get used to it."

"Okay," I said, "I will enjoy it. It looks like Becki and Melisa have been used to this way of living."

They are so good. They look so grown up eating their swanky meal and wearing their new jewellery.

Melisa had finished her meal and put her cutlery down. "

Uncle Jacob, can we get used to it as well, please? Mummy and the horrid man would never let us eat out in restaurants. If they were eating out we had to stay home in our bedrooms, didn't we Becki?"

Becki looked up and said, "Yes, that is true. That man didn't want us with him, he said we would make him look ridiculous carting two unruly kids around to restaurants."

"Mummy would cook us nuggets and chips then put us to bed. She said we had to stay in our rooms, but we didn't, did we, Melisa?"

"No, we didn't, as soon as they had gone out I used to go into Becki's room, and we would play till we heard them come home then I would go back to my room and go sleep."

Scott looked truly shocked, "are you telling me that they went out and left you on your own?"

"Yes they did Daddy, at least once a week," said Becki.

Scott looked furious, Caroline was holding his hand,

"Calm down my darling. "There is nothing you can do today but tomorrow I suggest you ring the man that is dealing with this case and let him know. That will be enough on its own to give you custody."

He turned to Caroline and kissed her. "Thank you my love, I will do that. Now girls I promise you that will never happen again. If Caroline and I are going out to eat you will be with us unless it is somewhere that children can't go then I will employ someone to come and stay with you until we get back. That is a promise, and you know I don't break my promises."

"Thank you Daddy they both said. Sometimes we were really frightened."

"I'm not surprised," he said. That is an awful thing to do to children, I don't care how old they are."

"Uncle Jacob and Auntie Ella are in love Daddy, did you know?"

"Yes, I did know that, he said. What makes you think it though Melisa?"

"Uncle Jacob told me. He kept kissing her and I said it was dirty, but he told me it's not dirty and he loves to kiss Aunty Ella because he loves her to the moon and back."

Jacob looked over to Scott and raised his shoulders, "She's not wrong bro," he said.

The girls' ice creams arrived, and they tucked in. I wouldn't be surprised if Flora had refused to let them eat ice cream after what they had just told us. I thought I was the only one who had lived a bad and sad life but apparently not. Flora has been a very selfish woman and doesn't deserve these beautiful girls. "I wonder what she made of the newspaper reports and photographs from yesterday."

We had all eaten enough without dessert so once the girls had finished we set off for a nice walk through the streets of Paris. I was really getting into this holiday thing. Paris is fabulous. So many amazing buildings and people everywhere. I began to notice people watching us, some were taking photographs on their phones. Jacob certainly has a lot of fans. I had thought that being in another country they wouldn't know him. How wrong was I. He just walked and ignored them, putting his arm around me and kissing me often.

We then headed back to the hotel, we thought the girls would need a rest before our evening meal then another walk through the hustle and bustle of the Paris streets.

The following day we would be going to Euro Disney. Our car would be picking us up at ten o'clock in the morning. Jacob said to put on flat shoes that would be comfortable all day. He said it would be a long and busy day.

"Do you feel up to it my love?" he asked?.

"Well, if I feel tired I will have to sit down, and rest won't I." The girls were so excited. They said they hadn't been to this one before, but Daddy and Uncle Jacob had taken them to the one in Florida. Jacob bent forward and whispered in my ear, that's in America if you were wondering.

I was actually, I still don't know what this thing is but by this time tomorrow, I will know.

Our afternoon nap consisted of making love with my wonderful husband, twice. We did manage to have a brief nap before having a shower then dressing for the evening meal and walk. I was still full from lunchtime but I would do my best. After all, I have to eat for three.

We had a lovely meal, once again the girls were perfectly behaved. I noticed how some of the other diners were watching us. I thought, God, I hope no one asks him to sing or we will never get out of here. Thankfully that didn't happen. Once we had finished eating we got up and went to leave the restaurant but before we had reached the exit someone stood up and shook Jacob's hand, it was Andrew, the guy that wanted him to take his show to America.

Jacob was gracious with him.

"What are you doing here?" Jacob asked?.

" Well, after your last show in London, I bought my family over here for a bit of a holiday before heading home. I guess this is your honeymoon. How did the wedding go?"

"Actually, Andrew it all went splendidly. We all had a great day. This is only part of our honeymoon though. We are taking the girls to Disney tomorrow then on Wednesday we are all driving to my house in the South. We will be there for about six weeks or so then when we get back we are moving into our new home."

Andrew turned to me and kissed my cheek then shook hands with Scott and kissed Caroline.

"Can I introduce you all to my wife Annabelle?"

The introductions were completed, and Jacob said,

"If you will excuse us then Andrew we are taking the girls out on the town for an hour or so before bed. I think we will all be having an early night as tomorrow will be a big day for them all."

I noticed Andrew pulled Jacob towards him. I couldn't hear what he said but guessed he was checking to see if Jacob had changed his mind.

"I told you Andrew, we are having some quality time together. Once the twins arrive we will be very busy so work will have to wait. I'm sorry, but that is how it is."

Andrew said, "well if you change your mind you know where to find me.

"I do and thank you, goodnight all."

There were three other couples sitting at Andrew's table, but he hadn't introduced them to us. Jacob turned to them and said, goodnight all, enjoy the rest of your stay. Still holding my hand he steered me away from Andrew and out into the foyer.

"He won't give up Jacob, he sees big pound signs when he sees you,"

"Tough said Jacob, I will do what I want when I want so he can just whistle."

I wonder if he will always feel that way. He is a born entertainer and just loves singing. If we have babies that cry a lot he might be pleased to get out of the house for a while. Time will tell.

Walking the streets of Paris in the evening felt very different to the afternoon. People were dressed in glamourous clothes and seemed very posh to me. Not all of them of course but there did seem to be an awful lot. I wondered if these were the people that Jacob would normally mix with. That question was answered about half an hour later.

A very tall skinny woman appeared as if by magic and pounced on Jacob. She tried to kiss him, but he moved his head away.

"Felicity, lovely to see you. What are you doing here?"

"Oh, been filming a commercial, finished today."

"Felicity, may I introduce my wife, Ella, Ella,

Felicity is an old friend of Cleo's."

I held out my hand to shake hers, but she just seemed to freeze and stood staring at me.

"What do you mean Jacob, wife? You're not married."

"That is where you are wrong Felicity. We held our wedding yesterday and this is the first day of our honeymoon. Do you remember my brother Scott?"

"Of course, Hi Scott."

"Well, we had a double wedding yesterday, Scott and Caroline were married as well as Ella and myself. It was the most wonderful day. We are

331

all very happy, I have waited a very long time to meet someone I can love and who loves me back, but Ella walked into my life and that was it. Love at first sight. We have been together ever since."

Felicity still looked as if she didn't believe what Jacob was saying. She turned and looked at me then looked back at Jacob. "Are you serious Jacob, you gave up Cleo for this?"

I thought Jacob would hit her.

"I think you need to speak with Cleo to find out a few things, oh wait, you can't, she is in prison waiting to go to court on charges of assault and attempted murder."

Felicity's face was a picture.

"I take it you are not in touch with that idiot woman, if you had been then you would have known all about her fall from grace. It is over a year since I split from Cleo, she can tell you the reason why if you ever pay her a visit. Just be assured my reason was justified.

She is a vile woman and I never want to see her again. As for your derogatory term relating to my wife, she is a million times better than that loon Cleo and if you think differently then you are no longer welcome in my circle of friends. You may also like to know that Ella and I are to be the proud parents of twins in early December. Bye, Felicity."

We turned and walked away from her. What a horrid woman. From a distance, she did look very beautiful but when you got close you could see it was all make-up. Underneath it all she is a very plain woman with a very ugly nature.

"Bet you're glad to see the back of people like her aren't you my love? Much better off with plain old me."

"Ella, you are not plain, you are a stunningly beautiful woman. She is just a bitter and twisted has been. I never did like her anyway. She is one of Cleo's inner circle or was. If she hadn't heard about our split then she was never much of a friend."

"Forget about her, my darling. Come here and kiss me in Paris."

I did, with all my heart, how I love this man. I can see why he described himself as very lonely if Felicity was the kind of woman who would push herself onto him. He deserves so much better.

All this time Scott and Caroline had been watching and listening to the exchange. The girls were busy looking in a shop window.

Scott said, "I told you once before Jacob that she was trouble."

"You did Scott, I always knew it myself. Glad I never went there, no matter how hard she pushed. What a bitch."

"Right then girls, do you want to go further or are you ready for bed?"

" Just a little bit further, Daddy, please. Promise we will get up early tomorrow and be good all day."

"Okay he said, another thirty minutes then I think we should all head back."

The remainder of our walk was uneventful. Everyone that was out and about seemed to be having a good time. Didn't see any more of the delightful Felicity thank goodness.

We arrived back at our hotel and ordered hot chocolate all round. We sat in the lounge area as we had our drinks.

"This is a lovely hotel Jacob, have you stayed here before?"

"I have he said, a couple of times actually but never had a gorgeous woman with me then. Spent my nights all alone. I had done a couple of shows here, well just outside of the city to be truthful and Eddie had booked rooms here for me and the orchestra guys. I have to tell you though, I am enjoying this visit much more than the previous ones."

I held onto my man as we left the lounge and headed for the lifts. A group of women were watching us, and one called out, hello Jacob. He turned and waved to them.

"Goodnight ladies" he said.

"Can we have a picture please?"

He looked aghast, "God almighty," he said, "can't even get any peace on my honeymoon."

I nudged him, "Go on you grouch I said, make their day."

"Only if you come with me," he said.

"Okay" he turned towards the group and smiled that devastating smile.

"Okay ladies, just a quick one. Ella and I are on our honeymoon you know."

The one that looked like the ring leader said, "Really Jacob, I hadn't heard you had got married. When did this happen?"

"Just yesterday," he said. "We had a double wedding with my brother Scott and his lovely bride, Caroline.

That is them over there with Scott's two daughters from his first marriage. They were bridesmaids and very beautiful they were too."

"That's amazing Jacob, you kept it very quiet."

"Not really he said, I announced it to everyone at a couple of shows I was doing back in London a few weeks ago then we really went to town and got it all organised in three weeks. Must have been some sort of record I guess. Anyway, let me introduce you all to the love of my life, Ella. I am treating this wonderful woman to a lovely long holiday before she gives birth to our twins that she is carrying. I can't tell you how happy all this has made me. Then to top it all we find out that Caroline is also expecting twins. We should be kept very busy once these babies arrive."

The women were lovely. They congratulated us on our marriage and also on the twins. They all had photographs taken with both Jacob and me. They couldn't thank us enough. As we wished them a good night they called across to Scott and Caroline, "congratulations to you both as well." It is really nice when they get included, they could easily be left out, but Jacob's fans seem to genuinely like Scott, but what's not to like, he is great.

Finally, we were allowed to leave the group and headed towards the lift. We all piled in and headed for our floor. The girls were suddenly very tired.

Jacob said, "I was going to ask you if you wanted to join us for a cuppa, but it looks like someone's bed is calling."

"We will get these two tucked away in their beds then hit the sack ourselves I think. Goodnight and see you both in the morning."

I went over and kissed them both, then the girls. Jacob shook Scott by the hand then kissed Caroline and the girls. "Night, night all" we called. They went to their suite and we went to ours, for a night of love and passion.

I really can't leave this man alone and it would appear that he feels the same about me. We constantly have to touch each other, no matter who else is around.

As we entered our room Jacob picked me up in his strong arms and carried me over to the bedroom. He lay me down on the soft duvet that covered the bed. "Now my darling wife, this is our time. Just you and me, "I love being with other people most of the time, but these private times are my absolute favourites. Just you and me together in our own little bubble".

"Funny you should say that Jacob, these are my favourite times too." He began undressing me, slowly and carefully. I did the same for him. His necklace was glinting in the light from the bedside lamp. He held the links in his fingers,

"Honestly Ella, I absolutely love these gifts from you. They are very precious to me, as are you, my love." He rose above me and then began to fondle my breasts before finally taking each nipple into his mouth and sucking gently. This made me arch my back, such a delicious sensation running all through my body.

I pushed him gently so that he was lying on his back. I climbed over him, playing with his nipples. This he liked, I moved down the bed and took him into my mouth, moving slowly. He was very ready. I moved back up the bed and climbed over him once more, guiding him to my entrance. He slid inside me and I began to move. Almost at once that wonderful pulsing sensation began. I moved harder and faster until my orgasm broke all around him just as he exploded into me.

"Oh my God Jacob" I breathed, "I love you so much my darling"

He could barely speak, we lay there in a wonderful glow of happiness. Just the two of us, happy and content. Slowly we began to recover and just lay facing each other and gazing into each other's eyes. His are like pools of deep green water, so deep I could drown in them.

I suddenly felt very thirsty. "Do you fancy a cuppa?" I asked.

"I do" he replied. "You rest here and I will make it" he said. He went back into the lounge completely naked, I could hear him running the tap and moving cups around. He soon returned with two beautiful mugs of steaming tea.

"Can you get tea in any country?" I asked.

"You can yes, but some of it is very different to the tea that we like. Some of it is okay but others not so much. I requested a supply of English tea for our rooms, they must think I am very picky, but I don't care, my precious lady should have the drink she desires.

Whilst she is carrying my two very precious babies she will have everything she wants. Then once they are born she and they will have everything that their hearts desire."

"You spoil me, Jacob, I love everything you do for me, but I also love giving you things that please you so please don't stop me. will you?"

"Okay, my love," he said. "Let's just say that we will continue to spoil each other and also our children when they arrive. I don't know if I can wait till December, I want to see them now."

"Be careful what you wish for I said. They need to stay where they are for a while yet. They are very tiny at the moment. I will start to get big soon, very big with two of them."

"I don't care how big you get he said. I will love every inch of you."

"I wonder if I will ever get back to being this size again, I will need loads of new clothes again in different sizes."

"You can have as many clothes and in as many sizes as you want my love. Do you think it's too early to start buying baby clothes?" he asked.

"Probably, let's wait till we are in the house. It won't be fair to Scott and Caroline to fill their home with more of our things. We could look at all the things we will need on your computer, maybe even order things but not have them delivered till we move. Will that satisfy you?"

"Great idea, he said. We will have loads of things to get, won't we?. Two of everything."

"To be honest, Jacob, I have no idea what we will need. I think I will need to speak with Caroline, and she can advise me. If she doesn't know then I don't stand a chance."

"We will all find out together, he said. They are going to need just as much as us." He laughed, "we will need a big lorry to deliver everything."

"And a big bank balance I chipped in."

"Well between us I doubt that will be a problem, he said."

"I tell you what I have been thinking about, the charity gig I said I would do for the hospital. We said the beginning of December, do you think we should bring it forward a bit?"

"Probably I said, I doubt you will feel like singing whilst I am doing my bit."

"Are you worried about it Ella?"

"A bit" I said, "I have watched the animals giving birth many times and they usually manage okay. It's just the same thing, isn't it?"

"I guess so he replied. I will be with you anyway, there is no way you will be doing it on your own."

"Jacob, will you make love to me again, please?"

"I will my darling. I can't be close to you and not want you."

He reached for me and kissed me with passion. I felt his need of me pressing into my thigh. We kissed for a long time and caressed each other's bodies. Finally, he rose over me and pushed himself into me, very gently and with so much love. We rode together, pressing against each other. I could feel my orgasm building and building finally pushing me over the edge. Jacob exploded once more into me, it was wonderful.

"Jacob, I love you so much" I said,

"Ella, you are my heart and my soul my sweet girl, I love you too."

We broke apart and lay together, hearts beating fast in our chests. Finally, our breathing returned to normal, and we slept, wrapped in each other's arms.

I was learning to manage my hair a bit better now so that it didn't bother me so much. I could pull it into a band at the back of my head and generally it stayed there when I needed it out of the way. I had needed it out the way this past hour or so.

I woke with a start, Jacob was standing beside the bed just watching me.

"Morning my darling, how are you feeling this morning?"

"Fine, I think" I said.

"We don't have time for loving this morning" he said. "We will have to shower and get dressed quickly then grab some breakfast. Our car will be here shortly."

Of course, I had forgotten, we go to this Disney thing today.

Jacob said he had rung and made a booking for us and the girls were very excited. Couldn't disappoint them could we. I got up and jumped in the shower, Jacob had been in there whilst I still slept. I was soon dressed sensibly is how Jacob described my look.

I had some trainers on that were very comfortable so my feet should be okay. Of course, Jacob looked a million dollars in jeans and an open-neck, short-sleeved dark green shirt. I love to see him in green, it matches his beautiful eyes. He made sure his necklace was visible under his shirt. It does look good on him, so pleased I bought it for him. He is always moving the links around on his bracelet and now the necklace.

Once we were ready we made our way down to the dining room. Scott and Caroline were already there with two very excited young girls. They were all tucking into croissants and drinking juice.

"That will suit me fine as well I said."

The waitress soon appeared at the table with more pastries and another jug of fresh juice. We were soon finished and so got up and made our way out to the waiting car.

There was a second car following behind. Jacob said they were extra security and would accompany us on this trip.

"Why do we need extra security today Jacob?" I asked?.

"We went out and about yesterday and we were all fine."

"I didn't like the way that Felicity woman walked straight up to me on the street though. She could have been anyone and her being a so-called friend of Cleo, well it just spooked me a bit. Won't hurt to be extra careful with the girls being with us.

Being with me comes with a certain amount of danger I suppose. I try not to let it bother me too much but with what happened recently and then that last night, well it pays to be careful. There will be a lot of people around today as well. Stay close to me all day Ella, don't go wandering off will you?"

"I will stick to you like glue, promise."

I did stick with him all day, of course I did. This place was huge, and all manner of strange things were going on. Not altogether certain I liked it if I'm honest.

The girls were in seventh heaven. They went on lots of rides, and Scott and Jacob went with them on the bigger ones. I think they were as excited as Becki and Melisa were.

Our security men were discreet but kept close by all day. I did feel safer having them with us. Jacob had been right, it was very busy. Thousands of people seemed to be enjoying this Spring day.

We had burgers for lunch and big containers with some fizzy drinks in them. Not sure I liked the fizz so much. Made me burp a lot.

We stuck it out as long as we could but both Caroline and myself were feeling very tired. The girls were beginning to wilt as well so we called it a day and made our way back to the hotel.

It had been a good day, just very long and a lot of walking was involved. At least now I know what Euro Disney is.

It was good to get back to the hotel, I needed a foot massage for one thing. We arranged to have our dinners in our rooms. None of us could be bothered to shower, change then go down to the dining room, as nice as it is. Jacob ordered for me again as I still had no idea what anything was. Will need a quick lesson in reading French menu's I think.

We showered and then dressed in our night clothes. We sat around in the lounge just talking, holding hands and kissing, lots of kissing.

Our meals arrived bang on time and they did smell gorgeous. The waiters quickly laid up the table and set our meals before us. There was a bottle of wine as well. Jacob said that half a glass would be okay for me to sip with the meal, but he really did fancy a drink tonight. And why not, both he and Scott have been brilliant so far. They both deserved a drink. I had a sip of my wine and it was very nice. If I hadn't been pregnant I would have really enjoyed drinking it with Jacob but no, I won't do that. I will not risk my babies.

The meal was some sort of chicken dish in a wine sauce, so I thought that alone would be sufficient. I sipped about half of the wine that Jacob had poured for me then gave the rest to him.

He was looking a little tired. It had been a long day for us all. We finished our meal and Jacob put all the dishes onto the trolley it had been delivered on. He pushed it outside the door, came back in and locked the door firmly behind him.

We sat on the sofa again and Jacob massaged my aching feet. He has a wonderful touch. They were soon feeling like new. He had the bottle of wine still but wasn't drinking it.

"Don't you want the rest of the wine" I asked.

"No, I don't actually. I was really fancying a drink with my meal but then I realised I wasn't enjoying it so no, had enough."

"What are we doing tomorrow?" I asked?.

"Well, how do you fancy going up the Eiffel Tower."

I must have looked horrified. "You mean that great big thing you showed me yesterday?"

"That's it, we can go right to the very top if you are brave enough."

"No thank you very much, I think I have tried enough new stuff for now, going up that thing is one step too far."

"I thought that was what you would say."

"How about a river cruise then, that will be nice and calm? We can take in all the sites along the river then get off if you want to see something then get back on again when you are ready."

"Jacob, I think that sounds perfect, will the girls be happy doing that do you think."

"If not then they can do what they want, we are not joined at the hip" he said.

"It is our last day here so if they want to do something else they can. Tomorrow we have a long drive to our house, I think you will love it, I hope you do anyway. Once the babies are here I think we should aim to spend at least part of the year there."

"Let's hope I like it then" I said.

Jacob rang Scott and told him we planned to go on the river cruise in the morning. If they fancied it then they were welcome to join us but if they wanted to do something else with the girls then that would also be fine.

"Okay Jacob he said, I'll have a word with them then let you know in the morning. The girls are both fast asleep now, just about managed their dinner but couldn't stay awake any longer. We are both knackered as well so I don't think we will be too far behind them. See you in the morning. Good night."

"Right my darling, do you want anything else to eat or drink? If not I recommend an early night. What say you?"

" That sounds just right to me my love. I feel a little light-loving then a good night's rest. Would that suit you?"

"Sounds perfect," he said.

So that is how we spent our night in Paris, loving and sleeping. We woke refreshed the next morning, the sun was streaming through the curtains and it felt like a good day was dawning.

We showered and dressed then met up with Scott and Caroline in the dining room. We all went for a light breakfast, even the girls. They still looked a little tired, it had been a big day for them the day before. They had been having a few of those lately what with the weddings and all that excitement.

"Scott said he had rung Mrs H to check everything was okay. Vera was still staying with her and they had become firm friends. They are still full of the weddings and the parts they played in the day. They will dine on those memories for weeks he said. They had walked down to the pub a couple of lunchtimes for their meals, and they said how everyone was talking about the fabulous time everyone had.

She has collected all the papers she could find and is keeping them for when we return. Not a bad word has been spoken or printed so good one Ella.

The lads in the pub had a great night with the money you left for them, so they are all happy. The hotel rang to thank you for choosing them so she told them you won't be back in the country for a couple of months, but she will pass their message on."

"Also, you need to ring the police station later today. They will bring you up to date on what is happening with Madam Cleo."

"Oh God, I hope it's not bad news," said Jacob.

"I doubt it, bro, she has really gone too far this time," Scott said.

"There will be consequences to what she did. Don't worry about that. Just give them a ring later, you never know it might be good news."

"I do hope so," he said.

The girls had chosen to do something else for the day, so we were going river cruising on our own. We had a really lovely day. The sun was shining, and it was quite warm so the breeze blowing across the river was nice and cooling. We hopped off and on again a couple of times. We visited an art gallery, never been to one of those before but I found the paintings and artworks fascinating.

Jacob pointed out really famous landmarks none of which I had ever heard of. He bought me a book all about Paris and all the interesting places to see. It was in English so I would spend a lot of time reading it. Perhaps if we come back here again in the future I will understand it all then, maybe.

We had lunch sitting outside a lovely little pavement café Jacob called it. We sat there people watching, holding hands and being very loving towards each other. We attracted a bit of interest, well Jacob did, but no one really bothered us.

"You should grow a beard when we go to the house I said, then when we go back home no one will know who you are."

"Really, do you think that would work?"

"It might do," I said.

"I tried to grow a beard once before, but it wasn't a success, very patchy and had different colours. I gave up in the end."

I laughed at him, this gorgeous, masculine man of mine struggles to grow a bit of hair on his face. Unbelievable.'

When we arrived back at the hotel Jacob said, "I had better ring the police, see what they have to say."

We were in our suite, he went into the lounge area and sat on the sofa. I was in the bedroom trying to brush my hair. I think the dampness from the river has done something to it. It was flying all over the place. I could hear Jacob talking, he didn't sound upset or angry so maybe it was a good call.

I went into the lounge and stood behind the sofa, I reached over and began to massage Jacob's shoulders. He did feel a bit tense. With a little firm massage though he did begin to relax under my fingers. Before he had finished his phone call I moved my hand to the front of his shirt and began to undo the buttons. I put my hands on his skin, moving them around in a gentle motion. I found a nipple and began to play with it then used my other hand to find the other one. That was definitely a winner, he finished his phone call as quickly as he could then jumped over the back of the sofa and gathered me up in his arms.

He kissed me so passionately, he really does take my breath away. He picked me up and carried me through to the bedroom.

"Right Mrs Ryan, what is the meaning of all this playing with my body?

We were laughing and enjoying being together. Before long things got very steamy. Jacob had me out of my clothes within seconds begging for him to make love to me. He did as I asked taking me to new heights of passion. I felt my orgasm building then bursting from me with such a shudder, it was wonderful. Jacob then exploded inside me bringing me to a fresh climax."

"Good God Jacob, that was amazing. I didn't think our lovemaking could get any better, but I think you just scored a ten out of ten for effort."

We both fell back onto the bed laughing.

"We are pretty good together aren't we?" he said.

"I should say so. Bloody brilliant."

"Tell me something Jacob, has it been like this with your other lovers?"

"Err, no. There really haven't been that many you know and until I met you and fell so deeply in love with you, within minutes of meeting you, I might add.

No I have never experienced anything so spectacular. Right from that first time, I just knew it was different, special. Now I can't stand by you without wanting you, needing you. We really are the real deal, aren't we?"

"I should say so" I replied. I can't even think about being with anyone else, ever."

"That is exactly how I feel my love. Just the two of us, together forever."

We lay side by side for a while then I asked, "what did the police have to say?"

"Sorry, forgot in all the heat of our lovemaking. "She is pleading guilty, so we won't have to go to court thank goodness. She has been assessed by a psychiatrist and a report is being sent with her file to whoever looks at these things."

"Basically, they think she is suffering from some form of PTSD, that is post-traumatic stress disorder. The military very often suffers from it when they have been in war zones or stressful conditions. They think that all the mess she made of things firstly with me, then with Arlo has tipped her over the edge."

"The guy who did the assessment of her wants her to go for counselling and maybe treatment, depending on how she responds to the counselling. That will be the magistrates decision ultimately. She will undergo this counselling before going to court so that they can give a better idea of her mental state."

"I told the officer that I really didn't care what happened to her, but I wanted it to be put down legally so that she was not contact or be anywhere near me, you, Scott and his family or our children when they are born. He said that my request would be put before the magistrate, but it may be that I will need to take out some sort of legal thing myself if the magistrate won't do it. I will speak with Scott about it, he will be able to sort it all out."

"He did say that since she has had time to consider the things she has done and said she is mortified by her actions. She told them that since I finished things with her she has been drinking heavily and she feels that it is the alcohol that has clouded her judgement."

"I left him with no doubt as to my feelings about it all. I don't want it all going to court if I can help it, it will just drag it all up again and cause us all a lot of upset. If she just stays well away from us I can live with that. She won't get a second chance though."

"That is very generous of you Jacob," but I think it is the right thing to do. She does need monitoring though. If she starts going the wrong way again it needs stopping before it starts. You might not be so lucky next time."

"Or you, my darling, I can never forgive her for what she did to you. You are innocent in all this, but she chose to attack you and for no good reason. It was all over with her long before it had even started really.

It was the depression I was in bought on through overworking that made me vulnerable to her advances.

To be honest I didn't really like her that much and I have never loved her, never given her cause to think that I did but she chose to see things differently."

"Darling Jacob. You need to put all this behind you now my love. We have each other and will soon have our own dear family. What has gone before is in the past and there is nothing we can do to change that. However, what is to come in the future, now we can do something about that.

I don't know about you, but I want my future to be filled with you and our babies and all the love and happiness that I think we deserve."

"Oh, Ella, you are the most wonderful, precious woman I have ever known. I love you more than life itself. The world that I have been living in is not real, it is full of people who don't really care about me. They all want what I can give them. It's a very selfish life in many ways.

I know it has its rewards and they can be plentiful, but it also comes with a huge amount of pressure. I felt as if I had to keep performing for other people, not for myself."

"That is why I need to take this time to work out exactly what I want from this life I lead, from our relationship, from all these people who rely on me to help them make a living.

All I know for certain is that I want to be with you, with our children and also with Scott and Caroline and their growing family. I need you to keep a tight hold on me. If you think I am pursuing the wrong path then you need to tell me. I can't and won't mess this up, this thing that we have between us. This all-encompassing love I have for you. Being with you is the one thing that gives me complete happiness. The funny thing is that with you I don't even have to work at it, it all comes just so naturally."

"I know Jacob, we have both led very different lives. But I think that what we both bring to the table is what we both of us needs more than anything else. Our love for each other will see us through, even if there are some bumps in the road we will get through anything, together."

"Thank goodness you feel the same as I do," he said. How lucky are we to have actually met with both of us coming from such different places?"

"I know, it's incredible I said. To think how my life has changed in just a few weeks. I never dreamt in all my wildest dreams that I would meet someone as wonderful as you, my darling husband. Do you know what? I rarely think about Will and my past nightmare of a life. It's like my life began the moment I met you."

We were in each other's arms once more, kissing and loving then kissing some more. I suppose we have Will to thank for all this anyway. If he had changed lawyer then Scott would never have visited the farm and so he wouldn't have met Caroline and I wouldn't have met Jacob. Our lovemaking was so wonderful, gentle and fulfilling. My whole world begins and ends with Jacob.

We were lying side by side just taking each other in, Jacob stroking my bare arm and me caressing his beautiful face.

I suppose I should ring Scott to see where they are and find out if they want to meet here for dinner or go elsewhere. He went through to the lounge and found his phone. A short conversation with Scott confirmed that they all wanted to eat in the restaurant again. The girls had apparently really enjoyed eating with the grown-ups.

We arranged to meet them in the foyer at seven. I am really getting to grips with this lifestyle now. Good job I have all Will's money coming my way. We will probably need it if Jacob is going to be working less. We had agreed to get dressed up for this last meal in Paris.

As usual, Jacob looked amazing, I'm sure he would look fabulous if he dressed in a bin bag. In saying that when I saw Scott he too had scrubbed up well. The girls had their bridesmaids dresses on and looked lovely. Caroline always looks good, she can carry any style off and when I looked in the mirror I thought, well girl you don't look half bad yourself.

And so it was that this blended family of six entered the dining room. All the staff seemed to be in a bit of a dither. I imagine that is the Jacob factor coming to the fore again. They were falling over themselves to make sure he had everything he wanted.

He treats everyone well, he makes time for people then goes above and beyond to give them what they want.

Of course the staff are not allowed to ask for photographs or autographs. They are there to just serve and to do the best job they can. Jacob recognises this and will invite them to have photos taken with him. That way the bosses can't give the staff a hard time. Is it any wonder everyone loves him? Of course he speaks French and that helps a lot. It would appear that I am the only one that doesn't. Will have to learn a bit though if we are to spend lots of time here. Perhaps Becki and Melisa can teach me.

We spent a lovely evening, all six of us. The girls were telling us about their exciting day. Caroline said that when they were finishing the packing before coming over here they had insisted they would need to bring their pretty dresses because Uncle Jacob always takes them somewhere posh. They did look adorable and very well behaved.

I noticed how Scott was continually playing with his bracelet, just the same as Jacob does, although now Jacob has to play with his necklace as well.

I asked Jacob to order for me again. Not gone wrong yet so will keep this way of ordering going till I can actually read French, goodness knows how long that will take. Before meeting Jacob it took me all my time to speak English. Never anyone but Will to speak to.

I noticed how lots of people were taking an interest in what was happening on our table. Jacob factor again I guess. He really is a very handsome man, very striking with his coal black hair and emerald green eyes. He wears his hair a bit longer than most men do, it is a little bit curly and flops around his adorable face. I had better stop dreaming about this man or we will be leaving the table early.

I was expecting some of the people watching us to approach him for a word or a photo, anything to get close to my man.

These people watching must notice how he is constantly talking to me, touching my face, my hands, my neck, anywhere just to keep having contact.

The watchers waited until we had finished eating then first one came up to request a photo then another. Before long there was a small queue forming. Jacob didn't seem to mind he just spoke with the next in line and

then smiled for the camera. The whole thing didn't take longer than fifteen
minutes and there were a whole lot of happy ladies to show for it.

Eventually, he was able to sit back down next to me. He kissed me full on the mouth and I hoped they could all see. That is the bitch in me. I don't mind really, after all it is me he comes home to every night.

He leaned into me and said. "Did you see that blonde woman?" I turned to see who he meant.

"Yes I said, why?"

She pinched my arse he said.

"Really?"

"Yes, really. I said to her don't do that my wife is looking."

"Did you?"

" I did he said"

"And what did she say?"

"She said sorry she didn't know I was married. Cheeky woman."

I looked into his eyes and then said. "Shall I go and punch her lights out?"

"Please don't he said, here's me trying to keep everything low key then they start forming a queue. What is wrong with people? Do they think that I shouldn't have a private life?"

"The trouble is my darling you are too kind to them. You never say no."

"He whispered in my ear once more, and aren't you glad I don't?"

I burst out laughing and then realised all these women were now looking at me. If looks could kill I would drop dead on the spot.

Becki and Melisa were watching all this with interest.

"Uncle Jacob, asked Melisa, why do women always want to kiss you and have their photo taken with you?"

"Because I am irresistible he said, just ask Aunty Ella." We were all laughing, it took the sting out of the tension that had been building.

"Are you all finished?" Jacob asked.?

"We all said yes we were."

"Do you want to go up to your room or should we all risk a hot chocolate in the bar?"

The girls began jumping up and down, hot chocolate, please Uncle Jacob.

"Come on then, let's get out of this menagerie. I feel like a monkey in the zoo."

We all stood up to leave, the girls running and jumping their way into the foyer.

"Before you and I leave this room madam I want a full-on sexy Ella kiss."

I had to oblige, didn't I? He had his arms around me and pulled me into his embrace then gave me the nicest, sexiest kiss ever. As I came up for breath he kissed me again. We then turned and walked out of the restaurant with arms wrapped around each other.

We headed for the bar and Jacob summoned a waiter. I believe that what he asked for were six hot chocolates because that is what arrived a few minutes later. The girls were excited, they did look yummy. Caroline was looking at me.

"Goodness Jacob she said, what are you trying to do to me and Ella, if we keep putting all these calories in we will be getting huge."

That caused another laugh. Caroline and me getting fat, never.

A couple of the women from the restaurant had followed us through to the bar and just stood watching us. It's like living in a goldfish bowl when out with Jacob.

His actions didn't stop, he carried on kissing me although he hadn't spotted the women. He kept hold of my hand and kept picking it up and kissing the back of it, then he turned it over and tickled my palm with his tongue. I put my arm around his neck and pulled him in for another full-on kiss.

"Aunty Ella, why do you and Uncle Jacob keep kissing."

" Because we love each other and kissing someone you love is really nice."

"That's good then she said. Daddy and Mummy are always kissing as well and they said that they love each other, and kissing is nice, only Mum told us it was dirty, and we shouldn't do it."

"Well, I guess that is because you are both young but when you get older you will like it as well."

"That's good then" she said.

"Right then, are we all ready for bed?" I whispered in his ear, because I am."

"You, my darling wife, are insatiable, but I wouldn't change you for the world."

"That's all right then" I said.

I noticed we were still being watched, they had moved a little closer in the hope of hearing our conversation I should think.

"Jacob, do you know those women who are watching us? Don't turn around straight away. They were over by the bar to start with but now they are moving closer. I think they were with the crowd that had photos with you."

Jacob said, "okay folks if you are all finished let's get out of here. I have had enough of smiling for the camera."

He stood up then lifted me to stand by him, putting his arms around me. This was his chance to look at who was watching us.

"Oh God, not those idiots. They weren't with the photo brigade, I know who they are. They are part of the group that used to hang around with Cleo and Felicity. Hope they are not staying here. Will be glad when we get away from here. I bet Felicity has roped them in to find out what she can."

We all stood together, and Scott said, "do you want me to get them moved out of here Jacob?"

"Maybe he said, let's see what they do when we move into the foyer."

Right on cue, as we moved so did they. We walked into the foyer and Scott beckoned the assistant manager. He came over and Scott told him what had happened with these women.

I heard him say that "my brother is very accommodating with all his fans and never minds the interruptions, but this is ridiculous."

"He is here with his new wife and this is the start of their honeymoon. I would be obliged if they could be moved out of here if they are not staying in the hotel."

He shook the man's hand, and I noticed some money had changed hands. Money does speak then.

He walked over to the two women and spoke to them. They seemed to be protesting but the guy managed to convince them to move. I noticed them turn towards us as they were moved towards the main doors. They didn't look too happy, but they still had to leave.

I was beginning to feel that leaving tomorrow was a good thing. I had enjoyed most of this trip but just little things like these stupid women took the shine off it. Once we get to the house, which Jacob said is a long drive away, we will all feel better, and less visible.

We all piled into the lift to go to our rooms. We stood outside of Scott and Caroline's room making further plans for the next day. We would have breakfast at eight-thirty then our cars will be arriving at nine-thirty.

I had assumed we would all be going in one car but no, Scott's family will be in one and Jacob and myself in the other. I suppose that makes sense, after all, they will be leaving in two weeks, but we will be here for another month so will need a car.

We all said goodnight and did the kissing thing, Jacob was messing with the girls threatening to kiss them instead of me. They were squealing with laughter.

"No, Uncle Jacob, not allowed." You can only kiss Aunty Ella."

"Okay," he said, I suppose I will have to make do with her then if neither of you wants to run away with me."

They ran into their room still laughing. Scott said, "thanks for that bro, they will be laughing and screaming half the night now."

"That's okay Scott, no charge. Thanks for that downstairs, I hadn't seen them till Ella pointed them out.

My heart sank, they are a pair of nutters at the best of times. Let's hope we can slip away in the morning without any fanfare. Perhaps they would let us use the back entrance, the cars could be parked round there. Would make the whole thing more bearable."

"Leave it with me, Jacob, I will speak with the assistant manager shortly. He is very helpful. I will help Caroline get those two ready for bed then I will nip down and see if I can find him. Would make more sense to go that way."

"If you're sure you don't mind Scott, would put my mind at ease."

"Leave it with me, will let you know the plan at breakfast. See you both in the morning".

With that, we left them to their task, and we went to our room to begin our own task. We need to find time to pack all our clothes before the morning.

"Don't worry about it, my darling said Jacob, it will be done".

With that, he gathered me up in his arms and carried me to the bed. He soon had me naked then quickly got rid of his own clothes. He joined me on

350

the bed and then began nuzzling my neck, under my mop of hair. It sent shudders through my body.

"Oh, Jacob, you know exactly the right things to do to make me want you urgently."

"Right, urgent is it?"

"It is" I said.

"Better see what we can do about that then." He made love to me, gentle and slow.

"*Wow,* I said, this I like".

"So do I" he said.

I reached my climax quickly and then could feel it building once more. Jacob exploded into me at the same time as I was thrown over the edge once more.

We lay in each other's arms, slowly regaining our breathing. I love lying like this, looking into those beautiful green eyes. They speak to me and I love it. Finally, we slept.

We woke early, made wonderful love once more, had a shower then dressed for the journey. I began folding our clothes ready to put into the cases.

"What are you doing my love? he asked.

"Packing of course. We won't have much time after breakfast."

"Just leave it there, the packing fairies will sort it all out."

"What are you talking about I asked."?

"Well, my love, when we leave this room to go for our breakfast hotel staff will sweep in here and pack everything away for us."

"Are you serious Jacob?"

"I am," he said. The staff make a bit extra money by doing this service. I think it's brilliant. Worth every penny."

"It's a wonder you don't pay someone to wipe your bum," I said.

"Now there's a thought," replied Jacob. "Would you like to apply for the job?"

" Err, no, thank you."

"Come on my love, let's go eat then you can see how amazing this service is. Scott will have all his things packed for him as well.

"Okay, I wait to be amazed."

We went to knock for the rest of our group, but they had already gone downstairs. We took the lift and Jacob thought this would be a great time to kiss me.

"What is it with standing close to you? he asked?

"Whatever do you mean?"

He took my hand and placed it on his crotch area. Hard as a rock.

"Jacob, you can't walk into the restaurant like that," I said.

"What are you going to do about it then?"

"In here, nothing."

He wriggled and moved things around, so he at least looked decent. The lift doors opened, and we could see Scott waiting on the other side of the foyer. He had just finished speaking with the assistant manager.

We joined him and then went into the dining room. "Everything all right?" Jacob asked.

"Yes, fine now."

"What do you mean? Now?"

Come and sit down at the table and I will tell you. We made our way over to the table and greeted the others then placed our order for tea and croissants. Right then Scott, tell all.

"Well, last night I came back down to speak with the assistant manager about parking the cars around the back but before I could find him those two women were back and trying to get into the foyer. The security men on the doors knew they had been tipped out earlier and they were dealing with them but before anything could be done another woman turned up and started ranting.

It was that Felicity woman, she was very drunk. Couldn't tell what she was trying to say other than your name came out loud and clear as did Cleo. The rest was just mumbo jumbo. The manager himself had come through from his office and ordered someone to send for the police."

"They arrived quickly to be fair, they bundled all three women into a van and carted them off. It was only then that I was able to speak with the guy about the cars. The top and tail of it is they think that will be the best thing to do. I was just checking with him that everything is okay. He said the cars were there already as soon as we let them know they would collect all the luggage and store it away in the boots then send for us to come down here to be escorted out to the cars.

I will have to follow you out of the city though, not too sure of the roads around this part."

Jacob looked stunned, "why didn't you call me last night, I could have helped."

"I don't think seeing you would have helped the situation at all. You were better off doing whatever it was you were doing. It's all sorted now so stop worrying. The women are still sleeping it off in the cells. Bloody nutcases all three of them. I don't know what it is with you and women, but you certainly draw some nutters, present company excepted of course."

"Don't worry Scott, I know what you mean."

Will this situation get worse do you think I asked?"

"I bloody hope not said Jacob, we came here for a nice, restful break and now look what's happened. Thankfully I never told Cleo about the house over here. We should be safe there, it is very quiet and if no one knows we are around we might just get the peace we had hoped for. Our treat bringing you two here backfired, didn't it?"

"Don't worry about it Jacob, it is what it is. We will cope as best we can and I for one have enjoyed being in Paris so stop torturing yourself. If you keep worrying about everything you will make yourself ill and I won't have that do you hear me?"

"I do my darling, sorry, I just want to keep you safe and give you the best time, everything. I wish I was a postman or something sometimes. At least, no one would bother me then."

"I laughed at him. With those looks, I don't think so. Anyway, let's have our breakfast and then get ourselves sorted for this trip of a lifetime. Caroline and myself are really looking forward to it and I know these two girls can't wait. Melisa has offered to teach me how to swim."

Melisa was suddenly in the conversation, she had been listening to the exchange between her dad and her uncle.

"Uncle Jacob, it is only because you are so pretty that all these women want to love you, but it is Aunty Ella that has stollen your heart, I know that because you told me."

"I did tell you, that is true. Aunty Ella has stollen my heart and I love her to the moon and back. She means the world to me."

I know she does, I love it when you are happy. It makes me cry when you are sad."

"Well I had better stay happy then hadn't I."

"Yes please" she said.

We then ate our breakfast in silence, all with our own thoughts. Please God, let Jacob stay happy with me. I hate to see him so worried.

Once our meal was over we hurried back to our rooms. Jacob was right, our cases and bags were all stacked on a trolly ready to be taken downstairs. I did a quick check around to make sure nothing had been missed but no, it was all packed and ready to go. There was a knock on the door.

Mr Ryan your vehicles are ready, may we take your things down sir?

"Yes of course, thank you. We are coming now. Has my brother gone down yet?"

"Yes sir, they are all in their car waiting for you."

Jacob handed the man several notes which he took and put away in his pocket.

"Sorry your visit has ended so badly sir, I am told that the three women concerned are still being held at the police station, so you won't have any bother from them."

We had been moving from our room to the lift whilst this conversation was going on. Once in the lift it was just a few moments till we reached the ground floor.

"If you follow me sir you will soon be on your way."

"Thank you, you have all been amazing. I have arranged for all the staff to be given a small bonus each for all the care you have taken of us all. Hopefully next time we visit it will be without incident."

"I do hope so sir, we have always appreciated your visits in the past."

"Okay, here now. I will just load up your boot then you can be on your way."

Jacob opened the door for me to get in, I will never get used to these cars and driving on the wrong side of the road. I sat waiting and waving to the girls. Caroline gave me a thumbs up.

Jacob climbed in next to me then reached over and kissed me.

"Any regrets he asked?"

"With what?" I asked.

"Marrying me?"

"Jacob, why would I regret marrying you, I love you and I don't care what problems get thrown at us I will always love you. Now, get this car moving and take me to this amazing house of yours."

"Not just mine Ella, it is ours now we are married."

"Come on my love, let's get out of this city and find our own little love bubble. I will be with you wherever you go my love."

He reached over and kissed me once more.

"Okay, let's get this party started."

We set off from the hotel and the mood lightened the further from Paris we got. Jacob was right, it is a long drive, but the roads seemed good, so we sped along making good time.

We had a couple of stops for the girls to use the toilet. We had drinks and a bite to eat at lunchtime then set off for the final part of the journey. I had no idea what to expect. We were in an area that seemed quite remote.

I said to Jacob, "it looks like you are taking me back to the farm".

"Don't say that Ella, I want you to love this place not regret coming with me."

"That will never happen, I would be happy to be on the moon so long as I am with you."

"Almost there my love. Just this village to drive through then the house is just the other side."

As we left the village Jacob slowed and made a tight left turn onto a narrow lane. Not too far down the lane we drove through huge gates that were left open, a little further along we entered what appeared to be a courtyard of sorts. It was all lit up with beautiful lanterns. There were tubs of pretty flowers all around making it look a very friendly place.

We came to a stop beside huge doors set into a wall. The doors opened and a woman appeared, smiling and waving her hands about.

Mr Jacob, so happy to see you again. Been too long."

Jacob got out of the car and went over to the woman and hugged her.

"Magda, how are you? You look well."

"All good thank you Mr Jacob."

"I have a surprise for you Magda."

I had left the car and stood watching this tender moment.

"Ella my love, come here."

I walked over to him and he put his arms around me.

"Magda please meet my wife, Ella."

She looked at him then at me then back to Jacob.

"Wife you say, why you not tell me naughty boy. Ella, nice name she said. Let me look at you, she held out her arms then held me close to her. My lovely Jacob he has a beautiful wife, I so happy."

"That's not all Magda, we are expecting twins in December."

"Twins, really, I so happy. Let me hug you both." She did, Such a lovely lady.

Scott pulled up just then and jumped out of the car. He rushed over to Magda and hugged her.

"You look well Magda,"

"I am Scott and so happy for my Jacob. A wife and twins how wonderful."

The girls were out of the car and hugging Magda's legs. "Magda we are happy to be here."

"Scott said I have a surprise for you as well Magda."

"Caroline come here and meet Magda," she was looking from Scott to Caroline then back again.

"Magda meet Caroline, my wife."

"Another wife my goodness, you boys keep big secrets."

"We do don't we? said Scott but that's not all, we too are expecting twins in December."

I thought she would pass out she was so excited.

"My boys she said, how wonderful. Is it secret or can I tell Laurent."

"You can tell him of course just don't get spreading it around the village just yet. We want to have some alone time for a while. We have been in Paris for a few days, and it got a bit silly. Stupid women making things difficult."

"Of course you boys need to have alone time with your new wives. When did you get married? Or is that a secret too?"

"Last Saturday said Jacob, we had a double ceremony. You know us Ryan's we like to do everything together. I have a video of the whole day on my computer. The others haven't seen it yet. I thought we can all watch it together."

"Wonderful she said, now come on in, let's get you all settled. I have a meal ready for you all. I am so pleased to see my boys finally happy with such beautiful ladies. Come, come."

We all trouped into the house behind Magda.

"Jacob I said, this house is so beautiful. I imagined a small cottage when I thought about being here."

Jacob smiled at me and said, "there is a cottage in the grounds, it is where Magda and Laurent live. They keep an eye on the place for me."

"I said I think they do more than that."

"You are right, they do. Laurent looks after the grounds. He gets people in to do the big jobs, but he sorts the rest out. He's great, you will love him. Then Magda looks after the house, I haven't been here for over a year, so they have had the place pretty much to themselves. Since meeting you though my love I have been dreaming of the day I could bring you here. And now we are here together, my family."

Magda was fussing about in the lovely kitchen.

"You want hot drinks or wine or fresh juices?"

Jacob looked at me," what do you fancy my love?"

"Well juice would suit me, what about everyone else?" A rousing chorus of juice please.

Magda fetched a large jug of juice from the fridge and placed it on the scrubbed pine table along with glasses. The girls were all over it.

"Magda makes the best juice in the world" they said.

We all sat down, and Jacob poured out our drinks.

"The girls are right I said, this is delicious, and it was."

We sat around drinking our juice whilst Jacob and Scott were catching up with all the news from the village.

Jacob said, "I think it's about time us men bought all the luggage in. We can get sorted out upstairs then eat. If you are all up for it we can then watch some of the video. I have only seen the first few minutes myself, decided to wait so we can watch it all together. I am excited by the bit I did see though."

We all thought that would be a lovely way to spend our first night here. We all trouped out to the cars and unloaded all the cases and bags. Caroline and I were only allowed to carry the very light things. The girls attempted some of the heavier things but failed. Scott and Jacob soon had everything

357

upstairs and on the beds. Caroline and myself began taking all the things out of the cases and hanging stuff in the wardrobes or putting it in drawers. It was soon looking nice and tidy, and I was then able to look around at the space that would be our bedroom for the next several weeks.

"This house is amazing" I said to Jacob, "was it like this when you bought it."

He laughed, "no it wasn't, it was a tumbled down wreck if I'm honest. I did spend a lot of time here during the renovations, that is when I met Magda and Laurent. I had to eat out all the time because there wasn't any kitchen facilities.

Magda ran the local café then but was looking to retire, that is when I stepped in. She still wanted to work but not such long hours or heavy work. This keeps them both occupied."

"You are amazing Jacob, always thinking of other's."

"I try he said but at the time I really needed someone here all the time and the arrangement suited us all. They are a great couple, we suit each other I guess. Plus Magda is a great cook."

"Thinking of your stomach again? You're always hungry."

" Growing lad" he said.

"If you keep eating like you do, you will be overtaking me and Caroline."

"You my darling are getting very cheeky when talking about your husband, come here and kiss me in our new bedroom."

I did, our day had been long and different to any we have had since being together, but I still had time for some loving from my darling husband. Once all our stuff was stored away we spent half an hour in our bed with the door firmly locked.

We quickly showered and dressed then made our way downstairs. Everyone was there waiting for us, the table laden with food.

"Sorry, didn't realise you were all waiting for us" I said.

"Of course you didn't" said Caroline with a giggle. "Takes a long time to empty a suitcase."

We sat down with all the family and Magda took pizza's from the oven for the girls. They were excited with those.

"Now be careful you two, they will be very hot. Have some salad with your pizza please" said Magda.

The table was laden with all sorts of things from salad to quiche, there was chicken and ham and three types of bread.

"Come now, please you all eat".

We all loaded up our plates and began to eat. It was delicious and a lovely way to spend a couple of hours. The men had one glass of wine each then joined Caroline and I with bottled water.

Once finished eating Scott suggested that the girls get ready for bed then come down to watch the wedding video. I was a bit puzzled as to how we were all going to watch it on the computer screen.

I still hadn't seen much of the house. The outside space was one thing I needed to see and of course there is a swimming pool somewhere.

So far I have seen the kitchen, hallway, stairs and our bedroom. There is obviously more to see. Tomorrow will be soon enough though. I guess we can all sit in the kitchen to see the video.

Once everything was finished, food stashed and pots in the dishwasher, girls showered and in pyjamas we were told by Jacob that if we could give him a few minutes the film would be ready.

We were all excited to see what has been sent to Jacob. Although it is less than a week since our joint weddings it feels so much longer. We were all so wrapped up in the day that none of us could remember everything.

Magda and Laurent appeared, Caroline and myself were introduced to him. What a lovely man. He said he is so happy to see that his boys now have lovely wives. The girls had flown to him as he walked through the door. Obviously they think the world of him.

Jacob came back into the kitchen and embraced Laurent.

"So great to see you again said Jacob, I have wanted to bring my lovely wife here and now we have the excuse to come and to stay for a long time. I want us to come back here a lot from now on. Once our twins are born we will bring them with us. You can help me to teach them to swim."

"Of course I will said Laurent, I will love it. This house was meant to have lots of babies in it."

"Well Scott and Caroline will also have twins so with Becki and Melissa that makes six, will that do?"

"For now, yes he said. Maybe more later. Your wife she is lovely. So much beautiful hair. You make beautiful couple."

"Well, thank you Laurent, now come on, let's go and see this video. We are all desperate to see it."

Jacob led us down a long hallway with four doors off. At the end of the hallway was another door. Jacob swung it open and led us into a cinema room.

"That is one big surprise I said, I thought we would all be standing around the computer." They all laughed at me.

We took our seats and Jacob did something with his computer. All of a sudden the big screen lit up and there we all were. Me standing next to Jacob looking up at my new husband and Caroline looking up into Scott's lovely face. The girls were standing in front of us looking adorable.

"Okay said Jacob, ready?"

Yes, we all called. He set the computer to play, and we all sat back and re-lived that wonderful day. There was footage of us all getting ready, even Mrs H and Vera being made up. There was so much chatter going on, people everywhere.

Then it moved to the pub where it showed Jacob and Scott being trimmed and shaved, then Gregg and Eddie. It even showed the men getting dressed. I'm sure I saw a glimpse of Jacob's bare bum.

It then moved onto the church and showed the men arriving and walking up the aisle, they stood talking with Gerald, the vicar. Then they were standing with Gregg and Eddie, they all looked a little nervous.

Next we were all getting into the cars outside Scott's house. Our dresses looked lovely even if I do say so myself. Becki and Melisa kept laughing every time they saw themselves. Jacob had his arm around me and kept kissing me, as did Scott and Caroline. Magda and Laurent were watching the film but also all of us. They seemed so happy for us.

Once we arrived at the church the video went from showing the men at the alter then to us walking up the path towards the church, then back to the men before finally showing us all walking up the aisle to meet our men.

The whole of the service was there, and it was lovely. There were shots of the guests sitting in the pews and of the girls talking quietly together.

Finally the last of the church footage showed us all outside posing for photographs then getting into the cars for our drive to the hotel.

That piece finished and Jacob asked if we would like a drink before the next bit. Of course the girls did but we all refused. He quickly went to make them hot chocolates then came back to find us all talking about what we had seen. We all loved it,

Magda and Laurent thought it was the best wedding they had ever seen.

Once we were all sitting back down Jacob set the rest of the video to play. It showed us getting out of the cars then going into the hotel and being greeted by the manager. He walked us through to the room we were having the meal in. There was footage of the guests arriving and being served drinks then finding their seats.

Once we were all seated and the meal was being served the screen went blank for a moment then came back on in time for the speeches.

Jacob was there singing *'Somewhere'* for all the guests. There was a lot of laughter and a few tears from us all. Funny how you live through something like that then forget a lot of what happened. This video will be amazing. I told Jacob we will play it on each of our anniversaries.

"What a fabulous idea" he said, and Scott and Caroline agreed.

It then took us into the dance hall and showed people dancing to the disco then of course Jacobs mini-concert. There was footage of the band members getting ready, tuning their instruments then beginning to play the intro. Magda was holding her hand to her throat, not really knowing what was to come.

Once the band stopped playing and Jacob began singing she turned and looked at Laurent, he held her hand and kissed it. I could see tears in her eyes, someone else that loved his voice.

No one spoke at all whilst Jacob sang, I was holding on tight to him, loving the feel of his arms around me.

Then when he asked me to join him for our song and he asked me to dance with him. What a magical moment that was. You could see people standing, just watching and listening, some with tears streaming down their faces. It really was a very special moment and now I can re-live it every day if I want to.

Of course it all had to end then the camera had taken video shots of all the guests, once again dancing to the disco.

The final shots were of us all getting back into the cars and driving off into the sunset to begin our new lives as married couples.

The screen went blank, and Jacob switched on the lights. Magda was in full sob by this time. Laurent had his arm around her. They too seem to be very much in love. Magical to see older people still caring and loving each other.

"Well, what do you think?" Jacob asked

"Bloody brilliant" was Scott's reply.

Caroline and I just looked at him, tears streaming down our faces. Of course, the girls thought it was fantastic and said they were the stars in a film now.

Magda and Laurent were speechless for a while. Laurent was the first to re-gain his composure.

"Well boys we think that the film is fantastic but the love that you all share is just what we have hoped for. It is a very long time since either of you have been happy but now we won't worry over you. Now we know for sure you both have what you deserve. A lifetime of love."

"Next, we need to know all about how you all met but I guess that will have to wait for another day" said Magda. "These two little angels look ready for bed."

Bless them, they have had a very long day and travelling makes you tired, but they were determined to watch the video to the end.

"We will take them up I think" said Scott "but before I go can I ask you to order a copy of that for us to keep, please?"

"Already done Scott but it's not actually finished yet. They sent this rough copy over for us to check, see if there's anything we want taking out. Once we okay it they will make it into a proper film with titles and lists of those attending, all sorts of little bits and pieces added. Once we are happy they will make as many DVD's as we want. I'm sure Magda and Laurent will want one as will Mrs H and Vera. We will have to ask the guests who were there if any of them want a copy. We could even send those press guys one." We all laughed but I thought that might not be a bad idea.

Scott carried Melisa and Caroline was holding Becki's hand and steering her towards the door.

"Goodnight they all called, see you in the morning."

We all wished them goodnight and then sat for a little while longer chatting with Magda and Laurent. They seem so happy for us.

Magda said she had worried about both of them for so long. Scott was in a bad place after Flora had left him then the awful thing that the horrid woman had done to her poor Jacob. It isn't any wonder they both suffered.

Jacob said "there is more to the tale regarding Cleo, but it will have to wait for another day. I for one am bushed. Do you want tea to take up with us darling" he asked me.

"That would be lovely I said but let me make it."

"No, I will do it" he said, "what about you two, do you want a drink making?"

"Thank you Jacob but no thanks, we will get off now and then make a drink back at home."

"Okay if you are sure" he said. "Don't get rushing in the morning, we might all need a lie-in after today. We don't want you pair rushing about after us, we can all take care of ourselves."

Magda said, "yes Jacob I know you can, but I love looking after you all. I will just carry on and do as I always do."

"Goodnight then both." She came over and kissed us on the cheek. I noticed how she put her hand on Jacob's face. This woman loves my man, she is the mother he and Scott no longer have.

We went through to the kitchen and let them out into the night.

"How far is their cottage Jacob?" I asked.

"Just around that corner, there see where the light is shining."

"That's lovely I said, being so close."

"They have been both mother and father to me and Scott ever since I bought this place. I wanted them to come over for the weddings, but I knew it was no good asking them. Neither of them will leave the village. It has been their way for a good many years. I was wondering whether we should have a party to celebrate our marriages with the village families. They all know us and will be thrilled for us once word gets around."

"That is a lovely idea Jacob, see what Scott and Caroline think about it in the morning. If we can plan a double wedding in three weeks then I'm sure a party can be organised in two weeks."

"Don't forget though he said, we had Sam helping us."

Jacob locked up and we made our way up the stairs.

"How many bedrooms do you have here Jacob I asked.

"We have six all told, it's a big place. I will show you around tomorrow. There is quite a bit of land that comes with it as well, but I let a guy from the village look after it.

Magda has what she wants for them and also for us when we are here. Other than that he sells what he can. I think he is happy with the deal. I don't charge him for the land, does him a good turn, which means he can provide for his family and it does me a good turn as I don't have to look after it or pay someone else to tend to it."

"Clever I said, win, win all round."

We had reached our bedroom door, we stopped for a second and listened, all was quiet. The girls were so tired they would have gone out like a light, but Caroline and Scott looked tired as well. It had been a long drive, we will all take some rest for a day or two. Jacob certainly needs to rest, he even performed on his wedding day, bless him.

I loved the DVD of our wedding. Wonderful to keep and be able to look back on over the coming years.

Jacob had opened the door to our bedroom and the sight of the bed drew me in. I guess I was feeling tired too. The door had no sooner closed behind us than Jacob had me in his arms. He was kissing me so tenderly.

"I have really loved watching that video tonight he said. So much that you miss on the day."

"I said that is exactly what I was thinking. It was like doing it all over again."

He began undressing me, kissing me all the time.

"Are you not tired tonight?" I asked.

"No, not at all, are you?"

"I am a little I said but not that tired that I can't make love to you my darling." And so for the second time today, we made love in this beautiful bed in the heart of the French countryside.

We finally fell asleep lying in each other's arms. Tiredness finally catching up with us both.

We slept so well, it was after eight before we woke. The sun was blazing through the shutters, and a beautiful day was waiting for us but first on the agenda was a little loving from my husband. I still can't believe how much I enjoy having sex with this man when just a few weeks ago I dreaded bedtime.

I rarely think of Will now. He is definitely in the past, Jacob is my today, my tomorrow and my future.

Once we were up and showered I looked for something summery to wear, I hadn't bought much with me as most of my clothes were for the winter and Spring. I have a couple of loose tops that will do for now but only jeans or trousers, I could do with a skirt or something.

"Jacob is there anywhere in the village that sells clothes" I asked?

"No, but if you can hang on till tomorrow we can drive into the next town. There are clothes shops there, why?"

"Well apart from a couple of tops I don't have anything for warmer weather. I think the jeans will be a bit warm. I bet Caroline isn't flushed for summery stuff either."

Jacob was looking at me, "If we are staying around here today you could wear one of those tops and just your knickers."

"Jacob, I couldn't do that".

"Why not he asked? There's only us here and I've seen more than your bum."

"What about Scott and Laurent?"

"Well my dear I am certain they have both seen a lot more than your butt."

"I will ask Caroline what she is wearing, I'll put my jeans on for now."

"Okay, but you will be very hot. We can get you some shorts and strappy tops and a couple of bikinis when we go into town."

"What are bikini?" I asked, dreading the answer.

"Well, let's see, I suppose it's similar to a bra and pants, you use them to sunbathe or go swimming."

"But I can't swim Jacob"

"You will before we leave here, you'll see."

I really wasn't too happy about learning to swim. I have never been in anything bigger than a bath before. Perhaps Jacob will forget about it, maybe.

For now, it will have to be jeans though, I grabbed them from the wardrobe and pulled them on. Not worn them for a few weeks.

"God they must have shrunk in the wash" I said.

I simply couldn't pull the zip up. Jacob was watching me.

"I don't think they have shrunk at all" he said.

"What I asked, are you saying I'm getting fat?"

He laughed at me.

"Not you getting fat my darling girl, our babies growing."

I took a deep breath, why didn't I think of that? Of course, it's my growing babies.

"I have noticed how things have been feeling a little snug lately" I said.

Jacob pulled me into his embrace.

"This is really happening my darling, now I can see how you are blooming. I tell you what, let's forget what I was going to do today, I will take you clothes shopping and Caroline as well if she wants to come. I can't have you squeezing into things that don't fit."

"Jacob, I would really appreciate that. I suddenly feel really fat. I know I'm not really fat yet but that's just how I feel. How will I feel in six months time?"

"Well, my darling, in six months' time you will be very close to giving birth to our beautiful children, then once they are born you will get back to being a slim and lovely young woman, well eventually you will. I guess it won't happen overnight. Come on, let's have breakfast then see if Caroline fancies a shopping spree."

Caroline laughed when I said I couldn't fasten my jeans.

"I am struggling as well she said. Scott said he would take me clothes shopping as well. I wonder if the girls want to shop or stay here with Magda."

That question was soon answered. stay with Magda is what they want to do so we ate a hearty breakfast and then pulled on the loosest fitting dresses we could find. Still felt odd though. The last time I had put this dress on it was really loose.

We all met up in the courtyard and climbed into Jacob's car. It still feels odd sitting by Jacob whilst he drives. I had got so used to sitting in the back of any vehicle that was taking us to the theatre or anywhere else we needed to go in London.

He tells me he always drives over here. Not so well known in France so he feels a degree of freedom. We flew along the narrow roads and were soon in the town. Jacob parked up and then we set off to find clothes shops that sold big sizes.

How could I think it would be that simple? Maternity clothes require a whole store dedicated to this temporary state. Thankfully there was such a store in this town so we could be kitted out with everything we needed for now.

We had managed to find several pretty dresses as well as tops and skirts, trousers and underwear and of course some bikinis.

I thought they would look ridiculous, but Jacob said they would be perfect.

Caroline and I had decided we would wear one of the dresses each and put the clothes we had been wearing in with the rest of the new stuff. These new dresses certainly felt better. It made me realise just how uncomfortable my clothes had become.

"I am going to be huge" I said to Caroline.

"Don't worry my friend she said, I will be huge with you."

Jacob took us to a lovely little café and bought us lunch. We sat outside and really relaxed. This seemed such a normal thing to do. It would be impossible back in England. Jacob would be swamped with fans. Yes he loves them, and he would be nothing without them but leading a normal life was next to impossible. We will have to make the most of our time here.

We were back at the house just after lunch, so Caroline and I took our new clothes up to our rooms, swiftly followed by Jacob and Scott.

The girls were in the pool and were squealing their heads off. Jacob said we should make the most of this time. Once the girls knew we were back they would be all over them looking for presents. Two new swimming costumes had made their way back with us of course.

We did make the most of their absence, spending a good hour making love and just being together. I guess that Scott and Caroline were doing the same. I really love these moments, just us, being together. I am so contented being with the love of my life.

Jacob got up and went over to the pile of clothes that were waiting to be put away. He moved a few things about then found what he was looking for. He held out one of the bikinis.

"Here, put this on, we can go in the pool for a while to cool off."

"Oh, Jacob, I'm not sure about this" I said.

"Don't worry my darling, I will be with you and being in the water will be good for you."

"Okay" I said, I had noticed that my flat tummy was no longer flat but what Jacob called my little 'pop' belly. I know it's not obvious yet to anyone else, but I am beginning to like this feeling of being pregnant. I have been lucky so far, not been sick at all just felt a bit nauseous a few mornings but that seems to have passed. I like it I decided.

I put on the bikini and then looked at myself in the mirror, not bad at all I thought. When I turned sideways my little tummy showed but face on not so much.

We walked down to the pool holding hands. Magda was sitting in the shade under a parasol, but Laurent was in the pool with the girls. They were still squealing their heads of and having a whale of a time.

Jacob and I stood by the side of the pool, I shivered.

"Are you cold my darling" he asked.

"No, not at all, just scared."

"Nothing for you to be scared of." "Come." he held out his hand and I took it. We walked to the other end of the pool and I noticed steps leading down into the water. That's good I thought, at least I don't have to jump in.

"Come on, just hold my hand and walk down into the water, you will find it very relaxing once you get in."

He was right of course. As I walked down the steps I realised that the water wasn't very deep at this end so I could go in up to my waist and my feet were on the bottom.

"Right said Jacob, still holding my hands, let me hold you here and just let your body relax and your legs and feet come up to the surface. I promise I won't let you go."

I felt quite brave by this time. Jacob walked back and forth from one side to the other holding my hands and letting the water hold me up.

It really is a lovely feeling. I noticed Scott and Caroline coming towards us. They waved and then went up to the other end, sliding into the water and then swimming from one side to the other.

They were playing with the girls and each other.

Laurent had got out and wrapped a towel around him. He went over and sat with Magda sipping something cool in a glass.

I asked Jacob if he wanted to go and swim with the others.

"What and leave you here on your own, no chance" he said.

We did a few more widths then I said I would just stay by the side where a rail was situated.

"I can hang on to that" I said. "You go and show me how it should be done."

"If you are sure" he said. "If you hold onto the rail you can let your legs come up and just float there. It will all give you confidence."

He kissed me then swam off heading towards the others.

I did as he had said, held on and just floated. I was enjoying being in the water. I was watching the others all having fun together. Will I ever be able to do that I wondered? Looks easy enough. Jacob insists I will be swimming before we leave here so we will wait and see. I know he won't allow any harm to come to me.

We spent a long time in the pool with the girls, they all came down to my end where it was shallow, and we played with a ball and several other things the girls have there.

They haven't been here for over a year with all the problems that both men have experienced. That will change now though. We will be able to spend long holidays here once the children are born. The house is definitely big enough for us all.

Jacob had taken me on a tour of all the rooms, there is a huge lounge and a smaller one, very intimate I thought. There is also a formal dining room with the biggest table I have ever seen, not that I have seen many. The whole house is beautiful.

The cottage that Magda and Laurent have is lovely too. Not at all like a cottage really. They have three bedrooms a kitchen diner and a big lounge. Plenty big enough for the two of them Magda told me. They really love living here and they adore Jacob and Scott as well as the girls.

She said that they are so happy to see everyone settled now. They have worried about them both for a long time but more so Jacob, they kept in touch by phone all through his troubles and couldn't believe how low he had sunk. That is all behind him now though and she is so pleased.

Jacob and Scott had gone for a walk into the village to see what the residents thought about a big party. Apparently, they were all thrilled with the prospect of a party and also a chance to celebrate the two marriages.

They would get their heads together once back at the house and see what would be the best way to go about it. They want to keep it under the radar of the rest of the world but also to give everyone a good time. Will take some thinking about is what they said.

They shouldn't have worried, two days later some of the villagers turned up at the house with their plans for the party. Jacob and Scott wouldn't have to do a thing. All the villagers would be making the food and the local band would play so we could all dance. They did ask though if Jacob would sing a few songs for them. What could he say, if they were prepared to do all the arranging and cooking a few songs is the least he could do. He would need to rehearse with the band though. He has no idea what they are like or if they are any good or not.

That first week just flew by, and the party was arranged for the following week, on a Friday afternoon and into the evening and night.

Caroline and I were getting a little excited as were Becki and Melissa. Of course, they wanted to wear their bridesmaid's dresses which was fine by us. At least they were getting some use out of them, different to Caroline and me with our wedding dresses. Wouldn't be using them again that's for sure.

Jacob had organised a meeting with the band members to run through a few songs, just to get the feel of things he'd said.

"Can I come with you I asked, you promised to sing for me every day, but you haven't done."

"Too busy making love to you" he said.

I walked down into the pretty village with Jacob, and we all met up at the village hall.

Jacob was surprised by the band, he was expecting three or four locals with an assortment of instruments but what they were was pleasing to him.

They were amateurs of course but they were really good. Seven of them in total. Jacob got together with them and explained what he wanted. They ran through the songs he had chosen, and I so enjoyed just sitting there listening to his wonderful voice.

The overall sound was good, obviously not the same as his orchestra back in London but good all the same. Once they were all happy we left to walk back to the house.

"Jacob, I loved that, just listening to your beautiful voice. I think I could listen to you twenty-four hours a day, seven days a week."

"Blimey, he said, when would I sleep?"

We were laughing and kissing our way towards the house when a group of children approached Jacob and started laughing with us. They were lovely, I couldn't tell a word they were saying but they certainly remembered Jacob and he seemed to know all of them. He took some money out of his pocket and spoke in French to them. Their little eyes nearly popped out of their heads. He handed over the money to the one that seemed the eldest. They were full of thanks and went running off, squealing and shouting as they ran.

"What was all that about?" I asked?.

"I told them to take the money to the sweet shop and tell the lady that all the children in the village can have sweets until the money runs out. Should keep them going for a few days."

"Jacob, you are so kind to everyone. No wonder they all love you."

"Well it doesn't hurt to spread it around a bit does it" he replied.

Once back at the house Jacob passed on the information about the party to the others.

"Blimey! said Scott, that's amazing. Didn't know they had a band here, did you?"

"No, I didn't but they are very good. They go around all the local areas playing at get togethers then donate the money they get to local charities. Nice bunch of people, six men and a woman that plays the keyboard. They seem to love it, well I suppose they must do, or they wouldn't do it, would they?"

Caroline and I were soon accepted as the new women with the Ryan men. We would take a walk into the village and look around the few little shops, everyone spoke to us. I was clueless but Caroline could understand a bit. She said she had done French at school and then carried it on for a year at college, but it is a long time since she has used it, she has forgotten more than she remembers.

Between us and hand signals, we managed to get over what we wanted to say. The women all wanted to touch our tummies once they found out we were both pregnant. Apparently, it is for luck and also it is supposed to help any woman who wants to get pregnant.

All superstition Caroline said but we were happy to allow them to touch our expanding tummies. *It is only a week since we bought all our new maternity clothes but already we were more comfortable wearing them. Took the pressure off the bump. I'm sure I have got bigger in a week.* Caroline said the same thing.

Jacob loves looking at me naked. He says he can really tell now that the babies are growing strong. He puts his mouth against my naked tummy and talks lovingly to his children. He is so excited.

Once the party was over we would only have one more day with Scott and Caroline. They are due to fly back home on Sunday leaving Jacob and myself to continue our honeymoon alone. *I love all the family so much, but it will also be nice to have some time to ourselves.*

I have been getting braver in the water as well. Jacob said I must'nt overdo it. Just gentle strokes and floating in the water would be good but I'm not to try doing hard swimming. He is like a fish and he says that one day I will be the same but not until our little tadpoles are born, that's his new name for the babies.

The party day was approaching, and we were all looking forward to it. We knew lots of the villagers now and they too were looking forward to a good time. Jacob had given the leaders of the village a large amount of money to cover the expense of the party, but they had returned it to him saying it would be their wedding gift to us. How wonderful of them.

Jacob and Scott drove us into the town again to find some party dresses for the two fat ladies. Luckily they had some really pretty things, and we were soon rigged out and ready to go.

We all dressed up for the walk down to the village. Magda and Laurent looked really smart, and Scott always looked the business. Caroline and I had on our new dresses and the girls had their bridesmaid's dresses on. *Jacob however looked every inch the star that he is. His hair shone black like polished boots. His curls flopped about his head. He had on dark grey jeans and a shirt the same colour green as his beautiful eyes.*

We had spent all week just being together, making love, eating with our family relaxing in the pool and walking around the village. We were having the most wonderful time. It will be sad when the others go home on Sunday.

Our walk into the village for the party saw our really happy group skipping and jumping all the way. Not me and Caroline of course but all the other's. Anyone watching us would think we were all nuts. We were all singing as we made our way so everyone would know we were approaching. Of course, Jacob's voice rang out clear and strong above all the others. He can't help himself, he has to perform.

The village looked amazing, there were banners and streamers pinned up everywhere. There were loads of trestle tables set up under the trees in the village centre, all of them laden with trays of delicious-looking food. Others were full of drinks, some for the children and other for the grown-ups.

There were all sorts of games being played by groups of children and Becki and Melisa were asked to join in. They were having so much fun.

People were laughing and talking in groups. Music was playing from a disco set up on the edge of the grassy area in the centre of the village.

Some teenagers were dancing on the grass and were having a good time. Must be difficult for them to live so far out from all the action. They probably won't appreciate Jacob's little concert, not their sort of music I guess.

We had all eaten as much of the delicious food as we could manage. Caroline and myself had drunk as much water as we could. Jacob had joined us with water, but Scott had given in and had a couple of glasses of red wine. He looked on the good side of happy.

He and Caroline were very loving towards each other. I guess they are thinking about their journey home. They would love to stay but there was so much they needed to do back in Wimbledon. The girls schooling for one thing. Scott had found a teacher who would be going to the house three evenings a week until they caught up with the lost lessons over the past few weeks.

I had a word with Caroline when we were watching the girls play some sort of ball game.

"How are you feeling my friend I asked."

"Good, we have all had such a fabulous time here with you and Jacob. It will be odd being just a family of four when we get back. Got used to being all of us. Scott and I are really happy together and we are both so looking forward to being parents together. I absolutely love those young girls as well, but I will miss you."

She put her arm around my shoulders.

"We have become such good friends, haven't we? It has been a real roller coaster since that first meeting with you back at the farmhouse. Who would have thought we would end up here with these wonderful men and lives full of so much love?"

I squeezed her shoulders,

Caroline, it is like a dream. The life I led for twenty-five years changed overnight when you walked in then it changed again when I walked into Scott's house and met Jacob. I fell in love with him the moment I saw him, did you know that?"

"I did she said, that is exactly what happened when I first met Scott, now look at us. Two fat ladies."

"I know it would be great if you could all stay for the next four weeks or so, but I also know you have to get back for the girls and Scott has his big case he needs to sort out. Then his final decision about selling up. Do you think he will?"

"I think he will, yes. It's the best thing for us all but more than that it will be good for Scott. His practice worries him all the time which is not good. If he works for Jacob all that worry will be gone."

Time was marching on, there was such an air of expectation as the hour for Jacob's concert came closer. He left us to go and get ready with the band, but we had to promise to be there at the front when he started. Of course, where else would I be?

We had a little walk around then made our way to the village hall. It was filling up fast. Everyone wanted to see and hear my man. We made our way to the front but stood to the side. A few minutes later the band came onto the stage and began to play a short version of the intro that the orchestra played at the start of all Jacobs concerts.

They stopped playing and Jacob's voice began that wonderful song **'Somewhere'**. Halfway through the band began to play again and Jacob carried on singing getting more and more powerful with every line. Finally that last long note went on and on. Wonderful.

As he finished that song he began his routine, one lovely song to the next.

Eventually, he stopped singing and began speaking to the audience.

"On behalf of my wife Ella, my brother Scott and his lovely wife Caroline we want to thank every one of you from the bottom of our hearts for hosting this fabulous party for us. We have all had a wonderful time. As you know I have had the house here for many years, but it is only now that I have my beautiful Ella here with me that the house has become a home."

"I'm not sure if you all know this but Ella and I are expecting twins at the beginning of December, not only that, so are Scott and Caroline and from December onwards each time we visit here there will be four extra little people with us."

There was a huge round of applause.

"If I can just beg your time for a while longer. Ella, come here please my darling."

"The first time Ella came to a theatre to hear me sing she didn't know who I was. I had found an old song that said everything I wanted to say to her. I have sung this song quite a few times since but always to Ella, *Making Memories*."

Jacob held my hands and gazed into my eyes then began to sing this song that has come to mean so much to us both. I just stood and gazed at him, holding him close to me. As the song finished he gathered me into his embrace and kissed me with such a passion.

He walked me back over to the others and then returned to the centre of the stage to finish his concert. The villagers were loving every second of this show and so was I.

Jacob spoke, once again, "we all want to thank you from the bottom of our hearts for this brilliant party, we couldn't have wished for anything better."

"I would like to finish with another of our favourite songs, '*The Impossible Dream*,"

The music began and once again that wonderful voice rang out. We all had a lump in our throats and several of us had tears in our eyes. He really knows how to stir the emotions. As the song finished the crowd went wild. They would have kept him there all night if they could. He thanked them all once more then wished everyone goodnight.

He jumped down from the stage and came over to me, hugging me tight.

"That felt good he said, but this feels better."

He kissed me then and all the love we felt for each other was there for the crowd to see.

He climbed back up on the stage and went to thank the band. He told them they were brilliant and to never give up.

It is true, they are an amazing group of very talented people. How lucky for the villagers that they have this band locally and also my beautiful Jacob living amongst them.

We walked amongst the villagers and I spoke with many of them as best I could. Jacob speaks French like one of them as does Scott. Something else I will have to learn.

As the evening drew to a close we bid farewell to them all then walked back up to the house. Magda and Laurent were with us, they couldn't stop speaking of the mini-concert that Jacob had done. They never get to see him perform live, so it had been a real treat for them.

The party was still going on for some of the villagers, we could still hear them laughing as we made our way home.

Laurent said, "they have all had a wonderful time tonight boys and they loved to hear you sing Jacob. Also, they really appreciated you all mixing with them and chatting to them all. When you live a little way out of the village and are not here so often they can sometimes feel left out of things. Tonight they know that this is not so."

We all walked into the big kitchen and I put the kettle on. "Who wants what I asked?"

Tea for Scott, Caroline, Jacob and me but hot chocolate for the rest of them. The girls were still buzzing, they too had enjoyed the whole experience and said they didn't want to go home.

Scott explained, *"well neither do we but I'm afraid we have to. You two have a lot of catching up to do with your school work and I have a big case that I need to get through. Once all that is out of the way though and the sale of the business is completed we can ask Uncle Jacob if we can all come back again later in the year and before the new members of the family arrive. Will that suit?"*

"Oh yes please daddy," "Uncle Jacob can we please?"

"Of course you can, you know you are all welcome whenever you want to come, even if Ella and I are not here you can still come."

"But we love it best when you are here as well Uncle Jacob" they both shouted.

"In which case we had better try to be here all together again then."

We finished our drinks, wished Magda and Laurent a good night then made our way to bed. The girls were almost asleep as they walked up the stairs. I think it will be bath time in the morning, don't you said Caroline.

We kissed each other good night then went into our room.

"Come here my darling and love me" asked Jacob.

I went to him and put my arms around him, lifting my head so that we could kiss.

" Jacob this has been such a magical day and night. I have loved every minute of it, but your singing was by far the best. You must really miss it when you're not in something."

" I do sometimes, singing is my life really apart from you and this new life we are building."

"We must find a way for you to be able to do both my love. I can't deprive the world of listening to your beautiful voice. I want you all to myself but also need to share you. There must be a way."

"We'll not worry about it yet he said, I won't take on anything big before our babies arrive and then I want to spend a long time with you and them.

I have the charity gig for the hospital to do, must check with Eddie to see if they have a date sorted yet and a venue of course. Then we will have to rope in a few other people to give their services. We owe the hospital and the staff there so much. I think I will ask Scott to chase it all up for me once he gets back. That will be better I think."

Jacob was undressing me as we were speaking.

"You are really beginning to show now my love, do you still feel okay?"

"I do I replied, I feel really well. Pregnancy must suit me."

"I love looking at that little swell of your tummy, our little humans growing in there. I am so excited you know."

" I do know that Jacob, I am excited myself. I am a bit worried though, I have never even held a baby before, how will I know what to do?"

"Well, we will have to learn together won't we said Jacob. I have never had a baby before either. I did help with Becki and Melisa a bit but not all the time. Flora didn't like me much and she didn't like me handling her children.

It really rankled with her once they were old enough to make their own decisions. They would ask to come to see me whenever they could, and she hated it. Stupid woman."

"We will be able to do this won't we Jacob, I mean, two babies all at the same time."

"Listen Ella, we will do it all together then if it does get too much we will have to look at hiring someone. Just someone to help, not take over. We will have Vera to begin with so maybe the three of us will manage anyway."

"I do hope so Jacob, I want this so much for us. We have the chance of such a wonderful life together don't we."

"We do my darling girl. We will be invincible, the 'A' team."

Jacob made love to me, so gently. He is my heart and my soul. I love him so much. I know that we can do this together.

Saturday dawned, another beautiful day. We lay in bed stroking each other's arms and kissing, so much kissing. Before long Jacob took me in his arms then made love to me again.

This man manages to make me so happy in every way. *I have almost forgotten about the awful times I was so scared in another mans bed. The evil Will, I never want to be in that position ever again. Jacob will love and care for me always, I know that he will.*

We went down to the kitchen for breakfast, we were the last ones up as usual. They were all sat around the big kitchen table eating croissants and fruit and drinking big mugs of tea. Jacob fussed around me.

"What does my darling wife require for breakfast" he asked.

"I think I can go with the same as these good folk thank you."

"What are you going to do today" I asked Caroline.

"We thought we would walk down to the village to thank everyone again for yesterday. It was such a brilliant day. The girls fancy doing that then coming back and having one more afternoon in the pool before we have to pack all our things up ready for tomorrow. Do you two have plans" she asked.

"No, nothing special, we could walk with you then I would love to go in the pool again. I will get this swimming thing learned before we leave here. It makes me feel really light when I float in the water. Might need to do it a bit more often once this belly grows to its full size. I feel a bit like a whale now."

"So do I said Caroline, we will be a right pair together."

Once our food was finished we did all walk down to the village. It will be good to hear what the villagers thought to the whole affair. I guess Jacob will get a ton of praise, but it is only what he deserves.

The walk is good for us as well, not too far but lets us stretch our legs. Caroline and I are both appreciating the new maternity clothes we bought. So much more comfy than tight fitting things. I began to laugh as we were walking along.

"What are you laughing at they all asked."

"I was just thinking about those lovely gowns we have hanging up in the wardrobes back in England. Can you imagine what we would look like in them now."

"I doubt we could fasten them up said Caroline. Do you think we will ever be able to get into them again?"

"I doubt it" was my reply.

The villagers were all pleased to see us up and about. We thanked each and every one of them for the lovely celebrations of yesterday then asked them what they thought to it all.

Only good comments from them, then of course came all the praise for Jacob. They all said they had loved seeing his concert and thanked him for doing it. They would never get the chance to see him perform normally. Gracious as ever he said it had been his pleasure.

We bought a light lunch and sat on the grass in the centre of the village to eat it. Caroline and I had managed to get down, but I was wondering how we would get back up again.

Of course our menfolk lifted us up. We walked back to the house then all went to change for our afternoon in the pool.

Those girls absolutely love the water. I need to get some of their bravery. I still think like I did back at the farm. I couldn't do anything, wasn't allowed for one thing but was always so scared to do and to try anything new.

I had been moving a few feet away from the bar then doing a few strokes before grabbing it and pulling myself up. I will try going a bit further away, maybe able to do a couple more strokes.

Jacob was in the deep end with the others, the girls were squealing their heads off at something Jacob was doing. I tried my usual three strokes first and felt confident doing that so the next time I moved a couple of feet further away. Remarkably I did it, that felt really good.

Okay, I walked to the middle of the pool, still at the shallow end then launched myself towards the side. I did it, I really did swim and it felt so good.

I looked around and noticed the others watching me. I put my thumb up and they all cheered.

Jacob swam over to me and kissed me.

"Well done you, I told you it would happen before we go home. You are amazing. I love you my darling."

He made me rest for a while before doing any more, he said that being pregnant I shouldn't overdo things, just take it steady. He stayed with me in the shallow end and was making such a fuss of me.

I thought, here I am, twenty-five years of age and just managed to swim from the middle of the pool to the side when Becki and Melisa can do just about everything.

They stand on the side and dive in. They swim from one side to the other and back again without stopping and they play and laugh and jump about for hours without a break. If only I had been allowed to learn when I had been their age. Still, nothing is going to stop me now.

Jacob coaxed me to go into the deeper water, holding the rail so as not to frighten me. The girls swam over to me and said I was good. They assured me I would love it once I get my confidence up. Such old heads on young shoulders.

We got out of the water and sat on sun beds drinking fresh juice that Magda bought over for us. The sun felt lovely on my skin, but Jacob insisted on covering me from head to foot in sun cream. I put some on him as well.

I noticed that Scott and Caroline had been putting cream on the girls then on each other. We lay in the shade as it was too hot to be out in full sun, I think we all nodded off for a while.

Just time for one more session in the pool then we would have to go in and get some dinner ready for everyone. Magda had said she would cook but Caroline and I insisted that we cook for them.

Once our feast was ready we all sat around the big table in the kitchen eating, drinking (tea) and chatting. I love this way of eating, not at all formal but very special.

Once finished Caroline and Scott took the girls up for a bath and bed then set about packing their cases ready for the next day.

They would have to set off for Nice airport after breakfast. They would take the hire car then leave it there. Once back in England Jacob has organised a car to take them all back to their house. Hopefully it wouldn't take them long as the girls were due to go back to school the following day.

All the plans worked out, they left us on the Sunday morning. There were a lot of tears, but Jacob promised them that once they broke up for the summer we would all come back here for another lovely time.

They were pleased with that and so left without further tantrums. Jacob and I along with Magda and Laurent stood in the courtyard entrance waving them off.

Well said Jacob, "that's all the fun stuff over with, just you and I now my love. I have thoroughly enjoyed having them all here but now I am looking forward to it being just us for a nice long break."

Magda and Laurent were going into the village for the day to see friends, so we were completely alone.

We lazed around the pool enjoying the sunshine then went into the pool to cool down. I am getting very brave now swimming. I can do a full width without stopping and am very proud of myself. I won't push to do more yet though until the babies are born.

Jacob suggested we walk down to the village to eat at lunchtime, it was a lovely day. Just us two and whoever we decided to speak with. I am beginning to learn a few words of French. Nothing exceptional just everyday words. I am sure if I stay here long enough I will be able to pick it up.

In the event we stayed for another six weeks, we lounged around the pool, we swam every day. We walked into the village often and ate in one of the two café's. By the end of the six weeks my stomach had grown a lot, I could now feel those little humans moving and kicking a bit. Every day they seemed to be a bit stronger. Jacob would put his hand over my bulging tummy to feel the movements, he was fascinated with it. He would put his mouth over the little movements and talk to his growing children. He would tell them how much they were loved and wanted and what a beautiful life we were going to give them.

My hair was still being a problem, especially with all the swimming. It seemed to be permanently wet. Jacob promised to take me into Nice one day to get some cut off it. He said we could make a day of it if we liked.

He has told me a bit about Nice and all the posh people that go there, I was a little concerned that if someone recognised him the game would be up. He said not to worry, we will cope.

The day we drove into Nice I was a little on edge. Stop worrying my darling, if we are spotted we will just jump back in the car and go home. He has let his hair grow quite long now, his curls are still magic to me. I think I like it longer. I can run my fingers through it. He has a few days growth of beard as well, I can see what he means about growing a beard though. It is very patchy. He has a baseball hat on as well so he thinks he will get away with it. I'm not so sure.

We drove to the outskirts and parked up then walked to the hair salon he had rung earlier. They were lovely in there and couldn't understand why I wanted my hair cutting. I explained about it always being wet when we went into the pool so often and how I keep sitting on it. I am also concerned that once our babies are born It will just be too much.

"Did you say babies?"

"I did I said, twins, due in December."

"How wonderful she said. I can understand now why you want some of this cutting off."

Jacob came over and said that he loves my hair as it is, but it really is driving me mad, so he had reluctantly agreed to me losing some of it. It was agreed that she would cut it to about six inches below my shoulders. It will still be long enough if I want to put it up or just tie it back.

"Let's go with that then shall we, see what you think afterwards" she said.

"Okay" Jacob said, "hope I like it when it's done."

I hope he likes it as well.

She then asked me something that really took my breath away.

"The hair I cut off, can I have it to send to the people that make the wigs for cancer patients?"

"Really I asked"

"Yes really" she said. "This will make some lovely wigs, they will really appreciate it."

"Of course you can have it I said, take it all. I thought you would just throw it away."

"No way, it's too valuable she said. I will cut it off in one chunk then do the proper style for you. Are you ready?"

"I am I said, just go for it."

She brushed it all straight then held it together in one piece by an elastic band.

"Okay" she asked.

"Yes I said, do it."

She cut straight through the hair and it fell loose from my head. She held up the long tail of hair, still held together in the rubber band. It looked huge,

"Bloody hell I said, it's any wonder it felt so heavy all the time."

"Okay she said, let's get your beautiful locks cut into a proper style. First I want to wash it then cut it, then dry it. Will take about an hour if that's okay?"

"Fine by me I said, do you want to wait here Jacob or go somewhere else to wait."

"I will wait here my love. Not going anywhere without you."

The woman cutting my hair kept looking at Jacob as if trying to make up her mind if she knew him or not. I decided to help her along.

"Yes it is him" I said.

"Really, is he really Jacob Ryan."

"Yes I said he definitely is Jacob Ryan, and I am Ella Ryan, his wife."

"I can't believe it she said, I know you have a place somewhere in France but never expected you to turn up here. I promise not to let the cat out of the bag, I expect you want it to remain a secret."

Jacob said," thanks for that. We are here on our honeymoon actually. My brother Scott and his new wife were here with us for two weeks along with Scott's two children from his first marriage. We had a few days in Paris then came on to our house here."

"Ella and myself will be here for a few more weeks yet. Since we have been here she has learned to swim and all that hair has been driving her mad, especially in the water. *Hopefully having all this chopped off will give her extra stamina in the pool. Thinking about it I suppose all that weight must pull her down. I love it but I guess she is right, once I get used to it I expect I will love it just as much."*

The hairdresser said, "no matter what her hair looks like she will still be the same lovely woman underneath."

"I know that said Jacob, it's just that I have only ever known her with the beautiful long hair."

"It will still be long just not as long as before, but it will be a lot easier to look after said the hairdresser."

Jacob held his hands up, "I give in, let's see what you can do to make us all happy."

I had my hair washed then she set too cutting my hair into what she called a style. I have to admit it felt so much lighter. I'm sure all that hair dragged me down. It was so heavy. It took a while to do the cut but once finished she put some product through the hair then blow dried it. *I need to get one of these dryers, that will take a lot of wasted time away. It was amazing.*

I wonder why Caroline never told me about them. I could see Jacob watching me, he seemed very interested in what was happening. God, I really hope he likes it.

"Right," she said, all done. She picked up another mirror and showed me the back of my head.

"Amazing, Jacob do you like it?"

"I do my darling, it looks stunning. Do you think you will be able to do it yourself?"

"Well, I think I will need some of that stuff you put through it and also one of those dryers." Look how quickly it dries my hair."

"That's not a problem the lady said, we stock both."

We left the salon with two bags, one holding the new dryer and the other full of products and brushes.

"Thank you my darling," I said, "I know you wanted me to keep all that long hair, but I feel like a new woman now. My head feels so light."

"Okay, he said, I have to admit it does look fabulous and if it makes your life easier then it will be worth it."

"Now, do you fancy lunch? You can show off those new locks."

We walked down towards the main part of the town and found a little café. We ordered our lunch and then sat outside in the shade of a lovely old tree.

Jacob had reluctantly agreed for the lady at the hairdresser to take a 'selfie'. She promised to keep our secret.

Lunch eaten, Jacob asked if I wanted to go into the main part of the town. I could tell he was a little anxious. If crowds of people spotted him it would spoil the whole day.

"No," I said, "what I would really like to do is go home and see if this hairstyle works as well in the bedroom."

"Oh you do, do you? I think we might be able to manage that. Come on, let's get back to the car."

We were soon on our way home. Jacob said that before we mess it up with lots of loving he wants to take a picture to send to Scott and Caroline, see what they think. I can't stop moving my head around. It all feels so light and amazing.

The car ate up the miles and we were soon back home.   Magda was just leaving the house after preparing a meal for us for later. She looked at me as if she didn't know who I was.

"Ella, your hair is so beautiful," she said. "It was lovely before, but this looks so nice. Very modern and will be much easier to look after."

"Well, Magda, that is exactly what I was hoping for. It has been a real pain for me having to keep drying it, but this new style and my new hair dryer will make the job a lot easier."

She left to go back to her own home then Jacob led me up to our room.

"Right, he said, let's get all arty with this photo", he told me to sit in front of the mirror then he took the photo from behind.

"Let me see I asked, Jacob, that is so clever I said. You could see both the front and the back of my hair at the same time."

He had taken a few shots then looked through them to find the one he thought was the best.

"Right, let's give those two a surprise shall we?"

Jacob wrote a cheeky message to go with the picture then pressed send. Not long after came two replies. Caroline said "Oh, *Wow*! You've done it at last Ella. It looks amazing. I bet your head feels a lot lighter now."

Then Scott said, "just Wow, looks lovely."

Jacob then rang Scott to check on a few things over in England. The house is now all finished. Scott has been down to check it all over and it looks great he said. All your stuff from the storage facility is being delivered next week then I guess the new stuff you have on order can be sent. All the curtains and blinds are in and they look the business he said.

I was beginning to get excited at the prospect of moving into our new home. Jacob had told me about a tennis tournament that happens near to the house every year. He says we won't want to be there then, utter madness. Cars and people everywhere.

"Okay," I said. "Well, we can always stay in France when that happens."

"That's my girl," he said. "Always the practical one."

Jacob also asked if there was any more news on the Cleo situation. The last Scott had heard was she was going for psychiatric assessment, depending on what comes back from that will determine what happens next. She had also been recommended to go for treatment for alcohol addiction. Whatever happens he doubts we will have to go to court. She has admitted everything so it's just a case of waiting for these reports.

Scott said that he has heard from Eddie asking when we are expected back. He needs a face-to-face with Jacob regarding this thing in America. He says it is too lucrative to turn down.

Scott said that he told him he would pass the message on but not to hold his breath.

Also, the film that has been offered to him, there is a delay on the start date for filming so they are hoping that Jacob will change his mind and do the damn thing.

Jacob promised to ring Eddie and tell him exactly what will be happening.

Jacob said he also needs to speak with Eddie about the charity show he has promised to do for the hospital. He wants to know who else will be doing it.

He then asked about the girls, Mrs H and Vera. All were good.

Vera is so looking forward to starting her new job once we return.

He then asked if Caroline is okay.

"Yes, she is fine, the babies are growing as they should. Her blood pressure is a little high, so they are keeping an eye on that but otherwise everything and everyone is fine."

"Okay," said Jacob, "We will get back to doing what all newlyweds should be doing."

"Not gone of it yet then," Jacob?

"Not likely," he replied. "I can't get enough of my beautiful wife." Speak soon. Love to everyone.

He then switched his phone off and came over to where I was still sitting. He began running his fingers through my hair, "this does feel nice," he said. So soft and just like you my love, very sexy."

He soon found out just how sexy it was. We made beautiful love and then stayed in bed together for another hour.

Finally, we got up and decided to go for a quick swim before getting our meal cooked.

Amazingly, each time I go in the pool I feel more confident and stronger. Who would have thought it.

When I wear a bikini though there is no doubt about me being very pregnant. All at the front at the moment so two babies are making themselves known to anyone seeing me. Jacob loves it.

The remainder of our holiday consisted of us spending every second of every day together. We spent a lot of time around the house and of course in the pool.

We walked into the village often and ate in the local café's.

During the last week of our holiday, Jacob drove me back to Nice to see the same hairdresser I had seen before.

He had rung earlier to make an appointment, so we were expected.

She gave me another trim so I wouldn't need to bother for a while once back home.

She was delighted to see us again and asked for another 'selfie' now that Jacob's hair was even longer.

"I love it like this." He has even let his beard grow a bit more and it actually looks a lot better. The longer he leaves it the thicker it grows.

She had good news on my hair she had donated for making children's wigs. The people that actually make the wigs were thrilled, they were able to make several wigs and still have some hair left. I am so pleased it will be doing someone some good.

I bought more of the products she had recommended last time because they really did work.

We then said our goodbye's promising to visit again the next time we were in France. We told her we were hoping to come again in August when his brothers children would be on holiday from school.

Not too long till we could return I hoped. I really do love this life.

We once again made for the same café we had used previously and had a lovely lunch before heading back to the car then on to our home.

"I will really miss this place" I said to Jacob.

"So will I" he said. "We have had a really good long time together haven't we? I do love being with you my love"

"I know my darling I replied, I love being with you too."

"We will have a busy time once we get back won't we" I said. "Moving into the new house will be the next big thing to sort out. And you my darling have some decorating to do."

"I know he said, it won't take long but it's something I really want to do myself."

We should just about manage to get the new house how we want it then have another few weeks here in France then back to England whilst we wait for these two to make an appearance.

"Once we get home we must go to the doctors to get everything checked" he said.

"We have been a bit lax being here but with you feeling so well and you seem to be growing well, I hope it is all good news. We will sort it as soon as we can. Make sure all is well."

"I'm sure it is" I said. "The babies are moving about very well so they seem healthy enough to me. It will be good to get the doctors verdict on things though."

"Not long now till we are home" I said. "It will all feel very different won't it?"

"It will my darling, but we will still be together all the time, unless you have had enough of me he teased."

"I could never have enough of you" I told him.

We would be travelling back to the UK in four days' time. We needed to work out what we would be taking with us and what could stay here. We had accumulated a lot more stuff over the weeks we had been living here in France. A lot of things can be left in France though as we will hopefully return shortly.

We decided that we would just fill one suitcase each and leave the rest here. I also had all the new hair products to take back, but Jacob said to just take the basic things then we can buy more back in England.

We spent half a day saying goodbye to all our friends in the village then had a final meal with Magda and Laurent. Everyone was happy that we would soon be back.

The day we left we both felt really sad, but it had to be done.

"The house move won't do itself," I said.

We were up early, Jacob and Laurent packed the cases away in the boot of the car. We said a final teary farewell to them then set off for the airport in Nice.

Once again we were treated very well. As we arrived someone in uniform came to load our cases onto a trolly then take them through to wherever they needed to be. We were whisked off to the VIP lounge once again as a woman came to take the car away.

As we were hurried through to the VIP lounge we attracted a lot of stares from other passengers. We kept our eyes forward and followed our escort.

Once inside the lounge we felt a bit easier and managed to have a nice, comfortable wait. We were served tea and croissants which were very welcome.

Before long our escort came to take us through to the plane, once again being allowed on before everyone else. It is such a short flight but as now I was bigger than when we had arrived, and the seats are not particularly large I would soon be feeling uncomfortable.

I shouldn't have worried, once all the other passengers were on board we were able to take off. I was still a little nervous, this is only the second flight I have taken but It was unremarkable, and we were soon coming in to land back in England.

Again we were allowed to leave the plane before everyone else. Then hurried through all the things that need to be done when coming back into the country.

Our luggage appeared then disappeared very quickly. Our driver arrived at our side and walked us through the crowds and out to our waiting car. All done with little fuss, very professional.

We headed off, back to Scott's house, ready to be reunited with the rest of our family.

Once home everything happened all together, first thing we had to do was go and check the new house, make sure it was all ready for us.

Vera came with us, we were so surprised when we walked in. Scott had done the walk through with the builder to make sure it was all in good order.

All of Jacobs furniture that had been in store was there, in situ, even his beloved piano. Plus all the stuff that we had ordered before going to France had also arrived and Scott had put it where he thought it was meant to go.

All the kitchen things were there, cutlery in the drawers, gadgets in the places they should be. Vera said she hoped we wouldn't mind but she had sorted all that stuff out. Put it where she thought it would be best to go.

"Why would we mind" I asked, it has saved us a lot of time and work.

She has moved into her flat and she loves it. All the new furniture she had chosen had been delivered along with our things.

She said that all the new sheets and duvet covers were here, she had washed and ironed it all along with the towels, tea towels, tablecloths and napkins. She said the beds are all made up, you can move in tonight if you want.

We were gobsmacked. All the way home we had been talking about how we would tackle the move.

"All this is marvellous" we said.

I told her that I had been dreading it.

"Nothing to worry about now" she said.

Our first night back we did stay with Scott and Caroline, the girls were desperate to see us. We had a nice evening, catching up with them all. Caroline had grown as have I. She said her babies were getting very active as were ours.

The girls were really happy to have us back and then we told them that all being well we would be going back to France again in August. Depends how Caroline and myself are really.

The following day Jacob and Scott took our cases down to the new house along with a few things that we had left in Scott's cupboards and drawers.

We had a doctor's appointment in the afternoon, so we had lunch and a catch up with Mary and Gregg in the pub.

Mary told us that they have reached an agreement with Gregg's sister and her husband. They are not only going to move in and help run the place but are also buying into the business so that is a lot of worry removed for them.

Jacob and I went together to the doctors. I was seen by the midwife first and she did all the checks, urine, blood pressure a physical examination and all was well.

She rang the hospital to tell them that we were back, and we were put in at the same time that Scott and Caroline were booked for in three days' time.

They will be doing another scan and if we want to know the sex of the babies they should be able to tell us then. Caroline's blood pressure has been stable for the last couple of weeks, so all looks good there.

Our move into our home had gone well, especially with all the work that Scott must have done to make sure it was all ready for us.

His business is being sold to the three senior lawyers that have been working for Scott, it should all be finalised before the babies are born.

Scott's big case that he had been working on was now over with a successful outcome for his client.

Becki and Melisa have caught up with their schoolwork thankfully. They really liked the teacher that had been to the house three nights a week for an hour each night to get them to where the rest of their classmates were.

Jacob is delighted that Scott is going to be working for him from now on. Won't be too much to do to start with but once Jacob gets back to working again then Scott will be kept busy.

Those first few weeks in the new house we were kept busy interviewing gardeners and cleaners.

Vera had the choice of cleaners as she would be the one in charge of them. She seems to be taking to the role like a duck to water.

Jacob did the interview for the gardener/handyman. The man he chose will fit in well. He was going to be taking us up on the offer of a flat that he and his wife would be living in. He said that his wife is a gardener as well, so they were both employed. It would need them both, the gardens are enormous.

Time was marching on, we will be back in France before long.

Jacob had been checking up on what is happening with Cleo. She did plead guilty but was still undergoing assessment on her mental state. She did seem to be remorseful for all the trouble and damage she has caused. Jacob says that he will be happy just as long as she stays away from us all, which she has vowed to do.

We all went back over to France and took Vera and Mrs H with us. They had both been working very hard on our behalf and deserved a treat. The house is plenty big enough for us all.

Jacob had promised that once we were there we can have a cinema night now that the wedding video is finalized. We can make a good night of it with Magda and Laurent there as well.

The people that had done the filming have done a remarkable job. It looks like a proper film now.

Once we leave France this time we won't be back until after the babies are born so Magda and Laurent are going to break the habit of a lifetime and will be taking a holiday.

All of Magda's family are from Poland although she was born in France. She has never met any of them but has now decided that if she doesn't do something about it now she never will. It will be at least February or March before we can go back so they will have plenty of time to have their trip.

We decided that we would wait until the babies are born to find out the sex, but Caroline and Scott wanted to know what they were having.

Both boys so that will make their family a nice even split. They are thrilled as are the girls. They are busy choosing names but if Becki and Melisa have their way the babies should have about six names each.

Caroline adores the girls, and they love her to bits. They see Flora occasionally but are always grateful to come back home. Flora seems to spend half her life travelling abroad now she doesn't have the girls to consider. Wonderful mother.

Jacob had been as good as his word and decorated the nursery himself. He chose all the colours, the furniture, everything that would be needed once these little people arrive. I left him to it and was thrilled to bits once it was finished. He was so proud of what he had achieved, it looks amazing.

It was decided that Caroline would have a Caesarion section. Her blood pressure continued to go up and down as she got further into her pregnancy. She was okay while resting but as soon as she started doing anything up it went.

She managed to carry them to just over the eighth month, she was enormous and was struggling to do anything, so she was admitted to hospital and gave birth to two healthy boys.

The operation went well, and she was soon able to hold her beautiful boys. They were a good weight for twins and so they were soon allowed home. Scott had employed a nurse/nanny to help for the first few weeks and that helped her so much.

The boys are named Daniel James and Edward Jacob. They looked so alike at birth that they had little wrist bands with their names on so that everyone could tell them apart.

I was enormous by this time as well and couldn't get comfortable. It felt like a football match was being played in there.

Poor Jacob, our sex life had altered somewhat. We needed to adapt positions so that we didn't crush our babies. We still managed to indulge ourselves most days, I can't imagine a life without this man and our wonderful life, sex and otherwise.

A week after Caroline had given birth my waters broke, and I was taken into hospital. All sorts of tests were done but I insisted that so long as the babies were safe and coping with the birth I would try to deliver them myself.

Jacob was amazing, he was with me every step of the way. Labour pains began just before midnight and I seemed to go from hardly any pains to full on labour within half an hour. This continued for a couple of hours and then I felt I needed to push.

I was taken through to the delivery room and our first child, a daughter was born at three in the morning. She was perfect and before I or Jacob could take it all in our second daughter was born at three twelve, another perfect little girl.

They were both good weights, six pound ten ounces and six pounds eight ounces.

"Jacob said, my darling, it's no wonder you were so big. They look huge. You are amazing, my love. Thank you for giving me these two beautiful children. I can hardly believe it. I am the father of two daughters. He had tears streaming down his face."

"Is it possible to take photographs of them sister?" he asked."

"Of course Mr Ryan, you are a lucky man. These two seem to be very healthy and they do have good lungs by the sounds of things. Let us get your wife cleaned up and comfortable then she can hold them whilst we take some shots for you. Congratulations to you both. A perfect family."

I was soon cleaned up and dressed in a fresh nightgown, I had been pushed down to a private room and our babies were brought in to us.

I could not believe what had just happened. These babies are gorgeous. They both have hair, black as coal just like their dad. They are identical as far as we can tell and so had wristbands with their names on them so we can tell them apart. Just like Caroline's boy's.

he midwife that had delivered them came in and asked if she could take their photo's for us.

Isabella Grace and Alicia Rose were the names we had settled on, of course Isabella would be called Bella and Alicia would probably end up being called Ali but that didn't matter because we loved all those names.

I held Bella in my arms then Jacob sat on the bed by my side holding Alicia, he looked so proud and happy. The midwife took several pictures then asked if she could be cheeky and have a photograph taken with us all.

Jacob said, "of course you can but can we ask that you keep it to yourself for a few days at least? We want to have some alone time before the rest of the world gets to find out.

Generally, the press is pretty good to us, but I think all this may just be a bit much for them to hold on to."

"Of course, Mr Ryan, this charity show you are doing for the hospital is an amazing gift to us and we are all very grateful. This photo will be for my eyes only."

In the event the whole team that had been present for the birth all had photos taken with their phones.

We were still smiling once they had finished.

Jacob and I were finally left alone with our daughters. We just kept gazing at them then at each other.

"We do make beautiful babies" he said "and my darling I can't thank you enough. How do you feel?" he asked.

"A bit like I'm in a dream actually. Did all that really just happen and are these two really ours to keep."

Jacob couldn't hold back any longer, he kissed me long and hard.

"Ella, you are the most amazing woman in the whole world. Well in my world at least. I love you so much. We are going to give these beauties a wonderful life. I can't wait to get you all home."

"Do you think we will manage?" he asked.

"Well, I guess we will soon find out. As long as you are with me my darling we will cope. Now, are you going to let everyone know our news or are you keeping it to yourself?"

"I suppose we will have to tell them won't we?

"I think that's wise," I said.

In the event we have coped, a case of having to really but I did have help of course. Jacob was with me all day and night and did as much as he possibly could. He was a dab hand at nappy changing and bottle feeding. He even bathed his daughters as often as he could.

Vera was a Godsend, although she had never had children of her own she seemed a natural with them.

I did breast feed but trying to feed two was awkward and very draining on me as soon as one was fed the other one would wake. We decided that I would feed one and either Jacob or Vera would bottle feed the other one then at the next feed we would change them round, the one that had been breastfed the first time would have the bottle next time. And so it went on.

By this time Caroline had healed and was able to come for a visit. Scott bought her in the car the first time leaving her boys with the nanny. She'd had the same problem and so had resorted to the same trick as me. We both kept this up for the first two and a half months then went over to the bottle full time.

This made life a bit easier as Jacob or Vera could help feed my two and with Caroline she had three options, Scott, Mrs H or the nanny.

I was resisting taking on a nanny, I really wanted to do it all myself but of course with two that wasn't possible. We will just have to wait and see how it goes.

Jacob had to leave the house a few times to sort out the charity show. He had meetings with his musical director and some of the band members,

Eddie had pulled out all the stops and had a really good line up of top acts, the tickets would cost a fortune but as it was all for the hospital no one minded paying.

Jacob was to perform the whole of the second half so that alone would attract a whole lot of fans and they would pay any amount to see him perform again.

He and Eddie along with Scott had a couple of meetings with some of the doctors from the hospital and also the hospital management.

Jacob said he didn't mind doing these things at all and would never take a fee, but he insisted that everything must be done properly, and he and Scott would have the final say in all that would happen. It certainly looked like being one hell of a night.

I so wanted to be there on the night but having two babies to care for I couldn't see how that would be possible, but Caroline came to the rescue.

The agency she had used to find her nanny could provide a nanny for me for just the one night if that is what I wanted.

They sent a lovely young woman along to introduce herself and to let her meet our daughters. "Why had I worried so much? She was amazing. She stayed with us throughout the day and saw how we were coping with the feeding and changing routines."

"Please don't worry Mrs Ryan, you have a good routine worked out so there is nothing for me to do but feed and change them as required. I have coped with worse believe me."

The evening of the concert was looming, Jacob had hoped it could be done before the births of the children but in the event it went ahead towards the end of January.

Caroline and I had to have new outfits having grown out of all the pretty things we have hanging in our wardrobes. We are both trying to get our figures back but not quite there yet.

Caroline left her family with Mrs H, the nanny and Scott whilst mine were left with the young woman that would be our nanny on the night of the show plus Vera.

Helena, the nanny said that she would make herself available whenever we needed her. Such a nice young woman.

We went into town, first time in months. Scott drove us in and dropped us off. First thing we did was to pop into the jewellers to meet with Julian. He was so pleased to see us.

"Please, tell me boys, girls or an assortment?"

We had managed to keep the news of our babies births under the radar for weeks which was lovely for us but of course they will all need to know soon.

"Two boys for Caroline and two daughters for me I said, and they are all doing very well."

"Congratulations to you both, couldn't be more pleased for you. And I must thank you again for allowing my fiancée and I to be at your weddings. It was the most magical day. I enjoyed catching up with Scott and my fiancée was completely in awe when she was introduced to Jacob. He was very gracious to her."

"It was our pleasure, Julian, so glad you enjoyed it. Will you be at the charity show next week I asked?"

"You bet he said, we have tickets for the third row, never been that close before. We are both excited to be going."

"We have set our wedding date for mid-June and would love it if you could all come."

"That would be lovely "we said. "I'll give you the address to send the invitations to but make it for your eyes only, please."

"Of course, I would never divulge such information. I feel honoured that you trust me with such information." "Now can I help you ladies with anything today or is this just a social visit."

We both said we had something in mind we wanted to make for our men, it's not urgent but just a little something we want to do for them. "Okay," he said, what is it you require?'

"So what we are thinking is some kind of disc or whatever that will fasten onto the chain that Jacob wears. We want the babies names engraving on whatever we choose."

Caroline said, "of course, I will need a chain as well and I have four names to be engraved."

We spent some time choosing what we wanted, and Julian promised he would have them ready to hand over to us on the night of the show.

Perfect we both said. The design I have chosen will mean that if we have more children in the future then they can be added easily.

Jacob is planning another night of celebration similar to the one we'd had after the final night of his shows in London.

Probably not as big but you are both welcome to join us we said.

Since returning from France we haven't managed to go to our favourite restaurant with all that has happened. Jacob is going to pop in one day to make his arrangements and give his apologies. He will also tell them about all the new additions we have to our families.

We have decided to do a press release to announce the babies births to coincide with the charity show. Maximum impact is what Jacob is looking for. Will all help to make more money for the cause.

Eddie has been approached by a TV company wanting to film the show and put it out a few days later. It will boost the coffers for the charity and give all fans an opportunity to see Jacob again. Not everyone will be able to go to the show after all.

He was a little reluctant at first but then agreed so long as the fee was a good one and all of it should go to the charity. That would mean him and Scott having to meet with a few more people before the night.

The show was an amazing success, all the acts in the first part of the show were excellent. Even the compare was both funny and clever with his words.

Caroline and I sat with Scott, Vera and Mrs H of course but also the big wigs from the hospital were there as well.

We spotted Julian and his fiancée and made our way over to speak with them and to collect our gifts for our menfolk. We were both feeling nervous for Jacob, it is a long time since his show closed and so much has happened.

They had decided to begin this show as they had all the other's. With Jacob singing on his own once the orchestra has finished their intro.

I really felt a bag of nerves for Jacob. I love him so much and just want everyone else in the world to love him too.

Things were a little different though tonight, after the close of the first half of the show the big curtains had pulled across the stage.

After the break the compare came on to the centre of the stage and made a short speech explaining a little of how and why this show had been put together.

He paid a lot of attention to all of the other stars in the show saying how everyone has given their time free to support this cause.

"As you all know the star of the show is who we should all thank as it has all been his brainchild. He is a very modest man and doesn't like to accept all the praise himself but if it wasn't for him and his brother Scott we would all be sitting at home watching the TV instead of sitting here waiting to be entertained by the greatest talent this country has ever produced."

"Ladies and Gentlemen, please put your hands together for the wonderful Mr Jacob Ryan."

What an amazing introduction, I bet Jacob didn't know that was going to happen. The audience was all on their feet clapping.

The orchestra began playing but the curtains remained closed. As the orchestra finished their intro Jacob's voice could be heard, singing *'Somewhere'*, the curtains began to open slowly and there he was, walking onto the stage and singing his dear heart out.

What really took my breath away was the huge backdrop behind the orchestra. Pictures of Jacob and I with our new babies in our arms and also Scott and Caroline with their son's, all of us proudly beaming at the camera's. There were also pictures of Becki and Melisa that had been taken in France.

My God, this man knows how to keep a secret. When had they decided to do this I thought.

Obviously Caroline had been kept in the dark as well because she too looked stunned. We looked at each other and both of us raised our shoulders to say, news to me as well.

The crowd were still on their feet, not knowing whether to clap or be quiet and listen to my husband sing. In the end most of them sat back down and just listened, as the song finished so the next one began and so it went for six big ballads. One after the other.

Finally Jacob went over to the piano and took a drink of water. He looks stunning in his evening suit once more. He had kept his longer hair and beard now it is looking more like a beard and not some random hairs on his beautiful face.

The audience were once again on their feet shouting, whistling and clapping.

"Wow, he said, what a welcome. Thank you so much." He then turned towards the photographs and said, "well, what do you think friends?

There is my brother Scott, his lovely wife Caroline and his two new sons, his older daughters are there as well look, a very lovely family."

"Then these were taken just a week later, my beautiful wife Ella and our amazing daughters, Isabella and Alicia. I can't begin to tell you all how happy we all are."

The audience had gone quiet whilst Jacob spoke but were now going mad again.

I have to admit the pictures are great. He must have had them done from the pictures the midwife took in the hospital. He's very sneaky at times".

"Right now let's move on, this next song is one that I began singing shortly after meeting Ella, it means as much to us today as it did back then. Ella my darling, come up here please.

Oh God I thought, not again. Caroline was pushing me up, "go on Ella, he wants you."

I took a deep breath and went to the side of the stage and climbed the steps shaking like a leaf. Jacob was there waiting for me. He held out his hand and I took it. He led me to the centre of the stage with his arm around my waist.

"Friends," he said, "my wife and mother of my twin daughters, Ella."

"This song is for you my darling" and then he kissed me. The music began playing then Jacob began to sing.

All the time he was singing he was looking into my eyes. I love this song so much, it really is our song.

As he finished singing he kissed me once again, full on the mouth then walked me back to the steps, helping me down them.

Before letting me go he kissed me once more then the connection was broken. I walked back to my seat with blazing red cheeks but still feeling so happy and loved.

His audience were all on their feet clapping and shouting. People were reaching over and touching my shoulders. I felt very special.

Jacob then got back to the rest of his show. It was wonderful hearing him sing once more. He does sing around the house and to his daughters and I love to hear him but hearing him sing in this environment just turns him into the star he is.

All too soon the show came to a close. The compare returned at the end to thank everyone once more, the stars for donating their time and the people out there for supporting all that they are trying to do by buying tickets and also donating their cash.

"He said that up to this moment in time they have raised a little over two million pounds but that is likely to rise over the coming days".

Jacob then thanked everyone once more. He said he was gobsmacked at the amount raised so far. You are all incredible.

Someone shouted out, one more song Jacob please. Other's soon followed. He put his arm up to silence them, okay, okay, what's it to be then. Of course, what else could it be, the wonderful song that says it all for us, *'The Impossible Dream'*. What a wonderful end to a brilliant night.

Transport to the restaurant had been arranged by Scott as he had done before. Caroline went in the car with Vera and Mrs H. They too had enjoyed it all. They both looked to be in a dream state.

All those coming with us were asked to remain in their seats for a while then once the theatre had emptied the rest of them got up and filed out to get on the coach.

Some of the other acts were joining us as were the two interviewers from the television thing we had done some months earlier.

Julian and his fiancée didn't look too sure.

"Come on you two," Scott said, "are you not hungry?

"Of course, Scott but we didn't think we would be included in your party."

"Of course, you are included, come on. I will be with you on the coach then Caroline will be coming in one car whilst Jacob cools down and has some pictures taken with his wife, then he always has to speak with his fans before he can leave but once that is done they will be arriving in their own car. Let's go party."

Once they had all left I went to find Jacob in his dressing room. His musical director and Eddie were both in there talking business I guess.

I crept in hoping I wouldn't be spotted but Eddie heard the door close behind me and called me round.

"Ella, come on my love. How are you and those two little munchkins doing?"

"We are all good Eddie, thank you. Mind you I don't know how I would have coped without Jacob. He is a natural with the twins and just loves doing things for them."

His MD, Tom said, "meeting you and having the children has certainly given Jacob a new perspective on life. I have known him for a very long time, but this is the happiest I have ever seen him. Did you like the backdrop he had made?"

"I did I said but it gave me a bit of a start when I saw it for the first time. I didn't know anything about it and then all of a sudden it was there in front of me. What will you do with it now?" I asked.?

"Not sure yet" Jacob said, "we could paper the lounge wall with it I suppose.

Once I go back to work, which won't be for a while longer he stipulated, Tom has suggested we have a video of you all that can play right from before the children were born up to whatever date that happens to be. What do you think my darling?"

"It's a nice idea Jacob but won't your fans want more of you and less of me and the kids?

"They will get what they are given then if they don't like it, tough."

I had moved over to stand by my man. He had his arms around me, pulling me into him and then kissing my neck. That simple touch had me wanting Jacob so much. *My post-natal had been a few weeks ago and so we had been able to start having a proper sex life once again. We had made plenty of time for us to be together during those last few weeks of the pregnancy, but with two babies taking up a lot of room it had presented us with a few delicate issues.*

Jacob had already showered when I arrived at his dressing room, so it was just whatever the two men were trying to talk Jacob into. He won't budge yet though. He says he hasn't waited all these years to become a father only to walk away and leave me to cope on my own.

Eddie said, "look Jacob, you can always employ a nanny for the kids and take them with you on tour."

Jacob stood up to his full six foot four inches and towered over Eddie. "I have made my decision and I am sticking to it. I have said that I will do some shows if they are not too far away and I can get home afterwards but you can forget any long runs for now, no matter where they are or how much they are willing to pay. My wife and my children come first now, so get used to it."

I felt myself colour, I hope they don't think it's me putting pressure on him. He will do what he wants when he wants.

Eddie looked over to where I was standing, "Can't you talk some sense into him, Ella?"

"Sorry Eddie, no I can't. Jacob will do what he wants and not until he is comfortable with what's on offer, you should know that. He needed a break, and he has had that, and I am sure you can all see the difference in him. He is now happy and healthy. I don't want to see him go plunging backwards again through overwork".

"Now, said Jacob, "let's go and eat."

We had been rather a long time talking and so we were all surprised when they opened the stage door to see so many people still waiting. Jacob had a beautiful dark green shirt on with a lighter green jacket over the top, teamed with his favourite black jeans. The green of his shirt so matched his green eyes. As we stepped out into the night there was a huge cheer and what appeared to be hundreds of flashes from the fans camera phones.

"Okay folks, can we form some sort of a queue so there isn't all this pushing and shoving. We will talk to you all briefly and you can take as many pictures as you want but we can't be all night. We have a lot of people waiting for us then we have to get home to our family."

With a bit of guidance from Eddie, Tom and security they were soon lining up and coming over for a quick chat and a photo. Lots of the women wanted to ask about our dear babies and they all said that they loved the backdrop. It made them feel as if they were part of Jacob's family too, which of course they are.

The months between Jacob's last show and this one hadn't put anybody off. If anything they were all excited to hear anything at all regarding Jacob's new life as a husband and father. Finally the last people were seen, and we were able to get into our car and head off to the restaurant.

As our car pulled up there were a few more fans waiting there. I think that they have all guessed that we would be heading there after the show and decided to chance it.

Jacob got out of the car first then turned to help me out. He had his arm around me all the time, this is how we spend most of our days, wrapped around each other. Our flame of love is still burning as bright as it ever was.

We quickly dealt with the fans and a few press guys that were hanging around. They still keep thanking us for the wedding invites. Guess it is still a novelty for them.

Jacob said to them, "Look guys we are going to be at least a couple of hours and it's cold. Don't get hanging around here all night. I'm sure you all have what you came for. There's nothing new to tell so you might just as well go home and have an early night."

"Okay Jacob they said, we will do just that and thanks for all the stuff you throw our way, it's really appreciated. Good luck mate and have a good night."

They went on their way and we managed to get into the restaurant. All our guests were waiting for us to arrive and once we got through the door they all stood up and began clapping.

Eddie and Tom had gone into the restaurant before us and so it was just us that needed to find our seats.

As before, Emile the manager was on hand to greet us. He escorted us to the back of the restaurant where we had sat before. Mrs H and Vera were sat together, they have become inseparable. Scott and Caroline were also on our table. Eddie and Tom along with Tom's wife made up the final seats.

As with our previous visit there with a large party the chef had devised another trimmed down menu. These menu's had been handed round and everyone had chosen their meal, just Jacob and I as usual.

"Just order the same for me that you have my love I said. Keep it simple."

The service was once again excellent. The meals were all cooked quickly then taken to everyone waiting. Wine was being served as were bottles of still and sparkling water. Just plain old water has become my go to drink, so I stuck with that. Jacob was so attentive to me, not that he is ever anything less. I love him so much. What a difference a few months can make to someone's life.

We all enjoyed a lovely relaxing meal with these friends and relatives of ours. The hospital big wigs seemed to be having a good time as did the doctors that had been with us on our last visit here. Many of them told us that this restaurant has become their favourite and they often dine here with friends or colleagues.

The restaurant manager had told Jacob the same thing when he and Scott had called in to arrange this night. He was so thankful for all that Jacob has done for them and their reputation. Some of the press guys turn up there occasionally as well if they have a special evening they want to celebrate.

The two interviewers from the TV show that we had appeared on were with us and were asking when we would both be able to go back on their show.

Jacob assured them that we would both be delighted to join them once again before too long.

Scott made a short speech thanking them all for their generosity and help in making this night so successful. He told them that the last he heard the total raised was well over two and a half million and they were expecting it to almost double once the TV show went out.

Scott sat down then the call went up for Jacob to say something.

"Really he asked. Don't you lot think I've done enough."

He did get up to speak eventually. He thanked everyone for their contributions to the night. He said how grateful he was to everyone at the hospital for all that they had done for him and his family this past few months. This was the only way I could think to thank you all. Let's hope that the money raised will do some good.

The guy that is the head of the hospital management, don't know what his title is but he seems very posh, got up and also made a speech. He said that it is only the way people like you all here tonight and particularly Jacob work to provide extra funds that the hospital is able to give the amazing treatments that they do.

Jacob and all the other celebrities that are here with us, thank you all from the bottom of our hearts. The show was amazing, my wife is hoping you will bring out a DVD of the night so that we can sit and enjoy it whenever the fancy takes us. Another round of applause.

I imagine Eddie will be on that first thing in the morning. After all the show had been filmed for the television company.

Once everyone had eaten their fill and drunk all they wanted it was time for us all to leave. We stood by the door to wish everyone a goodnight, they all climbed onto the coach ready to be transported home. Another brilliant and successful night thanks to my wonderful husband.

Jacob went to settle his bill with the manager who was once again in raptures over Jacob. As soon as your babies are old enough you must bring them here for their dinner he said. We promised we would do that.

Scott went home in the car with Caroline, Mrs H and Vera. We were all alone in our car as we sped homeward.

"I can't wait to see the children" I said to Jacob, he held my hand.

"I know exactly how you feel he said. I have kept thinking about them all night. I hate being away from them and from you my darling."

I remembered my gift I have for him.

"Here I said, they will be with you always now."

"What have you done now you naughty girl."

"Open it" I said.

He carefully undid the pretty paper then lifted the lid on the box. Inside were two gold leaves, on the back of each one was engraved the names and birth dates of our two daughters.

He looked up at me with tears rolling down his cheeks.

"Ella, these are beautiful."

"I know I said, they are to fasten onto your chain. You can carry them always now."

He pulled me to him, and the backseat of the car became a very steamy place to be. My God I thought, I want this man so much.

Once home we hurried to see our babies. They were sleeping soundly. Helena, the nanny who helps us out occasionally said they had been little angels. She was able to feed one before the other one woke. She said that she would have the monitor in her room tonight so that we could enjoy the rest of our evening.

She was staying over anyway so we might as well make use of her. She is very good with the babies, she has come with good references and would love to be with us full time.

I don't mind using her sometimes, but Jacob and I want to do as much for them ourselves as we possibly can.

When Caroline and I had been for our postnatal examinations we went together of course. Although her boys are a week older than my girls she had needed the extra week because she'd had a section. She had healed well apart from one of the stitches which festered a little. She had been put on a course of antibiotic cream and that had done the trick.

As we had waited for our appointments we were chatting. I asked her if she is happy with how things have turned out.

"I said the spotlight always seems to fall on Jacob and I feel bad that they have to take second place."

"Never think that, Ella. Scott is so proud of Jacob and it is only natural that he will be in the forefront of everything. He always includes us all in anything that he does or says and always listens to Scott's advice so there is no need for you to feel bad."

"As for us being happy, yes Ella, we are, very happy indeed. Becki and Melisa are amazing young girls, they love the boys to bits as well. Scott is so happy now that the business is sold, and he can now work for Jacob. They can talk through anything and come up with a good plan about everything. We all seem to have fallen into a very comfortable relationship with each other, with our children and with you and Jacob. Are you two really happy as well?

"Can't you tell how much I said, I have never known such love ever. Jacob is amazing and he really loves me and our babies. He really is amazing with them. I watch him at home, changing shitty nappies or feeding one of his girls, even bathing them then I look at the man he becomes once he is on the stage and I can't believe that he is all mine. He cried when I gave him those two gold leaves you know."

"He and Scott are so alike in many ways," she said. "Scott cried when I gave him the chain with those four gold circles with the children's names on them. He plays with it constantly as I've seen Jacob do with his. It is gratifying to be able to give something like that to men who seem to have it all. When all they really want is the love of a good woman and happy, healthy children. And that my friend is where we come in."

Caroline was called through to see the doctor then and I sat thinking about what she had said, she is right, that is all our men want and need and now they have it. I smiled as I thought about my wonderful husband. He is all I will ever want as long as I live."

Caroline came out smiling, "all's good," she said. "Ready to go again." "I can't wait if I'm honest", she said.

"Same here" I replied.

I was called through then and went in smiling. It was the same doctor I had spoken to before and he thought my way of asking the difficult questions was refreshing.

"Another Mrs Ryan, come in, let's get you sorted out now. Do you know I have often thought of that conversation we had a while ago. I loved the way you just came out with it. Will there be any more of those questions today do you think?"

I looked at him and smiled,

"Probably I said. "I can't help myself, sorry."

"Please my dear, don't be sorry, you just carry on being yourself. Now if you can pop behind the screen and remove your lower garments then jump up on the couch we can soon get this examination over with."

His nurse was in with him. I guess they need to be careful when doing these examinations.

"Now then Mrs Ryan, according to your notes from the hospital, you managed to deliver your twins yourself."

"I did" I said, "didn't take long either. Must be a natural mother. That's what happens when you are bought up on a farm."

He smiled at me, "Pity more people don't live on farms then if that's what gets you through."

He did the examination and said that everything was fine. "You didn't need any sutures either, I see." That's good. "Now have you decided what you are going to do about birth control?

"Well, Jacob and I were talking the other day and we think that we would like another child before too long. Not straight away obviously, we need to get back to our athletic sex life again for a while. I have really missed it you know. We still managed to do it most days, but we had to adapt, well you said we would didn't you. We didn't want to crush our babies."

"Anyway, that is beside the point. What we have decided to do is use condoms for a while then when we feel the time is right we can just stop using them. Caroline said that sometimes if you go on the pill it stops you from getting pregnant straight away once you stop taking it, does that sound okay to you doctor."

"It does he said, so carrying and delivering twins hasn't put you off?"

"Good God, no, I said. Jacob and I have so much love to give to our children and to each other it seems selfish not to have more babies to love, and Jacob loves kids. He is amazing you know, he changes their shitty nappies, feeds them and even bathes them. I was only saying to Caroline earlier I watch him do all these mundane things with the babies then he goes and does a show like he did the other night and it's like he grows to be ten feet tall once he steps on the stage. It was a wonderful show, I love it when he sings, have you heard him sing Doctor?"

"I have actually, my wife and I were in the audience for that charity show. We just went along to support the good cause really, but we were both bowled over. He is one very talented man. You were there as well weren't you Meg?"

The nurse said, "Yes, I was, I have been a big fan for years, but that show was something else. I loved it when the curtains opened, and all those photographs were there. He certainly is a very proud man. I love it when he gets you up on the stage and sings that lovely song to you. Makes me cry she said."

"Well, I have news for you, it makes me cry as well. I never know if he is going to do that but invariably he does. I love to hear him sing in a big theatre like that, his voice just bounces off the walls, but I also love to hear him sing to the babies. They just watch him, taking it all in I guess. By the way, it looks as if the TV company will be releasing a DVD of that show. I will buy one" I said.

They both laughed at me, "do you mean to tell me you don't get a free copy?" the doctor asked.

I said, "I would buy one as the money will go to the hospital, that's all."

"Very admirable of you my dear" he said.

I had a sudden thought, "I wish I'd known you were going to be there. After a big show like that Jacob takes a load of people out for a meal. He lays on a coach and everything. We go to this amazing French restaurant we know, and they treat us amazingly well. If I'd known you were there you could have come with us."

"That is a lovely kind thought, maybe next time?"

The nurse was looking at me and wondering if it was just the doctor I was speaking to or her as well.

I said, "You will be able to come as well." Jacob won't be doing much for a while but when he does I will let you know."

"Well, thank you so much, Mrs Ryan"

Please, my name is Ella"

"Thank you, Ella, we will wait for your call. Now what I suggest is you and your sister-in-law take yourselves home and make a real fuss of those men of yours."

"Don't worry, doctor," I said, "I have it all planned."

He chuckled, "I'm sure you do. Bye for now."

"Bye" I called as I left his room.

Caroline asked, "Is everything okay Ella?"

"Yes, fine, why?"

"You have been a long time I wondered if there was a problem."

"No, all good, we were just discussing getting home and getting jiggy with our men."

"Ella, you didn't did you?"

"Of course I did, the doctor and I understand each other."

Jacob and Scott had a meeting with Eddie in town, so we had left our babies in the capable hands of our nannies as well as Vera and Mrs H.

We were getting better at leaving them for short periods of time, it was inevitable that there would be times when they would have to be left.

We were home before the men, so Caroline came in for a coffee and a chat, babies do take up a lot of time and our days for chatting were now limited to the odd half hour here and there.

Caroline asked me if I was nervous about starting our sex lives up again.

"Not at all I said, can't wait. We never really stopped anyway, just had to be a bit more inventive so as not to crush the little ones."

"You sound as if you are nervous Caroline, did you stop having sex then I asked?"

"Well, not exactly stopped she said but you know it was different. Two footballers in your belly does present the odd problem. Now though we can get back to how it was before the babies were on their way and I really want that so much, but like I say it has been different and I did have surgery as well you know."

"I know," I said but you two love each other as much as Jacob and I do so where there's a will there's a way."

"I know you are right she said, silly of me to even think along those lines and you are right we do love each other very much. I am sure all will be well."

Caroline left to walk the short distance back to her house. I went to find my babies. Helena and Vera had taken them for a walk in the sunshine, but I heard them come back just before Caroline had left.

I went through to the lounge and there they all were, having cuddles on the sofa.

Well now, you all look as if you have had a good time without me, I said.

We have said Vera. These two have been very good, no crying at all. They love being pushed around in their pram.

Helena said "I can stay if you want to have some time with your husband."

His car had just pulled up and she said

"I reckon it's time for you two to have some alone time."

"Are you sure?" I asked,

"Yes, of course, there's no one else here, just us two. We can cope, go on make a fuss of your man."

I jumped up and ran into the hall to greet Jacob.

"Well, hello to you too," he said, I take it you have had a good morning."

"We have", I said, "all in good working order now and I have sold the children so come on up the stairs Mr Ryan."

"What do you mean, you have sold the children?"

"Joking" I said,

"Helena and Vera have them and they decided it was time for me to make a fuss of my husband, so here I am all ready, willing and able."

I took his hand and gently steered him towards the stairs.

"Are you sure Ella? I don't mind waiting a bit longer."

"You might not mind but I do, now get your arse up these stairs."

He beamed at me, "Right," he said, "better get myself sorted then. If my wife is demanding to be served then who am I to refuse."

We walked into our bedroom and closed the door. Jacob took me into his arms and kissed me, properly and thoroughly.

"Oh, Ella, I want you so much."

"Come on then, let's see if we can remember how to do it' I said.

Jacob picked me up then lay me down on the bed. He was kissing me, my mouth, my neck then once he could get my blouse off he kissed my breasts.

"Am I allowed to touch your breasts?" he asked?. "You know with you still breastfeeding I mean."

"I asked the doctor and he said that if you want to then that is fine, if you suck them it will stimulate them to produce more milk. It's up to you, though."

"Perhaps just a little," he said, "I have missed this so much. Just the two of us together, making love."

"Well, my darling husband, I have been missing you too, so let's get on with it shall we? All this talking is wasting time."

We made love properly, the first time in weeks. All this using your imagination and trying to find a position that suits is fine when there isn't a choice but now, well let's just say we spent a very magical couple of hours together.

It would seem that everything is still in working order. Jacob bought me to climax time and again, and I him. Finally we pulled apart and lay resting for a while just gazing into each other's eyes.

"I love you so much my darling," I said to him.

"And I love you too my love, my life, my everything."

We decided we should shower before going back downstairs. Helena and Vera were watching the TV when we ventured into the lounge. Our dear sweet babies were fast asleep in their cribs.

Jacob asked, "Who's for tea? A chorus of "yes", please give him his answer. He went through to the kitchen and put the kettle on. I followed him to help set the tray up.

"How was your meeting?"

"A pain in the arse if I'm honest he said.

Andrew keeps nagging Eddie to set something up for the States. I have told them till I'm blue in the face it's not happening, not yet at least. They don't seem to understand that I want to be here with you and our children. Once Andrew heard about the charity show we did he thought that was the green light to get me back working again."

There have been a lot of offers put on the table for taking that show on the road in the UK, also for taking it abroad, around Europe, Australia and the bloody States.

You know I turned a film down earlier, well the guy that was going to do it in my place has injured his back somehow and now can't do it so they thought they would try me again.

"Bloody pain in the arse."

"There are some other films that they want me to look at but all of them would take me out of the UK for several months."

"There's some more TV stuff on offer as well. Eddie thinks if I keep saying no they will forget all about me and give these things to other actors and singers."

"I told him to give it to whoever wants it because I don't. I got quite upset when he just kept going on about all the great opportunities I was letting slip through my fingers."

"What happens when the money runs out he had asked, they might not want to play ball with you then."

"Well if that happens they will have to find some other mug to play ball with, as for the money running out, well if it does there are plenty of jobs going in warehouses at the moment, I could give that a go."

"Thankfully, Sam was there as well, you remember him don't you?"

"Of course I do, it was because of his help that we managed to get our weddings sorted out so quickly."

"Well, he has been my personal assistant for a long time, and he remembers how ill I was with my mental state. Him, Tom and Scott were the only sane voices in my life back then. Those three saved me from going into a complete meltdown. I sometimes think that Eddie has forgotten all about that time. In the end I had to remind him of it and how very close I came to losing the plot completely."

"Anyway, between the three of us we have managed to make him understand that I really need this time to be with you and our girls. I have assured him that you and I will go through all these offers to see if there is anything we think we can do in the near future. If there is something then I will do it but on my terms, not his. He's not over the moon about it but he has had to accept it, I won't be bullied into anything else."

"That's fine by me Jacob, you know I want you here all the time, but I also want to hear you singing again, it would be such a waste if you didn't perform any more. I love your voice, you know I do but there are thousands of people out there that love you just as much. It will be just a case of finding a balance that works for you and for us."

"And there you have it, he said, balance, but Eddie thinks that the scales should be balanced his way a bit more. I have always followed his advice, done virtually everything he has asked me to do but not any more. I have rarely stood up to him before, finding it easier to back down myself and just do what he wanted me to do, but not any more, I think he gets it now."

I put my arms around him then kissed him with all the love I have for him.

"Tell him if the money runs out we can live on my money anyway, that might shut him up."

"Do you know what, I never thought of that?" said Jacob.

"Also we still have those jewels at the bank, we could sell them to keep us going a bit longer".

We were both laughing as we carried the tea things into the lounge.

Vera said, blimey! that little rest has put you both in a good mood, perhaps you should try it more often.

"Now there's a thought," I said.

EPILOGUE

Here we all are, three years down the line. I think that Jacob and I just about have our lives sorted. Our darling daughters are now just turned three years of age. They are adorable but mischief makers all at the same time.

This time last year I gave birth to our second set of twins, boys this time and the image of their dad. Noah James and Theo Jacob. Our home is so full of love for our children and also for each other.

Vera is still our head of house as we call her. She is amazing and simply loves working for us. She turns her hand to anything and loves nothing more than helping me with the children.

She set on two young women cleaners right at the start and they are still with us. They work part-time to fit in with their own families. Nice girls, the children love to help them clean, so we bought them each a mini cleaning set. Got everything they need to follow the girls around.

Helena has also joined us full-time and lives in one of the flats.

Once I was pregnant with a second set of twins it became apparent that I would need help. Helena is a first-class nanny and takes so much of the hard work of child rearing away from me. She and Vera get on well and often share the baby minding duties.

Our gardeners are still with us also and love living in their flat. No commute to work for them.

Our plans for a pool finally came to fruition two years ago. It is a great size, and our girls love it. They both swim well for their age and would go in there every day if we let them. We have started taking the boys in with us for short spells and they seem to love the water as well. It won't be long before they are off swimming on their own.

We try to get over to France at least twice a year, more often if we can fit it in. Vera and Helena always come with us and have really fitted in well with the people in the village.

Magda and Laurent are still living in their cottage and now travel to Poland once each year to catch up with Magda's relatives. Once she had taken the plunge and done it she loved it so much that now they travel outside of the village often. They even came over to the UK to stay with us a couple of times.

Cleo is another story, she had all the assessments to gauge the state of her mental health. Once a diagnosis had been given the courts were able to sentence her for the crimes she had committed against us. She was given a total of seven years with three of those years suspended. So in effect four years of which she would serve two.

Once she was released she tried to contact Jacob through Eddie. Of course, he wouldn't give her our address or telephone numbers. She must have forgotten about the house that Jacob had bought when he thought she was carrying his child but is now our family home. Once she had thought about it though she decided to give it a try. She had thought that Jacob would have sold it, but she was in luck. She apparently set up camp by the front gates and refused to move until Jacob came to see her.

Fat chance that would happen, we were all in France, so she was wasting her time. Finally, convinced he was inside and watching her she tried to climb the gates, got her foot caught and fell backwards injuring herself bad enough that she needed to be admitted to hospital.

It was whilst she was in there that she had another 'turn'. She was shouting and screaming that they would have to fetch Jacob. He really loved her and not me, she even tried telling them that our babies were hers and Jacob's, not mine. Of course, the hospital knew differently, after all the children had all been born there so the staff knew us well. Also, through all of the charity work that Jacob continues to do for them.

They became very worried about her and so she was assessed once more and then sectioned. She is presently being detained in a mental health facility somewhere up north.

Scott and Caroline are enjoying their lives together. They really are a lovely couple, and they adore their children.

Becki is due to go to secondary school in September but is deciding if she wants to go there or to a private school. I think that may win as she can come home every night and not have to board. Caroline said she hated the thought of her living away from home but this way she will get the private education without leaving her home. Melisa is still the mummy out of the two, she loves her baby brothers and plays with them for hours. The boys are very handsome, definitely got the Ryan gene.

Caroline has stayed at home to be a full-time mum, she said that she loved her job before but now all she wants is to be there for them all.

Flora is still a ship that passes occasionally. She will see the girls when it suits her, but they never want to stay away from Scott and Caroline. They have apparently put Flora in the picture regarding the stories she told them of their dad only wanting them for decoration at the wedding and once the new babies arrived he wouldn't want them any more. She said that she had only been joking, very funny joke.

Scott was able to get permanent custody of them easily, once the powers that be had read the files and of course the girls were both spoken to. They insisted that they wanted to live with their dad and new mum because they loved them. Their mum was more interested in herself. They even told them that their mother would often leave them in the house alone when she went out with the horrid man she lived with.

Now Jacob, my wonderful husband. We are so very much in love with each other. We both love our children so much and will do anything for them. He stayed true to his word and didn't do much work for the first year of our daughters lives. He had done a few charity shows and a couple of guest appearances on TV shows but nothing major.

He did work on a new album though, the DVD of the show had sold very well indeed so the album was a logical follow up. He did some of the work from home having converted part of the garage complex into a studio then went into the studios in London to finish it all off. It was a huge success, taking him and everyone else by surprise, but not me, I knew it would sell well.

Once the boys turned one, he did take on a few more projects, but nothing that would take him away from home. He said he needed to be back home with us all every night. The furthest he travelled for a show was an arena show in Birmingham and I had to agree to go with him. We travelled up there on the morning of the show then went to the venue in the afternoon for a sound check and a rehearsal of some new songs.

After the show, which was an amazing success we travelled back home. I think that was the night our twin boys were conceived. A couple of days later I began to feel queasy in the mornings, the same as with the girls. I told Jacob and he was over the moon. "Stay in the hotel and rest" he had said, this was another show, another night, another town. We had a hotel room so that he could take some rest before the show then once it was over we travelled home again.

"Not likely" I said, "I hear there's this fabulous singer on at the arena and I want to see him."

"Okay, he said, just stay by the side of the stage though, I don't want anyone bumping into you."

"I will" I said, and I did till someone shouted up from the audience, Jacob, where's Ella tonight?

"Oh she is here with me, don't worry about that. We are never very far away from each other."

"Come on then, let's see her. Don't keep her all to yourself. This was becoming a 'thing' at almost every show he did."

"Ella, he called, you are wanted." I crept out from behind the curtains and walked over to him, arms outstretched. I walked into his embrace and enjoyed the lovely kiss he gave me.

"Now sing that song to her about *"**Making Memories**."*

"Okay, okay, Tom, do you have the music for it?"

"I do," he said. A hush came over the crowd and the music began. Jacob looked into my eyes as he sang those beautiful words.

"Dance with me," he whispered. *I really must learn to dance properly* I thought, *all I can manage is a little shuffle hopefully in the same direction of Jacob.*

As the song ended Jacob hugged me to him. "I love you my darling" he whispered.

"And I love you too." He kissed me thoroughly then walked me back to the side of the stage.

They have done the video of us all and it plays across the curtains at the back of the stage, everyone seems to like it. There is footage of the weddings, then there are some lovely shots of Jacob playing in the garden with the girls and me watching them. They are all laughing their heads off. There will soon have to be some additions to it.

A few days later Jacob convinced me to do a pregnancy test, but I knew that I was pregnant, I just felt pregnant. I never gave a thought to it being twins again though, I mean no one has two sets do they? That is what I said to Jacob then again to Caroline when I let her in on our little secret.

Scott and Caroline had decided that their family was complete once the boys were born but Jacob and I always intended having more children. Caroline was thrilled for us but said that it was indeed possible to have more than one set of twins. Hopefully I won't be going through that awful ordeal with Cleo that told us we were in fact having twins last time.

I made an appointment with our GP to have the pregnancy confirmed and registered. Jacob came with me.

Each time he comes with me to the surgery there is always a lot of staring in disbelief and then talking behind hands. I feel like shouting, yes it is him, get a life, but of course I would never do that.

I had kept my promise to the doctor and his nurse when Jacob did another charity show for the hospital, I got tickets for them both and for their partners plus an invitation to the after-show meal. Each time we have been in since they have both thanked us again and again.

The doctor said that his wife can't stop talking about that night. How brilliant the show was and then the meal afterwards was just amazing. She still can't believe she actually met Jacob. The highlight of her life I think.

His nurse was equally thrilled with the night now each time we visit she makes a point of coming to chat with us. It is really lovely how good Jacob makes people feel.

"Well, doctor," I said, down to business. "I am pregnant again and yes we are thrilled. We only began trying for a week then I just knew it had worked. I think it happened on the night following Jacob's big show in Birmingham."

"Right then," he said, "I suppose you have done a test."

"Yes, two actually, we couldn't believe it had happened so quick. We seem to be able to get pregnant very quickly don't we? Mind you we do try a lot don't we Jacob?"

I looked round to where Jacob was sitting, he was just shaking his head. She doesn't get any better does she doctor?

"It's all right Jacob me and the doctor we get on well so we can tell each other everything."

"And everything is exactly what you do tell him. It's a good job I love you so much" he said. "I used to get embarrassed at one time but now I expect it, so it doesn't come as a surprise."

The doctor was smiling, "I just wish all my patients were as open with me. Makes my job a lot easier I can tell you. You wouldn't change her anyway would you?"

"Definitely not" Jacob answered. "I love her so much."

"And it shows," the doctor said. "You are a lovely couple, and your daughters are delightful. Hoping for a boy this time, are you?"

"We don't mind do we Jacob, if we have another girl then we can always try again can't we?"

"We like trying, don't we, my love?

Jacob just lifted his shoulders and said, "See what I mean. "She can be exhausting when she gets on a roll though. She won't give in till she gets what she wants. It's a good job I want a houseful of kids anyway he said. I would hate to be living in that great big house with just the two of us. It is a house made for children isn't it, my love?"

"It certainly is and the bedroom is made for making them isn't it," I said.

They just looked at each other and laughed.

"Come on then, let's get this examination over with." I removed my pants, pulled my skirt up and lay down on the couch. "Well, he said, "you are definitely pregnant, congratulations."

I jumped down and went to kiss Jacob. "We've done it again," I said.

Now then the doctor said, "Because of the history of twins in your family Jacob, I want to get Ella seen at the hospital sooner rather than later. I will ring them after surgery finishes at lunchtime then get them to ring you with an appointment. We have your number, don't we?"

"Yes, you do" I said, "do you think it will be twins again? I asked?.

"Could well be but let's not get ahead of ourselves, let's get you seen at the hospital then they will know more."

"Would twins be a problem?" he asked.?

"No, not at all," we both said. It is hard for a while, but we work well together and soon get a routine sorted."

"*Wow*, just think, me a father of four. Ella was brilliant carrying the girls and the birth went well so she should be okay if it is twins again shouldn't she?" asked Jacob.

"With how the first pregnancy went and with Ella being young and fit there's no reason to think she would have a problem this time but like I say, let's get her to the hospital and be guided by them."

Jacob managed to keep the news of our pregnancy to himself until it was confirmed at the hospital that I was in fact carrying twins again. Then it was announced to the world in much the same manner as the first time. He was doing a show in London again and the same ritual began, people shouting and asking where I was. As soon as I had reached his side he kissed me then turned to the audience and said, "This wonderful woman, my wife and mother to our lovely girls is going to make me a father again and yes, it is twins again. I am so happy I could burst," he said.

Of course, the audience went nuts at this news. Scott was working on a press release for the following day to let everyone else know. He was gradually taking on more of the work involved in setting these shows up and all that goes with them. There's also a lot of photo shoots required and sometimes I have to be involved with them. Jacob loves to have me with him and includes me as often as he can.

Sam is still very much on the scene and he and Scott work well together. Jacob just lets them get on with it. He knows that Scott won't do anything to force his hand and make him do stuff he really doesn't want to do.

He has ditched making movies for now. Everything that has been put forward has required him to do a lot of raunchy sex scenes. He says he won't do any more of those films, if a serious part comes up and he is happy with it then he will reconsider but until then he is happy to concentrate on the singing side to his career.

I am happy with that. I still can't bring myself to watch things he has done before we met.

So, all is going really well with his chosen path, he releases an album each year and then does a mini tour to promote it. The only time he will stay away from home is if I am with him, which I am beginning to do more often now the boys are older.

421

We have discussed having more children in the future but for now we are all happy and content.

Once the sale of the farm and land was completed, inheritance tax paid and everything from that life disposed of we set up trust funds for our children's futures. They will all be wealthy once they turn twenty-one. We were still left with a lot of money for ourselves. We certainly didn't need it.

We tried to give some to Scott and Caroline, but they are wealthy in their own right. Scott's house was the family home and so it passed to Scott on the death of their parents. His sale of the family business brought them more money, their sister Ingrid had half once all the taxes had been paid but it still left them with more than enough.

Caroline had suggested that once our babies are grown up then she and I could write that book that was mentioned. I couldn't do it on my own, but she had always nurtured an ambition to write. It may happen one day in the future, just not now.

Jacob is patron of several charities and so we made hefty donations to them and also some other worthy charities that do good work for little thanks.

The jewellery is still with the bank, we are not sure yet what to do with it. I certainly won't wear it again. Maybe in the future, it can be sold, and the money used to give someone a better life.

Occasionally I look back at the life I had before, and it feels like it happened to someone else.

It just goes to show, that no matter how bad things get, with the help of a good partner and friends things can turn out better.

Just hold on in there and dream.